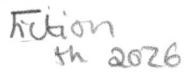

The Choice

Book 2: The Identity Thieves Trilogy

Karen Howard

Published by Leaf by Leaf
an imprint of Cinnamon Press,
Lytchett House, 13 Freeland Park, Wareham Road, Poole, Dorset, BH16 6FA
www.cinnamonpress.com

The right of Karen Howard to be identified as author of this work has been asserted by her in accordance with the Copyright, Designs and Patent Act, 1988. © 2026 Karen Howard.
Print Edition ISBN 978-1-78864-857-8
British Library Cataloguing in Publication Data. A CIP record for this book can be obtained from the British Library.

All rights reserved. No part of this publication may be reproduced, stored in a retrieval system, or transmitted in any form or by any means, electronic, mechanical, photocopying, recording or otherwise without the prior written permission of the publishers. This book may not be lent, hired out, resold or otherwise disposed of by way of trade in any form of binding or cover other than that in which it is published, without the prior consent of the publishers.

In the EU, we are fully compliant with GPSR (General Product Safety Regulation). Our EU GPSR Authorised Representative, via Inpress Books, is LOGOS EUROPE, 9 rue Nicolas Poussin, 17000, LA ROCHELLE, France
E-mail: Contact@logoseurope.eu

Designed and typeset in Adobe Caslon Pro by Cinnamon Press.
Cover Design Adam Craig.
Cinnamon Press is represented by Inpress.

Karen Howard grew up roaming the Malvern Hills and sampling the delights of Wiltshire. Despite her early love of literature and history, influenced by the books of James Herriot, she chose a scientific path, moving to Plymouth to begin her higher education. Having gained a PhD, she pursued a career in environmental chemistry, publishing a raft of factual papers and ultimately working for a global consultancy.

She travelled widely, spending eight years living partially in France, and began to write creative fiction. Karen takes inspiration from favourite wild and tame landscapes as well as drawing on personal experiences and an unbridled imagination.

In 2014 she self-published her first novel, *The Gimmel Ring*. In 2022, whilst working on the *Identity Thieves Trilogy*, she was awarded an invaluable Cinnamon Pencil creative writing mentorship. *The Search*, the first book of the trilogy, was shortlisted for the Cinnamon Press Literature Award 2023 and New Voices 2025. The second in the series, *The Choice*, was shortlisted for the Cinnamon Press Literature Award 2024. Karen is now working on the concluding novel.

Since retiring in 2021, Karen devotes most of her time to writing, walking and travelling. She lives in Shropshire with her husband and Border Collie.

For my father and in memory of my mother

The Choice

Chapter One

Plymouth, England, 30 May 2018

Mari drove from the waterside inn to a quiet residential side street in West Hoe, squeezed her Mercedes between two parked vehicles and cut the engine. Fear tumbled and lurched in her stomach and her hands were shaking. That she'd been accosted and screamed at was unnerving, but being confronted by Suzette's mirror image in such a hostile manner alarmed and distressed her. The woman's anguish clawed at Mari's heart—*Tell me where Suzette is! She's my twin, for God's sake!*—while guilt and anger flooded her senses.

Mari fumbled in her handbag for the pack of cigarettes she kept there for emergencies. She'd been trying to quit but hadn't been able to let go of her backup support. She found the packet and took out a cigarette, shoving it in her mouth while she felt around for the lighter, which evaded her fingers. 'Fucking hell,' she shouted. In a fit of pique she tipped the bag's contents onto the passenger seat. Having lit up and inhaled deeply a few times, she ran one quivering hand over her hair, tidying stray wisps behind her ears and patting her French twist, trying to steady.

Her hands were still trembling as she reached for her phone and saw she had a couple of missed calls from

Xavier. She dialled his number and his phone diverted to voicemail. *Bloody hell*, she thought anxiously, *he's in the meeting, he could be hours*. She noticed she had a voicemail and listened. It was from him.

He spoke with urgency. 'Mari, listen, we need to talk. My meeting should be finished within a couple of 'ours. Can we meet straight after? I know we'll see each other this evening but this cannot wait. Text to say where you'll be and I'll join you.'

She rested her elbows on the steering wheel and put her head in her hands, trying to think. Ash fell onto the upper sleeve of her green cotton blouse and she raised her head, brushing it off quickly. Her mind was whirling with thoughts and questions. She tried to catch hold of one and deal with it before moving to the next.

If those women had noted her in Malvern with Xavier and had also been at the inn where they'd had lunch today they must be pursuing either her or him. Had Suzette's sister tracked her to Plymouth or had she been hunting Xavier and encountered her, for the second time, by chance? Mari concluded they were following her, since Xavier was in France most of the time. It was obvious now the woman who'd approached her in the ladies' room of the eatery, speaking about Xavier, wasn't a private investigator working for her husband. But, she reflected, her initial assumption had been understandable given Gerren's increasingly resentful behaviour over the last few weeks and that had originally unsettled her. Now she knew she was being hounded for a far more ominous reason. A quiver of panic emerged from the knot in her stomach and began to flutter.

Mari had only seen Suzette once, in London with

Xavier, but the likeness was undeniable. It shocked Mari to her soul to hear the woman talking about searching for her sister. Thinking about it sent fresh dread through her body, making her limbs go cold. She felt slightly lightheaded and wished she had brandy to hand. It couldn't be, after all this time? Christ, it didn't bear thinking, yet here she was, trapped in a thirty-year old tragedy. All those years apart from the man she loved and, just as they'd found one another again, their past was threatening to catch up with them.

Myriad emotions swept through Mari, disrupting her reasoning. Her feelings tumbled, dust in a wind storm: immense love for Xavier, yet anger at him for the intrusion of his family into her life once again; resentment at Gerren for the years of bland soulless marriage; bitterness at having convinced herself comfortable monotony was better than any alternative; anxiety at the possibility of losing her home; dread of what might come to pass in the following days if those women continued to pursue them. Her life was on a cliff edge.

Mari lit another cigarette and tried to still her mind. The nicotine enhanced her dizziness as she hadn't smoked in a while. She wanted to go home, to lock the door behind her and shut out the world, to sit with a refreshing gin and tonic on her secluded terrace in the sunshine, gazing quietly over the water. But she knew something had to be done and first she would need to talk with Xavier.

She looked at her watch. Xavier would probably be another hour in the board meeting with Pierre. She tried Fran again. On hearing Fran's bright tones Mari uncharacteristically burst into tears. It was some moments before she could speak properly. Between sobs she told her friend everything that had happened since she'd left Fran a voicemail on exiting the restaurant: that Suzette's sister had approached and grabbed her arm; how the other woman had stopped her from closing the car door; how they'd questioned her over Suzette's whereabouts and accused her of lying—she had been, of course, and the frightening thing was they knew this and seemed to be following her.

Fran confirmed she'd received Mari's earlier message about the stranger trying to find out how well Mari knew Xavier and she'd sent Pierre a text, telling him to warn Xavier. She spoke calmly and slowly. 'Listen, Mari, don't panic. Go around to the back of our house and put your car in the garage. The key is in the usual place. There'll be room for Pierre's car too and I'll park on the road. In case anyone's tracking Xavier—I'm not saying they are but in case—I'll warn Pierre to conceal Xavier in the back of his car. They can drive in and shut the gate and no one will be able to see Xavier, or you for that matter, entering the house. We can all talk about this later and decide what to do. Okay?'

Listening to Fran's even, composed voice made Mari feel slightly better. She imagined the tone Fran had used was normally reserved for dealing with worried clients in Chambers. She was reminded she didn't have to handle any of this alone; the four of them would always support one another—the promise they'd made. 'Thanks, Fran,' she sighed gratefully, 'what would I do without you?'

'You never have to thank me, you know that. Anyway, we're all in this together, one way or another,' Fran responded wryly.

Xavier lay low in the back of the Maserati as Pierre drove. Worry had, long ago, drawn lines between his eyebrows and he felt these creases deepen with resentment and anger. *Merde*! Here he was, after three decades, having to hide like a bloody criminal. He tried to calm himself. That much was true, technically, but he'd only done what he knew was right.

Inside Pierre and Fran's elegant four-story Georgian home, overlooking the Tamar estuary and Mount Edgcumbe, Pierre went to the kitchen to make coffee while they waited for Fran. As Xavier entered the living room Mari ran to him like a child and he gathered her in his arms, holding her tight against his body and stroking her hair.

Mari spoke agitatedly, staring past Xavier at the polished wooden floorboards. 'For a moment I thought I'd seen Suzette again. Her sister is so like her. She's following me, Xavier, she's bloody stalking me! She kept asking me about Suzette. She tried to stop me from driving away. She actually put her hand on my arm.' She gave Xavier an anguished look. 'Then she screamed at me. Christ. I had to get out of there.'

Xavier was visibly shaken, but his tone was controlled. 'I saw 'er too this time, out of the car window as we were leaving the car park. There's no doubt it's Suzette's twin.'

'Did you mention…'

'No, of course not.'

Mari momentarily covered her mouth with one hand. 'She sounded so desperate. Her scream; it tore through me,' she said, moving her head slowly from side to side.

Grim determination showed on Xavier's face and he spoke as if through clenched teeth. 'Pierre 'as 'er registration number. 'E's asked Fran to check 'er details.'

'Can she do that?'

'She's a barrister, remember. She 'as… connections.'

Mari turned to the window. The Cornish coast across the estuary was bathed in sunshine. 'Do you remember that day?'

Xavier's eyes followed Mari's and his face softened fleetingly with the recollection. 'We all visited Mount Edgcumbe; I've never forgotten it—'ow could I? It was the day I fell in love with you.'

Mari continued to stare out over the water and her voice took on a distant quality. 'Knowing what you know now, would you do the same again?'

Xavier sat on the little window seat in front of her, cradling his head in his hands, reflecting. Eventually he raised his head and shrugged. 'We all did what we thought was for the best.' He paused. 'Would you?'

'So much fallout; so many consequences; so many lives affected,' Mari uttered sadly. 'No… I wouldn't. We should have left it to the professionals.'

'Do you mean taking the child or… right from the beginning?'

'The beginning, the Lesters, everything,' she answered.

Xavier grabbed her hand. 'Listen, Mari, you only ever tried to 'elp.'

'Yes, but what good did it do? It wrecked us, didn't it?'

'I'm going to take care of this,' Xavier urged, anger surging through his words like the Severn Bore, swelling second by second. 'I'm not going to lose you all over again.'

The living room door opened and Fran walked in. Pierre followed close behind with a pot of coffee and four mugs, which he placed on their smoked-glass coffee table, returning to the kitchen for warm home-made banana bread. They gathered on the two large mink velvet damask sofas, facing one another across a generously-proportioned and exquisitely-woven Persian rug. The aromas of fresh coffee, banana and warm sultanas drifted comfortingly between them.

Fran smiled thoughtfully at Mari and Xavier as she poured the coffee and indicated they should help themselves to cake. 'Between us we will deal with this,' she stated resolutely.

Xavier nodded and Mari managed a half-smile.

'First, we have to establish beyond doubt it was definitely Suzette's twin sister,' instructed Fran, thumbing through emails on her phone. 'You two are obviously sure. Pierre obtained the car registration number and I've had it checked out. Mmm… yes… here it is.' She looked up to find the others all staring intently at her in anticipation of the verdict.

Fran took a deep breath. 'The Toyota Prius being driven by Suzette's doppelganger is registered to a Sarah Lester,' she pronounced.

'I knew it,' declared Xavier. 'Sarah was the name written on the other cot.'

Fran looked at Xavier empathetically. 'The address recorded in association with that registration is in Malvern, Worcestershire,' she continued.

'Well that makes sense,' Mari stated, 'as it's where I saw her first.' She turned to Xavier. 'Today she said she knew you and I had spent a weekend there. It was as if she was threatening me, wanting me to know she'd been following me. How the fuck did she find us here? How long has she been pursuing us? I mean, what does she know?'

'I can't believe 'er parents would have told 'er anything,' Pierre stressed, 'knowing what they 'ave to lose.'

'Per'aps they've lied to 'er,' suggested Xavier bitterly, draining his mug of coffee and refilling it. 'Per'aps they told her a story with the characters swapped around.'

'We're assuming Jake and Lena are both alive and well,' Mari pointed out. 'They're a similar age to us, so I expect they are, but who knows. I mean it's possible Sarah discovered something about Suzette following their deaths; documents, diaries maybe.'

'They'd 'ave been bloody stupid to write anything in a diary,' Xavier expressed disdainfully.

'A deathbed confession maybe?' Mari suggested.

Fran raised a hand to halt the discourse. 'As far as I can tell, both of them are alive,' she affirmed.

Xavier and Mari looked at their friend in surprise.

Pierre indicated his head towards his wife. 'She's always a step a'ead,' he smiled.

'They're both on the full electoral register,' Fran explained, 'though their address details aren't on the open register. I checked this afternoon.'

'Going back to what Sarah may or may not be aware of; only six people know for definite it was Xavier who took Suzette,' Pierre said assuredly, taking another piece of cake. 'Whatever the Lesters may 'ave told Sarah, she couldn't 'ave found Xavier and Mari through any of us. If she'd discovered Alain, she'd 'ave found Suzette already.'

'It doesn't matter at this stage what she thinks she knows,' Fran stated assertively. 'She can have no proof of the kidnap. We must decide what to do next. As far as I can see we have several options: we can do nothing and await her next move; we can warn her off; we can warn her parents off; or we could tell her the truth.'

'I don't think we can sit around doing nothing,' Mari answered edgily. 'At the very least Sarah will find out where we live and continue to pursue us. I'm sure of it.'

'Yes, we 'ave to stop 'er some'ow,' Xavier agreed, nodding determinedly.

'How would we warn her off?' asked Mari apprehensively, hugging a scatter cushion to her chest.

'I can't see what information of any substance she'd 'ave on any of us,' Pierre answered. 'So we could put the frighteners on, tell 'er if she continues to ask questions she'll get more than she bargained for. It's true.'

Xavier nodded. 'We can threaten unimaginable consequences. She doesn't know what she's getting into.'

Mari spoke quietly. 'I don't want her to be frightened. I just want her to go back to her life and leave us to ours. If we tell her the truth, we'll expose ourselves and we'll hurt her and others. There's been enough damage. I think her parents should be warned off, anonymously, and they can deal with it.'

'I agree with Mari to a certain extent,' declared Fran. 'But we have to consider how we'd deliver a warning and we're making an assumption Jake and Lena have a good relationship with Sarah or any influence over her. Another option would be to give Sarah a legal harassment warning. Although it may not be effective, it would show her we're unafraid of her accusations. If that doesn't work, I might vote for warning the Lesters off. But...' she paused, looking at each of the others in turn, '... there's an elephant in the room. Doesn't she actually have the right to know the truth?'

They all reacted at once.

'Jesus, Fran!'

'What?'

'Are you serious?'

'Alright, alright, I'm simply putting it out there,' Fran responded, raising her hands. 'I think we should consider it as an option.'

'Yes, but there are huge consequences. How can we possibly tell her?' Mari answered, aggravated.

Xavier sensed Mari was looking to him for immediate support, but he avoided her eyes, staring down at his feet, buying time while trying to consider Fran's observation. *If it were Suzette, how would she feel?*

Pierre broke the silence. He spoke calmly, his initial disquiet at Fran's suggestion having subsided. 'I think I can see where Fran is coming from. What has kept us all safe all these years?' he asked rhetorically. 'The fact we're all in it together, the Lesters included.' He shrugged. 'They didn't report their child missing at the time—they moved, disappeared. Why should it be any different now?'

'We're not dealing with the Lesters now though, are we? We're dealing with the daughter. We don't know what she might do. We don't know what she's been told, or found out,' answered Mari forcefully.

'I'm not disagreeing, but we 'ave to remember her parents are implicated. Would she want to expose them?' Pierre countered.

Xavier considered Pierre's question then shook his head. 'Maybe not; 'owever it would be a big risk,' he argued. 'We don't know 'ow she might react. She might want some kind of revenge. I can't be accused of kidnap.' *And I can't risk losing Mari.*

'Yes, it's not straightforward,' said Fran. 'If we warn Sarah off by emphasising her actions will harm her parents, that presupposes she loves them and cares what happens to them. Whatever their relationship in the past, she might now hate or resent them. We certainly can't risk a written threat Sarah could take to the police.'

'I think the fact Sarah 'as started pursuing me after all these years implies something 'as gone wrong with our safety mechanism,' Xavier noted.

Fran spoke decisively. 'Right, we're all agreed telling her the truth is risky. So, I suggest we try and warn her off with a verbal threat of legal action on the grounds of harassment, for starters. I can deliver it.'

Pierre sighed discontentedly. 'I don't like the thought of you 'aving to engage with 'er. You're the only one of us she 'asn't seen.'

'She won't know who I am. I'm merely a legal representative. I really think it's the best course of action at the moment. Okay?'

The others nodded.

'But if she persists, we'll 'ave to deal with 'er in another way,' warned Xavier.

Later that evening, after dinner, Fran took Mari into her office in the basement. The sun, low in the sky, shone through the glass patio door, filling the room with a diffuse amber glow. Fran unlocked the bottom drawer of her desk and took out a large brown envelope. 'I'm sorry,' she said, handing it to Mari.

Mari tore open the packet and removed its contents. Her features were stony as she looked through the photographs. She glanced up at her friend. 'When were they taken?' Her tone was cold.

Fran looked at Mari sympathetically. 'A few weeks ago... after you'd told me Gerren was backtracking on the house and beginning to make accusatory remarks. I... uh... know people.'

Mari nodded slowly and tapped her lips with an index finger. 'I can't pretend I don't feel anything,' she reacted, 'but we're both going our separate ways anyway. I guess his accusatory tone with me was because he's been trying to cover his own tracks. Where does she live?'

'She's in Noss Mayo. She's a divorcee with two grown-up kids.'

'Oh. The house looks nice,' Mari responded flatly.

'It has a view of the water.'

'So... he doesn't need mine then.'

'No.'

Mari put the photos back in the envelope and gave Fran a hug. 'Thanks.' She turned to leave the study but turned back, holding the packet aloft. 'Why these?'

'Insurance,' replied Fran.

As Mari was leaving the room Fran called after her. 'Everything's documented, you know. I mean... what happened before the Lesters left Plymouth. We have records. They're... locked away.'

Mari gave Fran a reluctant smile. 'I wouldn't expect anything less from you,' she said.

Chapter Two

Newton Ferrers, England, 2 June 2018

The brooding clouds of earlier had been melted by the strengthening sun, as candyfloss over a flame. Mari's mood, however, remained like the dawn sky. She was sitting on her limestone-flagged terrace facing the southern sunshine, gazing along the turquoise creek towards where it curved gently towards the sea. She stared but did not see, her mind elsewhere and in another time.

Mari took another sip of pinot grigio and lit a cigarette. She would put the cigarettes away again soon but not today. Her mind had drifted to the troubles with Gerren in their early marriage. They had been so happy when first married but, after eighteen months of trying for a baby, the dark miasma of infertility crept into their relationship, enveloping Mari and settling over her as a blanket of despair. Disappointment had grown with every month of failing to become pregnant and with it grew anxiety, an intense worry there was something wrong: they wouldn't simply be able to have children like everyone else they knew; they couldn't take it for granted like hundreds of thousands of other couples. Mari had become locked into exhausting cycles of hope and failure, optimism and desolation. Her desperation affected every part of her life until she was consumed by desire for a baby, the yearning pervading her dreams and almost every waking moment. Hope had kept her going; the possibility that this month, or maybe the next, their luck would change.

However, after extensive hormone monitoring and treatment, examination of her sex chromosome, assessment of her thyroid and adrenal functions and a diagnostic laparoscopy, finally came the dreaded diagnosis: primary ovarian insufficiency. POI; it rolled off the tongue, masquerading as a relatively straightforward condition treatable with tablets or a change in diet, like PMT or IBS. In Mari's case the POI was significant and chronic. The problem lay with her follicles, preventing her ovaries producing and growing eggs. She still remembered the date she was told this; fifth of September, 1982. Experts at the hospital had informed her that hormone replacement therapy to increase her levels of oestrogen could treat her menopause-like symptoms and guard against osteoporosis; however, she would not be able to get pregnant naturally.

She and Gerren had few options. The birth of Louise Brown four years previously had acted as a positive focus for Mari's thoughts during the months of investigations. She remembered clearly the sensational headlines: "Test Tube Baby is Born", "Wonder Baby", "Baby Brown gives Hope to the Childless". Along with the newspaper reports came a call for an evaluation of the implications for infertility treatment and the accompanying religious and humanitarian ethical controversies, muddied by the Brown's £20,000 contract with Associated Newspapers. But no matter the negative views of some, Mari had clung to her belief in science; if the technology had worked for someone else there was a chance it could work for her, although expensive.

However, with her diagnosis it had been made clear there was no chance of growing a child in her womb. Despite further research, IVF was still in its infancy; trials were ongoing in a few places but the process was extremely complicated and depended on many factors, so the success rate was low. She was told experimental research on in-vitro fertilization of donor oocytes had begun, however there had been no reported successes. Mari was devastated. To have believed with unbridled optimism in the solid foundation of medical science, only to have that possibility crumble beneath her like solid ground in an earthquake, had shattered her.

They'd been told their one choice was whether or not to adopt. Gerren was against adoption. He'd told Mari he felt he couldn't love someone else's child as he would his own. She'd vehemently disagreed but failed to change his mind. 'We can do so much together without children,' he'd said, 'and we'll be better off financially.' He believed they should accept their fate and look upon it as an opportunity. He hadn't used the 'G' word, but Mari sensed religion had played a significant part in Gerren's decision. Gerren had been brought up Christian and still attended church occasionally, whereas she was an atheist, choosing to believe in the inherent goodness of mankind; they didn't discuss it. Her husband trusted in His will, particularly, it seemed, when it was aligned with his own desires. She believed you made your own luck, if you were fortunate enough to be able to influence your circumstances. Mari intensely resented Gerren for refusing to consider adoption, becoming bitter at him for allowing his beliefs to affect her life in such a momentous way. She'd considered leaving him but despite her resentment she'd still loved him at the time, enough to hope he'd change his mind.

Mari poured herself another glass of wine, took several mouthfuls and closed her eyes for a few moments, tilting her head slightly to the sun, relishing the warmth on her face and the kaleidoscope of colour on the inside of her eyelids which intensified the tighter she shut her eyes. It had been like bereavement in a way, giving up the hope. Coming to terms with the realisation she'd never have a child had been the most difficult thing she'd ever done. She still remembered her feelings and regrets as if it had been last week: never to feel a life grow inside you; never to make a child you can nurture and guide, educate, share experiences with, laugh with, give to, provide for, see mature into adulthood with their own life and loves, marriage and children. It wasn't until after she'd left Xavier she'd finally relinquished the hope, once it had become a choice between Gerren or being completely alone.

Mari had mourned for a long time. Eventually she'd decided something had to replace the loss of hope; something had to fill the cavernous void. Gerren had continued to work hard in her father's engineering business and had been promoted. Likewise, Mari had thrown herself into her career, working long hours, vigorously marketing her services to potential clients and volunteering for as many trips away as she could handle. Their social life revolved around the pub, although the people they'd socialised with were mainly Gerren's friends from the darts team and the local football squad. So she'd taken up sailing again, joining a club and finding the activity absorbing and thereby therapeutic. She'd made new friends there and slowly the pieces of her life had begun to come back together. However, her relationship with Gerren never fully recovered.

Gerren had been behaving increasingly resentfully over the last few weeks and was now contesting their previous agreement that she would buy his share of the house just as she'd organised the release of the funds. Neither of them wanted to sell. Some months ago they'd both come to the same conclusion, their marriage had simply run out of steam. At that point they'd agreed on a divorce. When Gerren decided he would move out there had been no bitterness, only a mix of sadness and relief on both their parts. But recently Gerren had been back-pedalling on their arrangement for the house, making thinly veiled remarks, hinting at misbehaviour on her part. Mari was damned if she was going to let him accuse her of adultery. Their marriage had been unequivocally over before Xavier had come back into her life.

A warm breeze played gently around Mari's body, cooling her face and neck. She flexed her toes, enjoying the wafts of air between them. Her metallic red nail varnish caught and reflected the sun, glinting as prettily as the sparkles of silver on the rippled surface of the water below. The occasional stronger gust was accompanied by the sound of halyards slapping on their masts as sailboats moored in the creek swayed and shifted. Mari found the sound comforting. It reminded her where she was; her haven. She lit another cigarette, hoping the nicotine and wine would help to calm her mind but her thoughts insisted on drifting back into the past, to the source of her present anxiety.

She'd taken to Lena and Jake Lester. Mari recalled the first time they'd met, when Gerren had invited the couple to dinner one evening in February '82. Jake worked for Gerren and they got along well. 'You'll like them,' he'd told Mari and their friendship budded and blossomed from that moment on.

It was not until Fran met Pierre and Mari came to know Xavier the following year that the opportunity arose and the plan was conceived. It would have benefited them all, if it hadn't gone so disastrously wrong. That Lena had betrayed her, Mari felt unforgivable. In the end it was not simply the betrayal but the ensuing consequences and the actions they'd had to take to deal with them that had ruined her life. How different it would have been if she'd run away with Xavier, as he'd implored. Perhaps they would have adopted children and she might never have had the idea which sparked the scheme that had led to such devastation.

After living with it so many years, since she'd set eyes on Sarah Lester the bitterness Mari had eventually managed to bury deep within had welled again. Bitterness that knotted her intestines and tore at her heart, that clenched her fists and pulled her muscles tight so her teeth were gritted and her body compressed.

Mari took a deep breath, aware she badly needed to relax. She finished her wine and reached for the cigarettes, but the pack was empty. The sun had moved westwards and the lush, undulating wooded hill across the creek was beginning to cast shade onto a section of her terrace. She moved her lounger into the sunlight. The afternoon had been surprisingly hot, given the morning had been so gloomy and, even now at nearly six o'clock, her body was glowing with perspiration. She decided what she needed was distraction and to cool down.

She knew better than to swim into the creek half-tipsy but the blue-green water looked so inviting. She slipped off her skirt, leaving her light cotton chemise on over her bra and pants, and trod carefully down the steep stone steps to the water. The steps continued beneath the surface but were slippery, so she held the wooden rail placed alongside for that purpose. Normally she'd have dived in, the shoreline as familiar to her as the lines on her face, but she knew the combination of wine and cold water could present dangers. Gradually she eased herself into the creek, gasping with the chill, until she stepped off the bottom stone and trod water. Her feet and legs quickly became numb in the spreading coldness and the rest of her body followed. She dipped her head under the surface for a few seconds before emerging, shaking her hair and wiping water from her face.

The plunge was sobering and her body tingled with renewed freshness as she mounted the steps to the terrace. She'd come to a decision: if Sarah Lester continued to harass them, she would take matters into her own hands and handle the girl. What she would do, at that point she had no clue, but she wasn't going to be a victim again.

Chapter Three

Birmingham, England, 2 June 2018

Xavier was driving to Birmingham airport under a sullen sky. In his rearview mirror he caught the occasional glimpse of clouds parting, revealing small patches of blue; however his route took him roughly north-east under a perpetually steely cloud cover. He was travelling faster than the warm weather front. Tomorrow he would be home and the forecast for Cahors was hot and sunny. He was at least looking forward to a relaxing late-afternoon swim in his pool, though not much else.

Nowadays he had mixed feelings about his returns to France. He loved his country and greatly valued his life there but hated leaving Mari. Today, however, the regret and yearning which accompanied leaving Mari behind were intensified by anxiety; a fear that recent events would cause her to back away from him again.

He recalled the time when Alain and Fayette had entered the equation; the plan they'd all made. After that Mari had seemed to be looking to the future a little instead of trying to live merely in the present. It was as if a glimmer of hope had crept back into her life. Xavier had a good idea why but hadn't asked her any questions. He was glad of it, for he wanted her to be happy and fulfilled.

He'd known she loved him—she'd said so often enough—but he also believed, for her, part of what they shared was escapism, a distraction from her deep desire for a child and the life with her husband which constantly reminded her of it. Although he knew Mari's love was genuine, the force behind it hadn't been entirely in his favour.

Throughout their involvement with Jake and Lena, until they'd disappeared, he and Mari had shared many happy times. There were moments when he sensed Mari might leave her husband and start a life with him but she hadn't been ready to make that decision until immediately before her friends vanished. After they'd all been betrayed Mari had done her utmost to help him locate the runaways. It had taken them nearly two years and during all that time he'd never felt it was appropriate to ask her to make a permanent commitment to him.

Mari had insisted on being part of the resolution. Xavier hadn't wanted her to take risks, so had initially been against any action on her part. Eventually, he'd had to admit he needed help abducting the children and piloting the getaway boat as he didn't have a licence. However, he'd promised her if they were caught, he would swear he'd blackmailed her into doing it. Was it revenge or closure she'd wanted? He believed it was the latter but had never been entirely sure; guilt affects people in strange ways.

Knowing her situation, he should never have let her do it. She'd wanted to right a wrong but it had destroyed them.

Xavier pulled into a parking bay at the airport, dropped the car keys into the executive hire bureau and walked to the on-site hotel. He felt stiff after the two-hundred-mile journey and was looking forward to a hot shower and a glass of wine. The clouds had now cleared, though the sun had dropped below the city skyline and the air was cool. He brought his mind to focus on the present. All that was over thirty years ago, though the memories could still incite heartache he'd rather forget. Since a chance meeting with Mari a few months ago at a party hosted by friends of Fran and Pierre—he had a strong suspicion the situation had been engineered—he and Mari had rekindled their relationship and had become supremely happy. As soon as Mari's divorce came through, they planned to go travelling then live between their two houses in Devon and the Midi-Pyrénées. In all of the previous years he'd never loved anyone as he loved her.

He would never relinquish Mari again—whatever it took and whoever was hurt in the process.

Chapter Four

Issigeac, France, 3 June 2018

Xavier sat at his round table on the edge of the square trying to keep his emotions in check. His hand shook as he drained the last of his coffee, the only outward sign of the seething fury he felt within. His other hand was clenched so tightly his short nails bit into his palm. Issigeac was a popular place to stop when collecting or dropping someone off at Bergerac airport, especially on a Sunday when there was a market. He'd often seen people he knew there. The blonde spiky hair had caught his eye first. He'd almost made the same error as Mari when she saw the girl in Great Malvern, thinking she was Suzette. Then he'd caught sight of the man accompanying her and realised they'd met before on the hill above that town. He deduced they were following him. It hadn't been difficult; he'd woven through the narrow streets, occasionally doubling back and looping around, and they'd always been two or three stalls behind him. But how in God's name had they located him here? Judging by their naive behaviour he doubted the man accompanying Sarah Lester was a detective; he guessed the guy was a husband or a boyfriend from the way they acted together. He was also sure they hadn't been on the same flight as him. So how the hell had they found him? There was one possible answer—they must have been waiting for him at the airport, which meant someone in his company had given out his schedule.

Xavier ordered a beer and a plate of bread and pâté and tried to think clearly. They hadn't approached; perhaps they didn't want to make a scene; perhaps they wanted to follow him to see whether he would lead them to Suzette. The girl, Sarah, had clearly not been deterred by Fran's verbal warning.

Xavier wanted to bang his fist on the table, to roar, to walk across the square and confront the pair. He'd noted the addition of hats, which made him more furious. Did they think this was a game? Didn't they appreciate they were playing with people's lives! Xavier had seen red the moment he'd caught sight of her and now she'd become the focus of thirty years of regret and sorrow. Suddenly she was to blame for the rift with his brother, the loss of his lover, his years of loneliness. He wanted to rage at her.

A waiter brought his order and he paid the man. He took a gulp of the cold amber liquid in front of him and tried to calm himself. The vehemence of his feelings shocked his usual rational sensibilities. He swallowed several more mouthfuls of beer and picked at his bread. He wasn't hungry but needed to soak up the alcohol. After some minutes, he took a deep breath and forced himself to think logically. In difficult situations, Mari would always try to put herself in another's position.

He glanced across the square seeing Suzy in her green summer dress. Sarah looked away quickly. *Suzy... Sarah... Elles sont identiques*!

Returning his gaze to his glass, Xavier thought

momentarily of Alain and realised Sarah was likely to be as desperate to find her sister as his brother and Fayette had been to get the children from the Lesters. Gradually a degree of empathy arose in his consciousness and he shook his head slightly as he began to feel surprisingly conflicted. Nevertheless, he thought, Sarah and her husband, boyfriend—whoever he was—were solely concerned with the lives of Sarah and Suzette, but he was concerned not only with his own life and that of Mari, but also Alain and Fayette, Pierre and Fran and Suzy. He must protect them, all of them.

He finished his beer. He felt weary of the guilt and responsibility weighing on him for years. He recalled Fran's words; *Doesn't she actually have the right to know the truth?* Perhaps it was time. On the other hand could he really trust her with the knowledge of his having kidnapped her sister? It would be like having a primed bomb wandering around the perimeter of their lives, not knowing if or when the explosion of disclosed truth would come and with it the threat of destruction. *But then again*, Xavier said to himself, *this is the case whether I tell her or not, as she's likely to find the truth some other way. So if I help her, I might retain control over the situation.*

He needed more time to think, to discuss it with the others, so he would have to create breathing space. The overhead sun glared relentlessly between the cool stone buildings. He looked at his watch; it was nearly midday. The waiters were laying tables for lunch. Xavier knew his pursuers would either have to move or order a meal. He waited until he saw Sarah's partner go inside the café, then made his move.

He assumed Sarah would be less keen to follow him

alone and thought a degree of hesitancy on her part would give him the opportunity to slip away. Although the village was relatively compact, he knew the maze of lanes and passageways well enough to secrete himself somewhere. Hopefully they'd spend sufficient time looking for him to allow him to retreat to the car and depart unnoticed. He took a small back lane from the square and turned several times, walking quickly. Finally he sidestepped through a covered cobbled passage leading into a small private courtyard. Standing with his back against the nearest inner wall, to his right, he was invisible from the narrow walkway entrance. It was quiet, the windows of the enclosing houses shuttered against the dazzling sun.

Almost immediately he heard something like the slap of a shoe or sandal on cobblestone. Surely it couldn't be… could it? Perhaps it was a local resident. In a few seconds whoever it was would exit the alleyway. It had better not be them. Xavier's heartbeat amplified and frustration welled. *Just fuck off and leave me alone.*

As Sarah stepped out of the passageway, fury, born of exasperation, overwhelmed him once more. His palms were sweating, his fists clenched. He hadn't wanted a confrontation, but she'd given him no choice.

'Fucking stop following me or I'll 'ave you arrested.'

As she whipped around and looked up at him he saw the fear in her eyes. He realised she was on her own, vulnerable.

She stepped backwards from him, further into the courtyard, all the while talking about Suzette. Her words were trembling and hurried and seemed to come at him all at once. He caught some of them.

'I'm trying to find my sister. I think you know where she is. I thought I knew your face... from a long time ago. Your friend, Marigold, seemed to think I was Suzette and she mentioned your name—she said "have you come with Xavier."'

He tried not to panic. 'Why the 'ell should I know your sister?'

Stop persisting with this! You don't know what you're getting into; how many people will be affected.

He continued to prevaricate and found himself shouting furiously. 'You know my face because you've been following me around. You 'arassed my friend and you're 'arassing me!'

He walked towards her. 'You were warned to stay away or there would be consequences. You understand? *Comprenez?*'

Then she slipped on the cobblestones and fell, plainly damaging her ankle, and he saw Suzette in pain lying on the ground before him then trying desperately to stand and move away from him. His rage died. It shocked him to hear her ask him not to hurt her. He checked himself. *This is not who I am, an intimidator of women.*

She was perceptive, like Suzy. 'When you look at me you see her,' she said. 'We're identical, we're family. I have a right to know her.'

As they sat a little way apart on the warm stones overlaying the ground he tried to think clearly. Sarah's phone kept ringing and Xavier knew he didn't have much time until her partner would come storming into the courtyard. He had to find out how much she knew. As they talked it became clear Jake and Lena had lied to their daughter; that, apart from there being no death certificate, she didn't have any explicit evidence of anything; a questionable memory of seeing him when she was very young but no proof of what had taken place or who was involved. However, that she mentioned Pierre's fertility clinic rang alarm bells. She had been dogged in her investigations. As a terrier worrying the squeak out of a toy, she was bound to discover the truth at some point.

But what would she do with the truth? She was in danger of dismantling her own life, quite apart from the damage she could inflict on all those he loved. Infuriation clawed at him once more and his attempt at persuading her to back off took on a threatening tone.

'You 'ave no idea what you 'ave stepped into. Things aren't always as they seem, so forget what you think you saw. Your sister is well and she is 'appy. She 'as 'er life and you 'ave yours. You want to ruin that?'

His angry words did not have the desired effect; she became even more insistent and determined to locate Suzette. Her voice had a sharp edge.

'The truth is important. Don't you think she has a right to know she has a twin?'

His voice rose heatedly as exasperation boiled into fury. 'Oh, and what do you think would 'appen then? Did you intend to waltz into 'er life, tell 'er she's your sister and play 'appy families? You from England and 'er in France; you don't think there'd be questions? She's where she belongs, living a contented life with 'er 'usband. You want to come in and blow all that apart? Go 'ome. Go back to your own life and be 'appy!'

Sarah shook her head. 'I can't.'

The more irate he became the more she dug her heels in. *Merde!* Suzy could be like this; determined, obstinate, unyielding. *Like my brother*, he thought ruefully. He had a sudden vision of Sarah with Jake and Lena, envisaging the aftermath of the exposé. What would the truth do to her? He imagined Suzy in Sarah's position and a hint of sadness infused his frustration. He had to try again.

Moving towards her he put a hand on her arm. 'It would be worse for you, much worse, not to mention for your parents, believe me. Why do you think they lied to you? To protect you. If you know what's good for you, forget all about this.'

But it was useless.

'I can't simply forget I have a twin sister,' she exclaimed.

Suddenly the boyfriend stormed onto the scene, threats ensued and Xavier had to back down or risk being punched.

Now, under the shade of a large umbrella, at the *Café de Thé* with Sarah and Ben—he'd silently thanked God Ben hadn't hit him; fit as he was the muscular younger man looked powerful—Xavier wondered what Mari, Fran or Pierre might do in his situation. He considered his brother, Fayette and Suzy. Thoughts tumbled through his mind like sand through an hourglass.

This girl was going to stop at nothing to get at the truth: if he walked away today, she'd simply reappear somewhere else. He badly wanted to talk with Mari but couldn't bear to worry her. His friends trusted him to do what was necessary, what was right for them all, but ultimately it was his decision; they all had a great deal to lose, however, assuming he could keep Mari out of it, only he—and Jake and Lena of course—would face punishment for their crimes.

It was clear Ben and Sarah didn't trust him at all and why should they? He didn't trust them either at the moment. He thought again of what Fran had said and recalled Pierre reminding them that the threat of disclosure worked both ways, which was why the Lesters had remained silent all these years.

Xavier felt drained; weary of the anxiety, tired of the past, exhausted with the stress of it all. He set down his glass and slumped against the back of his chair. He just wanted to look to the future, with Mari, without anything hanging over them. He wanted to purge his life of this poison.

He concluded his only option was to tell Sarah the truth. But if this was going to have an acceptable solution everyone would have to agree he would do things his way. He had to be in control.

As they ate their lunch, he formed a plan. He did not want Sarah rushing off to find Alain and Fayette or pursuing Suzy, once she knew the truth. He was concerned how they would all cope, particularly Suzy. He would need to tell people in his own time and manner. He realised there would be nothing to stop Sarah and Ben disappearing and taking a taxi, but he hoped to engender trust on the journey to Cahors and thereafter. If they were willing to let him drive them, that would be a good start.

As they walked to the car park after lunch, Sarah hobbling between the walking sticks which he'd obtained for her, Xavier announced he would drive Sarah and Ben in his car and they would have to trust him.

On entering the imposing *Cathédrale Saint-Étienne* in Cahors, Xavier faced the altar and crossed himself.

Although he'd been raised a Catholic he'd left that behind him; he hadn't attended a service for years. However, he couldn't help but undertake the ritual when he entered a church. Somewhere deep inside he felt it would be unlucky and disrespectful not to do so, although he didn't analyse why. He preferred not to think about religion: he simply tried to be a good person and treat others with kindness and respect—*at least most of the time* he thought ruefully. He walked on, past the choir towards the medieval cloistered garden, indicating Sarah and Ben should follow.

He'd been thinking constantly about what and what not to impart and how to start and had decided to tell enough of the truth as was necessary, not mentioning the nature of his relationship with Mari or her part in taking Suzette. He would also protect Pierre and Fran as much as he could. But where should he begin?

Chapter Five

Plymouth, England, February 1982

Mari finished dribbling the Marie Rose dressing over the prawns and placed the glasses of prawn cocktail into the fridge. She looked at her watch. Their guests were due in five minutes. She hurried into the lounge to plump sofa cushions and found Gerren fiddling with the record player.

'They'll be here any minute, Gerren. Could you please set out the drinks?' she asked for the third time, her request sounding more agitated than she meant.

He didn't look up. 'Yes, sure. As soon as I've finished cleaning this needle. Have you been dusting the records with the new brush before playing them, like I showed you? It's important, you know. This is all fluffed up.'

She exhaled noisily, ignoring his question, and went to the dining room herself to extract alcohol and glasses from their walnut-veneered sideboard.

'Don't fret, angel,' he called after her. 'They're very laid back. You'll like them.'

The doorbell rang and she delayed answering, lingering in the kitchen so Gerren would get there first to make the introductions. It was silly to be nervous, she told herself. Jake worked for Gerren and by her husband's account they got on well. But she'd not met Jake or Lena and was hoping this wouldn't turn out to be an evening of stilted small talk.

'Come in, come in,' Gerren was saying. 'Let's take your coats.'

Mari joined him as he shut the front door against a blast of freezing wind.

Gerren introduced them all as they stood at the foot of the stairs in the narrow hallway of their mid-terraced house. 'Lena, Jake, Mari,' he indicated obviously.

'Hello, nice to meet you both.' Mari smiled politely as she took Lena's big old Afghan coat and held out her hand for Jake's weather-beaten leather jacket.

'Hi, Mari,' Lena exclaimed enthusiastically, beaming as she straightened the long, flared sleeves of her capacious brushed cotton dress, which had rumpled under her coat. 'Tis great to finally meet you. We've been lookin' forward to this, ant we, Jake?'

Jake stepped forward, took Mari's outstretch hand and shook it energetically before giving her his jacket. 'Bloody freezin' out there, in't it? Cold enough to make yer balls shrivel,' he grinned. 'Still, nice an' warm in here.' He handed Gerren a bottle of Blue Nun. 'Here you go. I dunno what we're eatin' but this'll go with anythin'.'

'We also got this un,' added Lena, pulling a bottle of Mateus Rosé from her brightly coloured woollen shoulder bag. 'You can use it afterwards for a candle.'

Mari instantly unwound, relieved. The couple had no airs and graces, unlike some of Gerren's other colleagues and their spouses. She beckoned they follow her into their front lounge, where Gerren offered them drinks.

'Who's driving?' he inquired.

'Neither of us. We came down on the bus to Mutley Plain an' walked from there. 'In't far from the bus stop, is it?' Jake observed.

'We don't tend to use the buses much,' Gerren replied, pouring drinks. Lena had a Cinzano Bianco and Gerren joined Jake in having a cider. He gave Mari a brandy and Babycham.

As they relaxed around the coffee table nibbles, Mari felt increasingly overdressed in her new shoulder-padded cocktail dress. Jake wore a baggy brown jumper and jeans and even Gerren had a sweater on over his shirt. Mari excused herself. She was in their bedroom, dress pulled down inside-out to her waist, trying to cut out the pads with nail scissors when Lena popped her head around the door.

'Oh, sorry, Mari. I was lookin' for the bathroom. The cold weather always make you want to pee more, dunt it?' she laughed cheerfully. 'Are you having a spot of trouble there? Can I help?' Without being asked she entered the room and held a hand out for the scissors.

Mari overcame a momentary flush of embarrassment and grinned. 'It's a new dress. I hadn't had time to remove these. I don't like shoulder pads but they seem to be in everything,' she explained hastily.

'I know what you mean,' Lena replied as she deftly snipped at the cotton stitches. 'We're not all bloody Sue-Ellen Ewing, though I wouldn't mind her money,' she chuckled. 'There y' go.' She handed Mari the superfluous items. 'They'd be useful to a skinny teenager to stick down her bra. You an' me have no need of 'em,' she added, placing her hands on her ample bosom and nodding towards Mari's.

Mari laughed as she pulled her dress up and wriggled into the arms. 'Thanks, Lena, I really didn't want to emulate Joan Collins. Can I get you another drink? Oh, the bathroom's just on the right.'

They all continued chatting amiably over dinner. Mari noted Gerren didn't serve the white wine provided by their guests, choosing a superior Chardonnay. So she made a point of opening the rosé they'd brought. A hearty casserole of slow-cooked beef in red wine followed the prawns, which was well received.

She found herself really taken with the Lesters. Lena's disposition was like her loose-fitting hippie clothes; colourful, comfortable and slightly scatty. It seemed to Mari Jake was astute and practical with a kind, laidback temperament. They were keen walkers and Jake was a member of a climbing club, so they spent a lot of time on Dartmoor. The couple rented a small house in the north of the city, trying to save for a place of their own.

'This is a smart house, nicely painted. I always liked this row of terraces. When d' you move in?' Jake was saying.

'We've been here three months,' Gerren answered, popping the last roast potato onto his plate. 'Before that we were living in a house owned by Mari's parents.'

'Gerren did most of the decorating,' Mari said proudly. 'He'd rather do it himself than give me a paintbrush. I don't mind painting large spaces but I hate doing the fiddly bits, skirting board etcetera.'

Gerren inclined his head towards her, looking at Jake. 'My angel's a bit slapdash,' he mocked.

Mari raised her eyebrows at her husband, sardonically. 'You're the engineer, you're used to detail.'

'Well, it's a lovely home,' Lena interjected. 'Very comfortable.'

'A man's got to have his castle, eh Mari?' Gerren stated brightly, glancing at her, then smiling at his guests. 'She wants to start a family,' he divulged indiscreetly, reaching out to put an arm around her shoulder and giving her an enthusiastic hug, which pulled her sideways. 'But I agree with her father; there's plenty of time for all that. Got to build our careers first. Can't let our education go to waste, eh, Jake?'

Mari arranged a polite smile on her face but her stomach contracted. She'd not been using contraception since they were married, though hadn't told Gerren as she knew damn well what he'd think about that—she'd thought it better to tell him after she'd conceived. The timing of her periods had always been haphazard but when she'd failed to become pregnant after a couple of years she'd seen a doctor. She'd then been referred to a specialist clinic and the appointment was now only days away. She'd have to be honest with her husband but this evening definitely wasn't the right moment.

'Just because men can't multitask, doesn't mean women can't,' she pronounced in a faux disdainful tone.

Lena giggled. 'Too right.'

'Anyway,' Gerren continued bluntly, 'we'll need a larger house first. Can't have little Thomases running around this one, cluttering up all the space with their toys.'

'This seems pretty roomy t' me,' Lena declared affably. 'It's much bigger than ours.' She nudged Jake with an elbow. 'Dunt you think so, my luvver?'

Jake nodded good-naturedly. 'Mmm, yeah, loads of space in here for a little un.'

Gerren's features indicated he didn't agree. He shrugged. 'It's only our first house; a steppingstone to a better place,' he remarked cheerfully. 'We want a view of the sea, don't we, Mari? Got to set your sights high, Jake.' He winked. 'Anyway, before that, I need to upgrade my HiFi. I've been looking at a Denon amp. Only the best for my angel. D'you know Denon, Jake?'

'Er, dunt think I do, Gerren,' Jake responded, as if he couldn't quite recall a particular model.

'Ah, you should look at it. I tell you what, when I get one you'll have to come and listen to it. Sublime sound quality.'

Jake mumbled something into his beard.

Mari's smile remained fixed, though inwardly she shrank at Gerren's insensitivity. Jake and Lena clearly coveted a house such as theirs and from what she'd learned that evening they were a long way from achieving it.

Later, helping Mari with the washing up, Lena confided that although they both enjoyed their current jobs—she was a primary school teacher—their dream was to have their own business selling outdoor gear for camping, fishing and the like. She asked Mari not to mention this to Gerren as she didn't want him thinking Jake wasn't committed to the engineering work, because he was.

Mari agreed it was good to have a goal, however distant. Privately, her thoughts returned to her forthcoming fertility consultation. Right now, she seemed as far away from having a child as Lena and Jake were from their camping business.

Plymouth, England, April 1982

Mari and Lena were enjoying a relaxed evening at Mari's house while their menfolk were occupied elsewhere. Lena had opted for hot chocolate and they'd curled up at either end of the sofa to enjoy their drinks and graze on biscuits.

'You on the wagon too?' Lena chortled.

Mari turned down the corners of her mouth and shook her head. 'I'm seeing a fertility specialist. I've been trying to get pregnant for ages and it's just not happening.'

Lena's smile disappeared. She moved closer and threw her arms around Mari. 'Oh my luvver.'

As they hugged, Mari experienced not only the comforting physical embrace but felt herself enfolded in such tender affection she could only think of it as a kind of love. Surprised, she sensed an unspoken depth of understanding which hitherto had been missing in her life. In turn, this gave her the strength to fight her welling tears and retake control of herself. At last, she knew she could unburden her anxieties without fear of reproach.

They drew apart and she smiled gratefully at her friend. 'I had an initial consultation at the hospital in February,' she explained. 'The first thing they wanted to do was to test Gerren's… you know… to do a count and check motility.' She emitted an ironic 'hmph' and shook her head, shrugging. 'I suppose I was expecting that,' she added resignedly, 'though I was kind of hoping they would investigate me first.' She heaved a sigh. 'So of course I had to tell him.'

'Fuck,' said Lena, her eyebrows raised.

Mari could see from the look on Lena's face she had recalled their conversation over that first dinner in

February and realised exactly where Gerren stood.

'Jesus, Mari, that must've been difficult. Poor you. An' poor Gerren,' Lena continued empathetically.

Mari nodded. 'To say he was shocked is an understatement, which is fair enough. Though, to be honest, he told me it wasn't so much the fertility problems that upset and disappointed him, but the fact I'd deceived him. Marriage is supposed to be an equal and honest partnership, he said. Everything he does is to make our life together successful.'

'Mmm, but o' course we all measure success in different ways,' Lena responded perceptively.

'Exactly. I tried, and failed, to make him see my view of accomplishment is very different to his and to that of my parents. But he's right about my dishonesty. I should have been candid from the start. I apologised, of course.'

Reluctantly, Lena nodded her agreement. 'But I understand why you kept it from him,' she stated supportively. 'I sense he would never have agreed to actively try for a little 'un.' She put a hand on Mari's and squeezed it. 'Everyone thinks children are a given, but sometimes it can take a while. Considerin' what I know about yer husband, I can understand why you didn't see the need t' upset the apple cart afore you had to.'

Mari expressed a look of gratitude.

'So, how're things between you now?' Lena asked.

'Well, Gerren grudgingly agreed to participate in whatever medical tests are necessary but only, he said, because he loves me. He's still unwavering in his opinion about this not being an appropriate time to start a family.'

'At least he's on board,' Lena responded encouragingly.

Mari nodded. 'Anyway, we've had the results of his tests

and they're all fine. Nothing wrong. So, they'll start investigating me now.'

Lena squeezed her hand again. She didn't respond with a platitude. There was no point in saying "It'll be alright," as both understood full well there was no way of knowing what the future held.

Lena simply said, 'I'll always be here fer you.'

Mari's fertility investigations began. Her blood hormone levels were measured, she was tested for chlamydia, underwent an ultrasound scan and was referred for a laparoscopy. Despite their private difficulties, or perhaps because of them, she and Gerren saw a lot of Jake and Lena. A week before her surgery, on a Saturday afternoon, Mari called on Lena for a coffee and a chat. She and Lena were sitting at Lena's old Formica kitchen table when Mari sensed an unfamiliar uneasiness in her friend.

Lena took a discernible breath. 'I've somethin' t' tell you, Mari. I've been puttin' it off as I know how tough things are for you right now. I really dunt want t' upset you but I need you to know… I'm pregnant. I'm sorry, my luvver.' Lena reached out, clasped her hand and gave it a squeeze.

Despite Mari's stomach lurching and tumbling as she listened to Lena's disclosure, and the waves of anguish echoing though her mind, making her feel slightly lightheaded, Mari was truly delighted for her friend. 'Ah, Lena, that's wonderful news,' she exclaimed. 'No need to be sorry,' she insisted emphatically. 'I'm so pleased for you and Jake.'

They hugged, Lena rocking Mari gently for a moment. 'They'll get t' the bottom of it. You'll see,' Lena whispered encouragingly.

Mari drove home, shut the door on the world and wept.

Pregnancy suited Lena, she was a natural earth mother. She blossomed, the extending curves of her body complementing her round face and curly brown hair. She was considerate and supportive of Mari and sensitive to her situation, allowing Mari to conduct their friendship on her terms. However, the fact of Lena's pregnancy became increasingly difficult for Mari while she herself was undergoing numerous fertility tests. As her anxiety grew, she felt increasingly isolated from her friend, unable to relate to the physical and emotional changes Lena was experiencing or share in her joyful expectations. But, despite this, she still endeavoured to see as much of Lena as she could manage.

Once little George entered the world that October, Lena made it clear to Mari she had open access to them and could take as much or little as she chose. Mari was acutely aware of Lena's deep empathy for her circumstance and was grateful. There were occasions when Mari craved Lena and the baby's company and they spent many happy hours together. However, at other times she couldn't bear to be in the company of a child and Lena understood.

Chapter Six

Plymouth, England, January 1983

As Xavier entered the restaurant he felt a welcome waft of warm air on his cold face and hands. He wiped his feet on the well-worn bristle mat and took off his coat, shaking it near the doorway to avoid wetting the polished floorboards of the old, converted wharf. Outside the meagre snow had turned to sleet, as was often the case in Plymouth, and the wind whistled around the timeworn Barbican buildings and whipped up the water in the harbour. Xavier looked around for Pierre, the college friend he had just driven down from London to visit for the weekend. The low-lit room stretched back quite a way and various seating areas with candlelit tables were partitioned by old oak beams. To his left an open-tread staircase led through the wooden ceiling to an upper storey from which came murmurs of conversation and the chink of glasses. A bar boasting ten ciders, guest ales and a multitude of wines was positioned at the back of the room. It was past eight p.m. and the eatery was buzzing. Xavier couldn't see Pierre, so he bought himself a pint of St Austell Hicks Special and checked the room upstairs.

Pierre was sitting at a small table in a corner by a window that looked out over Sutton Harbour. His distinctive, blonde-highlighted brown curly hair and red bandana stood out in the flickering light. He rose as Xavier walked over to him. '*Bonsoir, mon ami*!' he grinned as they shook hands. They continued to speak in French. Pierre looked at his silver-strapped digital watch. 'Hmm, not bad, you must have been flying!'

'I left London at lunchtime and called to see a client on the way,' Xavier smiled, placing his pint on the table. 'That way I can use the hire car for business and for pleasure. You're looking good, Pierre—who is she?'

'Ah, she's whoever I want her to be' Pierre laughed. 'These lovely Devon girls, they can't resist a French accent.'

Xavier discerned his friend knew how attractive he looked in his pristine black leather jacket, worn over a teal v-neck jumper and tight-fitting stone-washed jeans.

'What is it the British say? Snap!' Xavier chuckled as he slung his leather jacket over a chair and sat down. 'What's tasty here? I'm starving.'

'Everything; the chef is French! The fish is especially good, mmm, very fresh,' Pierre replied, putting a thumb and two fingers to his lips and kissing the air.

They perused the menu and ordered the crab starter with sea bass and monkfish to follow and Xavier chose a bottle of Chenin Blanc from the refreshingly excellent wine list. Then they caught up on each other's news and reminisced about their days at university.

They had both studied at Imperial College in London, Pierre reading medicine and Xavier biochemistry. Pierre was now twenty-eight, three years older than Xavier, and on completing his studies had stayed in England, obtaining a position at a London hospital and specialising in women's health. He was a highflyer, having achieved a first-class degree, and was now five years into a nine-year specialist training programme in obstetrics and gynaecology with the aim of becoming a consultant. He had taken a position at Plymouth's large teaching hospital in Derriford and, eight months earlier, had also become involved in research into infertility at a private clinic. He worked hard, lived well and was highly motivated by both.

They had met at a university French Society function, whilst Xavier was in his first year, and become fast friends. At first their connection was common nationality and interest in medical science but they soon bonded on many different levels including their love of rugby, art house cinema, post-punk music and gastronomy.

The crab was delicate and sweet and tasted of the ocean. Pierre poured them both a second glass of wine as a waiter brought the fish main dishes. Sharing their platters so both could enjoy the mild, meaty monkfish and the moist, buttery seabass, they continued recollecting and exchanging news about their families. It had been a while since they'd seen one another.

On finishing his degree Xavier had returned to France, where he'd begun to carve a career in pharmaceuticals. He was currently based in Lille, which allowed him easy access to Paris, Brussels and London. He'd discovered that the field of business development excited him and his persuasive manner was conducive to marketing, so was edging himself into that sphere. Originally from the Midi-Pyrenees, Xavier hadn't missed south-west France as much as he thought he would. He'd been glad of the opportunity to spread his wings and study in another country. At the time he'd had few qualms about leaving the onus for assisting his mother with the care of their aged father to Alain. His younger brother lived locally and seemed to accept his role without complaint. As their papa became less able, Alain took care of all the practical things he could no longer manage. However, when their father had passed some months ago Xavier regretted spending so little time at the family home over the last few years. He loved his mother fiercely and wanted to support her as much as he could, so he travelled to see her every other weekend. It was time-consuming and tiring but, nevertheless, he chose to do that rather than look for a position nearer to home. He felt conflicted; he wanted to care for his family—after all, he was the eldest son and he'd realised he should no longer leave the responsibility solely on the shoulders of his younger brother, who had his own problems—but he also wanted to maximise his opportunities with the company he worked for, which meant an increasing amount of commitment and travel in Northern France and Southern England. So he was working hard to progress as quickly as possible, sparing as much time as he could to help his grieving mother. Money wasn't an issue; the family home was safe, his mother well cared for and his papa had left both of his sons a sizeable inheritance. Nurturing was what the family needed and he was doing his best to provide that, at least on a part-time basis.

Spending time in Devon with his friend had therefore become a rare occurrence and Xavier was determined to make the most of this weekend. They had been tempted by the dessert menu and were waiting for the arrival of *tarte tatin* and *crêpes suzette*.

'Have you thought any further about my proposal?'

asked Pierre, sharing the last of the wine between their two glasses.

'Actually I have,' replied Xavier, 'I've thought about it a lot over the last couple of weeks. I agree it could be good to invest in a developing area of medical treatment. I think my father would approve of me using the money for the benefit of others. But he'd also want me to be prudent.'

'Ha, I remember he was a judicious businessman,' Pierre stated fondly.

'Yes, he was. I can hear him now saying, "Have fun, work hard, may your love life be carefree and your spending be cautious".'

'Indeed.' Pierre grinned. 'I've tried to live by those rules, except I haven't quite managed the last one.'

'Yeah, I noticed your new watch. I must admit to the occasional blow-out myself. Thankfully we're no longer poor students subsisting on bread and soup.'

'Speak for yourself. NHS pay for junior doctors doesn't go that far when you've an expensive course and exam fees to pay for.'

'Ah, so I'd be supporting your wining and dining if I invested in the clinic,' Xavier laughed.

Pierre smiled. 'The clinic doesn't pay me much at the moment. I got involved to gain more research experience and to be at the cutting edge of new medical approaches to infertility. I'm going to be a consultant before I'm thirty-five, you know, and then I'll be like a pig in clover, as they say here.'

Xavier chuckled.

'No, seriously,' Pierre continued, 'the clinic has considerable talent and expertise. They're pushing the boundaries of what's possible with IVF and I'm really excited to be part of it. But as I've said before, they need more capital for research, to be able to offer additional services to more patients and to bring in further experts. I'd like to work there full-time when I've finished my MRCOG.'

Xavier gave him a quizzical look.

'Member of the Royal College of Obstetricians and Gynaecologists,' he clarified.

'Can't you move there before your specialist training is completed?'

Pierre shrugged. 'I'm not sure. I think it'll depend on whether I can satisfy the training requirements. I'm looking into it.'

Xavier leant forward, elbows on the table. He tapped his clasped hands against his lips. 'I'd like to invest,' he said earnestly, 'but I want to talk with your CEO about possible risks, the reliability of earnings and the long-term viability. You know I'm not in it for the short term, and the clinic is in the vanguard of medical research, so over the long term hopefully the return should significantly outweigh the risk. I also need to discuss the investment capital. As you know, my father left me quite a bit.'

Pierre nodded, pleased. 'Sure. I'll try and get a meeting for some time this weekend. Failing that, what about Monday morning? You're not leaving until lunchtime, are you?'

'First thing on Monday would be fine,' Xavier confirmed. 'I've a client to visit in Bristol on Monday afternoon on the way back to London.'

'Great,' Pierre replied happily. He looked at his watch; it was nearly ten o'clock. 'Then I suggest we celebrate your investment of millions with some more drinking.'

'Correction, *possible* investment and not quite *millions*,' Xavier countered, laughing. 'Will a hundred and fifty thousand pounds do, sir?' He inclined his head in a mock bow.

'Shit, that's over a million francs!'

Xavier laughed. 'Yeah, it sounds better in francs, doesn't it?'

'God, Xavier, that would be amazing.'

'Well, let's see what your CEO has to say.' Xavier smiled.

'Come on, we're going to celebrate anyway. I prescribe drinking, dancing and women susceptible to our charms,' exclaimed Pierre, pulling on his jacket.

'Where are we going?'

'The GX club.'

They walked a short distance around an inlet of the old harbour and entered an old, grey-painted building on the quayside. It was as dark inside as out, but they followed the resounding music, ascending a narrow staircase, at the top of which were a man and woman taking money and staffing a coat room. They entered the nightclub through a door to their left and headed to the brightly lit bar. Beers in hand, they found themselves a table on the far side of the large shadowy room.

Raising his pint, clinking Xavier's glass and shouting over The Stranglers singing about a European Female, Pierre admitted, 'We're going to regret this in the morning—grape and grain.'

'Who cares about the morning?' Xavier yelled back. 'To success,' he toasted.

'It comes in many forms.' Pierre inclined his head towards a group of girls a few tables away.

Xavier followed his friend's gaze and laughed. Taking several large swigs of beer, he said, 'You're on.'

'Just like the old days,' Pierre replied.

They joined the dance floor and manoeuvred nearer to where the girls sat, performing their best moves to Prince, Elvis Costello and The Jam. As soon as the DJ played Kraftwerk the women jumped up enthusiastically to dance. Then came Human League and Soft Cell and the floor became crowded, giving Xavier and Pierre an excuse to intermingle. They continued dancing for a while, making eye contact with the women and throwing flirting looks their way. Xavier noted Pierre and one red-haired woman exchanging remarks and getting on quite well. He himself was struck by a pretty, dark-haired girl dressed in a pink crop top and a short red skirt with knee-high boots worn over lacy black tights. Her mass of long permed hair, worn high to one side, belied something about her that was more sophisticated than the rest of her appearance. Her beautiful dark eyes and full red lips complemented her fine sculpted cheekbones and she moved gracefully. They exchanged smiles. The music changed to The Specials and Xavier signalled to her he was going to the bar and asked if he could get her a drink. To his delight she nodded and followed, weaving around the edge of a group of people enthusiastically throwing two-tone shapes.

As they waited to be served, they exchanged names and niceties. The woman's name was Mari, and she and her friend were on a girls' night out to celebrate a birthday. On arriving back at Xavier's table Pierre and the redhead joined them.

Pierre grinned, first at Xavier then at his companion.

'This is Fran,' he said in English. 'Fran, meet my good friend Xavier.'

Xavier nodded. "Ello.' He turned to Mari and began 'This is Pi…' when she interrupted him.

'Pierre, yes, hi, Pierre.'

'Oh, you know one another?' remarked Xavier, slightly taken aback.

Mari laughed. 'Yes, we've met Pierre before, haven't we, Fran?'

Fran chuckled and patted Pierre on the leg. 'Oh, yes, we know Monsieur Pierre, who doesn't keep his promises,' she said mockingly.

Pierre pretended to look hurt. 'Ohhh, I told you, my aunt called in unexpectedly that afternoon and I couldn't turn 'er away. I 'ad no way of letting you know. I'll make it up to you.'

'Hmm,' retorted Fran, taking a mouthful of lager. 'Will you now?' she said cynically. 'Perhaps these Frenchmen are all the same?' she remarked, directing the comment to her friend. 'What do you think, Mari, should we let them dance with us?' She threw Xavier a sideways glance, raising her eyebrows.

Xavier grinned. 'Let me say I'm not my friend's keeper, and, unlike him, I would never let a girl down.' He took Mari's hand momentarily and looked into her eyes. 'Especially one as pretty as you.'

Mari dipped her head to one side in mock appreciation. 'Ahhh, so charming.' She smiled at Xavier, not swayed for a moment.

Xavier raised his glass and toasted her without answering. To Pierre he spoke in French, 'You cheat! You already knew her.'

'Let's say we have some... er... history,' Pierre chuckled, responding also in French. 'You haven't done badly so far.'

'I hope we're not some kind of crass bet,' Mari interrupted hotly in fluent French. 'Because if that's the case you can forget it.'

Xavier and Pierre simultaneously raised their eyebrows, first looking at one another and then at Mari.

'No, not at all,' protested Xavier hastily in French. 'I'm usually a bit shy, so Pierre was just... encouraging me.'

'I didn't know you could speak French. You speak very well,' Pierre added sheepishly, smiling.

Mari turned to Fran. 'They assure me they haven't been betting on us,' she explained with a mischievous look. Then, to the two men, 'Don't you know it's impolite to speak in a language not all of us can understand?'

Fran gave her friend the slightest of winks. They could easily handle these two.

"Ow is it that your French is so good?' Xavier asked Mari, genuinely interested.

'I have a degree in languages and work as a business translator,' she rejoined, 'French and Spanish, mainly.'

'Her job takes her all over the world,' Fran stated, proud of her friend.

'Well, not quite. Mainly Europe and Canada, very occasionally South America.'

'Where did you study?' asked Xavier.

'Here, Plymouth,' Mari answered, taking a sip of her gin and tonic.

'And what do you do, Fran?' Xavier inquired.

'I'm a trainee solicitor.'

'Intelligent and beautiful,' chortled Pierre, trying his

arm around Fran's shoulders and giving her a quick squeeze.

She didn't move away. 'Mari and I have known each other since we were at school,' Fran said to Xavier.

Xavier nodded. 'Pierre and I were at college together in London. I'm sure he must 'ave spoken of me many times. He 'as always… 'ow do you say… looked up to me,' he laughed with false immodesty.

'It's really the other way around,' joked Pierre, 'although 'e likes to be the centrepiece.' He downed the remainder of his pint and jerked his head towards Fran. 'You want to dance?' She nodded and they joined the floor, where XTC's senses were working overtime.

'What do you do, Xavier? What brings you to Plymouth—just visiting Pierre?'

Mari seemed to be studying Xavier's tanned face whilst he answered her and he sensed she liked what she saw.

'I'm in pharmaceuticals. I 'ave clients in the South-west and in London. I came to see Pierre for the weekend. It's been a while since we 'ad the time to catch up.'

'Ah, so you're both scientists,' she smiled, pushing a stray curl from her eye.

He gazed at her beautiful mouth, itching to press his lips on hers, to feel them part. Instead, he took a gulp of beer.

'C'mon,' she grinned, jerking her head towards the dancers. They bopped to Haircut 100, boogied to Duran Duran and twirled to Adam and the Ants. For the next couple of hours Mari and Xavier ceased dancing only to refresh their glasses.

At about one-thirty in the morning the DJ relaxed the mood and played a few slow songs. Xavier took both of

Mari's hands and, with arms outstretched, they swayed to the gentle recurring rhythm of the Stranglers' 'Golden Brown'.

During the next song, a Foreigner track, Xavier drew her closer. 'May I?' he said. From the way she moved, he guessed she was cautiously allowing herself to be held by him, placing her hands first on his shoulders then casually around his neck. Although she was tall for a woman, she was looking up at him.

As they shifted under the softly-coloured lights Xavier found himself whispering the words of the song into her ear, *'I've been waiting for a girl like you…'* He didn't mean to; it was clichéd, but he was so struck by her that Foreigner's lyrics suddenly fit his feelings. He buried his face in her hair and drank in her perfume. As the song faded, he moved his head back slightly to look at her and she did the same. As they kissed softly his body tingled. He wanted to press his lips hard against hers, to explore her mouth with his tongue, but she pulled away and he realised he needed to be gentle, to treat her with respect, to take things slowly. She gave him the sweetest of smiles and they continued slow-dancing until they ran out of music.

Chapter Seven

Saturday dawned cold and sunny. There was no sign of the fierce breeze and sleet of the day before. The morning was calm and the sky a gorgeous cornflower blue with not a cloud in sight. The shimmering silver sea gently licked the rocks around the Sound and the walls of the harbour.

While leaving the nightclub in the early hours, Fran decided it would be fun for the four of them to meet for a late breakfast. Mari and Fran were first to arrive at Cap'n Jaspers on the quayside. Since it was so cold they each bought themselves a mug of coffee and found a bench near the tiny shack to sit and wait for the men. The Victorian fish market, designed to look like a pretty railway station, was closed. However, as it was a lovely day, there were plenty of people around and the eatery was busy. A wooden seagull suspended from the apex of the blue-and-red-painted hut rose and dipped cheerfully, welcoming customers to the pretty cabin constructed of little more than old hardboard doors with scalloped plywood edging.

As they warmed their hands on their hot mugs Mari spotted the two men in the far distance, walking towards the inner harbour from the Hoe. Both were tall and lithe with skin tones of olive and honey; they made a handsome pair.

'You have to admit, Xavier is bloody gorgeous,' Fran remarked.

'Fran, I'm married,' Mari responded, though she didn't disagree.

Fran raised her eyebrows and tilted her head at Mari. 'Well, it didn't seem like it last night. I see you've got your wedding ring on again this morning.'

'Yes, well, it doesn't exactly encourage men to dance with me and I wanted a bit of fun,' Mari replied sheepishly. She looked down at her ring, stroking it with her thumb. 'You know I love Gerren,' she said pensively, 'it's just sometimes I need some fun, in a different way I mean.'

Fran laid a hand on her friend's arm. 'Mari, you know I'm fond of Gerren,' she said guardedly, 'but I have to say he can be… just a tiny bit… boring sometimes. You know what I mean.'

Mari sighed. 'I suppose so.'

Fran's laughter lines crinkled. 'A model railway, Mari, come on.' She smiled softly.

'He is an engineer.'

'Yeah, but he's also a grown man with a beautiful wife who he needs to appreciate more.'

'Hmm.' She and Gerren didn't go clubbing. He wasn't one for dancing, preferring to frequent the local pub and play darts. These days their local was ten miles out of town, so, on the rare occasions when she met girlfriends, she stayed over at Fran's flat and exuberance was high on the agenda.

'Well, anyway,' Mari continued, batting her hand as if discouraging a persistent fly, 'I had a lot of fun last night. I must admit Xavier is good looking.' She recalled the moment his beautiful dark brown eyes seemed to see through the veneer to the essence of her. She'd melted a little. A pleasant frisson arose within, evoked by the memory. She giggled. 'It was a lovely kiss. And, my friend, Pierre is attractive too.'

'He's a bit of a one for the ladies, but I think I could hook him if I wanted to.' Fran grinned.

It was Mari's turn to raise her eyebrows. 'What's not to like?' she remarked, matching her friend's grin.

Fran turned slightly to look away from the approaching men. 'Here they come,' she whispered.

As Xavier and Pierre approached the fish quay, Xavier experienced a rush of adrenaline. He hadn't been able to stop thinking about Mari all night and consequently hadn't slept much. He'd finally sunk into a slumber at about six-thirty. Pierre had woken him at ten-thirty and he'd just had time for a quick shower before they set off for the Barbican from Pierre's flat in West Hoe. They'd walked quickly yet he couldn't help stopping to admire the beautiful view, across the glinting water, of Drake's Island and beyond to the open sea. On the Hoe, where Drake had famously stood hundreds of years ago, people were enjoying the sunshine, walking their dogs, pushing their toddlers in prams or carrying them on shoulders, playing ball games or simply sitting on benches looking at the scenery.

Now he was so close to Mari again Xavier felt nervous and hung back, letting Pierre make the approach. His friend always behaved calmly, almost nonchalantly at times; he had a lot of self-confidence.

'*Bonjour*, ladies,' announced Pierre, throwing his arms

wide. "Ow are you this fine morning?' He took Fran's hand and kissed it in a flamboyant gesture.

'Fine, now we have our hands around hot mugs,' joked Fran.

Pierre looked at her sideways for a moment then placed his hands over his heart. 'No, anything but a mug,' he cried in mock indignation.

Xavier didn't understand but smiled anyway. "Ow is the coffee?' he asked Mari, rubbing his cold hands together. 'I'm dying for some caffeine.'

'Good,' she replied, 'warm.'

Xavier nodded. 'This place seems to be popular.'

'No fancy restaurant this morning,' Pierre stated, 'but the best breakfast in town. What are you girls 'aving? Can you manage 'alf a yard?'

'Don't be so rude,' Fran chuckled. 'Tck, he's so boastful,' she continued, looking at Xavier, who laughed.

'What is this yard you are talking about?' Xavier asked Pierre.

'Come *mon ami*, let me show you the menu. It's their speciality; devised for 'ungry fishermen.'

Fran bought a large bacon and egg sandwich and Mari chose a hot mackerel roll, while both men decided on two jumbo sausages with onions in half a yard of baguette. Large mugs of steaming coffee perfectly accompanied the feast. They sat on a bench overlooking a multiplicity of vibrant fishing boats with masts and rigging stretching skywards and colourful buoys dangling casually towards the water, their decks stacked with nets, coiled rope and lobster pots. For a while no one said a great deal—they were too busy enjoying their breakfast in the sunshine. It was established that nobody had any particular plans and

Mari wasn't expected at home, so Fran suggested they take a walk in Mount Edgcumbe Country Park along the coastal path, an idea met with unanimous approval.

As they walked up the coastal road to where Xavier had left his car at the foot of the forbidding Royal Citadel walls, they passed the Mayflower steps from which, as Mari explained to Xavier, the Pilgrims had left for America in 1620. 'I bet they didn't 'ave such a good breakfast,' he remarked.

Receiving directions from Fran, Xavier drove them the short distance to Stonehouse, where they caught a small foot ferry across the River Tamar to Cremyll. During the crossing Mari pointed out various local landmarks but Xavier couldn't concentrate on what she was saying. As she indicated with her hands he noticed she was wearing a wedding ring. He could have sworn she hadn't had a ring on that finger the evening before and she'd not mentioned a husband or boyfriend. The joy in his heart began to evaporate but he quickly blocked its escape route, telling himself all might not be what it seemed; she'd kissed him, hadn't she? She was here with him now rather than at home with someone; perhaps she was a widow or perhaps separated. He saw laughter in her beautiful eyes and felt warmth in the way she spoke to him and wanted so much to enjoy her company. So he decided to ignore the ring for the time being—he would ask her casually about it later.

Within ten minutes they were disembarking at a hamlet next to a small beach backed by large grassy areas, woodland and a nice-looking pub.

'Now you can eat a proper Cornish pasty,' Pierre chuckled to Xavier, looking provocatively at Mari and Fran, who were Devon girls through and through. 'You know there is a rivalry between Devon and Cornwall about 'oo makes the best pasties,' he explained.

'Ah, much like the contention between French and British cheeses,' remarked Xavier. He grinned at Mari. 'Of course, although there is a lot to recommend English cheddar nothing can beat good cave-aged Roquefort, consumed with grapes straight off the vine and a glass of red wine,' he stated mockingly, adding 'in the sunshine.'

Mari gave his arm a light thump. 'I beg to differ,' she stated in an equally authoritative tone, 'mature Stilton eaten with slices of ripe pear and enjoyed with a glass of homemade sloe gin simply cannot be beaten.'

Xavier tilted his head in acknowledgement of a good case. 'Mmm, sounds lovely, I'll 'ave to try that combination.'

They took a path into the Mount Edgcumbe estate and, following the South-west coastal route, entered through a gatehouse into an Italianate garden with an impressive Georgian orangery at one end and, at the other, a handsome pair of sweeping stone steps capped with ornate balustrades and graced with three Romanesque statues. Four circular flower beds surrounded an imposing central mermaid fountain.

'We could come here on the way back and have some tea in the orangery,' remarked Fran, rubbing her hands together. 'Their cakes are delicious.'

'Don't you ever stop thinking about food?' jested Pierre, patting his stomach. 'I'm still full of sausage.'

Xavier noticed Fran glancing at Mari, rapidly raising and lowering her eyebrows as if to say 'I wish I was!' which elicited a smirk from Mari. 'We'll see,' she said, 'who can and who can't resist a cream tea in a couple of hours.'

They took a path through mixed woodland and across pasture through another formal garden, laid out in geometrical shapes defined by box hedges around a shell fountain, ending at the sea edge on top of an old semicircular gun battery jutting out over the rocky shoreline.

'This was built to protect Plymouth from the French,' Mari stated provocatively. 'Though I'm glad we let you in nowadays,' she laughed.

They continued along the shoreline through landscaped woodland, alongside a series of sandy beaches and past several historic follies and stone seats, eventually turning eastwards from the coast to circle back across pasture embroidered with trees and grazed by wild deer.

All the while, Xavier and Mari talked about many things, getting to know one another casually without trying. They explored their artistic and political likes and dislikes and activities that excited them, their love of the countryside and historical architecture, taste in wines, college days, love of their professions and the accompanying hard work ethic.

Xavier summoned the courage to ask the question that, all the while, burned in his gut. His heart began to pound. 'I noticed your wedding ring. Do you 'ave an 'usband?'

Mari declined her head and her mouth turned downwards for the briefest moment. 'Yes.' Her tone seemed to be touched with a trace of guilt. 'He, Gerren, works for my father's engineering company.' She stalled.

Xavier felt something plummet inside. He forced the best smile he could manage and tried to adopt a casual-yet-interested timbre. 'Ah, so 'e's an engineer then? Is that 'ow you met, at your father's workplace?'

'Yes, er, and no. We were at school together but he's a year older. We started dating in the sixth form before he left to study engineering in Plymouth.'

Xavier nodded. ''E didn't go far away then.'

'No, we both decided to stay local. He had a comfortable home with his parents and…' she shrugged, 'he wanted to stay near me. I had a good life at home too, but once I had my place at college my father bought a small house, which we shared with two other students. Gerren and I only paid bills, which allowed us to save for a deposit on a house of our own. My folks helped us with that too.'

Xavier realised his lips were pressed tightly and hoped she hadn't noticed. 'That's very, er,' he struggled for an appropriate word, 'generous of your parents.'

'Well, it was a good investment for them,' she explained straightforwardly. 'My mum's a GP and they're not short of a bob or two. They're fairly well-off,' she added in response to Xavier's quizzical expression.

Xavier nodded. *An engineer like his beau-père with a job and house given to him by his beau-père. Very expedient*, he thought. 'So, 'ow long 'ave you been married, if you don't mind me asking?' he ventured.

Mari cleared her throat slightly. 'About four years.' She qualified, 'Since I was nineteen.'

Xavier wondered why she'd revealed her age. Could he hope she was hinting she'd married too young and was regretting it? He wanted to change the topic but there was one more thing he needed to know. 'So 'e doesn't come dancing with you, this 'usband of yours?' he shrugged in a questioning manner.

Mari's expression changed to marginally sheepish. She

shook her head, not looking at him 'We have, er… different social lives.'

Xavier decided to try to put the fact Mari wasn't free out of his mind and simply enjoy her company. Having a friendship with her would be better than nothing and, after all, who knows what could happen in the future. They made one another laugh and had a great deal in common. There were similarities in their upbringing; both fathers had worked hard to build their businesses from nothing—Xavier's in property development and Mari's in construction—and had instilled the value of industriousness. Both Xavier and Mari valued their good fortune at having been raised in what they considered idyllic locations. Mari's love of the sea and sailing, wild rugged cliffs, little sandy bays, rock pools, the smell of saltwater and seaweed and walking on Dartmoor stemmed from being nurtured in Plymouth and, later, in Newton Ferrers, an old farming and fishing village on the beautiful Yealm Estuary. Xavier had grown up amidst vineyards and forests hosting deer and wild boar, rivers rushing through deep limestone gorges and medieval towns whose dwellings protectively surround their active market squares, radiating out via networks of narrow lanes and passageways. Xavier's love of walking and climbing, white-water kayaking, cooking fresh market produce and his respect for, and knowledge of, traditional architecture all originated from his childhood.

All the while they were chatting, Xavier endeavoured to keep Mari at an emotional distance but failed. He longed to stroke her hair, to gently take her face in his hands and kiss her full mouth, to hold her to him and feel her tremble under his touch. He wanted her so much but he realised Friday night—when she'd let him dance so close to her—had been a one-off. That would be their only kiss. She was married and he had to respect that. Here she was, walking beside him, but she might as well have been on another continent.

After a couple of hours the four of them arrived back in the formal gardens surrounding the striking red-stone Tudor mansion and unanimously decided to head to the orangery to warm up with tea and cake. Mari found herself not wanting their outing to end. She was most definitely having fun. She had a coffee and walnut slice, Pierre ordered lemon drizzle cake for himself and Fran, while Xavier wanted to try a warm Cornish pasty. As they enjoyed their tasty tea and elegant surroundings they discussed their plans for the days ahead. In confidence, Xavier told her and Fran about his scheme to invest in the clinic and that he'd be visiting clients in London for a few days before returning to Lille. Pierre said he had an assignment on subfertility to finish within the next couple of weeks and Fran had a social welfare law vocational elective to complete as part of her part-time legal practice course. Mari was reticent about her activities. She was due to be translating at several London meetings, however, she didn't want to mention she'd be in the capital at the same time as Xavier. She had realised she didn't quite trust herself with him. This was a shock, so, as a protective measure, she decided to impart information prudently, simply stating she had a lot of meetings coming up and changing the subject. They then discussed what they should do that evening. Mari said she would have to go home but the others all begged her to stay another night.

'C'mon Mari, it'll be fun,' pleaded Pierre. 'You can all come back to my flat. We'll get beers and fish and chips—obviously a lot later,' he revised, patting his stomach. 'And watch movies—I have a VCR and I've loads of stuff recorded from the TV. Or we could play naked Twister,' he kidded, patting Fran's backside before she shot him a repelling look.

'Is Gerren expecting you back?' Fran asked her quietly. 'There's a phone box in Cremyll; you can always ring and check.'

Mari nodded. She didn't want to go home but was concerned to know Gerren's plans. 'It would be nice to stay another night. I'll have to see.'

While Mari rang home the others waited for her by a castellated stone kiosk next to the slipway. The daylight had faded but an old-fashioned street lamp radiated enough light for them to double-check the ferry times.

Having talked with her husband, Mari exited the phone box smiling. 'Gerren has a darts match this evening in our local pub, so he'll be out anyway,' she announced, walking towards them. Cheers went up from the other three. 'But I'm not playing Twister, naked or otherwise,' she added. 'I'll have to leave after breakfast tomorrow because he's arranged for us to have Sunday lunch with his parents.'

'The boat comes every 'alf 'our, but the last one isn't until seven. Per'aps we could sample the delights of that pub,' Xavier suggested.

'*Bonne idée, mon ami!*' Pierre agreed, patting Xavier on the back.

The girls grinned at one another. 'Last one in buys the drinks,' cried Fran, making a dash across the road.

They spent an hour or so drinking Cornish ale and recounting entertaining stories.

'D'you remember phoning me pretending to be from the Women's Institute?' Fran asked Mari, at one point.

Mari chuckled. 'I couldn't resist it, not after you told me about that client who was a real pain. What was her name?'

'Walker, "the talker",' Fran replied with a groan. 'I received a call from a member of the WI, with a strong Scottish accent, inviting me to give a presentation on conveyancing—that's the legal part of buying or selling a property,' she explained to Xavier and Pierre. 'She said she was arranging an evening of talks on career choices and I'd been recommended to her by Mrs Walker. She was so enthusiastic, I was finding it hard to say no.'

Mari giggled. 'I asked you to talk about your passion for conveyancing.'

'Yeah, as if anyone could get passionate about that,' Fran chortled. 'When you told me my slot would be between a bus driver and a tax inspector my heart sank even further. You really had me fooled.'

'What 'appened,' asked Xavier, laughing.

'I knew she'd be too polite to refuse. Once she'd agreed I owned up,' Mari grinned.

Pierre raised his glass. 'To English wit,' he toasted, then finished his pint. 'Let's 'ave another.'

A little while later, they emerged, somewhat unsteadily, out of the cosy inn into the cold night air and made their way onto the ferry. Since they were all over the drink-driving limit, they walked the mile or so from Stonehouse to Pierre's flat, picking up supplies from an off-licence and fish and chip shop en route. A highly enjoyable evening ensued during which they discovered Mari's penchant for peanut butter and banana sandwiches and Xavier's proclivity for animated dancing.

At about two in the morning their beds were calling. Fran chose to spend the night with Pierre. As her friend followed him into his bedroom without a backward look, Mari threw an involuntary glance at Xavier and found him returning her discomforted look. There followed an awkward silence.

Mari suddenly felt rather sober and tried to ease her self-consciousness by looking around for signs of where Pierre might keep spare bedding.

'I'll take the sofa,' Xavier announced quickly in a slightly embarrassed tone. 'You 'ave my... I mean the guest... room.'

Mari's pulse was racing. She nodded gratefully.

'Pierre keeps bed stuff in 'ere,' Xavier indicated with a wave towards a flat-top pine trunk in one corner of the living room on which sat a number of scientific magazines. 'Let me 'elp you.'

Thankful for something to do, Mari went to the trunk, removed the journals and rummaged inside, pulling out a pillow and quilt, which she passed to him. As they went into the spare room to swap the bedding, she avoided looking at him and sensed he was doing the same. But as he turned to leave the bedroom their eyes met briefly and he threw her a broad beam.

'Bonne nuit Mari. *C'etait une journée pleine de plaisir.'*

She returned his smile. 'I enjoyed today too. *Bonne nuit.'*

Mari woke at regular intervals, her thoughts centred

on Xavier. She considered how he made her feel—desired, joyous, special: sensations she hadn't experienced in quite a while. She imagined his strong muscular body and craved his hands upon her. He was only a few feet away. She was sure if she went to him he would be more than willing. But she knew it would be wrong. Despite their difficulties she did not want to betray Gerren; she would not. Therefore each time she awoke she made herself turn over and go back to sleep.

After breakfast the next morning she said her goodbyes and drove home to be with her husband.

Chapter Eight

London, England, January 1983

In London, on Tuesday, Mari's meeting went well and the clients were pleased. They invited her out for dinner that evening but she politely declined, saying she had plans. Sometimes she needed a break between clients to regroup and concentrate on preparing for the next task. On this occasion she was well-prepared for the next two days. So, fifty minutes later, having showered and changed, she found herself emerging from the Marble Arch tube station and crossing the road to stand under the triumphal monument in the corner of Hyde Park. It had been another cold day and the sky was clear. The four columns bordering the three arches were lit prettily from below. Once a pristine white, the marble had yellowed with age and exposure to air-born pollutants, conveying a warmer quality to the structure.

Mari gazed through the crowds and traffic, not into the park but towards Great Cumberland Place, where Xavier had said he usually stayed in London. A cautious voice in her head warned her this was not a good idea; she would be fanning hot embers and was bound to get burned. However, an artful voice asserted itself; they were just friends—they would only have dinner—what harm could it do? Sagacity wrestled against desire as she crossed the road hesitantly.

She entered the hotel and was approaching the reception desk when she realised she didn't know his surname. She stopped in her tracks for a few moments to concentrate. Fran wouldn't know it either and she certainly wasn't going to phone Pierre. She thought hard and remembered Xavier had talked about his family in the sense that they were hard-working. He had said something like *I have the family work ethic*, mentioning his family name; it began with a D. What was it? Demars? Doucet? Ducat? No, that wasn't right. Dubois: that was it. He'd said *I have the Dubois work ethic*.

Mari waited for a receptionist to become available then approached the desk, tidying her wind-wafted hair with her fingers.

'Hello, I wonder if you can tell me if you have a Mr Xavier Dubois staying here. So silly of me, I think he booked at this hotel but I'm not certain.'

'I'll just check for you,' replied the thin pale-faced man, running a finger over a list of names and signatures in a large book placed out of reach behind the reception desk. 'Ah, yes,' he answered in a formal tone, 'we do have Mr Dubois with us this week.' He gave Mari a brief polite smile.

Mari's heart pounded against her rib cage. She tried to keep her voice steady. 'Could you possibly tell me which room he's in, please?'

'Sorry, madam, we don't give out guests' room numbers, but I can phone him. Who should I say wants to see him?'

'Uh, say it's a friend, please. I'd like to surprise him.'

'Just a moment, please.' The man dialled a three-digit

number and waited. There was no reply. 'I'm sorry, he doesn't appear to be in his room.'

Disappointment flooded through her.

'I can have a message delivered if you like.'

Before Mari could decide whether she wanted to leave a message the receptionist had clicked his fingers and a bellboy appeared. The dark-suited man gave him a hastily scribbled note and sent him on his way. 'Is there anything else I can help you with?'

'Um… no, no thanks.'

She wasn't sure what to do next and looked at her watch. It was five past seven. Xavier had probably already gone out for dinner. Perhaps he was with a client or even another woman. Mari's confidence faded. She looked around and noticed a bar on the other side of the spacious foyer. She decided to get herself a drink and sit in one of the comfy leather armchairs in the lobby near the entrance, telling herself she'd wait until she'd finished one drink.

About fifteen minutes later she was taking the last sips of her Cinzano Bianco when she noticed a familiar form walking towards the reception desk. The pounding in her chest began. He showed a piece of paper to the man Mari had spoken to, who subsequently cast his eyes over the lobby then pointed in her direction. Unexpectedly Mari felt an intense shyness. What would she say to him—*I was just passing*? It sounded ridiculous. There was no time to think. He was in front of her with a surprised look on his face.

She was flustered but managed, 'Hi!' She needn't have worried. He threw his arms around her in a big hug then stepped back to look at her, a wide grin on his face.

'Mari! Wonderful to see you! What are you doing 'ere... ah, I don't mean 'ere at my 'otel, but 'ere in London?'

'Um, well, some meetings came up and I thought... perhaps... I'd look you up,' she responded brightly, with false confidence.

'That's great.' He bent his head towards hers and spoke quietly. 'I was in the shower when the phone rang but they pushed a note under my door. I could not think oo it might be. I don't know anyone in London now, apart from clients. I'm glad it's you.'

'I wondered if you might like to have dinner—if you don't have other plans, I mean.' Mari tried to sound casual.

'I'd love to. I was going to go out by myself, maybe see a film. I'd much rather spend the evening with you.'

He was open, honest and self-assured, which Mari found refreshing and delightful.

The air was cold on their faces, imparting a ruddy glow to their cheeks. Xavier thrust his hands into the pockets of his winter coat. Mari was glad to be wearing her leather gloves. She pulled at her woollen scarf so it fitted closely around her neck and chin and linked her arm with his.

They walked down Oxford Street, threading through boisterous crowds of busy people scurrying home from work, doing late-night shopping, on their way to restaurants and bars, or simply sightseeing. The wide road, heavy with double-decker buses, cars and London taxis, was lit by streetlamps and myriad vehicle lights, countless shop windows and neon advertising, so the period architecture above the modern shop fronts was still clearly visible. With their cornucopia of styles from Renaissance and Neo-Classical through Gothic and Queen Anne to Art Nouveau and Post Modern, the buildings proudly exhibited their history. Concrete and steel stood side by side with red brick and terracotta, glass frontages alongside Ionic columns and stone statues. A multitude of pillars, gables, domes, spires and clustered chimneys stretched upward into the night sky.

Eventually they turned south into Soho. Some narrow streets were already festooned with red lanterns for the upcoming Chinese New Year and the air was charged with a cheerful buzz of impending celebration.

'You know the fifteenth of February will be the year of the Pig,' said Xavier. 'All the babies born this year will be crying because they're 'ighly emotional and intuitive enough to know 'ow to get attention.' He laughed. 'Personally, I'm a dog, which means I'm loyal and bring good fortune,' he smiled. 'Which animal are you?'

'I don't know. I've never thought about it,' Mari replied, fascinated. 'I was born in 1960, so what does that make me?'

Xavier thought for a moment. 'Well, the animals go in twelve-year cycles, so two after a pig is… er… you're a rat! If you were born after Chinese New Year,' he added.

'Oh,' responded Mari, disappointed. 'I don't think I like the sound of that'.

'No need to be sad about it. Rats are incredibly charming,' Xavier replied, 'and also cheerful and adaptable and therefore popular!'

'That's okay then,' Mari laughed. 'I could have guessed, actually—that's me all over.'

They spent the next few hours enjoying a delicious Chinese meal, talking and laughing, telling one another more about their childhoods, their hopes, ambitions, triumphs and disappointments. It was so easy to talk to him—Mari found herself confiding things she'd only talked about with Fran and, to some extent, Lena; feelings she'd tried to lock away. She told Xavier she couldn't have children and that the fault was with her; Gerren was refusing to consider adoption; she'd never know what it was like to be a mother or grandmother, and how those thoughts sometimes ate away at her like acid on metal until she was able to sequester them in a corner of her mind.

He touched her hand and said he was sorry, he understood how difficult it must be, his brother, Alain, and sister-in-law, Fayette, were also struggling to have children.

Inwardly, Mari was comforted by Xavier's empathy. She wanted to ask him more about Alain and Fayette's difficulties—it was clear his comprehension of her suffering was born of personal family experience. But she began to feel vulnerable; weakened, as if she'd opened a wound and truths and emotions were bleeding out, exposed. At that moment she needed to regain control.

She drew herself up, shook her head and shrugged. 'We've thrown ourselves into our careers,' she stated. 'Gerren seems content.'

He looked at her sadly but responded positively. 'Although children are the focus of many people's lives there's a lot of other enjoyment to be 'ad in life—'owever you may 'ave to work 'arder to attain it.'

Later, Xavier insisted on walking Mari back to her hotel. At first she protested politely, saying she didn't want to inconvenience him; in fact she didn't want the evening to end, so eventually agreed and was privately glad. Her hotel was in Westminster so they caught the tube to St James's Park and walked from there. They strolled, arm in arm, a pretension against the cold, enjoying the heightened familiarity the pose afforded. Neither was in a hurry to reach their destination. At length, however, they came upon an imposing building of red brick and white stone with wrought iron balconies and a central arched entrance.

'This is me,' said Mari reluctantly.

'Your clients must really appreciate you,' remarked Xavier.

'What can I say—I'm charming and popular!'

'Ah yes, the adorable little rat,' Xavier laughed then changed his tone. 'I really enjoy being with you,' he declared seriously.

'And me with you,' Mari reciprocated clumsily. *You are so refreshing and exciting.* Her dark eyes sparkled and her features reflected the delight she felt within.

She thought for a moment then threw the last vestiges of caution aside. 'Will you come in? A final drink perhaps?'

They both knew what was being offered.

'Are you sure?' he responded considerately, though longing was palpable in his eyes.

Her heart was thumping, blood racing through her veins causing a moment of light-headedness. She steadied herself against the wrought iron railings and nodded. 'Yes, quite sure.'

They took two glasses of wine up to her room, each prolonging the pretence of an innocent nightcap. The room was stylishly and simply furnished in tones of cream and beige with a floor-to-ceiling window at the far end and large double bed in the centre.

Xavier took Mari's drink and placed it with his own on a wooden desk by the bed. He turned back to Mari and she sensed the desire filling his body as wine flowing into a glass, spilling over. He reached her in two strides and put his arms around her. Then, withdrawing, he gently took her face in his hands and kissed her full mouth.

His hands on her body and his mouth upon hers, an intense yearning swept through Mari. She abandoned herself to desire, craving the touch of his fingers, the heat of his body, letting herself drown in the sensations he was creating deep within.

They stood, undressing one another slowly, each savouring the anticipation and discovery of the other in the muted lamplight. Running a finger down the line of her long neck he found the roundness of her full breasts, his caresses radiating quivers over her skin. She breathed his natural musk, moving her hands lightly over the firmness of the muscles in his arms and chest then began tracing the line of dark hairs below his navel leading tantalisingly downwards.

He let out a strangled groan then stepped towards her again, enveloping her in his arms. *'Tu es si belle,'* he murmured into her hair.

They lay together then, on the fresh cotton bedclothes, and he came to her. She gave herself completely, arching her hips upwards to meet him and moaning with the utter, exquisite, loss of control, as he melted into her.

Neither wanted to stop; again and again their bodies came together during the night, melding like warm chocolate.

By the morning they were bound.

Chapter Nine

London, England, June 1983

Since their first liaison, Xavier and Mari had met in London several times when they'd succeeded in scheduling their work meetings in the capital simultaneously. They both incorporated extra time into each trip, enabling them to spend the occasional afternoon together in addition to evenings. They always booked separate hotel rooms but merely for the sake of appearances.

Their sex was uninhibited and impassioned, as addictive as chocolate with a bottle of red wine. Afterwards they talked for hours, each absorbing the other's life; loves and passions, hopes and goals, fears and anxieties. Quickly Xavier came to know Mari and she him.

One morning, as the first rays of sunlight intruded through a gap in the heavy brocade curtains, Xavier lay in bed listening to Mari humming happily in the shower. He rolled over into the warm patch bestowed by her body and laid his face on the sheet, inhaling her perfume. His hand on the empty space reminded him of how it was when he was apart from her: alone, abandoned. He'd never felt like that with any other woman. His longing was an invisible force pulling at his chest and throat, silently reaching out to her through the ether. Sometimes he ached with it. Yet when they were together his heart knew pure bliss and joy danced through his stomach as sunlight on water.

Xavier wondered if she felt the same. He thought she did. He believed something wonderful had happened between them, he was not merely a distraction from her deep desire for a child, and her life with her husband which constantly reminded her of it. He loved her and he'd made up his mind to tell her.

She emerged from the bathroom in a white towel, her long black hair glistening. Xavier patted the bed beside him and, taking her comb from the bedside table, ran it through her curls, gently separating the strands.

He told her then how he felt. '*Tu es tout pour moi, mon amour. Quand je suis avec toi, mon cœur chante.*' You are everything to me, my love. My heart sings when I'm with you.

He kissed her hair. 'When we're apart I spend each day waiting for the next time we're together.' He shook his head and heaved a despondent sigh. 'I feel like I can't even breath without you.'

She turned to him with glistening eyes, opening her mouth to speak but he put a finger to her parted lips.

'Let me say this or my courage will fail.' He smiled tenderly and took her slight hands in his, gently stroking the backs of them with his thumbs. 'I know you're with…'—he couldn't bring himself to say Gerren's name—'I mean, you're not free… but you're 'ere with me now and that says something to me. And you 'ave passion for me, which says something too. I just need you to know 'ow I feel.' He paused. 'So if you want to make a life with me I will be there for you.'

A tear made its way down her cheek and she disengaged a hand to wipe it away then reached to touch the side of Xavier's face, her fingertips soft against his morning stubble.

'I would share all my days with you if I could. I love you, Xavier. You must know that. I love you and I want to be with you.' Her voice began to fracture. 'But my life is complicated… and…' Her words descended into sobs and she reached out and clung to him.

He held her then, tenderly rocking her from side to side. '*Ma petite Souci,*' he murmured.

After a while, when her tears had dried and she'd regained her composure, she moved apart and looked up at him with a troubled expression. 'I'm sorry Xavier. I know how unfair on you this is and it's my fault.'

He made to protest but she cut him off. 'I don't regret what we have; not one bit. But I do feel sorry for making you unhappy—in the times when we're not together, I mean. I know it's wrong but somehow I can't help myself. I need to be with you.' She sighed sadly. 'The thing is, despite the difficulties between me and Gerren, he's my husband and I still love him—though differently to the way I love you. I… I love you both.' She looked away from him.

Thus far Xavier had carefully avoided mentioning children, knowing it would be unfair on her; *un coup bas*. But he felt as if he were clinging onto a cliff; a scree, shifting under the weight of his words and actions. He needed to use everything to gain a foothold.

'Just so you know… I mean I'm not trying to put any

pressure on you…' he began tentatively. 'I would be 'appy to… adopt a child with you.' He meant it.

He waited for a response or acknowledgement, his heart pounding. Had he stepped too far?

Mari said nothing, but threw him a faltering smile and squeezed his hand.

As they said goodbye, they agreed not to make any decisions and simply to carry on spending time together; to keep their lives as they were, for the moment. While it was far from ideal it avoided the unthinkable—that they should part.

Chapter Ten

London, England, December 1983

No sooner had Mari entered her hotel room than the phone rang. It was Xavier, via the reception desk. '*Coucou* Mari. Sorry but I'll be about 'alf an 'our late.'

'No problem,' she answered brightly. 'I'm going to have a shower anyway. Ring room 325 when you've checked in and I'll come to you. We still have time for a drink before we head out.'

She washed and dressed in an raglan-sleeved sweater dress, belted at the waist, which was both warm and flattering to her figure, all the while quivers of anticipation rippling through her body. She'd been able to contrive an extra night away on the pretext of attending a late Friday meeting. She and Xavier would dine in Covent Garden and enjoy the Christmas lights and window displays in Oxford and Regent Streets. They planned to spend the majority of Saturday together before she caught her train back to Plymouth. She couldn't wait to be with him.

As she pulled on her over-the-knee leather boots the phone rang again. Xavier confirmed his room number. As she replaced the receiver a mischievous smile crept onto her face. Guessing he'd have requested a bottle of wine she dialled 3 to confirm. Then she phoned his room. 'Mr

Dubois, its Niamh from Room Service,' she announced in a strong Irish accent. 'I apologise but the Bordeaux you ordered isn't available. We do have a 1981 Chateau Lafite Rothschild which I'm sure you would enjoy.'

'Oh, *dommage,*' came Xavier's disappointed response. 'Hmm, 'ow much is the Chateau Lafite?'

'It's thirty three pounds, sir, but well worth it,' Mari said, keeping her tone impassive.

'Thirty three,' repeated Xavier, the price catching in his throat. Mari began to vibrate with suppressed giggles. 'That's... er... I'll... er...' he stuttered.

Mari continued. 'As I said, I'm sure a man such as yourself would appreciate it. And I'm sure the lady in room 325 would too.'

There was a moment of silence before realisation dawned. 'Mari? You devil,' he chuckled. '*Dieu.* I nearly 'ad an 'eart attack.'

'Am I not worth a bottle of Chateau Lafite Rothschild then?' Mari teased.

'Hmm, I think you should come to my room and I'll tell you,' he laughed.

Xavier had ordered their breakfast to be brought to his room and it had just arrived when he received a call. Mari was pouring coffee as Xavier answered; it was Alain. Mari couldn't hear what Alain was saying but she could tell he was upset. She experienced a rush of anxiety. She knew Alain and Fayette had finally managed to conceive—Xavier had cautiously mentioned it, though hadn't shared further details for fear of upsetting her. She'd genuinely been pleased for them and had told him about her relationship with Lena, convincing herself, as well as him, she could be happy for friends who had what she could not. As she caught Alain's troubled tone, she hoped to God it wasn't bad news about the baby.

Xavier swung his legs out from under the covers and sat on the edge of the bed with his back to her. His head dropped as he listened to his brother, responding intermittently. '*Ah Alain, je suis vraiment désolé. Comment va Fayette?... Mon Dieu, vous avez tous deux tant souffert. ... Y a-t-il quelque chose de pratique que je puisse faire pour vous aider?... L'as-tu dit à notre mère? ... Non—alors, laisse-moi lui dire pour toi. Au moins tu n'auras pas à voir sa tristesse.*'

Mari understood from Xavier's side of the conversation something awful had happened to Fayette and Alain and that they'd suffered in the past. Xavier was suggesting he tell their mother so they wouldn't have to face her yet. He was offering practical help, but it seemed there wasn't anything else he could do.

When the call ended Xavier turned to Mari. His eyes were glistening. 'Fayette 'as lost 'er baby,' he stated simply. He put his head in his hands and was quiet for a few moments.

Mari's stomach lurched. It was as she had feared. She put a hand on his shoulder. 'Oh, Xavier, I'm sorry.'

Eventually Xavier looked up and shook his head despondently. His face was drawn with sadness. 'It is the last of five. The doctors 'ave told 'er there is something wrong with 'er uterus. She 'ad an x-ray. It seems there is something interfering with the embryo developing. *Fibromes.* I can't think of the English word—my mind 'as gone blank.'

'Fibroids,' Mari said gently. 'Can anything be done?

Xavier shrugged. 'Alain's understanding is they're quite large. She 'ad an internal examination.'

'A laparoscopy or a hysteroscopy perhaps?' The terms were all too familiar to Mari.

'The last one, I think. Apparently as long as she's not in too much pain she could just wait until the *ménopause*, when they might reduce in size. Or she could 'ave an *'ystérectomie.'*

'God, I'm so sorry!' Mari's own grief, covered only by a light coating of life, brimmed and surged. She felt Fayette's pain. To have experienced that devastating loss five times and now to have lost all hope too must be utterly unbearable. Tears welled and she wiped them brusquely.

'It is an illusion of choice. There is no option that gives 'er what she wants,' Xavier grunted, staring at the carpet, before registering who he was talking to. *'Jésus*, Mari, I'm really sorry. I didn't think.'

She shook her head. 'It's okay.' She gave a deep sigh. 'You can tell me anything, you know that. It's with me all the time. This can't make it worse for me. It's just… more… vivid.'

'I didn't tell you about Fayette and Alain, about… you know… the other times, because I didn't want to upset you. This call took me by surprise.' Xavier wore a look of remorse. He got back into bed and stretched out an arm so she could snuggle into his shoulder. He kissed the top of her head then her mouth as she tilted her head briefly towards him.

They stayed like that for a while and it was some time until she spoke again, her voice distant, distracted. 'Your coffee will be cold now. I'll pour some more. We should eat some breakfast.'

She extricated herself from his embrace and went over to the side table on which their breakfast tray had been placed. Under a crisp white napkin were croissants and Danish pastries. She tipped Xavier's cold coffee down the sink in the bathroom and poured him a fresh cup and one for herself, placing them on the bedside tables. Handing him a glass of orange juice and the pastries and crawling back into bed, she said, 'You know, there might be another way for Fayette and Alain.'

'What do you mean?'

'Well, you should talk to Pierre, but I was told over a year ago there had been some experiments involving fertilisation outside the woman's body using eggs from a donor, although it wasn't successful at the time. You've heard of Louise Brown, the test tube baby, haven't you?'

Xavier nodded. 'Yes, of course.'

'Well, my understanding was the mother's egg was fertilised by the father's sperm and the embryo was put back into the mother's womb. So if the new experiments work it would be possible for someone to donate an egg, which would then be fertilized by the father's sperm and placed in the mother's womb.'

'Okay. I follow—but it wouldn't be the mother's baby, only the father's.'

'In that case, yes.'

'That could work for you too, couldn't it? I mean, if you didn't mind the baby not being yours genetically speaking.'

'If it's scientifically possible, it might.' Mari's eyes were brighter. 'I know I can't produce eggs, but I don't know whether or not I can carry a child. There might be a chance.'

'Would Gerren want to do that?' asked Xavier, hesitantly.

A shadow crossed Mari's face. 'I… er… don't know,' she shrugged.

'I'm sorry,' Xavier said again. 'I shouldn't 'ave asked. It's none of my business.'

Mari didn't reply. She finished her coffee.

She could see Xavier thinking hard, but confusion pulled at his brow. 'I don't see 'ow that could 'elp Fayette though, if she can't carry a baby.'

'Well,' responded Mari slowly, tapping the edge of her plate with a middle finger while her mind was shaping the idea, 'if a woman's body will accept an embryo that doesn't contain her genetic material but only her husband's, why shouldn't it be possible to implant an embryo that's not from her or from him?'

'What do you mean?'

'Well, if a woman can become pregnant from a donor egg fertilised with her husband's sperm, then it should be possible for her to receive a donor egg fertilised with someone else's sperm.'

'Then it wouldn't be the couple's baby at all.' Xavier still couldn't see how this could help Fayette.

'Surrogates have been around for centuries. The difference is normally a surrogate woman is impregnated—one way or another—with the sperm of a man who's not her husband, she becomes pregnant then gives the baby up as soon as it's born.'

Mari's reasoning suddenly registered with Xavier. 'Oh, I see! You mean, because it's possible to make an embryo in a test tube, an embryo from Fayette and Alain could be implanted into another woman to carry.' He tilted his head in recognition of a smart theory. 'It's a good idea, but we don't know whether it's technically possible. I mean the surrogate mother's body might well reject the embryo. It would be like putting a foreign body in there. Perhaps that's why you were told it 'ad not worked.'

'Yes, maybe,' Mari agreed. 'But what if it did work? Wouldn't that be wonderful? I don't know Fayette but even so I can feel her desire for a child, Xavier. It can overwhelm every other aspect of your life.' Pain and longing showed clearly on her face.

He nodded. 'I'll talk with Pierre. If anyone knows what's possible and what 'as a good chance of success, 'e does. I could not bear to falsely raise Alain and Fayette's 'opes after what they've been through.' He heaved a guilty sigh. 'I feel so bad, leaving Alain to cope with Papa before 'e died. Alain was always there for Maman, while they were trying to 'ave a family of their own and I was looking after myself.'

Mari attempted to ease his regret, putting a hand on his. 'It's not your fault, Xavier. You couldn't have changed what happened, even if you had been there. You had to go away to study.'

He shrugged away her placation. 'I expect they were all under a lot of pressure. I 'ad weekends. I should 'ave been there to 'elp. I owe 'im a great debt.' He gave her a wry smile. 'Maybe there is a way I can repay it now, thanks to your suggestion.'

During the long train journey home, Mari couldn't stop thinking about human egg donation, Xavier's words echoing: *That could work for you too, couldn't it?* Who in the world would contemplate donating eggs? Why would it occur to anyone to do so? It would take a particular kind of woman to allow her biological child to be born to someone else. Perhaps the sister of someone in need? She didn't have a sister. She would need to ask a friend. But who could bear being close to their genetic offspring while they're raised by other parents? She couldn't ask Fran as she and Pierre didn't want their own children, which was ironic considering Pierre's choice of career. She couldn't imagine bringing up a son or daughter who was Fran's child. That would create an impossible situation for her friends and indeed their friendship.

Her thoughts turned to Lena, the archetypal earth mother. Fourteen months had passed since George was born and during that time she'd become close to Lena once more, had learned how to be happy for her and Jake, had become fond of George. Might egg donation be something Lena could contemplate? Mari didn't know. She did know her friend had felt the power of a mother's love and appreciated the pain Mari felt at being unable to experience that. So maybe—if her friend didn't have to watch her biological child grow up the daughter or son of Mari, unable to disclose her true relationship with the child. Maybe—if she moved to France…

Cahors, France, December 1983

Alain replaced the receiver and turned to his wife, curled up on the settee, her hands around a mug of hot chocolate. 'Xavier says he will tell Maman. We won't have to see her yet.'

A tear made its way slowly over Fayette's sculptured

cheekbone. Another followed, then another. She didn't move but continued to stare through the glass-topped coffee table at the Persian rug below, its woollen pile intricately woven into a tree of life in ochre, red and green. 'It's just as well my parents are dead,' she uttered wretchedly, 'I would have been such a disappointment to them.'

'Don't say that, my love.'

'It's true, you know it.'

He went to sit with her, enfolding her in his arms. Sadly, she was right about her parents. With his mother it would be the opposite. 'Maman will suffocate us with kindness,' he said ironically.

'She'll mean well but it will be unbearable. I don't want to talk about it.'

Alain glanced towards the long multi-paned windows where the white morning light was illuminating elaborate frost formations on the glass. 'It's a nice day. We should dress warmly and go out.'

Fayette shook her head despondently. 'I don't want to see anyone I know.' She laid her head in his lap and sobbed. 'I want to hide from the world.'

Alain gently stroked her feathered blonde hair. He looked around the large living room of their apartment. They'd loved it so much when they'd bought it three years ago with a share of Fayette's inheritance. In the centre of town on the main street, close to the shops and cafés, the restaurants and the theatre, it had suited their lifestyle. They even had a small garden terrace on the roof of the draper's shop below. Fayette had discovered her flair for interior design and had furnished the old characterful rooms in an elegant modern fashion, their high ceilings perfect for the graceful floor-sweeping chintz window coverings and hanging baskets overflowing with bright green ivy and maidenhair ferns in contrast with the soft pastels on the walls. There was plenty of space for his extensive Hi-Fi and a large kitchen/diner in which to engage with their love of world cuisine. But now every room seemed tarnished with their disappointments and pain. Recently, Fayette had barely been outside except for medical appointments and she'd neglected their home. To Alain, the flat seemed almost like a tomb of their making. They both badly needed a change.

He ran one hand through his quiff and gave Fayette's shoulder a squeeze. 'Dry your eyes, my love. We'll get out of this stuffy room, get some fresh air and feel a little better. We'll drive to Bouziès and go for a walk by the river. We could have a bit of lunch there.'

'I'm not hungry,' came Fayette's muffled reply.

'You don't have to eat. We'll have a hot drink. Come on, it'll do us good.'

With a great effort Fayette raised herself from his lap and wiped her wet face with her hands. 'Okay, if you want.'

Alain stood and helped her to her feet. He held her face in his hands and kissed her gently on each of her swollen eyes and then her mouth. 'We will get through this. We need a fresh start, something new to focus on—and we're going to begin today.'

Chapter Eleven

Plymouth, England, December 1983

Their partings were always a wrench—this one in particular, since Christmas was looming and Xavier had to face it without Mari. Not only that but, increasingly when alone, he couldn't help picturing her with Gerren. He had arranged his final business meeting of the year for Monday morning before returning to Lille. He'd drive to his mother's house in the Lot region later that week. He'd decided it would be easier to discuss medical matters with Pierre face to face and that also gave him an excuse to accompany Mari back to Plymouth on the train. Before the train reached Plymouth, they had gone into the corridor to say their goodbyes away from windows and prying eyes. Gerren would be at the station to meet her. Xavier tried to swallow the lump in his throat as he watched Mari walk away from him along the platform; he couldn't wait to get to Pierre's flat, where he knew he could dissolve it in alcohol.

Pierre welcomed him like a brother. It was late but Xavier hadn't eaten for hours so Pierre produced a selection of cheeses to consume with bread and a bottle of wine. Xavier told Pierre about Fayette's medical condition and asked his advice. As was always the case when alone, they spoke in French.

'With respect to treating Fayette, as the fibroids might reduce in size during the menopause, if she's not in pain and doesn't have abnormal bleeding she could wait until then,' Pierre replied. 'Or she could have them removed but that would involve a hysterectomy. There's a new laser technique for the treatment of persistent haemorrhaging but it's not widely available at the moment and anyway it works by destroying the endometrium—the lining of the uterus—so that would also preclude her from becoming pregnant. But if the fibroids are a problem, I mean other than preventing pregnancy, she should have them removed.'

Xavier sighed glumly. 'I think that's basically what her consultant has told her.' He took another large mouthful of Merlot. 'I've been discussing with Mari whether there are other options for Fayette. Mari was told last year there'd been some kind of experiment using IVF on donor eggs but it wasn't successful. Do you know anything about that?'

Pierre nodded. 'Yes. A paper was published by an IVF group in Australia, back in March, reporting a pregnancy established in an infertile woman after the transfer of a donated embryo fertilised in vitro with sperm from a donor. Unfortunately the pregnancy failed after ten weeks. But still, I think it's only a matter of time. We're doing our own research, too. It's successful in animals.'

'Really?'

'Yes, it's a technique used in animal breeding.'

'Are you getting anywhere with your research? How close are you?'

Pierre shrugged. 'Hard to say. We're trying to mimic a

complex system with hormone treatment at exactly the right doses and times in an intricate mammalian body where a range of other factors could affect the outcome. Moreover, each trial takes a long time. But anyway, it wouldn't help Fayette, I'm afraid,' he raised his eyebrows, tilting his head slightly to one side, 'but it could help Mari, at some point in the future. I guess that's not what you want to hear though, is it?' he paused, 'unless she leaves her husband.'

Xavier's face wore an expression of concentration. 'Let's put that to one side for the moment. Do you think it's possible for an embryo from Fayette and Alain to be implanted into a surrogate woman who would carry the child?'

Pierre thought for a few moments, tapping one finger on the stem of his wine glass in deep contemplation. Xavier waited patiently. He'd watched Pierre problem-solving; he had to work through all the actions, impediments, complications and ramifications, before giving a considered opinion.

At length Pierre responded. 'Obviously we've been focussing on the treatment of infertile women, but if we can achieve success in that regard—and I believe we will—technically it should be possible to implant an embryo into a perfectly healthy woman. The ovulation of the two women would need to be synchronised so the body of the surrogate is at exactly the right stage to receive the donated embryo. There've been attempts to use frozen embryos in IVF treatment but the freezing and thawing processes often cause permanent injury to the cells. A paper reporting the first human pregnancy from a frozen embryo was published last October by the Australian team, which was an exciting step forward, but unfortunately premature rupture of the amniotic membrane caused the woman to lose the baby at twenty-four weeks. But they reported the failure wasn't linked to the cryopreservation of the embryo, because the fetus appeared normal at week twenty-four.'

'So you're saying it might be possible?' Xavier replied, trying to provoke a clearer answer.

'It's a complicated process,' Pierre rejoined. 'There are other considerations. For the surrogacy process to work you'd have to be sure successful pregnancy in the surrogate woman was the result of the transferred embryo and she hadn't inadvertently conceived with her own husband.'

'That can be done, can't it?' asked Xavier. 'People have paternity tests.'

Pierre nodded. 'The testing is more reliable than it was. There's a technique called human leukocyte antigen typing, or HLA typing. It's used to match patients and donors for bone marrow transplants. It's about eighty per cent accurate.'

'So the surrogate woman and her husband don't have sex for a while and get paid,' remarked Xavier glibly.

'I'd have to be paid pretty well not to have sex,' Pierre joked. 'Seriously though, there are significant ethical issues to consider—for example, there are medical risks associated with pregnancy and how would the parties manage a situation where the child is born with a defect?'

'I understand there could be all sorts of issues and problems to overcome,' Xavier replied earnestly, 'quite apart from the fact that assisted reproduction is against the rules of the Catholic Church. I guess there'd have to be some sort of legal arrangement. Maybe Fran could look into it?'

'I think we're probably getting a little ahead of ourselves,' Pierre observed. 'We have to succeed with the embryo donation technique first. Then we can think about the other aspects. For now, the most important thing is Fayette's health. If she has to have a total hysterectomy the surrogacy idea is academic.'

'God forbid that's the outcome.' Worried as he was for Fayette, Xavier couldn't stem his growing feeling of hopefulness. Despite his reasonable cautiousness, Pierre was clearly excited by the scientific developments. The possibilities for Alain and Fayette, and for himself and Mari, filled Xavier with anticipation.

Chapter Twelve

Lille, France, January 1984

Noël had ensued as a sober affair for the Dubois family. For Xavier and Alain's mother, Vivienne, it was only the second Christmas without her husband and Xavier could see she was also finding it hard to conceal her sadness at her son and daughter-in-law's news. Xavier was missing Mari and trying to stop himself imagining her having a cosy time in Devon with Gerren, though failing miserably, unsure whether he'd be facing a future without her. It was all Alain and Fayette could do to converse with anyone. The family had spent two days together before dispersing to their respective lives.

A few days into the New Year, Xavier received an enthusiastic call from Pierre.

'There's an exciting paper coming out in *Nature* this month, though I wish we'd got there first. The Australian IVF group are reporting that in December a 25-year-old woman with premature ovarian failure became the first person to successfully deliver a pregnancy using a donor egg! It was fertilized with her husband's sperm.'

Xavier was quiet, assimilating the implications; he couldn't quite believe it for a moment. 'That's fantastic! Does this mean your team will be able to do this now?'

'We have a call with the Australians tomorrow and a team meeting on Friday. I can tell you we'll be doing all we can to replicate their success. We're also liaising with research groups in Norfolk and Cambridge. There's a lot going on.'

'So the surrogate idea may not be so improbable after all?' Xavier responded eagerly.

'It should be possible. We must work towards it, but I'm optimistic.'

'Pierre, that's the best news I've had for what seems like a long time.'

'How's Fayette?'

'Alain told me if she has a hysterectomy she doesn't have to have her ovaries removed. She and the consultant are discussing whether she'd benefit from having her uterus removed at this stage. If she goes ahead with the operation, will she still be able to produce eggs?'

'If she doesn't have her ovaries removed and they're fully functional, she'll still ovulate,' Pierre explained. 'They should continue to follow the regular monthly menstrual cycle so the retrieval of eggs should be possible. But I think if she doesn't have to have an operation at this time that would be the best outcome. Would it be helpful if I talked with her?'

'Not yet,' replied Xavier hastily. 'I think I should broach the subject with Alain first then leave it with him. I'll get back to you if it's something they'd consider. The possibility is exciting though, isn't it?'

'It certainly is.' Pierre told Xavier he'd talk about it with his colleagues and let him know of developments. He'd also ask Fran to investigate the legal aspects of surrogacy.

On replacing the receiver Xavier experienced a tremor,

a dancing in his stomach. All was not lost for his brother and Fayette, and if it worked for them maybe some kind of assisted reproduction could for Mari. He sensed Gerren was not as keen to have a child as Mari; maybe she could be persuaded to leave Gerren and have a baby with him? As he picked up the phone again to ring Alain hope burgeoned as a heliotropic sunflower bud blossoms in the sun.

Fayette was curled on the sofa under a hand-knitted woollen shawl Vivienne had given her for *Noël*. The television was on, but she wasn't watching, the images merely swirls of colour to her unfocussed eyes. Alain was in the hallway talking to his brother on the phone. She had shut the living room door to keep the heat in before crawling back to her nest. A half-empty glass of red wine stood on the table beside her, which she sipped intermittently. *They're having a long conversation* she thought vaguely.

The door burst open and Alain came in, excited. 'There's a possible way for us to have a baby of our own, Fayette,' he exclaimed rapidly. 'I just spoke with Xavier and he's been talking with his friend Pierre who is a fertility specialist and…'

'Whoa, slow down,' Fayette interrupted. 'Xavier has been talking with another consultant on our behalf?' she asked incredulously. 'But we know I can't carry…'

'I know, but Fayette listen,' Alain continued enthusiastically, 'there's been a technical break-though; there's another option! It's not without its issues of course—we'll have to discuss all of that,' he waived his hand impatiently—'but there's definitely hope.'

Fayette was overjoyed to learn there could be another way for them to have a child of their own. They spent the next few hours considering all the information Xavier had given Alain, recognising while in principle they desperately wanted to try surrogacy, a significant barrier lay in their path: all forms of assisted reproduction, being considered artificial fecundation, are against the teachings of the Catholic Church. Neither of them were practising Catholics, although both had been brought up in that faith.

Over the next few days, Alain researched legal texts which confirmed their suspicion that surrogacy was prohibited by law in France, with criminal consequences for transgressors. If they were to go down this route, they would have to find a surrogate abroad. Fayette understood why Pierre had chosen to pursue his career in the UK. Alain spoke several times with his *maman*. She'd become like a mother to Fayette too, over the years, and Fayette recognised how important it was for Alain to share his thoughts with her. A dutiful Catholic, Vivienne believed because IVF and surrogate motherhood separate procreation from normal sexual function they are immoral. Children are a gift from God, she said. However, she also admitted she found herself troublingly conflicted, her disapproval on religious grounds set against her strong desire for Alain and Fayette's happiness and, to be honest, her own longing for a grandchild.

However, they were dismayed when Alain discovered that a child born to a surrogate mother in another country would be refused registration on the French Civil Register and effectively not exist in the civil system and have no legal identity or civil rights under French law. This would affect every aspect of the child's life.

This was a colossal blow for her and Alain. For a time, it seemed their hopes had once again been crushed almost into oblivion. In terms of the law, if they wanted a child that was genetically theirs, they had only two options: make a new life in a country that legally permitted surrogacy or commit a criminal act by falsifying the truth.

Neither option was palatable, so over the next few weeks they discussed the situation only with Xavier. It was then they decided to talk with Pierre, face to face.

Chapter Thirteen

Plymouth, England, April 1984

Xavier made himself available, meeting Alain and Fayette at Heathrow and driving them to Plymouth. They had arrived on a rainy evening. Sea mist swallowed Plymouth Sound and its encompassing coastline and dampness hung depressingly in the air. Thus far Devon had not recommended itself to Alain and Fayette, who had left Toulouse airport in warm, bright spring sunshine.

Pierre and Fran welcomed their three guests warmly and chatted for a couple of hours over glasses of Pinot Noir and delicious *coq au vin*. After a dessert of pear tart with clotted cream they withdrew to the sitting room with coffee and earnest discussion began.

Firstly, Pierre explained to Alain and Fayette the law firm employing Fran were the legal advisors for the clinic—though she didn't usually get involved in this side of the business—so the clinic would naturally use her firm to produce legal agreements.

Then Pierre began to elucidate the IVF process, before introducing the complications of surrogacy. They spoke in French. Alain's English was passable and Fayette had studied the language at school, however such was the technical nature of the conversation it was important to understand exactly what was being said. Consistent with her methodical nature, Fayette took notes. Xavier remained with them; he needed to understand the procedure in more detail, partly so he'd be better equipped to support his family in the months to come, but also because he wanted to explain it to Mari, who was also eager to learn the specifics. Fran busied herself with clearing up, leaving them to their medical discussion. She'd been looking into the legality of the process; her role would follow.

After an hour or so and many questions, Fayette and Alain were content they understood the complicated medical procedure and the risks. Just to be sure, Pierre asked them to summarise.

Fayette recapped from her notes, trying to keep the trepidation welling inside from tainting her voice. There would be many tests and drugs and invasions of the most intimate nature. She and Alain would need to undertake multiple blood tests to ensure they had no adverse medical conditions which could be transferred via an embryo to the surrogate mother. She would be treated with drugs to stimulate follicle growth and increase the number of eggs produced by her ovaries. She would have daily injections and either Alain would be shown how to administer them, or she'd need to attend the clinic every evening as well as every morning—Fayette wasn't sure whether she wanted Alain sticking needles in her buttocks. Daily blood plasma tests would determine the doses of hormones she would receive. Her ovaries would be monitored via vaginal ultrasound scanning and urine samples taken to track hormone levels. After the diameter of her largest follicle had reached 18 millimetres, she'd be given another hormone injection to help the eggs to mature and trigger ovulation. Then egg collection would take place. The tests, treatments and timings had to be so precise, Fayette foresaw how their lives would be dominated. But, although apprehensive, she knew she had to embrace this opportunity, or she'd regret it forever.

All the while Pierre nodded comfortingly, interjecting the occasional 'Hmm' and 'That's right' as Fayette gave an accurate account of the IVF protocol his clinic was using.

At this point, she continued, she'd be sedated and all of her eggs collected via a needle inserted through her abdomen and into each ovary. Meanwhile, Alain would produce a sperm sample which would be quality-checked, concentrated, and subsequently mixed with her eggs. Any fertilised eggs—in other words embryos—would be left to grow to the four- or eight-cell stage. Only the best one or two would be transferred to the surrogate.

Pierre then explained the medical risks, the worst being hyperstimulation of the ovaries, which could cause abdominal bloating, nausea, diarrhea, and in severe cases shortness of breath, chest pains and difficulty with urination. Fayette glanced nervously at Alain, hoping to God she wouldn't suffer any of these. Alain looked as worried, but squeezed her hand reassuringly. She sensed Pierre was being careful to be realistic, not only about side effects, but the chances of pregnancy, even if they could produce enough embryos of the right quality. In their case the overall chance of success would depend on not only her physiology and response to the medications but those of the surrogate and both women would be subject to medical risks.

'You also have to realise,' Pierre said, 'although in

Australia a woman has had her husband's baby using a donated egg, which is the first time the birth of a baby not biologically related to the mother has been reported, we would be attempting something new in lawful terms; a combination of IVF and traditional surrogacy, where the surrogate would be carrying a child she has no connection to at all. I'm sure you're aware there are legal and ethical considerations as well as biological challenges.'

Fayette opened her mouth but, seeing an almost imperceptible shake of Alain's head, halted, recognising he would deal with that issue later.

She and Alain both nodded soberly. Alain spoke for them. 'We understand. This is going to be challenging in many ways.'

Xavier shot her and Alain a sympathetic look and raised his eyebrows but said nothing.

Pierre went on to outline his clinic would need to discuss the synchronisation of the menstrual cycles of Fayette and the surrogate woman, so an embryo transfer could take place at the right time. 'I'm confident all of this could be done,' he stated encouragingly. 'However, my colleagues and I will need time for proper discussion of the details.'

Just then the door opened and Fran joined them, bringing a fresh pot of steaming coffee and a chocolate selection box. 'I thought you might need these,' she smiled.

It seemed they were all glad of the interruption and helped themselves readily.

'Quite apart from this,' Pierre emphasised, between bolstering sips, 'you would need to consider an appropriate and willing surrogate mother who would not only be prepared to undergo the process, with the inherent risks, and give up the child, but also understand and accept the experimental nature of the procedure. She would need to be fit and healthy, with no significant medication use and a demonstrable history of normal fertility.'

Again, Fayette and Alain nodded their understanding. Inwardly Fayette's thoughts whirled like a dust devil. Comprehension and action seemed impossibly far apart. There were so many obstacles and challenges. Where and how on earth were they going to find such a woman? She'd hoped Pierre or the clinic might have been able to suggest someone. Clearly this wasn't going to be the case. A mix of dismay and anxiety cast a tight band around her chest. She swallowed purposefully to clear the restriction in her throat, attempting to reach the hope and excitement that had sustained her at the beginning of this journey. *A baby… our baby* she reminded herself. *I'm not giving up now.* Gradually the negative emotions were surmounted by her innate tenacity, which, she realised, had clamped her jaws so tightly her teeth had begun to ache.

'If a child is born as a result of the procedure,' Pierre was concluding, 'the parentage must be confirmed. There is a test, but it's difficult and uncomfortable for infants because a relatively large blood sample is needed—I hope this will change in the future.'

Pierre leaned imperatively towards her and Alain, over the coffee table. 'I have to say, if you decide to go ahead, I and my colleagues will do our utmost to deliver a successful outcome,' he pronounced fervently. 'This is an exciting time for the advancement of infertility treatment.

But there are many factors outside our control. You must be aware the psychological stress for all concerned will be significant. All parties must be prepared for this and able to cope with it.' He took a deep breath and sat back.

Fayette silently sought a reaction from her husband, her eyes conveying her decision. Alain's serious expression reflected a burden of knowledge and weight of purpose. He drained his coffee, took hold of Fayette's hand and looked squarely at Pierre.

'We want to go ahead. We understand the risks and appreciate there will be tough times ahead as well as difficult conversations and decisions,' he stated forthrightly. 'I've no doubt you are aware—since you made the decision to pursue your fertility work in the UK—of France's view of IVF and that surrogacy is not accepted there. This presents a significant obstacle to us in terms of finding a surrogate and is also why we have come to you, here in England. We can't ask any of our friends to be a surrogate. We are hoping your clinic will be able to recommend a suitable person.'

'I am, of course, aware of the Catholic Church's view on assisted reproduction,' Pierre replied. 'But I'm content if the process is carried out in the UK, where surrogacy is accepted, there should be no problem.' He repeated this in English for the benefit of Fran, who was sitting with her notes, awaiting the end of the technical exchanges.

At this, Fran shook her head slightly. 'Sorry, I can't entirely agree. Pierre, will you translate for me? According to the research I've just completed, the legal situation isn't that straightforward. I understand surrogacy is unlawful in France. However, in the UK there are no laws governing surrogacy; the process is legal and the birth can be registered in England. But you also need to be aware that in the UK historically the legal assumption is the woman giving birth to a child is that child's legal mother. So, you might need to formally adopt the child, which would require the birth mother's formal abandonment of her parental rights.'

On hearing this Fayette was dismayed and she could see Alain was equally shocked.

'But the child would 'ave to be legally ours from the beginning!' protested Alain. 'If we 'ave to formally adopt the child from the surrogate mother it will still not be recognised under French law, and we want our child to be a citizen of France, otherwise it will not 'ave the same rights as us. It will not legally exist!'

'That is a problem if you want to continue residing in France,' Fran returned evenly.

'Would it be possible for Alain and Fayette to adopt the child as though it was not born to a surrogate mother?' Pierre asked hastily, directing his question to Fran then translating. 'I mean, some women give their child up for adoption shortly after birth. That wouldn't be unusual. So the surrogacy and adoption wouldn't have to be linked and they could presumably register the child as a French citizen.'

Fayette shook her head determinedly and Alain glared at him, so he raised his hands, attempting to defuse their obvious frustration. 'It was only a thought.'

'The child would be ours, so we shouldn't 'ave to adopt. It should 'ave our name,' Alain returned curtly. 'We considered adoption, but we 'ave not been married for ten years and neither of us is over thirty-five, which is the requirement under French law. I've no idea what the rules are 'ere.'

Fran shot him a sympathetic look but remained composed. 'In England adoption is governed by the 1983 Adoption Agency Regulations, with the Local Authorities acting as adoption agencies,' she explained. 'So it would be difficult for you to demand the adoption of a specific child without declaring the mother was a surrogate. Even as the genetic parents, as you are non-British nationals you would need to reside in the UK and a Hague Convention adoption order would be the relevant process. In this case, the adoption law of the applicable convention country, in other words France, would have to be complied with.'

'If you choose to declare the surrogate mother, you could adopt, but the child would initially be a UK national. A thirty-two-week welfare supervision period would be needed before parental informed consent could be granted and an authorised UK court would need to be satisfied that the adoption law of France was obeyed. As you've just told me you don't yet qualify under French adoption law, this does not appear to be an option for you at the moment. May I ask when you expect to meet the French adoption rules?'

'We're not waiting another ten years before one of us is over thirty-five,' Alain exclaimed, exasperated. '*Merde! Pourquoi ça doit être si difficile!*' He banged his fist on the table.

Pierre looked taken aback. Xavier placed a hand gently on his brother's arm. Fayette, who was used to Alain's volatility, sat still, silently imploring Fran to come up with a legal solution. The woman's face was as unreadable as a blank sheet of paper.

Fran remained calm, considering the matter. 'I suppose in your case if the child has no genetic link to the surrogate mother, if you were proved to be the genetic parents, we could make a case for you being the legal mother, Fayette. There aren't precedents, as this is a new situation. Obviously, there'd need to be a detailed surrogacy agreement. We'd need to address your rights as the genetic parents and those of the surrogate mother and other concerns. It's complex, there is a lot to consider.' She went on to clarify this wasn't a legal area she or anyone in her practice had experience of, although she'd been studying the subject recently. Traditional surrogacy was a minefield, she said, and it appeared that arrangements had pretty much been conducted on a case-by-case basis.

Fayette ran a finger around the base of her wine glass, deep in contemplation as she listened to Pierre's translation. All this talk of adoption and legal definitions. It was a nonsense, she thought. After all, the word surrogate meant a stand-in, a temporary substitute, someone deputising for another. A surrogate mother was a proxy. In her mind it was clear; she would be the mother and Alain the father. She shook her head slowly, gave a shrug and spoke quietly in French to Alain, who nodded his agreement and spoke slowly in English.

'We don't want to make a big fuss about the surrogacy. We must simply register the child as ours.' It was his turn to shrug. 'It would be ours, that is not a lie. The French authorities will not know that Fayette 'as been pregnant or not. We will 'ave to stay in *Angleterre* for a few months anyway. Women 'ave babies in foreign countries; it's not unusual.'

Fran frowned at this. 'I told you in the UK it's assumed

that the birth mother is the legal mother. I believe we would need to lawfully challenge this to be clear about the legal identity of the child. The place of birth is on the birth certificate and it's common for the birth to be registered at the hospital by the mother before she leaves, although this doesn't have to be the case.'

Alain shook his head adamantly. 'No. If there is a legal challenge there is a fuss. And if there is a fuss it could become known to the French authorities there is a surrogate. And what 'appens if the challenge does not work? We would 'ave to adopt the child anyway, then we are back in the same situation. No, it cannot 'appen like that. The birth must take place at your clinic, Pierre and we will register the child as ours. Then we will get the certificate transcribed onto the register of the Consulate General of France in London.' He shrugged. 'Then there are no questions and everything is simple.'

Fran and Pierre looked at one another silently. It was clear they were both unhappy, Fran in particular, about becoming involved in activities necessitating dishonesty and likely to be considered illegal.

Sensing this concern could be a serious barrier, Alain brought the financial factor to bear. 'Obviously we would compensate the clinic generously for the necessary work, in addition to all the medical expenses of course, and a substantial fee for the surrogate. I understand, Pierre, there 'as already been a significant investment in the clinic from my family.' He glanced at Xavier, who looked down at the carpet, trying to remain neutral.

Pierre shifted in his seat, leaning forward as if preparing to stand. 'Well,' he said in a tone indicating the discussion was concluding, 'there is clearly a lot for us all to think about. I suggest we do so and arrange a follow-up telephone call in a couple of weeks. Is that okay with everyone?'

All present nodded their assent.

As Fayette and Alain prepared to leave, Xavier caught Pierre in the hallway. Laying a hand on his friend's arm, Xavier spoke quietly in French. 'My family really would be grateful if there's any way you can make this work. I know there are probably a hundred and one problems to overcome, most of them technical, but if you succeed, think of the kudos for the clinic. A seminal publication—with all the participants anonymous, of course. Think what it could do for your reputation and for our business.'

Pierre patted Xavier on the back. 'You can be sure I understand how important this is, not least for Alain and Fayette. I think it can work if we concentrate on our own roles and keep the medical and contractual aspects separate from the registration of the birth—*if* a child is born. Obviously, I need to protect the clinic from any wrongdoing. Fran's bound to feel uneasy; she's a solicitor. Let me talk with her. I'm sure I can bring her around.'

'Thank you, Pierre, my friend,' Xavier shook his friend's hand warmly.

Pierre grinned. 'It's an exciting opportunity.'

Chapter Fourteen

Later that night Pierre and Fran lay awake in bed listening to nocturnal noises, the city slackened but not asleep: a patter of rain on the windows; the hiss of tyres on wet roads; the occasional distant horn; a long yowl followed by the shrill shrieks of a cat fight.

Fran spoke first. 'I know how important this is for you,' she said, staring at the ceiling through the gloom.

'Mmm. I can't stop thinking about it,' he replied, turning onto his side to face her, one crooked arm supporting his head.

'It is technically possible, isn't it?'

'Yes, there's no reason why not.'

Fran sighed and rolled over to look at him, curving her legs towards her belly. 'I can't be involved in a deliberate fraudulent act.'

'Would it *really* be fraudulent?' Pierre tested the water, 'I mean, Alain and Fayette would be the genetic parents—the surrogate would only be a carrier.'

'Technically yes, but not legally,' she disputed. 'I believe it would be duplicitous.'

'You said the law 'ere assumes the birth mother is the legal mother. 'Ow important is the word 'assumes'?'

'There are no laws concerning surrogacy, but you know there's been a lot of discussion around the legal and social problems raised by IVF and related technologies such as freezing embryos. Also, what about that government committee set up in July '82 to consider surrogacy and human-assisted reproduction?'

'Yes, I know; the Warnock Committee. They 'aven't delivered their report yet,' Pierre replied. His tone had a hint of disdain. 'We consider the IVF services we provide and the research we do entirely ethical and take that seriously. We 'ave to balance the sensitivities of some against the vast benefits for childless couples. I'm aware there's a call in some circles for parliament to legislate. I worry about it and so do my colleagues at the clinic. Did you know the Australian Group 'ad to stop their research programme on IVF with embryo donation? Although a government committee in Victoria looking at the ethical and legal issues of egg donation recommended continuing the work, the state government didn't lift the moratorium! The same could 'appen 'ere. Personally, I think we should continue our development as much as we can before anyone tries to stop us. We wouldn't ever freeze an embryo or use it without the parents' consent. Currently freezing doesn't work well, but we should try to improve it; think of the benefit for women oo 'ave to be treated for cancer and will no longer be able to produce eggs.'

'I suppose the government will eventually issue a set of guidelines that all medical practitioners will have to stick to,' Fran answered.

'Yes and that is entirely reasonable provided there's a sensible and comprehensive technological discussion as well as the ethical and legal debate.'

'In my reading around the subject of surrogacy I sensed a lot of disapproval among scientists and doctors as well as legal and religious organisations—I was quite surprised,' Fran said.

'Well, it's an emotive subject,' responded Pierre rationally, 'and up to now the surrogate mother 'as always been the genetic mother as well. Giving away your baby is generally frowned on. People always judge others by their own standards without understanding all the facts of each case. Fayette and Alain are desperate for a child of their own and if there's a kind and generous woman out there oo is prepared to 'elp, and 'er husband is also very understanding, to me that's a wonderful example of true 'umanity.'

Fran heaved a sigh. 'Yes, I agree. As long as it's carried out above-board. With the birth mother, the surrogate, being the genetic mother, there's never been any reason to question the assumption she's the legal mother. In this case the legal process is formal adoption. I suppose in the case of a woman receiving a donor egg then carrying the baby she'd want to be the legal mother, so again there would be no reason to question that. But Fayette's situation would be different.'

Pierre thought for a moment. 'What if the surrogacy agreement doesn't mention anything about what will 'appen regarding registering the birth? What it if just states the baby must be 'anded over? Alain and Fayette would 'ave to be confirmed as the genetic parents of course but that should be more of a formality if the agreement also states the surrogate and 'er 'usband must not have intercourse at any time during the whole process. I mean, your involvement would end once the agreement is drawn up and signed. If everyone sticks to the agreement there wouldn't be any need for you to 'ave contact with any of them after that, would there?'

Fran was unconvinced. 'Hmm. But then we'd be leaving out one of the most important aspects of the document; the legal identity of the child! I could make a statement addressing the genetic parentage and leave the rest to be inferred but that wouldn't afford the child legal certainty and protecting that child is the most important aspect of this from my point of view. Also, it may not stand up to a legal challenge, which is where my reputation and that of my firm could be damaged.'

Pierre persevered. 'Yes, but you could make it clear to both couples they'd be signing up to a particular set of circumstances and procedures and once they'd signed, they couldn't go back on the agreement. Tell them—in writing if you want—what the proper course of action would be to establish the legal identity of any children but make it clear they're on their own after that.'

'I could do all of that. But that wouldn't legally protect the child, Pierre.'

'Yes, but if we establish Alain and Fayette are the genetic parents and they rear the child, what further protection does the child need? I bet there are 'undreds of children out there whose real fathers aren't oo their mothers say they are. In our case, we'd be sure!'

'Hmm, you have a point. I'll need to do some more research then decide how to handle it,' Fran answered. She yawned, stretched her long legs and turned onto her back.

'Per'aps... you could do it privately; don't run it through the firm,' Pierre offered tentatively.

'Oh come on, Pierre,' she returned, slightly irked. 'My firm handles all the legal documentation for the clinic, you know that. That can't just be bypassed. How would you protect the clinic if Alain and Fayette register the child as theirs and ignore the surrogacy?'

He raised his head, propping himself on one elbow. 'We'll be involved clinically, but do we really need to get involved beyond that? Except to provide the surrogate mother with medical support after the birth if she needs it. The clinic will be excited about the opportunity; we 'ave a lot to gain from this if we're successful. I'm sure, as Alain and Fayette will be contributing to our research funding, we can be discreet about the process. If everyone is in agreement, we're not doing anything wrong.'

She snorted. 'I doubt my colleagues would see it that way. That sounds a bit like the clinic taking a bribe for looking the other way on the legal issues of the surrogacy; at least that's what you would expose yourselves to being accused of if things go wrong and there's a legal challenge. I understand your enthusiasm for this opportunity, I really do, but don't let it obscure your judgement. And anyway, if I took this on personally it would put me at risk if there was a legal challenge down the line. I certainly wouldn't want that. Would you?'

'Of course not. I just don't see why there should be a legal problem.'

'Hmph.' It was so like Pierre to become focussed on a goal almost to the exclusion of everything else. His tenacity and passion were qualities she loved but he could be exasperating. She shrugged. 'In any case you'll have to discuss everything with your management.'

'I will,' he assured. 'Why don't you talk with Mari and see what she thinks of the situation? You sometimes talk through dilemmas with 'er.'

'Alain and Fayette don't want anyone else to know.'

'You can keep it anonymous. According to Xavier, though, she was the one oo suggested surrogacy in the first place.'

She turned onto her side to face him again. 'Did she? I didn't know that. She's not mentioned it to me.'

'Ah, well, I don't know what's going on there. I don't know whether Xavier's talked with 'er about it since. But she's a clever woman. Maybe she's thinking about donor embryos for 'erself'?

'I can't see Gerren going for that,' replied Fran dismissively. 'He seems to be quite happy with the life he's carving out. I think sometimes he forgets he has a wife.'

'That's a bit 'arsh, returned Pierre kindly. 'From the few conversations we've 'ad, 'e seems to want to provide for 'er as well as 'e can.'

'Yes, well, providing material things is different from understanding her emotional needs,' Fran retorted protectively. 'The fact she's having an affair is proof of that!' Then she softened. 'Gerren's a nice guy—I like him. It's just he's a bit… well… bland. He seems to need less out of life than Mari. Quite honestly, I think they're growing apart.'

It was Pierre's turn to roll over onto his back. Their bed was warm and cosy, a feeling accentuated by the rain driving against the window. ''E loves 'er, you know.'

'Who?'

'Xavier. I expect Gerren does too, but I was talking about Xavier.'

Fran's face took on a concerned expression. 'I believe she loves him too. I don't know what she'll do. I think she's still fond of Gerren and doesn't want to hurt him.'

'Do you think she'd consider trying for a baby with Xavier, say if Gerren is against using a donor egg?'

Fran shrugged. 'I honestly don't know. Maybe. I think she'd certainly consider using a donor if she could carry the child herself. I suppose it could be a tipping point in their marriage; on the other hand, perhaps Gerren might be persuaded if he realises Mari would be heartbroken if there's an option of trying for a child that's his at least and he refuses. Perhaps if he knows there's a good chance of success it could make a difference. I don't think he wants to adopt. Has Xavier said something to you about wanting a baby with Mari?'

'No, but I sense 'is enthusiasm for the scheme is maybe not all on be'alf of his brother and sister-in-law, or the clinic. I've known 'im a long time. I believe 'e would love to make a family with Mari. Per'aps he is trying to show 'er something of this.'

'Well… it seems you all may have something to gain from this plan succeeding; Alain and Fayette, you, Mari and even Xavier. Now you have to find a surrogate.'

Chapter Fifteen

Plymouth, England, May 1984

Lena was hanging out the washing while George played with his dumper truck in their tiny back garden. Every so often a ray of sunshine peeped through the protective cottony cloud, highlighting flashes of copper in the toddler's unruly hair; George had inherited Lena's curls with Jake's colouring. The day was breezy and bright and the clothes would dry in no time, which was just as well as she had a load of nappies to do. She would have loved to use disposable ones but they couldn't justify the expense. Lena was still feeling an echo of the vibration from the twin-tub, which she'd leant on to stop it travelling across the kitchen floor while spinning. A week ago she'd left it while she went upstairs to change George and the damn thing had pulled itself from the sink causing the drainage pipe to leak all over the floor. She and Jake were saving for an automatic front loader, but it would cost nearly a month's worth of Jake's salary and was taking some time. Nevertheless, setting money aside regularly was good practice and they'd managed to save three-quarters of the cost of a new machine, so it wouldn't be too long until her Monday washday became a thing of the past. Once George started going to school she planned to return to primary teaching, which would ease their finances.

The grey tabby cat from next door had made himself welcome among the blooming peonies in the flower bed under Lena's front window. Something having caught his eye, he jumped up and ran across the lawn. In turn, his movement caught George's eye. The cat lowered the front half of his body, haunches high and swaying slightly, ready to pounce.

'Sameee!' chuckled George, clambering to his feet and going after the animal, chubby legs wide apart, jerking one foot forward then the other, swaying unsteadily from side to side, his arms outstretched.

His stalking having been interrupted, Sammy resumed a more dignified upright position, shook his head and ran out of the toddler's reach, nimbly scaling the wooden fence and settling himself on top of a post, tail swaying.

As he threw his head back to watch the cat climb the fence, George fell backwards onto his bottom with a thump then flapped his arms. 'Samee,' he repeated, pointing at the cat and looking at Lena disappointedly.

Lena laughed as she scooped him up and gave him a kiss. 'Sammy dunt want t' play right now, sweetie. You gotta be gentle with him.' She set George back down next to his truck, placing a couple of brightly painted wooden blocks into the dump box before returning to her basket of washing.

She was pegging up the last of George's corduroy dungarees, absent-mindedly humming a tune by the Pointer Sisters, unaware the telephone was ringing until she felt a pull on her long Indian cotton skirt. 'Mummy, bell; Mummy, bell.' George tugged insistently, looking up at her, his blue eyes wide with determination.

'Is it the telephone, George? Well done fer letting Mummy know. Come on, my lovely, let's go an' answer it.'

Lena picked him up and carried him through their modest kitchen and into the hallway. Setting him on her knee as she sat on the stairs. It was Mari, who wanted to talk about something face to face. There seemed to be some urgency. Lena suggested meeting in her local park, however Mari wanted to come to her house so they could talk in private. As she put the phone down Lena hoped Mari was alright; that nothing was wrong. Yet her friend hadn't seemed depressed or upset, rather nervous and hesitant, which she found odd.

Mari arrived forty minutes later flustered. Lena offered her tea from a pot. 'I've just put George down for a nap. We'll have t' sit in the kitchen I'm afraid cos I've gotta keep an eye on that thing, or it'll take itself off,' she laughed, waving a hand towards the washing machine.

Mari sat with her hands around the warm mug. 'I've got something to tell you… and something to…'

Lena found her friend's body language confusing; her voice faltered though her eyes sparkled with excitement.

She gave Mari a kind smile, patting her on the arm. 'Mari, this is me yer talkin' to. C'mon, spit it out.'

Mari took a deep breath. 'Well, do you remember the friend of mine, Pierre, who's a fertility specialist? He's been discussing exciting new developments in assisted reproduction with another friend, Xavier—you don't know him—with the aim of trying to help Xavier's brother and his wife have a child. The thing is, not only could this new process help them, but it could also help me.'

As Mari began explaining the technical

breakthrough—the woman who successfully delivered a pregnancy using a donor egg—Lena was thrilled to think perhaps, at last, Mari might have a chance to have a baby with Gerren. She was fascinated such a process could be possible.

As Mari outlined Alain and Fayette's circumstances, Lena felt immense sympathy. They must be going through hell. Picturing George asleep upstairs, she tried to imagine what five miscarriages could do to a person; it would crush her.

When her friend spoke about surrogacy, she thought it terrific poor Fayette and Alain might have a different kind of opportunity to have a child. She considered it an incredible way for a childless couple to have their own offspring and agreed it was marvellous and selfless of someone to help make that dream possible.

At length Mari finished speaking and took hold of her hand across the table. 'Well, what do you think?'

'It's bloody amazin' what scientists can do these days!' she replied. 'I'm so glad yer friends will have another chance. Sounds like they really deserve happiness. An' I think it'd be absolutely wonderful if ee were able to have a baby, Mari.' She squeezed her friend's hand. 'What's Gerren's take on this? Have you told him yet?'

Mari shook her head and leaned forward earnestly. 'No... I mean... would you do it? Would you be the surrogate?'

Lena sat back in her chair, shock resonating. 'Bloody hell, Mari. Yer askin' *me* to have Fayette and Alain's baby? Lordy!'

Mari threw her a sheepish look. 'I'm sorry, I didn't make it very clear. And I didn't mention the financial part.

The surrogate would be paid a lot of money.' She nodded to emphasise this. 'A lot. You could do so much with it. Start your own business, like you've always wanted. You're a wonderful person, Lena. You always seem to be able to empathise with people. You're caring and compassionate. I know it's a huge ask, but I thought it might be something you'd contemplate and the money would be life-changing.'

Lena rested her face in her hands for a few moments, elbows on the table, her eyes downwards, unfocussed. 'There's a great deal t' think about, Mari. It's bloomin' complicated is what it is. Obviously I'd need t' talk with Jake.' She looked up. 'How much would this payment be then? Y'know, if it's somethin' we might consider.'

'Forty thousand pounds.'

'Fuckin' hell!'

After a few moments Mari spoke again. 'There's one more thing. If you do decide to go ahead… and if it's a success… would you contemplate donating eggs to me?'

Jake arrived home at around five-forty. He was tired and not in a particularly good mood. He generally tried to keep work matters firmly in the workplace but occasionally they boiled over into his home life. This was one of those days. Lena was busy feeding George fish fingers with potato and broccoli. She put the kettle on while Jake sat at their kitchen table pulling funny faces at his son, who gurgled with delight while trying to stuff a large chunk of potato into his mouth. Nowadays Jake's whole world was George and Lena and his *raison d'être* was providing for them. Usually when he walked through the front door to be greeted by his son's chubby face his professional problems would melt away but this evening he was finding it difficult to shrug off the day.

Lena placed a mug of hot tea before him and laid a hand on his arm. 'Bad day?' she smiled empathetically.

He shook his head briefly. 'It dunt matter.'

'C'mon luvver, ee can tell me.'

Jake sighed. 'It's bloody Gerren again.' Glancing at George, he clapped a hand over his mouth. 'Sorry, love.'

'Dunt want him pickin' up bad words,' she chided softly. 'What's Gerren done now then?'

'Oh, he's a blinkin' pain in the backside. One minute he's yer best mate and the next he's remindin' you he's yer boss. I never know where I stand with him,' Jake grunted unhappily. 'Nowadays he never misses a chance fer one-upmanship and I'm really sick of it.'

'He's not that senior to you, is he?' asked Lena, continuing to feed George the last of his dinner. The little lad banged his plump fists on the plastic tray of his highchair after every mouthful.

'Oh, he's goin' right t' the top. He married the boss's daughter an' he never lets anyone forget that. He acts as if he's there already.'

'You've got a thick hide, my luvver,' Lena responded sympathetically. 'You just use it to shield him off. He's not better than you.'

'Yeah, well, I know that, but it's not just me; I feel sorry for the others below me. At least he throws me a bit of respect now an' then. He treats some of the others like they're all good fer nothin'. It really gets my back up.' He bent to gently stroke George's cheek with the back of one finger as the toddler drank his milk from a beaker with a spout. 'He's a real guzzle-guts tonight, isn't he?' he smiled.

Lena laughed. 'He has a healthy appetite, like someone else I know!'

Jake returned to his exasperated thoughts. 'I mean, there's nothin' wrong with ambition but you don' have to stand on everyone else to get there.'

'You have ambition,' Lena stated softly. 'Your ambition is to set up yer own business and you've got t' focus on that.'

'Yeah, well, that's not goin' t' happen any time soon. That's lookin' more and more pie in the sky, if you ask me,' returned Jake despondently.

Lena leaned across the table and grabbed Jake's hands. 'What if there was a way of earnin' a lot o' money, enough to fund a new start, an outdoor shop like we always wanted?' she said earnestly. 'If we had the money, would you do it? Would you leave Thomas Engineerin'?'

'O' course I would. But that's a dream, love. We can't even afford a washin' machine at the moment. The interest rate looks to be goin' up again and, judgin' by the way house prices are risin', it's goin' t' take years to save a deposit on a home, let alone a business. Anyway, we have George t' think about. I can't go throwin' away a good job. Don't you worry about me; I'll keep me head down and get on with it.'

Lena squeezed Jake's hands and rose from the table. 'Want a beer?'

'Sounds good, thanks. Come on, little feller, eat yer greens,' Jake encouraged, offering George a small floret of broccoli.

Lena opened two cans of Sam Smiths, gave one to Jake and sat at the table again. 'There is a way,' she said quietly, 'for us t' earn forty thousand pounds.'

'What? Where did you hear that? What do we have to do, rob a bank?' Jake responded cynically.

'It's not a wind-up,' Lena answered, shaking her head. 'I had an unexpected visit from Mari today.'

'Mari hasn't got forty thousand,' Jake interjected.

'Listen, Jake. This is serious. Hear me out.'

While she talked Jake unconsciously drew in his chin and raised his eyebrows, his eyes widening. Once she had finished, the air between them was thick with silence. Jake continued to stare at his wife, a thousand thoughts tumbling around his mind, all fleeting, none forming slowly enough for him to capture and absorb.

'Oh, say somethin', my luvver,' Lena eventually prompted apprehensively.

Jake took a deep breath. 'I'm just a bit... shocked, is all. I mean... you've just told me you could... well... effectively rent out yer body fer forty thousand pounds! Bloody hell love, I don't rightly know what t' say.'

'You make it sound like prostitution,' Lena said, crestfallen. 'It's nothin' like that.'

Jake laid a hand on her arm. 'I know, love, it's just... well there's a lot t' think about. Have you really considered this seriously?'

'I've been doin' nothin' else all afternoon.'

'I mean, you'd be carryin' someone else's child... then you'd have to give it up! Could you honestly do that?'

'I'm not sayin' it would be easy. I'm sure that part of it would be bloody difficult,' Lena returned, cupping her hands over George's ears as she swore, then lovingly smoothing his hair. 'We'd have t' be really focussed on our own family and goals.'

'Hmm... I don't know. Yer emotions would be all over

the place—remember how you were with George? Anyway, don't you want another baby of our own?'

'Yes, but we could easily afford to have another child afterwards,' she countered.

'There's a certain amount of risk associated with pregnancy, isn't there? You'd be puttin' yourself at risk for someone else.'

'It's a lot o' money.'

'Lena, I don't know. It doesn't feel right.' Jake's thoughts were slowing to a shuffle so he was at last able to identify each question individually. 'What happens if the process dunt work and you don't become pregnant? How many times would they want you t' try? Or say you are pregnant an', God forbid, somethin' goes wrong and you lose it? I mean, does the money depend on you deliverin' a healthy baby? What if the child has a disability? Fuck, there are so many what ifs! What about yer health, Lena—yer emotional health? Imagine carryin' a baby inside you for nine months, with all yer motherin' hormones racin' about, an' as soon as you give birth, just like that, it's taken away from you. I can't begin t' understand what that must be like. I'd be worried fer you the whole time.'

'I know there are a lot of questions,' Lena responded considerately. 'I've been askin' myself the same things all afternoon. Mari said all our questions would be answered by the clinic. This is only a preliminary step, t' see if we'd have any interest at all in bein' a potential surrogate couple. We'd have to meet a consultant at the clinic t' discuss everythin'. I'm sure ee'll answer questions we haven't even thought of.'

Jake nodded his understanding. Then he asked, 'Why

is Mari involved?' A wave of fear came over him. 'God, it's not Mari an' Gerren is it? Because there's no way…'

'No, absolutely not!' Lena interrupted hastily. 'I wouldn't do that for yer boss an' I wouldn't ask you to either. No, she doesn't know them. It's relatives of a friend, someone Fran knows, apparently. Mari thought of us because we love children, because I'm fit an' healthy an' obviously fertile, an' because my first pregnancy was a breeze compared t' what some folk go through…' she hesitated, '…an' because she knows we could do with the money if we want t' set up our own business.'

'Does Gerren know?'

'No, an' Mari's not goin' to tell him either. It's all confidential. No-one else has to know.'

Jake snorted. 'It would be hard to keep it a secret if you got pregnant.'

'I know. I haven't thought how we'd deal with that yet. We'd have to talk t' the clinic. Look Jake, there are so many issues, but we'd be helpin' an infertile couple to have a child. We have George. It's awful to think what it must be like not t' be able t' have a baby; Mari's talked about it enough. For me, bein' a surrogate mother would be like… well… like fosterin' a child, an unborn child; takin' care of it until its parents were able to. I would just have to keep remindin' myself I wasn't the real mother. People foster children and give them up. I'm sure they must form bonds which then have to be broken. It's a big thing, I know, but it's also a lot o' money—money we could do so much with. It's a huge opportunity, one that isn't likely t' come around again. We have t' decide whether it's right fer us.'

Lena wiped George's sticky hands with a wet cloth before lifting him out of his highchair. 'Look, I need t' get this little man to bed. Let's carry on talkin' over dinner.' With a swish of her skirt she had gone, leaving Jake alone with his beer and thoughts.

Chapter Sixteen

Mari sat in a deckchair on her lawn, with the remains of a glass of Piat D'Or, enjoying the last of the unusually warm evening sun before it disappeared behind next door's sycamore tree. Gerren was out playing in a darts match and she and Fran had just spent a couple of hours nattering over a light supper of warm quiche with garlic potato wedges.

Mari's thoughts were all over the place. Fran had been updating her on the tricky situation concerning the surrogacy and how she and Pierre had attempted to resolve it.

Fran said Pierre had discussed the situation, the benefits and risks to the clinic, with his CEO who stated his duty was to ensure the clinic is legally protected as well as ethically unimpeachable. Because of the obvious benefits the CEO, Giles Blenkinsop, agreed to authorise the technical procedure with the proviso Fran handled the surrogacy agreement on behalf of her company's legal team and if anything went wrong Pierre must be prepared to shoulder the responsibility on behalf of the clinic. He also stipulated the donation from Alain should be made anonymously and any payment from Alain to the surrogate must be separate from the clinic's IVF fee and not involve the clinic. Pierre hadn't mentioned that Alain and Fayette wanted to register any resulting children as theirs. Pierre didn't believe there was a reason to involve Giles, though Fran disagreed.

Fran had shared her concerns with Mari. Giles had told Fran he trusted all current legalities would be covered in the surrogacy agreement. He also assumed she and her firm would envisage and address any potential complications. He realised this was a new area for the legal team but was confident they could handle it. Fran felt under pressure to participate, since Giles had given the go-ahead and specifically requested her involvement. But he wasn't aware of the added complexity of child identity and Pierre had implored her not to mention this to Giles as he wanted to keep this under the radar, for fear of losing the opportunity to try the technique. Fran's professional head told her this should be openly discussed but her heart willed her to support Pierre. So, to limit liability to herself and her firm, she'd decided to deflect any potential legal challenge from Lena by including a statement in the agreement to the effect that any child identified as Alain and Fayette's will be legally theirs. Fran trusted if Lena was willing to sign up to Alain and Fayette having legal and social rights to the child, then she would respect the agreement and there should be no challenge. It was a risk as she doubted this would stand up in court.

The more she and Fran talked, the more Mari had appreciated the legal complexity of the process and the more apprehensive she had become thinking about potential egg donation for herself at some point in the future. She wondered what Gerren would say—deep down she knew; it would be such an impediment to him, adding to his already strong feelings against having a child with a donor, he'd never approve. She kept seeing the image of Lena's shocked expression when she'd mentioned egg donation, knocked for six at the thought of sharing a child, genetically, with Gerren and watching him or her being brought up by them. Perhaps if she wasn't with Gerren, she told herself; maybe if she made a life with Xavier... But then she imagined the hurt she'd cause Gerren and tried to shut her desires away. At least for now.

A few days later, Fayette and Alain were informed Pierre was in charge of their case and it would be overseen by the clinical director. Fayette was apprehensive, almost to the point of panic, about meeting the Lesters and she knew it would be a challenge for Alain too. Up to this point, 'the surrogate' was just a term, a name for a carrier, a stage in a long complicated reproductive process that was tangible every step of the way, particularly the conception, which for most was impalpable. Fayette had existed in a reality in which she was the driving force: her body was in control and she had to accept the consequences of her own making, however involuntary. Now she would be giving up a rite of passage, the enactment of the natural role of a woman, her perceived entitlement to grow and bear a child. Now there would be two physicalities on which her happiness would depend and her attitude would need to be generous regarding the culpability of another if anything went wrong.

Now, sitting in a private waiting room at the clinic, Fayette felt a strange mixture of resentment and selfish guilt at involving another woman, a stranger, in her all-pervading intimate ambition. She experienced an urge to get up and walk out but her intense desire for a child, a force equally as strong, kept her there.

The door opened and Fayette came face to face with Lena, a curvy, maternal-looking lady. She and Alain sprang to their feet. Beaming, Lena walked straight up to her, arms wide, and gave her an enormous hug. As they parted, Lena grabbed her hands and squeezed them. She spoke earnestly.

'Hello Fayette. 'Tis so good t' finally meet you. Jake an' I,' she indicated to her husband, hanging back by the door, 'we're so pleased t' be able to help.' Turning to Alain, she held out both hands. 'It really is a privilege, y' know.'

Alain returned her smile and kissed her formally on each cheek. '*Enchanté.*'

'Oh,' she giggled, 'two kisses. Better take note, my luvver,' she chuckled, inclining her head towards Jake, who moved toward them.

Jake shook Alain's hand firmly and did the same with Fayette, hesitated, then kissed her roundly on both cheeks. 'When in Rome, so t' speak,' he winked, his eyes twinkling and laughter lines creasing. He stepped back and Fayette noticed him slide an arm around his wife's waist, drawing her close to him.

Lena glanced lovingly at her husband then smiled at her and Alain. 'Technology t'day is absolutely amazin', int it? I mean, what we're all about to do. We're so honoured you chose us. To have a child is the most precious thing in the world an' it means a great deal t' be able to give you that gift, to turn yer hopes into reality. I'll do my very best fer you.'

Fayette felt drawn towards them and relief flooded through her, so she was slightly overwhelmed. 'We are very grateful,' she managed to respond. 'It is a big thing to ask. You 'ave to be sure.'

Lena nodded assuredly. 'We'll make a good team.'

Pierre entered with a pot of coffee, a plate of shortbread biscuits and a bowl of fruit. He smiled easily at everyone.

'Sustenance for the team. I'm going to leave you a while longer, then return to answer any more queries you might 'ave on the IVF process. After that Fran will be 'ere to go through the contractual side. I know you 'ave each discussed this before with us but being all together for the first time will trigger more questions. It's important to 'ave any worries addressed now. Then you can all make a final decision on whether to proceed.'

As Pierre left the room, Fayette glanced at Lena hesitantly then took control of the coffee tray, pouring for everyone. They sat chatting, getting to know one another, and Fayette thought how open, generous and kind Lena was. If she had been at all nervous, she hadn't revealed it. She'd put her and Alain at their ease, despite this being a unique situation for her, which can't have been easy. Her giggle was infectious and soon had them all laughing. Lena's love for her little boy radiated from her like warmth from the sun. It was clear to Fayette that Lena and Jake were close and he was enormously supportive of his family.

Here was a woman with whom she felt able to share the bond of motherhood.

Fayette and Alain shared their feelings of appreciation with Lena and Jake and said goodbye to the couple. Before they left the clinic Fran mentioned she wanted a private word, so they resumed their seats in the waiting room.

'I'll get straight to the point,' Fran said seriously, looking at Fayette and Alain in turn. 'As you know I'm not comfortable with your wish to falsely register any children resulting from this procedure.'

Alain sat forward to protest but Fayette laid a hand on his arm gently. 'Let 'er finish speaking.'

Fran smiled at her. 'Thank you. I understand formally adopting a child born of a surrogate mother will not work for you. I'm just trying to explore any other options. For example, might it be possible to obtain French citizenship for a child after a period living in France?'

Alain shook his head. 'No, I mean, yes, but only after the age of eighteen. That is much too late. We 'ave discussed this,' he replied frustratedly. 'When a child is born abroad from a French parent, the parent 'as to record the birth in the French civil register. We 'ave three options. One,' he pointed a finger exaggeratedly toward Fran, 'we can register the child in England as our own—it would be, biologically. Two, not register it at all then apply for a court judgement to register 'im or 'er in France. 'Owever we'd still 'ave to lie, as a surrogate is not accepted and 'aving a birth certificate stating us as the parents will be more straightforward than applying for a French court judgement with no birth certificate. Or three, wait until 'e or she is adult, when 'e or she could maybe apply for French citizenship by naturalisation. This is not acceptable. See? There is only one option for us.' He sat back, folding his arms defiantly.

Fayette inclined her head to one side, the corners of her mouth turned down, her eyes fixed on Fran. She shrugged and spoke slowly, considering each word. 'This will not be in the surrogacy contract. You will not be involved. This is our decision.'

Chapter Seventeen

Plymouth, England, June 1984

Lena and Jake sat side by side at their kitchen table examining the final draft of the surrogacy contract. The lengthy document encompassed the procedure and the responsibilities and expectations of all parties, together with their informed consent. It covered three potential cycles or attempts, with the option of opting out between cycles, and detailed the known obstetric risks. A maximum of two embryos were to be implanted at each attempt. Agreed attitudes to an abnormal baby, to amniocentesis and abortion on medical grounds were incorporated. Fayette's behaviour during the IVF and Lena's conduct during the pregnancy were outlined. There was to be no drinking or smoking, no taking of drugs unless specifically prescribed by the clinic. All parties would be subject to health screening and the limitations of Jake and Lena's conjugal activities were included. Payments of the clinic fees and medical expenses were detailed. Separate compensation for the surrogate couple was included in an annex. Lena and Jake would receive their payment in four instalments three months apart. They'd receive an initial two thousand pounds if the embryos didn't implant, to compensate for the tests and shrugged and spoke slowly, considering each word. 'This will not be in the surrogacy contract. You will not be involved. This is our decision.'

Chapter Seventeen

Plymouth, England, June 1984

Lena and Jake sat side by side at their kitchen table examining the final draft of the surrogacy contract. The lengthy document encompassed the procedure and the responsibilities and expectations of all parties, together with their informed consent. It covered three potential cycles or attempts, with the option of opting out between cycles, and detailed the known obstetric risks. A maximum of two embryos were to be implanted at each attempt. Agreed attitudes to an abnormal baby, to amniocentesis and abortion on medical grounds were incorporated. Fayette's behaviour during the IVF and Lena's conduct during the pregnancy were outlined. There was to be no drinking or smoking, no taking of drugs unless specifically prescribed by the clinic. All parties would be subject to health screening and the limitations of Jake and Lena's conjugal activities were included. Payments of the clinic fees and medical expenses were detailed. Separate compensation for the surrogate couple was included in an annex. Lena and Jake would receive their payment in four instalments three months apart. They'd receive an initial two thousand pounds if the embryos didn't implant, to compensate for the tests and embryo transfer. On Lena becoming pregnant, if the procedure then terminated for any reason they would be recompensed on a time-related pro-rata basis and the payments would start again from the beginning with each new cycle. Lena would have no legal or social rights to any consequent children that were biologically confirmed as Alain and Fayette's. There was to be no disclosure of the identities of participants in the surrogacy arrangement to any outside party, including any resulting children, during the process or at any time in the future.

Lena twiddled her biro between her fingers as she read the final paragraphs. She reached the bottom of the last page. 'Are you happy t' sign?'

'It seems t' reflect what we agreed.' Jake leant back in his chair, stretching momentarily. 'I am if you are.'

Lena beamed, signing underneath her printed name and dating it.

Jake returned her grin as she passed him the pen. 'I still can't quite believe it. Think of it, Lena, we'll be able to have our own business! We'll be able t' set up wherever we want; obviously where there's a lot o' tourism an' people are interested in outdoor pursuits. I'm thinkin' Cornwall. Yer Mum would like that. Not too far but far enough to begin a new life away from the city.' He added his signature to the document.

'Without lots of questions from neighbours and people at work,' Lena added.

Jake laughed cynically. 'My parents might even come and stay once in a while if they can drag themselves from their "marvellous" Dorset and my good-fer-nothing brother. How they're taken in by him, time an' time again, I dunt know. He's a wrong un conducting business in a shady world. He's always come between them and me. We always end up bloody arguin' about him.'

Lena caught his hand and squeezed it. 'Once you've got yer own business they might show you a bit more respect. We won't tell them if I get pregnant though.'

'No,' Jake agreed, 'it's not like we see 'em often. They'd never understand an' anyway I think we're better off not admitting the truth to anyone.'

'Except my mum,' Lena stated firmly. 'I'm tellin' her no matter what. I can't lie to her, Jake. She'd be heartbroken if we let her believe we'd lost a child. Anyhow, she wouldn't say anythin' an' I'm sure I'll need her support, you know, when the time comes.'

'Well, I don't see why you couldn't tell yer Mum,' Jake agreed. 'Mari knows what's going on and she's not mentioned in the contract.'

'Exactly.'

'There is still one thing I'm really concerned about,' said Jake, looking serious.

Lena's cheerful countenance fell away. 'What, my luvver?'

'I dunt know how I'm goin' to fulfil my part of the bargain an' keep my hands off you, you lovely woman! Come here!'

He grabbed her arm and pulled her towards him so she ended up on his lap. She laughed as he flung both arms around her and fondled her ample breasts through her loose-fitting colourful cotton top.

'I hope yer not goin' to keep yer hands off me!' She looked around at him with a mischievous smile. 'There are plenty of other ways of havin' fun, y'know.'

Jake raised his eyebrows. 'I'm not sure I can remember.

I think you'll have t' show me—right now, in fact.' He slid a hand under her skirt and she giggled loudly.

'Yer ticklin' me!'

'I'll do more than tickle you, you wicked woman.'

'Shhh; c'mon, let's go in the front room. I dunt want t' disturb George.' She moved from his lap.

He grabbed her buttocks playfully. 'Lead the way, Jezebel.'

A second meeting between Fayette, Alain and the Lesters had gone well. Extensive screening had found no medical contraindications and Fayette's cycle was to be prolonged for eight days with hormone tablets to synchronise with Lena. There was now an agreed start date.

Pierre had told them he'd been checking and re-checking results, facts and processes and had concluded everything was in place. It was obvious to Fayette he felt a deep responsibility for the success of the process, which reassured her. They were all ready to begin.

Fayette was sipping her morning coffee sitting at the brightly-lit breakfast bar in their newly rented modern home in Mainstone on the north-eastern edge of Plymouth. The location was perfect: not far from the clinic and Plymbridge Woods were at the end of the road. She'd already been jogging through the beautiful ancient oak woodland and alongside the cool rushing river. She and Alain had found a furnished place—it would have been too costly to buy everything they needed—and she was awaiting the delivery of a few of their pictures and ornaments from France, which would make it feel more like home. The internal walls of the spacious rooms were as light as the freshly painted brilliant white exterior, lending themselves easily to personalisation.

She reflected how fortunate they were Alain was able to manage his business of buying, renovating and selling property over the telephone. His team were all experienced and knew what to do, which meant he shouldn't have to visit France much over the next nine months.

She made a fresh cup of coffee and took it to the conservatory to sit in a comfy wicker chair amidst padded floral cushions. The room afforded a lovely view of the long garden, which was planted with shrubs along its borders and overhung by a stand of beech trees at the far end. She could imagine sitting here on a winter's day, the air warmed by sunlight through glass, cradling a baby on her lap—her baby! She wanted nothing more. Over the last weeks the longing had consumed her, so she could barely think of anything else. Born of her grief at losing the last baby and the subsequent glimmer of hope delivered by Xavier with his New Year news—hope that had now burgeoned to a propitious beam which encompassed and held her in its spotlight—her yearning had intensified. She couldn't wait to begin the medication.

Two days later Fayette began taking the hormones designed to delay her period.

Fran arrived home on the 26, June, to find Pierre sitting in the dining room, with a large glass of red wine, looking strained. She threw him an understanding smile, sat and poured herself a glass. 'The Warnock Report?'

He nodded unhappily. "Ow did you guess. It was signed off today.'

'I know, but I don't have any details yet. What does it say?' she said anxiously. 'Is it as bad as we feared?'

Pierre nodded and pushed sheets of paper across the table towards her. 'We don't 'ave the full report yet but Giles got the press release. 'E called a special meeting for all our staff.'

Pierre went on to say they'd discussed a summary of the report of the Warnock Committee on the inquiry into the social impacts of infertility treatment and embryological research. He and his colleagues were extremely concerned about some of its recommendations, including the limitation on the use of human embryos to the first fourteen days after fertilisation and the proposals that the UK government write laws detailing criminal liability for professionals and others who bring about a surrogate pregnancy and that surrogacy contracts are made illegal and unenforceable in law.

'The committee 'as completely rejected surrogacy,' Pierre exclaimed. 'They think women might be tempted to contract out their pregnancy for the sake of vanity. 'Ave you ever 'eard anything more ridiculous?'

As she listened, Fran filled with dismay. 'It's going to be in the papers tomorrow, isn't it? I'll have to telephone Fayette and Lena.'

'Yes, you should, Fran. But listen, you know as much as I do, unless the government acts upon the findings of this committee, their advice will remain just that—advice. We 'ave no idea if this will be taken any further. After today's discussion the conclusion of the clinic's management team was to put aside our concerns for the time being. Giles will request your legal input, Fran, but I'm telling you the clinic wants to proceed with the surrogacy. So please reassure the Dubois' and the Lesters. I'll talk with them too, if that will 'elp.'

Fran leaned over the table and squeezed Pierre's arm. 'I'm sure it will.' She heaved a sigh. 'I think this could be the beginning of a rocky road but we're all in it together, fighting the same corner. And we make a great team.'

Chapter Eighteen

Plymouth, England, July 1984

On the second day of her cycle Fayette began to take hormone tablets and receive injections into her buttocks every afternoon at four o'clock, mainly administered by Pierre but occasionally by Alain, who turned out to be surprisingly good at putting her at ease while inserting the long needle and driving the liquid painfully into her muscle. She visited the clinic at seven-thirty every morning in preparation for blood and urine tests and the ultrasound scan and watched with fascination and some trepidation as Pierre measured her enlarging follicles on the computer screen. As she needed a full bladder for the vaginal ultrasound, she rose every day at six o'clock so she'd time to drink plenty of water following her initial toilette and first coffee. A couple of times she'd misjudged it, nearly having an accident, and had relieved herself on arrival at the hospital then sat and drank cups of cold water from the machine in the waiting room to refill her bladder.

The process was relentlessly invasive and intimate. She'd had internal examinations and procedures before but the frequency and intensity of invasions into her body of needles and probes initially felt awkward and unnerving. The private parts of her body were no longer that. However, seeing other women in the waiting room, knowing they were likely going through similar embarrassment, normalised the situation.

Fayette became aware of her body like never before: her ovaries busily producing egg cell-containing follicles which grew and grew as the days went by, deflecting pulses of inaudible high-frequency sound waves during scans to prove they were there; her body chemistry changing with the rising levels of all the necessary hormones; the blood pumping through the superficial veins in her bruised inner elbows; the reflexive tightening of the muscles in her bottom whenever a needle was inserted.

On day eleven it was confirmed Fayette's eggs were almost ready for harvesting and two days later she was given a hormone injection to assist their maturation for collection after thirty-six hours. She'd been informed there were quite a few promising follicles. She felt excited and positive: her body had seemed to respond well to the treatment and she was looking forward to the harvest of their combined efforts. Alain would then get to play his major role. He'd supported her every step of the way, caringly accompanying her to the clinic, tenderly holding her hand through the scans, deftly puncturing her skin with needles.

Alain kissed Fayette on her forehead as she lay in a bright medical room waiting to be sedated. A tall thin consultant with glasses, a friendly female nurse and Pierre were all making their final preparations.

Pierre explained to them Fayette's abdominal wall

would be anesthetised locally and her bladder filled via a catheter with isotonic saline so her follicles could be effectively visualized on the scanner. 'I will then collect your eggs using a needle that will be passed through your vagina and into each ovary under ultrasound guidance,' Pierre continued. 'With the needle I will puncture each mature follicle to aspirate the fluid inside. I'll examine this immediately under a microscope.' He smiled kindly. 'Do you 'ave any questions?'

Fayette's nerves tightened her facial muscles and knotted her stomach. She shook her head. Alain squeezed her hand.

'The whole procedure will only take around thirty minutes,' Pierre said cheerily. 'You can relax, Fayette. Mr Goodall, Nurse Underhill and I are with you and there is nothing to worry about. In the meantime,' he looked at Alain, 'you'll be shown to a room from which you will subsequently emerge with your semen sample. Four 'undred million sperm cells, each carrying twenty-three chromosomes,' he grinned.

Alain left the room. As the sedation took effect, Fayette heard herself murmur 'that's a lot of chromosomes.' *Alain's ability to create something of his own flesh and blood, to pass on his family genes*, she thought and smiled.

Nurse Underhill passed Fayette a second cup of tea, offering the same to Alain. They were sitting in a warm, comfy recovery room on a large sofa. In front of them, on a low pine coffee table, was a plate of hot buttery toast.

'You might experience cramps or a little bleeding but it shouldn't be anything to worry about,' said the nurse. 'If you have any concerns though, just ring the clinic.'

Pierre appeared, sat opposite them and nodded encouragingly. 'The egg collection 'as been successful you will be pleased to know. There were a good number of mature ova. Alain, your sperm sample was good quality. This 'as been concentrated by centrifugation and mixed with Fayette's eggs. We will know more in a few days.'

Fayette heaved a thankful sigh, grinning at Alain as he did the same.

Alain held out a hand and shook Pierre's, forcibly. '*Merci*, Pierre, *merci beaucoup!*'

As they left the clinic under a blue sky, Fayette's relief dominated a whole array of other emotions vying for supremacy: satisfaction, excitement, hopefulness, anxiety, nervousness. She could tell Alain was experiencing similar feelings. They'd completed their part of the process and were eager to know the outcome. Would they have at least one fertilised egg of sufficient quality?

After three days of fretful waiting, Fayette and Alain received a call from Pierre asking them to come to the clinic. When they arrived, Lena and Jake were also there. There were hugs all round. Pierre informed the gathered ensemble there were two good-quality eight-cell blastocysts available for transfer. They were all delighted, Pierre included, though he warned against celebrating too soon—a challenging stage of the process, that some considered the most difficult part of the IVF procedure, was still to come.

Pierre stated by monitoring Lena's hormone levels he'd confirmed adequate synchronization with Fayette's cycle and she was ready to receive the embryos.

That afternoon two miniscule multi-cellular structures, the basis of human life, were introduced onto the lining of Lena's womb via her cervical canal by means of a catheter, with no need for anaesthesia; it was a simple process, Pierre had told them, taking less than fifteen minutes, though its simplicity belied the complex variables influencing any subsequent establishment of pregnancy.

Alain and Fayette were waiting outside the clinic for Lena and Jake as they emerged into the late afternoon sunshine, Lena hosting the precious cargo. The two men shook hands and the women hugged. The tacit bond now binding them lay thickly in the air between them, undeclared. Both couples were acutely aware of the significance of this moment but unable to utter anything more than, 'Good luck,' although their eyes signalled responsibility and courage.

On returning home Fayette felt bereft. Her part in the making of a child was over. She'd relinquished control: she would no longer attend the clinic every day, there was no need for pills or injections, no requirement to give her blood or collect little pots of urine. She'd been cut loose to float in an excruciating sea of uncertainty for two weeks.

Lena felt the weight of responsibility in her abdomen, cognisant of the two tiny embryos entrusted to her. As she went about her daily tasks, she occasionally placed a hand on her belly, attempting to silently communicate warmth and kindness as if she were already pregnant and welcoming the developing baby. She was fully aware these early-stage embryos were only a group of cells which might or might not have attached to the lining of her uterus. As the days went by, she tried harder to detach from what was going on inside her. *What will be will be*, she told herself. Like Fayette, she was helpless to do anything about it.

Plymouth, England, August 1984

At last the day came when Lena was called in to give the blood sample that would show whether she was pregnant. The couples had decided to unite to hear the result. They waited nervously in a private waiting room furnished with soft beige linen-covered chairs and embellished with large verdant potted plants. A tropical fish tank stood in one corner, a ploy to lure and relax the restless mind.

Fayette's stomach lurched as Pierre entered. She clasped her hands to hide their shaking. Lena placed her water glass on the glass coffee table in front of her and grabbed Jake's hand. Pierre's features wore a cheerless expression and he had an unusual air of despondency. Fayette knew he didn't have good news. She wanted to scream at him to delay him from imparting the verdict; anything to cherish her hope a little longer.

Looking uneasy, Pierre sat and took a deep breath. He shook his head slightly to lessen the blow, his gesture conveying his message before he delivered the words. 'I'm afraid Lena's pregnancy test was negative. I'm so sorry; it didn't work this time.'

For a few moments the silence was palpable. Fayette tried to speak, but found her mouth dry. She lifted her water glass slowly, buying time, delaying when she'd have to say something. Her disappointment was a grey blanket of lead, crushing her spirit, constricting her lungs. It seemed to her she was on show, the person in the room expected to respond.

The others were looking at her. She regretted her decision to have Lena and Jake in the room. She wanted badly to be alone with Alain. She felt him squeeze her hand. Then he spoke resignedly, 'I'm sure you did your utmost, Pierre,' he said sadly. 'Thank you. We all know the odds are against us.' He looked at Fayette then at Lena and Jake. 'We all did our best, didn't we?'—everyone nodded—'and we'll try again, won't we?' It wasn't a question.

Lena and Jake nodded. An escaped tear made its way down Lena's cheek and she quickly wiped it away, not wanting to indulge her sadness in front of Fayette. She was acutely conscious she'd failed Fayette and Alain. They'd played their part; they'd made the beginnings of a baby and she couldn't complete the process. She was responsible for their distress.

She was compelled to let them know how she felt. 'Fayette, Alain, I'm so, so sorry. You put yer trust in me and I let you down! I don't know what went wrong, but I'll try again fer you, I will.'

She moved to stand in front of Fayette, bent and hugged her, slightly awkwardly.

At her touch Fayette began to cry softly. 'It is not you,' she whispered. '*Merci*, thank you.'

Pierre addressed the four of them with professional compassion. 'Okay, please listen to me,' he said kindly and intently. 'I know this is disappointing, but you 'ave to understand it's no-one's fault. There are a lot of reasons why a blastocyst may not implant. It's not uncommon for them to 'ave flaws, even those that look good under a microscope, and implantation is another part of the process we can't control. Both you ladies are young and 'ealthy, so you still 'ave the best chance of success, even though that may be only twenty-five per cent. Fayette and Alain, I understand you wish to try again, is that right? Lena and Jake, I sense you might be willing to undergo another attempt, yes? But you've all just 'ad the bad news, so I suggest you 'ave some time to think about it. We will arrange separate appointments for you in a couple of weeks or so. You'll each be able to discuss your thoughts with me in private and we'll take it from there. Is that okay with all of you?'

Fayette took a deep breath and straightened herself in her chair. She held Pierre in a determined gaze while she spoke firmly. 'For myself, I 'ave no reservations to try again. I cannot give up now,' she glanced briefly at Alain, who smiled at her supportively, 'and I know Alain feels the same. We can take the two weeks, but our answer will not change.' She turned her attention to Lena and Jake. 'Of course, you must decide what you feel.'

Jake looked questioningly at Lena, who nodded. 'We had already decided what we'd do if, you know, it turned out not to work this time,' he responded earnestly, leaning forward in his chair. He reached for Lena's hand. 'We'd like to help you, to try again.'

Fayette sensed for the past weeks, as she'd dared to hope again, she'd been living in a split reality: in the actuality of her existence and in an ideal world full of optimism in which she saw herself as a mother. She'd imagined herself curled on the sofa by the fire cradling her sleeping baby or joining friends and their toddlers for morning coffee near the local market, gently rocking her infant in its pram as they chatted. The outcome of the first IVF cycle had instantly and mercilessly plunged her into her former life, devoid of children, barren and bereft, down into the deep black well of desolation once more.

Hope is a fickle friend that balances on a razor edge, Fayette thought bitterly. Besides providing sustenance for dreams and expectations, it feeds yearning and hunger. To keep hope alive requires energy and courage. She had to search deep within herself to find the smallest thread of tenacity to which she could cling until it slowly grew into a sturdy rope of resolve with which she could haul herself out of the abyss.

She didn't quite know how she'd come through those first few weeks after the failure of their first IVF attempt. Alain had driven back to France to conduct business and liaise with his team. He'd asked her to go with him, but she'd declined, feeling it was better to stay in England within the surroundings necessitated by their mission. If she returned to France, she told him, she might not want to come back.

They would have to wait two months to allow her menstrual cycle to recover and find its natural rhythm again before embarking on another course of treatment. She volunteered part-time at a charity shop, kept herself fit and waited impatiently to begin again.

Chapter Nineteen

Plymouth, England, November 1984

Sleet threw itself against the windows of Fayette's kitchen as she waited for Alain to gather his keys and wallet. She'd never experienced so much prolonged rain as there'd been this autumn. She'd had to stop jogging in the nearby woodland weeks ago, having pulled a muscle slipping on one of the perpetually wet leaf-strewn paths. Once her calf had recovered, she'd taken up swimming instead. The world outside was continuously enveloped in a cloak of mist. As the weeks had gone by, she'd grown increasingly impatient to begin her treatment again, the sole reason for having to remain in England's dankness.

They'd reached mid-November. Today was day one of her cycle and she was feeling positive. At last she could be doing something towards their goal. They set out for the clinic in the cutting late-autumn freeze.

It had been decided that once Lena had ovulated, she too would receive hormone treatment, to assist in thickening the lining of her uterus and preparing her for pregnancy. This was a trial—the clinic hadn't adopted this procedure before and discussion of the potential benefits in IVF research circles was only beginning.

The intensive treatment began again. Fayette and

Alain immersed themselves in the invasive process of hormone injections, blood taking, bladder filling, urine collection and ultrasound scanning. Drugs, schedules, dos, don'ts, crazy hormones, body imbalance, trepidation, optimism, frustration, stomach pain, bruising, clocks ticking, tiredness, stress, hopefulness, more stress...

As the days went by, Fayette prayed with every fibre in her body to a God in whom she didn't believe.

Two days before Lena began her treatment it was Jake's birthday. They arranged a babysitter for George and treated themselves to a rare evening dining out. They started at their favourite pub on the Barbican then went to a steakhouse chosen by Jake. Lena substituted apple juice for cider while Jake took the opportunity to quaff several ales, thoroughly enjoying Lena's enforced sobriety and chauffeur service. Outside a sudden storm whipped through the narrow streets, rattling old loose-fitting windows and whisking the water in the harbour. Within the restaurant the atmosphere was warm and relaxed and their surf-and-turf platters were tasty. Over dinner they talked about their plans, allowing themselves a little freedom to imagine what their life together could be like living in a little house of their own and running their business in a friendly community somewhere by the sea. They would have a decent-sized garden for George to play in and, when they were settled, make a brother or sister for him.

Hitherto, except for the evening on which they'd signed the surrogacy contract, they'd sought to maintain a pragmatic outlook, limiting such extensive dreaming. However the £2,000 payment for Lena's part in the first

IVF cycle had boosted their hopes, along with their bank balance. They'd at last been able to buy a new washing machine and had paid off their car loan. The remainder had been diligently deposited in their new savings account. Jake's birthday was the excuse they needed to relax and celebrate before plunging back into the stresses of the next surrogacy attempt.

On returning home, and having released George's sitter from her task, they were both in high spirits.

'One for the road!' Jake declared, swaying slightly as he shuffled towards the kitchen cupboard, where he kept a bottle of whisky for special occasions. He caught his foot on one of the legs of the pine table and almost overbalanced, managing to keep himself upright by grabbing the edge of the drainer at the expense of an earthenware mug.

'Shhhh, Jake. You'll wake George,' Lena half-scolded, half-giggled, as she bent to pick up the pieces of pottery. 'Good job this weren't one of me favourites. I dunno about the road, more like last one afore bedtime if you ask me.'

'Ah, now that's a thought.' Jake replaced the bottle, unopened.

'What is?'

'Bed, woman! Bed and a cuddle. Those puppies have been bouncin' around all night, dyin' to be played with, and I'm the man for the job.'

'Is that right?' Lena countered mischievously.

'Yep—it's me or the dog walker.'

Lena laughed. 'What's he like, this dog walker?'

'You hussy; come here.'

Grinning, Jake grabbed Lena's hand and led her into the hallway and up the stairs to their bedroom. He collapsed on the bed trying to take his trousers off, so she did it for him.

They were eager to touch and be touched. Jake fought to get her bra off, the dexterity of his fingers temporarily diminished by alcohol. Then at last her breasts were free and Jake began to pleasure himself between them.

Some moments later Lena felt his tongue move down her body, licking and nibbling, until he came to rest between her legs. She groaned, squirming under his touch. She badly wanted him inside her, but knew it was not allowed. He halted a moment, teasing, and she moaned, arching her hips towards him. Stroking her rhythmically with his fingers, one finger inside, he stopped again. She reached for him, but he'd left her side and was rummaging in his bedside drawer.

'Jake, we can't,' she exclaimed.

'It'll be okay; I've got a condom,' he answered, trying to reassure her.

'We mustn't, even with a condom.'

'It'll be fine. I'll be careful.'

He positioned himself between her legs again, resuming his gentle caresses with one hand, and she let her eyes close and her body relax once more, giving herself up to the pulsing deep within. He covered her with his body and they kissed, love and lust driving their desire for one another, for fulfilment.

'I love you,' he murmured hoarsely into her ear. 'I need you; I need to be inside you.'

She moaned at the thought of him plunging into her. She was close, but he'd moved his hand to her breasts again. 'I love ee too,' she sighed, 'so much!'

'It'll be okay,' he repeated, 'nothing can get through

this.'

Somewhere in the back of her mind, far away, a voice warned of breaching the contract, but at that moment it was overpowered by her intense desire for Jake. She raised her arms above her head, signalling submission.

They held each other in the afterglow, as sated and contented as cats with cream.

Following the egg collection and fertilisation Pierre informed Fayette and Alain they had three grade-one embryos. According to their surrogacy agreement only two could be transferred to Lena. Now the question was whether the two couples wished to revisit that decision. They all knew there was a greater chance of success if three embryos were used; however, that allowed the chance of triplets and pregnancy in excess of twins brought significant risks which could necessitate embryo reduction. Fayette and Alain, Lena and Jake decided unanimously to restrict the transfer to two embryos. Fayette asked Pierre if there was any way he could keep the spare embryo, as she hated the thought of it being destroyed. She and Alain understood its viability might not endure but they would rather he tried. Pierre gladly agreed, adding encouragingly that the clinic was working on improving the freeze-thaw method. Lena had already begun her hormone treatment and two embryos were subsequently transferred.

The difficult waiting period began. Lena told Fayette she felt this time would be better than the last as she was actively contributing by being treated with the additional hormones to give her the best chance of a well-prepared womb. Fayette had asked Pierre to communicate the outcome to her and Alain in private before they met with Lena and Jake, as she felt she'd be able to manage the situation better that way.

Plymouth, England, December 1984

The afternoon Fayette and Alain were called into the clinic was wintry and bright. An overnight hoarfrost had lingered that morning, crystals adorning naked tree branches and icy needles protruding sharply from red-brown leaves. By mid-morning a cool sun had done its best to dispel the ice, though in the woodland the advancing winter persisted and Fayette felt the crunch under her boots as she took herself off for a short walk to calm her nerves.

On entering the clinic they were shown to the same waiting room as before. They were not alone for long. Pierre entered, beaming, shook Alain's hand and kissed Fayette on both cheeks. 'Congratulations!' he announced with gusto. 'Lena's test was positive.'

'*Mon Dieu!*' Fayette sat abruptly, her hands to her mouth. Her smiling eyes met Alain's as he sat alongside and threw his arms around her.

'Of course, it's early days,' Pierre was telling them in French, 'but we have confirmation Lena is pregnant. We'll follow up with an early ultrasound viability scan in a couple of weeks and a further scan at about ten weeks. At that point we'll be able to confirm whether there are one or two foetuses.'

Pierre's voice came to Fayette like a whisper through wool. She couldn't focus on what he was saying, wrapped as she and Alain were in their joyous moment.

Pierre left them alone while he went to fetch Lena and Jake from a consulting room. As all three entered the waiting room hugs and kisses abounded. The atmosphere was of profound elation. They shared the joy of accomplishment and augmented anticipation of a successful outcome.

'*Merci, merci, Lena, mon amie incroyable,*' Fayette exclaimed as she embraced her friend.

Lena beamed. 'I couldn't be more delighted fer you!'

Fayette and Alain returned home in a mist of euphoria and celebrated that evening over a bottle of Cahors Malbec brought over from France. Alain telephoned Xavier to impart the wonderful news.

About half an hour later Xavier received a call from Pierre with the same information. Xavier had to wait until the following morning to telephone Mari at work but by then she already knew about the exciting development as Lena had revealed the good tidings. Everyone was thrilled.

Two weeks later Fayette accompanied Lena to the clinic for her first scan, which confirmed the pregnancy was progressing normally. Seeing Fayette's expression of rapture gave Lena a warm, loving feeling in her stomach. The fact she could help this woman to experience motherhood bestowed on her a feeling of kinship unlike anything she'd experienced before.

Chapter Twenty

Cahors, France, December 1984

Christmas was a wonderful time of celebration for the Dubois family, entirely different to the muted gathering of the previous year. Fayette and Alain joined Xavier and some old family friends at their mother's house for five days of eating and drinking, with a modicum of walking to assuage their consciences. It seemed that rain had been banished over the festive season and the sun daily anointed the countryside with its winter blaze, so the happy sextet could enjoy their long lunches on the veranda.

Fayette warned Xavier not to tell his mother about the surrogate pregnancy yet. She and Alain wished to wait until after the twelve-week scan, when they would hopefully be reassured the baby was developing normally and there was significantly less chance of miscarriage. Optimism usually won over anxiety, although their past experience was never far from Fayette's mind and she knew Alain was experiencing the same concerns.

As usual, Lena, Jake and George spent a relaxing Christmas with Lena's mother, Judy, in Cornwall. Their house was too small for overnight visitors unless George slept in their bedroom and, in any case, they loved visiting her mum, so took every opportunity. Lena had grown up in the village of Polperro twenty-five miles from Plymouth, where Judy still ran the post office, nowadays on her own since Lena's father had sadly passed six years previously. Most of Lena's friends had dispersed in pursuit of jobs but she still knew many people in the friendly community and frequenting the pubs at Christmas time was especially fun. Lena's father, David, had been raised in a fishing family but turned his hand to boat trips as tourism rapidly increased, effectively replacing the fishing industry. Lena and Jake considered offering boat excursions could be a useful sideline to their planned outdoor pursuits business during the summer months. Her mum still had the boat, which they took out in temperate weather. George loved the sea, as did they all; she and Jake couldn't imagine living anywhere far from the ocean.

Lena's mum had always been supportive of her and now was no exception. Judy was delighted to hear about their life-changing plans and accepted the news of the surrogate baby calmly and understandingly, offering to help whenever she and Jake needed it. Judy loved her grandson dearly and it was clear to Lena she hoped one day to have another grandchild. Her mum had admitted being concerned that Lena would find it incredibly hard to give up the baby, however, said she knew her daughter had the mettle to do what was necessary as long as she had the support of her family.

Pierre and Fran celebrated Christmas and New Year on their own, making the most of the rare opportunity of a few days off together in dry bright winter weather to engage in some hiking on Dartmoor and enjoy the seasonal ales and warm firesides offered by numerous old country pubs. Fran was thrilled for all their sakes and wondered whether Mari might now consider trying for a baby using a donor egg. They hadn't spoken about it to date, as both women had been busy in the run-up to the Christmas holiday. They planned to meet soon, which Fran was looking forward to.

Fran loved that Pierre was over the moon about the success of the IVF process thus far and understood the few colleagues at the clinic who were aware of the trial had also been delighted with the establishment of a surrogate pregnancy following embryo transfer. It seemed to Fran this positive news, however fragile, had afforded a much-needed boost to Pierre and his co-workers who were under pressure from the increasingly threatening political climate.

Since July, they had been progressively more concerned as debate on the Warnock Report had found little support for embryo research in the Houses of Commons and Lords, most speakers drawing staunchly on anti-abortion rhetoric. There had followed an opposition campaign initiated by medical experts and supported by certain members of the Medical Research Council. However, the introduction of Enoch Powell's Unborn Children (Protection) Bill in early December, seeking to ban all embryo research, making it impossible to improve assisted reproduction techniques, complicated the situation and gave the clinic serious cause for concern. Pierre and his colleagues had joined the pro-research campaign and were following developments closely. Any government initiative to introduce legislation based on the Warnock Committee's recommendations—notably the creation of a licensing committee to oversee assisted reproduction and scientific investigation—was in danger of being hijacked by this even more conservative private member's bill.

Pierre had told Fran he was determined to put his fears to one side and enjoy Christmas and, to her relief, he seemed to be doing just that. There was time enough in the new year to worry about the second reading and vote on the bill, which would be taking place on the 15th of February.

At Christmas Mari and Gerren split time off work between their families as usual. Mari had wanted to do something different this year, suggesting since they frequently spent time with both sets of parents, perhaps they could spend a few days away at a country-house hotel. However Gerren insisted on the customary family events; his parents for Christmas Day lunch and high tea, hers on Boxing Day, and an afternoon and evening of darts with friends at their local pub the following day. Christmas wouldn't feel right, he'd told her, if they went away. Mari felt increasingly frustrated. Although she was happy to spend time with family and friends, to her each of the days felt scarcely different to an ordinary Sunday. Nevertheless, she agreed and decided to take advantage of Gerren's celebratory frame of mind to discuss the advances in assisted reproduction.

The morning after Boxing Day, as they enjoyed a delicious late breakfast of smoked salmon and scrambled eggs, she broached the subject. She told him of the publicised success almost a year ago of a woman achieving pregnancy using a donor egg fertilised with her husband's sperm. She emphasised how the procedure was becoming more common and the fertility clinic in Plymouth had successfully performed a similar procedure and asked him how he might feel about trying for a child of their own in the same manner.

Gerren was taken aback. 'To be honest love, I thought we'd moved on. I'm sorry, I really thought you were content now… you know… with the way things are. We've made a good life for ourselves, haven't we?'

Mari couldn't help but issue a deep, disappointed sigh, tears pricking her eyes. She lowered her gaze and pushed her fish around the plate with her fork, trying to maintain a calm expression. 'We didn't have this option before. If this had been possible, I'd have wanted to try it. Our only choice at the time was adoption or nothing. If you had the chance to have your own child, wouldn't you want it?'

Gerren paused before answering carefully in a measured tone. 'The thing is, Mari, it wouldn't be your child—it would be mine, not ours. It'd be like having a baby with a stranger. Every time I'd look at the baby, I'd wonder who the mother was.'

'But if I was able to get pregnant that way, I'd be carrying the baby inside me… for nine months,' Mari pointed out; 'nurturing its development, contributing nutrients. He or she would have my blood, Gerren. I would be part of the child. I'd feel the child was mine. Don't you think that would make all the difference?'

Gerren's expression told Mari he'd made up his mind against the idea. 'I don't agree, Mari. It's just not the same for me. If, and it's a big if, you had a child, it would still have someone else's genes, not yours. And there's another consideration: IVF is an expensive process with less than a twenty per cent chance of success.'

Mari looked at him, surprised he should have this statistic at his fingertips.

He nodded in an irked fashion. 'Yes, I did some research, at the time you were having your tests. Mari, would it really be worth going through such an emotionally stressful and costly process with no guaranteed outcome? How many times would you want to try – one, two, three?' He shrugged carelessly, his tone becoming more dogged. 'We're building a good life; we're throwing our energies into different activities and having fun. Where do you want to be in five years, poor and sad after several failed IVF attempts, or comfortably off and having a great time doing things you couldn't if you had a child to look after?'

Anger rose within Mari and caught in her throat. She swallowed and pressed her lips tightly to prevent it from spewing out. She wondered whether Gerren had ever wanted children. Perhaps he even considered her infertility a bonus. After all, it allowed him to live the lifestyle he preferred. She took a deep breath and decided to try calmly and persuasively once more; she knew only too well how he could dig himself into a position. 'I don't think money is really an issue. I know IVF isn't cheap, but we both have good jobs and I'm sure my parents would help us. I just feel… I'd really regret it… if the technology's available and we didn't take advantage… if we didn't at least try. Surely we could discuss it and agree how many times we'd be willing to give it a go, how much time and money we'd be willing to spend? I know we have a free and easy lifestyle now, Gerren, but think how much a child, your child, could enrich our lives! Please, give it some consideration.'

Gerren shook his head. 'I'm sorry,' he replied firmly, 'I just couldn't love a child in the same way not knowing who its mother is. You might feel it would be yours, but that's not the same as it actually being yours, having your characteristics. As I said, for me it wouldn't feel the same as having a baby that's ours, mine and yours.'

'Many would say a child's mother is the one who gives birth to it,' Mari retorted, infuriated.

'I'm sorry,' Gerren repeated brusquely, 'I can't help the way I feel. Maybe if you were able to produce your own eggs and we undertook IVF it would be different, but I can't have a child with a stranger.' His eyes left her dismissively and he went back to reading the paper.

Mari felt as if she'd just been punched in her barren ovaries. The level of acceptance of her infertility she'd gradually managed to cultivate over the last two years was shattered. Grief for her non-existent child, for the possibility of a life with children, for the hope so recently kindled and now annihilated, welled until she ached with it. In that moment she was unable to feel or think about anything else.

She had to get out of the house, away from her husband, from everyone. She rose from the table, sending her chair backwards with a crash, collected her coat and car keys and walked out.

Chapter Twenty-one

Plymouth, England, January 1985

On Friday, 4th January, Fran read the alarming headlines in the daily newspapers: *Baby for Sale on the Way*; *Commercial Surrogate Mum in Labour*. Christ, she thought, this is it.

Pierre was at a conference in Newcastle. She tried to get hold of Lena and Jake but couldn't reach them. Fayette and Alain were in France and she figured they were unlikely to have seen these reports, so decided to wait and see what the next day would bring.

Further developments followed on Saturday: *Kim Cotton, Britain's first commercial surrogate mother; Surrogate Baby Born – Place of Safety Order Sought for Girl*; *Baby for Sale, Wife May Face Court*.

Pierre was still out of town, but she reached him on the phone that evening. 'My God, Pierre, this has hit the public consciousness hard. It's pandemonium! Have you seen these headlines? *Babies Born to be Sold*; *Sold for Carpets and Curtains*; *No Better than Prostitution*; *Wombs to Rent*.'

Pierre grunted despondently. 'We 'ave been talking of nothing else. This public outcry against Kim Cotton, it's frightening.'

Fran agreed. 'Yes and from what I've read she's shocked and totally unprepared for this uproar, poor woman.'

''Ave you been in touch with Lena?'

'I tried calling several times; they seem to be away. I'll keep trying. I've spoken with Fayette—they saw the news on French television, but I don't think they're aware of the vitriolic headlines in the UK papers. They're heading back next week. I'll meet with them and Lena and Jake as soon as possible.'

By Monday, MPs across all parties had expressed significant concerns about commercial surrogacy, pressurising the government to act quickly. Pierre and Fran sat with a bottle of whisky reading the evening papers, exchanging worried looks: *Fowler Moves to stop Baby Sales*; *Fowler Plans to Ban Baby Agencies*; *Baby Sale – Fowler Acts*.

The next day, Pierre was summoned to a confidential emergency meeting at the clinic. There were only four people in the boardroom: himself, the CEO, the financial director and the clinical director—all those who knew of the surrogacy arrangement between the Dubois, the Lesters and the clinic. Prior to the meeting, the CEO reminded Pierre only he, Pierre and the Financial Director had knowledge of the source of Alain's 'anonymous' donation to the clinic, while neither the Financial Director nor the Clinical Director were party to the surrogacy fee payment by Alain to Lena, as this was detailed, deliberately, in a separate confidential annex to the surrogacy contract.

The CEO, Giles Blenkinsop, a tall, grey man who wore his many years of medical experience unpretentiously and with grace, made the situation and his opinion clear. 'This is potentially an extremely difficult one for the clinic,' he stated soberly. 'Firstly, it's imperative we always regard any donations in support of our research—over and above the usual fees for treatment, in situations where this is relevant—separately from any arrangements made for the treatment of a patient. Secondly, you're all aware we are engaged in a surrogacy IVF process. On no account should this clinic, any member of staff working for this clinic or any member of their immediate family, be linked with the provision of a recommendation to a patient of any woman willing to be a surrogate or with receipt of payment for surrogacy services. Is that clear to everyone? We can't risk anyone, staff or the public, misconstruing that donations, investments in the clinic, or fees received, are linked with surrogacy services.'

Pierre and the others nodded.

Giles turned his attention to Pascoe Newton, the firm's exacting financial executive. 'Pascoe, I would like to make you aware there is a financial contract between Alain Dubois and the surrogate, Lena Lester, however it is entirely separate from the finances of this clinic; deliberately so.' Without pausing, he shifted his focus to the clinical director, Gareth Townsend. 'Gareth, whilst you're aware of a contractual arrangement for Dubois to pay a surrogacy fee to Mrs Lester, my understanding is you have not seen the details, correct?'

Townsend, a tall wiry man, originally a fell runner from Yorkshire, nodded.

'Good,' replied Giles, 'let's keep it that way. My own view,' he continued austerely, 'is we have acted in accordance with our client's wishes and done nothing wrong. Paid surrogacy is not against the law in Britain—not yet anyway. To be attempting a new procedure, implanting a genetically distinct embryo into a healthy woman acting as a surrogate for our patient, who cannot carry her own child on medical grounds, is, I believe, a natural and worthwhile step forward from the treatment of an infertile patient with a donor egg. In this context it is entirely reasonable that a surrogate be paid for her time and effort. However, judging by the current outcry, perhaps fuelled by some of the sensationalised headlines we've seen recently, we can anticipate swift action from the government. We'll need to keep a close eye on developments over the next days and weeks.

Pierre, you and Fran talked the two couples through the surrogacy agreement; obviously Gareth and I contributed to the clinical aspects of the document and my understanding is the legal and ethical aspects are thorough. I will be meeting with Fran to discuss how it may be legally impacted by the current political situation. I also need to know who else knows? How watertight are we?'

'The agreement is compre'ensive,' assured Pierre, glancing supportively around the table at his colleagues. Townsend indicated he agreed. 'As for oo knows about it at Wilkins and Farrell, my partner, Fran, assisted in drawing up the document and a colleague of 'ers did the QA, I believe. Of course it will be on file in their records but, anyway, all client work is absolutely confidential. I 'ave to tell you it was a close friend of Fran's, oo is… ah… connected… with Alain Dubois' brother, oo suggested Mrs Lester as a possible suitable surrogate and first spoke with 'er about the opportunity. I believe she and Mrs

Lester are friends. No-one else knows—confidentiality is covered in the contract. Our clinic is not mentioned by name; regarding the treatment costs, the text just stipulates that payment of clinical fees and medical expenses is the responsibility of Dubois.'

'This friend who suggested Mrs Lester—I assume she isn't covered by the contract and neither is Alain Dubois' brother. How do you intend to ensure their discretion?' demanded Pascoe Newton, concern knitting his luxuriant eyebrows.

'I know Xavier Dubois well,' Pierre replied, 'e 'as 'is brother's interests in 'is 'eart from the beginning and, don't forget, 'e 'as a significant financial investment in this clinic. My partner Fran 'as been friends with Mari for years— that is the lady oo suggested Lena Lester. She cares about the wellbeing of both 'er friend and Fayette Dubois. She will not mention the arrangement to anyone else and she would not wish to damage the reputation of this clinic. I think in time she might wish for fertility treatment 'erself. But in any case I will speak with both 'er and Xavier.'

'Hmm. I'm not keen on loose ends and potential loopholes,' Newton responded. 'Playing Devil's advocate, you can see how this arrangement could appear rather cosy; investments and donations to the business from your friends, Pierre, a friend of yours proposing her friend as the surrogate and beneficiary of a sum of money and your partner overseeing the legal agreement. Someone on the outside might question whether this was planned as a one-off or whether everyone stands to benefit from a series of surrogacy procedures, akin to the agency that recruited Kim Cotton. You might think this is an unfair remark but I'm trying to put myself in the shoes of an unscrupulous reporter. I'd be the first to say the financial contributions from the Dubois brothers have been significant and highly effectual for the business.'

An awkward silence followed. Pierre gathered his thoughts; Giles raised his eyebrows at Newton, who realised he'd inadvertently revealed to Townsend that Alain Dubois had donated to the clinic and Townsend began to look annoyed.

Newton spoke first, directing his comment to Giles. 'I'm sorry but I believe it's important all senior management are aware of how this clinic is funded.'

'I concur, for the sake of transparency as well as effective management,' Townsend rejoined. He shrugged. 'Our duty is to the business as well as our external funders. In any case, we regularly discuss confidential matters in this boardroom. We're all used to handling sensitive information. I would appreciate it if this is how all such matters are dealt with between us in future: openly.'

Giles directed his initial response to his two senior managers. 'You're both right, of course. I apologise for keeping you in the dark, Gareth. Newton, I'm acutely aware of how this situation could appear, which is precisely why we're having this discussion, but I thank you for your candid opinion.' He switched his focus to Pierre. 'As you say, Pierre, Xavier Dubois is highly invested in this clinic and its reputation. The only person we cannot be sure about is your friend, Mari, I think you said. You need to make sure she knows how potentially critical this situation is and that she respects our policy of confidentiality.'

Pierre nodded. 'Absolutely,' he assured his colleagues.

The debate about the morality of commercial motherhood raged on in the public domain against the backdrop of ongoing political debate on the use of human embryos.

Fayette and Alain cut short their stay in France and returned to Plymouth. They were horrified when a court action banned the removal of 'Baby Cotton' from hospital, referring the case to a North London juvenile court. Each day they scoured the papers and listened to the news with increasing apprehension.

'Oh God, Scotland Yard have been asked to report on the circumstances of Baby Cotton's birth,' Fayette exclaimed one evening, dismayed at the day's new development.

Alain sat beside her on the sofa and heaved an angry sigh. 'It's unbelievable how they're acting like some crime has been committed. From what I've read, a surrogate mother in the UK is legally able to reclaim a child she's brought into the world at any stage—which is worrying from our perspective—but Kim Cotton isn't trying to keep the baby, is she? So she's not reneging on an agreement.'

'No, but as she's the biological mother, she's being accused of selling her baby. I think the authorities are concerned for the safety of the child. But I don't entirely understand why; they must know who the baby's father is and his circumstances.'

Alain shook his head in disbelief. 'New babies are taken home from hospital every day without anyone checking whether their parents are suitable.'

Fayette turned to Alain, tears welling, distress cracking her voice. 'What is this going to mean for us? What happens if our arrangement is exposed?'

He took her face in his hands and tenderly kissed each moist cheek. 'It means under no circumstances must anyone discover the truth about Lena's pregnancy, or else the law is likely to impose a similar court order on our baby,' Alain replied resolutely. 'And our plan to discreetly take the baby and register it as ours must work—that hasn't changed. It means our bond with Lena and Jake must remain strong and Pierre must fulfil his part when Lena goes into labour.'

Fayette wiped her eyes with her hands then nodded determinedly. 'We need to talk with Lena and Jake. They must be going through a similar hell.'

'Agreed. And soon.'

Lena and Jake were appalled by the press's treatment of Kim Cotton. Having followed her home from hospital, the journalists had remained camped outside her house.

'Jesus! Listen to this, Jake: *Norman Fowler, the Social Services Secretary, is planning to rush a bill through Parliament to outlaw commercial surrogate motherhood.*' Pouring their mugs of tea, Lena spilled the hot liquid over the kitchen table. She couldn't seem to stop her hands shaking. 'Shit. Get a cloth would you, luvver.' She hadn't slept soundly for days, even at her mum's where she normally felt relaxed, like on holiday.

Jake looked pale and drawn. 'Fuckin' hell,' he uttered, mopping the table with a dishcloth. 'Sit down, love, before you fall. You look like I feel. When we talk with Fran about all of this, we'll ask her where we stand. I mean, we've already had £12,000 from Alain an' you're due the next £10,000 in nine weeks.'

'Yes, an' another £10,000 three months after, an' more.

We need this money, Jake, if we're goin' to begin a new life like we dreamed of. But if this could soon be illegal, would we have to pay it back?' A shock of realisation crossed her face. 'God, Jake, could I be arrested?' Lena covered her face with both hands and wept.

Jake jumped up, came to her side of the table and bent to hug her. 'Hey, don't take on, luvver. It's not gonna come to that.' His words were meant to be comforting but Lena glimpsed alarm in his eyes.

'What if someone finds out I'm a commercial surrogate too?' she sobbed. 'There'd be a scandal. I couldn't bear for us to be treated like Kim Cotton. And what about poor George? We can't let that happen!'

Jake knelt before her, taking her hands in his, stroking them gently with his thumbs. 'No-one's gonna find out. We're not tellin' anyone, Fayette an' Alain need to keep this a secret an' we all signed a confidentiality agreement, remember? It's not in the clinic's interest to say anything an' yer mum's not about to. The main thing now is you try to relax, stop worryin' an' keep healthy. You must look after yerself an' the baby an' I'll take care of you an' George. Okay?' He smiled up at her compassionately.

She regarded him through tired blurry eyes. 'What we're doing will be against the law,' she whispered.

'We don't know for definite it'll come to that, Luvver, an' it's not illegal at the moment an' we're all in it together, so we're gonna make it work,' Jake responded firmly.

Mari had been following the developments with consternation, feeling almost entirely to blame for the situation in which Lena now found herself. As soon as the first headlines began to appear she'd visited Lena and Jake to convey her apologies and regrets. Of course they told her not to worry, they were perfectly fine, and things would be alright, but they all knew their platitudes bore little weight.

Chapter Twenty-two

Fran arranged a meeting with both parties but stipulated she would only discuss the arrangement as covered by the surrogacy contract. She would not be party to any subsequent private arrangement between the couples concerning registering the baby's birth. She'd spent the last week on tenterhooks. She knew her research and legal advice had been sound but now feared a potential misinterpretation of her involvement as some kind of surrogacy agent for which she'd charged a fee. She took steps within Wilkins and Farrell to ensure she would be solely responsible for the surrogacy agreement in the event of any trouble. Her decision not to name the clinic in the contract was vindicated and she was at least glad she'd insisted on that.

She kept abreast of the copious reports and rapid developments as the newspapers continued to report the unfolding Baby Cotton story and government ministers argued, some calling again for all 'embryo experiments' to be outlawed. She and Pierre were disappointed every day, but not surprised, by the Press's proclivity for sensationalist headlines. The phrase 'rent-a-womb' was bandied around. One newspaper report compared the situation to a tragic case in which a baby had been born without arms or legs, questioning whether the intended parents, the surrogate mother or indeed Barnet Social Services would have wanted Baby Cotton if she'd been similarly handicapped. The reporter presumed every commercial rent-a-womb deal would assume the 'merchandise' would be in good order, emphasising babies don't come with that guarantee.

Fran felt increasingly uncomfortable. However, she knew she'd produced a thorough contract, which had addressed the issues now being raised via the media, and was satisfied nothing significant had been overlooked. Although the decision for her to be involved hadn't been entirely hers, she felt she would be able to defend her judgment, if it came to that—although she prayed she would never have to.

She came home one evening to find Pierre clattering pots and pans in the kitchen, seething. He turned towards her, raising his shoulders and spreading his hands in his French manner, incomprehension written on his face. For a few moments he could hardly speak. Then: 'The bloody Marriage Guidance Council 'ave called for an end to secrecy about babies fathered by donor artificial insemination. They say the resulting children are illegitimate and fathers registering themselves as their parents are making a false declaration which could lead to prosecution for perjury!'

Fran made to reply that, in legal terms, the council were correct, however thought better of it.

'You know the reasons couples keep quiet about AID treatment?' Pierre continued testily. 'Children's welfare. And not only that but embarrassment. Many of them are worried what people will think if they discover the truth. So you tell me 'ow is this going to 'elp childless couples?

This 'as all got completely out of 'and.'

Fran sighed inwardly, shot him a sympathetic look and poured them both a large glass of wine. This, she feared, was only the beginning of a long ethical and political crisis.

On the 11th of January it was reported that the High Court Judge, Sir Justice Latey, ruling in the best interests of 'Baby Cotton', gave the natural father and his wife—the intended parents—care and control of the baby. On the 14th she was handed over and they took her back to America. A BBC Panorama documentary entitled *Baby Trade*, in which Mrs Cotton would put her side of the story, was to be aired on national TV that evening. Fran made sure Lena and Jake and Fayette and Alain were aware of the ruling and the programme.

As she and Pierre sat to watch the documentary, Fran's heart thumped and she hoped to God nothing would be said which would cause even more controversy.

Transfixed, Lena and Jake watched Kim Cotton stating she couldn't imagine not being able to have children and had never thought people might have trouble conceiving. "My children are my life," she said, "and if you're lucky enough to be able to give birth and have a child you should share your fertility."

Lena glanced at Jake and nodded. 'I must admit, it does feel good t' be able to do this fer someone desperate to have children.'

Mrs Cotton went on to say the money offered would be useful as she was a stay-at-home mum and it would help with the cost of the big project she and her husband had taken on to do up their house.

'She comes across as a straightforward, intelligent, caring person,' remarked Jake. 'She's been honest about the payment.'

'Yeah. It seems like she did it fer compassionate reasons but the money's handy as well.'

'Bit like us, d'you think?'

Lena heaved a sigh. 'To be honest Jake, I wouldn't be doin' this for strangers except fer the payment. Fer a very close friend maybe or if I had a sister in need—'cept I dunt have a sister. But there's one big difference: the baby I'm carryin' isn't mine. I'm pretty sure I couldn't give up my own child.'

Jake turned and hugged her. 'I know, love. An' even when it's not biologically yours it's still a part of you and it's goin' t' be tough. But I'll help you through it every step of the way. You can count on that.'

On the 15th of January Fran read the headline in the evening press, *Three More Rent-a Mums Pregnant*. 'Have you seen this?' she called to Pierre, who was in the kitchen preparing dinner. He looked around the door jam and shook his head.

'Not yet. Trying to get this in the oven before my stomach thinks my throat's been cut. Come tell me.'

Fran précised. 'The American Surrogate Agency, which recruited Kim Cotton, say three more babies are due to be born to surrogate mothers in Britain, the first of them in the spring. The agency's director has declared changes to the law won't make the problem of infertility go away. She says she's had hundreds of enquires from infertile couples and would-be surrogate mothers and she thinks couples will either go to America for babies or try to obtain them illicitly in Britain.'

Pierre nodded. 'She's probably right.'

'Yes, but listen. She also revealed Kim Cotton hasn't yet been paid her fee and the agency is taking legal advice because criminal charges against her are possible under the Adoption Act.' Fran provided a quick explanation, waving a hand in the air. 'That provides criminal sanctions against payment for the transfer of custody of a child with a view to adoption.'

'I suppose it's a good job Fayette and Alain won't be adopting then,' Pierre remarked gruffly.

Fran shot him a look. 'Hmm. This report goes on to say the agency director has criticised Kim Cotton for selling her story to the *Daily Star* for a reported £20,000.'

'Can't say I blame 'er,' Pierre retorted as he slid a delicious-looking lasagne into the oven.

'Yes,' Fran agreed. 'At least, after all the vindictive press coverage, she gets to give her side of the story and get paid for it.'

'The clinic's been doing AID for years without politicians or anyone else wanting to ban it,' Pierre stated, opening a bottle of wine. 'What's the difference between a woman 'aving a child of 'er own with donor sperm because 'er 'usband's infertile—which is essentially surrogate father'ood—and a woman being the surrogate and giving the child to the biological father?'

'Technically I agree. But donor sperm and eggs are the building blocks. That's different to giving away your own child for money.' Pierre's expression turned sour and Fran raised her hands. 'I know, I know, I'm just playing Devil's advocate.'

'You know there are urgent calls for the government to

establish a licensing authority governing assisted reproduction procedures and human embryonic research?' Pierre said.

'That's not necessarily a bad thing per se, though, is it?' Fran returned. 'I mean if it's underpinned by sound scientific and ethical principles and considers the huge benefits to human health and welfare.'

Pierre grunted. 'There is supposed to be a—'ow do they put it—"mature and compre'ensive consideration of all related issues in order to inform permanent legislation". God knows what we'll end up with.'

The time had come for Fran's arranged meeting with the Dubois and the Lesters at her and Pierre's flat. It was a foul evening; intensifying wind and rain presaging a coming Force 8 storm. Both couples arrived apprehensive.

Fran had made steaming pots of coffee and hot chocolate and once they were all settled, she began. 'I know the last few weeks have been stressful.' She raised her eyebrows. 'That's probably an understatement.'

The others smiled nervously.

'So let me outline the current legal situation as I understand it and then you can share your thoughts and questions. Okay? Pierre will translate so we're all absolutely clear.'

The couples nodded.

'Right, this started with the Government inquiry into human fertilisation and embryology, which, as you know, culminated in the Warnock Report published last July,' she said. 'That concluded surrogacy contracts are unenforceable and hence should be illegal, because in cases where a surrogate mother changes her mind and decides to keep the child any court would be unlikely to insist on a separation of mother and child on the grounds of a prior contractual agreement. Also, because the Warnock Committee believe surrogacy arrangements are legally unenforceable, they say this is guaranteed to cause confusion about parentage.'

'*C'est stupide,*' Alain exclaimed. 'Just because something is not enforceable in every situation should not make it illegal.'

Fayette laid a hand on her husband's arm and Fran cast Pierre a look. This was not going to be easy.

'Surely if there's a contract which clearly states who's the donor, who's the recipient, what's been donated an' everyone has signed it, then it should be bloody obvious who the parents are,' Jake interjected.

'Did the Committee consider our kind of situation?' Lena asked earnestly, leaning forward in her chair. 'Y' know where the surrogate mother isn't biologically related to the child. 'Cause it seems odd to me a court would rule in favour of a surrogate when the baby isn't actually related to her.'

'Yes,' Fran replied patiently, 'chapter eight of the report includes all forms of surrogacy, including your situation. The definition of surrogacy they use is a woman who carries a child to term for another person or couple, whether she contributes to the genetics of the child or not.'

'Hmph.' Lena re-settled herself.

'The report contains a lot of very detailed discussion and deals with all aspects of infertility treatment as well as embryological research,' Fran stated evenly. 'It's been a comprehensive inquiry and surrogacy is only one aspect of

it. The Warnock Committee does recognise, in most cases, a surrogacy agreement would be kept, but they say the courts would treat such agreements as contrary to public policy, so in cases where one party breaks the agreement, the court would not assist the other party. However the courts do have jurisdiction over children so in any dispute they would act in the child's best interests in all the circumstances of the case. So, if the carrying mother changed her mind and decided she wanted to keep the child, the Committee say it is most unlikely a court would order her to hand over the child against her will.'

Fran decided to let both couples absorb this explanation before continuing. She didn't feel it necessary to outline some other of the report's conclusions: that, in cases of a dispute, a court would not order the surrogate mother to return any fee paid to her under the terms of the agreement; that the present state of the law makes any surrogacy agreement a risky undertaking for those involved.

After a few moments she added, 'You can, of course, read the report for yourselves—though it's over a hundred pages long so I would focus on chapter eight—because several different views were considered and it might help you to understand why they reached their various conclusions, even if you don't agree with them. But remember, this was published last year and it's still only advice. Can I top anyone up with coffee or hot chocolate? Then we can focus on the current state of affairs.'

'Chocolate for me please, Fran,' responded Lena.

'Coffee please,' said Fayette.

Alain and Jake remained silent until Pierre offered beer, which they gratefully accepted.

Fran poured the hot drinks. 'Okay. As for the current situation—and I emphasise this strongly—surrogacy, commercial or not, is not illegal at present. And neither is arranging a surrogacy contract or participation in a surrogacy procedure. However, the fact that we have all agreed to keep this process confidential plays in our favour. There is no knowing what legal developments might ensue in the coming months.'

'Yes, we've all gotta keep this a secret,' Lena stressed. 'I've had nightmares thinkin' what would happen if the papers got hold of my name.'

Fayette viewed Lena compassionately. 'Please do not worry. You 'ave to keep calm for the sake of the baby. No one will say anything. We all 'ave much to lose.'

A murmur of agreement echoed.

'I want to talk briefly on the subject of the legitimacy of the expected child,' Fran said. 'I believe UK law and, probably, also French law would consider the child illegitimate in relation to Alain and Fayette.' Before the couple had a chance to protest, she raised her hands. 'I know, I don't make the rules. My job is to ensure you're fully aware of the legal situation. This is an issue that could be solved by formal adoption, but therein lies a minefield. As discussed, surrogacy is not acceptable under French law and formal adoption of the child in the UK after having paid a fee for the surrogacy could be interpreted as 'buying an adoption', which is illegal. We've already seen that issue raised in the case of Kim Cotton. Anyway, formally adopting a child born of a surrogate mother won't work for Fayette and Alain.'

'Would it be possible for Alain and Fayette to adopt the baby in the normal way? I mean after Lena gives birth,

it. The Warnock Committee does recognise, in most cases, a surrogacy agreement would be kept, but they say the courts would treat such agreements as contrary to public policy, so in cases where one party breaks the agreement, the court would not assist the other party. However the courts do have jurisdiction over children so in any dispute they would act in the child's best interests in all the circumstances of the case. So, if the carrying mother changed her mind and decided she wanted to keep the child, the Committee say it is most unlikely a court would order her to hand over the child against her will.'

Fran decided to let both couples absorb this explanation before continuing. She didn't feel it necessary to outline some other of the report's conclusions: that, in cases of a dispute, a court would not order the surrogate mother to return any fee paid to her under the terms of the agreement; that the present state of the law makes any surrogacy agreement a risky undertaking for those involved.

After a few moments she added, 'You can, of course, read the report for yourselves—though it's over a hundred pages long so I would focus on chapter eight—because several different views were considered and it might help you to understand why they reached their various conclusions, even if you don't agree with them. But remember, this was published last year and it's still only advice. Can I top anyone up with coffee or hot chocolate? Then we can focus on the current state of affairs.'

'Chocolate for me please, Fran,' responded Lena.

'Coffee please,' said Fayette.

Alain and Jake remained silent until Pierre offered beer, which they gratefully accepted.

Fran poured the hot drinks. 'Okay. As for the current situation—and I emphasise this strongly—surrogacy, commercial or not, is not illegal at present. And neither is arranging a surrogacy contract or participation in a surrogacy procedure. However, the fact that we have all agreed to keep this process confidential plays in our favour. There is no knowing what legal developments might ensue in the coming months.'

'Yes, we've all gotta keep this a secret,' Lena stressed. 'I've had nightmares thinkin' what would happen if the papers got hold of my name.'

Fayette viewed Lena compassionately. 'Please do not worry. You 'ave to keep calm for the sake of the baby. No one will say anything. We all 'ave much to lose.'

A murmur of agreement echoed.

'I want to talk briefly on the subject of the legitimacy of the expected child,' Fran said. 'I believe UK law and, probably, also French law would consider the child illegitimate in relation to Alain and Fayette.' Before the couple had a chance to protest, she raised her hands. 'I know, I don't make the rules. My job is to ensure you're fully aware of the legal situation. This is an issue that could be solved by formal adoption, but therein lies a minefield. As discussed, surrogacy is not acceptable under French law and formal adoption of the child in the UK after having paid a fee for the surrogacy could be interpreted as 'buying an adoption', which is illegal. We've already seen that issue raised in the case of Kim Cotton. Anyway, formally adopting a child born of a surrogate mother won't work for Fayette and Alain.'

'Would it be possible for Alain and Fayette to adopt the baby in the normal way? I mean after Lena gives birth,

it. The Warnock Committee does recognise, in most cases, a surrogacy agreement would be kept, but they say the courts would treat such agreements as contrary to public policy, so in cases where one party breaks the agreement, the court would not assist the other party. However the courts do have jurisdiction over children so in any dispute they would act in the child's best interests in all the circumstances of the case. So, if the carrying mother changed her mind and decided she wanted to keep the child, the Committee say it is most unlikely a court would order her to hand over the child against her will.'

Fran decided to let both couples absorb this explanation before continuing. She didn't feel it necessary to outline some other of the report's conclusions: that, in cases of a dispute, a court would not order the surrogate mother to return any fee paid to her under the terms of the agreement; that the present state of the law makes any surrogacy agreement a risky undertaking for those involved.

After a few moments she added, 'You can, of course, read the report for yourselves—though it's over a hundred pages long so I would focus on chapter eight—because several different views were considered and it might help you to understand why they reached their various conclusions, even if you don't agree with them. But remember, this was published last year and it's still only advice. Can I top anyone up with coffee or hot chocolate? Then we can focus on the current state of affairs.'

'Chocolate for me please, Fran,' responded Lena.

'Coffee please,' said Fayette.

Alain and Jake remained silent until Pierre offered beer, which they gratefully accepted.

Fran poured the hot drinks. 'Okay. As for the current situation—and I emphasise this strongly—surrogacy, commercial or not, is not illegal at present. And neither is arranging a surrogacy contract or participation in a surrogacy procedure. However, the fact that we have all agreed to keep this process confidential plays in our favour. There is no knowing what legal developments might ensue in the coming months.'

'Yes, we've all gotta keep this a secret,' Lena stressed. 'I've had nightmares thinkin' what would happen if the papers got hold of my name.'

Fayette viewed Lena compassionately. 'Please do not worry. You 'ave to keep calm for the sake of the baby. No one will say anything. We all 'ave much to lose.'

A murmur of agreement echoed.

'I want to talk briefly on the subject of the legitimacy of the expected child,' Fran said. 'I believe UK law and, probably, also French law would consider the child illegitimate in relation to Alain and Fayette.' Before the couple had a chance to protest, she raised her hands. 'I know, I don't make the rules. My job is to ensure you're fully aware of the legal situation. This is an issue that could be solved by formal adoption, but therein lies a minefield. As discussed, surrogacy is not acceptable under French law and formal adoption of the child in the UK after having paid a fee for the surrogacy could be interpreted as 'buying an adoption', which is illegal. We've already seen that issue raised in the case of Kim Cotton. Anyway, formally adopting a child born of a surrogate mother won't work for Fayette and Alain.'

'Would it be possible for Alain and Fayette to adopt the baby in the normal way? I mean after Lena gives birth,

she can say she's givin' up the baby for adoption, without mentioning payment or that she's a surrogate mother,' Jake suggested.

'I dunt think it works like that, luvver,' Lena replied. 'You can't just choose who yer baby goes to. There's a system.'

'Lena's right,' Fran confirmed. 'An adoption would have to be processed through an official agency.'

'We're not adopting a baby that is biologically ours anyway,' Alain protested hotly. 'And our child 'as to be French.'

Fran acknowledged Alain with a nod and continued steadily. 'I'm simply ensuring you are all aware of the legal situation. Legally, the child's claim to French nationality will depend on proof of their natural parentage. Practically, since you have all agreed on blood tests to confirm parentage, this is not an issue; the issue lies in the declaration, or not, of the surrogate birth; in other words, the parents identified on the birth certificate. Further than this, I will not be drawn into a discussion and I do not wish to be a party to what you do.'

Fran left the two couples with Pierre while she went into the kitchen to replenish the pots of hot drinks. The situation had become something of a nightmare and there was no clean solution. She decided to make detailed notes of her part in the meeting and keep them on file with her copy of the surrogacy contract, just in case. She didn't want to know about any decision made by her guests. Eventually she opened the kitchen door, returning to the worktop for the two vessels. Quiet tones, she recognised as Fayette's, drifted through the doorway, though the timbre was unusually tenacious.

'…a lot of money, not only for you, Lena, but also for your clinic, Pierre,' Fayette was saying. ''Ow you say? Everyone is winning. We will 'ave our baby, you will 'ave money and no other person will know what we do.'

On her return to the living room, Fran felt relieved they'd chosen to keep the arrangement strictly private, for everyone's sake.

However, Alain suddenly stood and made an announcement. 'We,' he waved an arm in Lena and Jake's direction indicating he was speaking for both couples, 'wish to thank you, Fran and Pierre, for everything you are doing.' Then he looked directly at Fran. 'Especially as we will commit fraud. Only us in this room will know Lena will 'ave the baby at Pierre's clinic in private and we register the child as ours. Only we six know Lena receives a large sum of money for being a surrogate mother and it is also a secret we donated to your clinic, eh, Pierre.' Alain smiled, patting Pierre good-heartedly on the back. But shrewdness, not geniality, was manifest in his eyes.

Annoyance tore at Fran's composure; regardless of client confidentiality, knowledge of an offence which she might have to deny would tar her with the same brush. Alain was aware of this. He'd deliberately made her complicit. Was this an insurance policy? She politely returned his insincere smile. It was too late to extricate herself. Both she and Pierre were involved and their livelihoods might come to depend on what happened over the next few months, albeit in different ways. She concluded secrecy was the best way forward for all concerned.

Chapter Twenty-three

Plymouth, England, February 1985

Fayette sat by Lena's side as she lay on her back in the dimly lit room. Lena gasped as Pierre squeezed ultrasound gel onto her stomach.

'Bit cold,' he chuckled. 'Can you both see the monitor?'

Both women nodded and Pierre slid the probe across Lena's skin. A blurry, undulating, greyscale image appeared. At first Fayette struggled to make sense of it. A yellow box with curved edges materialised on the screen as Pierre chose an area to enlarge. More indistinct moving greyness. Then a clearer picture; a dark sack-like area containing shapes which shifted in and out of focus: a shrimp-like form with a slightly larger roundish mass at one end which looked head-shaped. Was it a head? Fayette could see other light grey areas against the black; spindly, there one moment then gone. Arms and legs? As Pierre continued moving the probe, the image on the screen transformed, other shapes coming in and out of focus. She glanced at Pierre who was wearing an odd expression, as if he were recalling a private anecdote.

Lena had also picked up on something. 'Is everything okay?' she asked nervously.

'Everything is fine,' Pierre grinned. 'In fact it's

marvellous. He brought the shrimp into focus again. 'Can you see? This is the 'ead and 'ere,' he pointed a pen to a tiny pulsing shape, 'the beating 'eart. And there are the arms and legs.'

Lena grasped Fayette's hand, squeezing it. 'Look at that. I'm goin' to be having yer baby!'

Fayette's anxiety, born of past bereavement, dissolved in a flood of relief, leaving her trembling. *Dieu merci* she said to herself. As she continued to gaze at the moving image she felt as if a shaft of sunshine had settled over her. 'That's wonderful,' she beamed, as she squeezed back. She was trying to process the news—what this meant for her and Alain—when the foetus began to diminish and distort. 'Wait, Pierre. Can we 'ave a copy of that image?'

'Yes, of course,' he smiled, 'but I want to show you this first. We just need to go further in… and… there it is. This one is 'arder to see as it's deeper, but there's no doubt. There's the 'eart beating, there's the 'ead and body.' He swivelled on his chair to face them. 'You're carrying twins, Lena.'

Fayette looked at Lena in amazement. And in the next few moments, the room, the screen, Lena and Pierre, all dissolved into a milky mass. Fayette was sitting in the conservatory, amidst her floral cushions, cradling, not one, but two tiny babies, one in each arm. She was gazing at one perfect cherub face then the other and Alain was standing over her, smiling, and she was filled with utter joy.

'Fuck!'

Fayette's reverie vanished with Lena's exclamation.

Lena's hands had flown to her mouth, apprehension displayed in her eyes. She smiled tentatively then spoke quickly. 'Don't get me wrong, Fayette, I'm thrilled fer you. I really am. We knew there was a chance this might happen, didn't we? I'm just a bit… nervous at the thought of carryin' twins.'

Fayette threw her arms around Lena as best she could, avoiding the scanning equipment. *'Naturellement,'* she empathised, 'but you will be cared for at every step. Isn't that right, Pierre? You will take good care of Lena. And I will be right by your side, Lena, you wonderful woman. I'll do everything I can to support you whenever you need it. I cannot thank you enough for this precious gift.'

Pierre nodded and smiled at Lena caringly. 'Absolutely. You 'ave nothing to fear, Lena. You are in very good 'ands. Now if you look at this image you can see there is only one amniotic sac present,' he indicated with his pen, 'and we can't see a membrane between the two foetuses, therefore in all likelihood Lena is carrying identical twins.'

Lena's brows came together in confusion. Fayette was also perplexed. 'But 'ow can implanting two separate embryos lead to identical twins?'

Pierre explained, first in English then in French to be sure Fayette understood, a fertilised egg, or zygote, can split while it is still a tiny collection of cells, as late as eight or nine days after fertilisation, and the later the zygote splits, the more likely it is the resulting embryos share the same placenta. Pierre reminded the women they had transferred two eight-cell blastocysts, or balls of cells, into Lena's uterus, and he went on to clarify that the split of one of these would have occurred sometime after it had implanted in the lining of Lena's womb. Once implanted, a ball of cells was termed an embryo, becoming a foetus at ten weeks, he said. As the ultrasound image indicated the foetuses shared a single gestational sac and placenta it was likely the split had occurred a few days after the transfer and the two self-contained halves had developed into the two foetuses they could now see.

Pierre advised them the pregnancy was developing normally, but from sixteen weeks Lena would have fortnightly scans to monitor for signs of abnormality, in particular twin to twin transfusion syndrome, a disease of the placenta that can affect identical twin pregnancies. He warned Lena to inform him if she experienced any sensation of rapid growth of her womb, sudden increase in body weight, abdominal pain, or uterine contractions, reassuring her she was being cared for by the best experts in the country. If she had questions or worries she was to contact him immediately, day or night.

Lena was bolstered by Pierre's expert diligence and Fayette's support. She trusted that between the two of them and Jake, and with her mother's assistance, she'd manage well. On seeing Fayette's elation, an immense feeling of satisfaction had pervaded; being able to give the gift of life was truly fulfilling.

Later that day Pierre discussed the scan with the clinical director, who agreed, although it was unusual to perform scans so frequently, it would be best to monitor and record the foetal development closely. They'd already drafted the beginnings of a scientific paper.

Pierre's delight at the success thus far, of their cutting-edge surrogacy procedure, was quashed two days later as he watched the evening news. In the House of Commons, the pressure had increased with the second reading of Enoch Powell's private members bill to ban all research on human embryos, contrary to the recommendations of the Warnock Report. As he listened to the report, Pierre experienced a rush of anger and dread, setting his heart thumping. The draft bill, requiring notification of every attempt to implant a human embryo, had passed with a significant majority and would proceed to the Committee stage for detailed examination. This would severely restrict IVF practice in the UK.

Pierre envisaged his colleagues' consternation and the similar reactions of many others in the scientific community. What was to be done?

Plymouth, England, Spring 1985

In early March it was reported that Norman Fowler intended to bring a bill banning commercial surrogacy before Parliament later that month with the intention of rushing legislation through with all-party backing before the summer. This would make it an offence, punishable by imprisonment or heavy fines, for commercial surrogate agencies to operate or advertise in Britain. Several Tory backbenchers called for a blanket ban on surrogacy.

Pierre and Fran existed in a constant state of alarm. Each knew their attempts at reassuring the Lesters and Dubois were futile. Everyone was thinking the same—this law could make their actions illegal; the words 'fines' and 'prison' were cited in the press.

Fowler's Surrogacy Arrangements Bill was subsequently backed on all sides of the House and passed with ease in both the House of Commons and the House of Lords with a view to its implementation before the summer parliamentary recess. Having followed the parliamentary discussions, Fran could at least confirm the Bill would not act retrospectively, however the Government had issued guidance to Local Authorities on how to act when discovering a baby had been, or was about to be, born as a result of surrogacy, whether or not money was involved, the general recommendation being to make the child a ward of court where he or she is considered to be at risk. Councils were therefore put on alert for new surrogate births.

Regardless of whether their surrogacy arrangements would be tainted with criminality, or the child deemed at risk, public knowledge of their agreement would presage disaster for them all.

Meanwhile the debate on IVF and embryological practices continued. Norman Fowler tried to reassure MPs and the public the government intended to submit a bill that autumn for the regulation of embryonic research, addressing issues arising from the Warnock Report. Frustrated by the government's inactivity, the Medical Research Council and Royal College of Obstetricians and Gynaecologists established a Voluntary Licensing Authority, VLA, announcing their plan to approve a code of practice and inviting all those engaged in IVF research to submit their work for approval and licensing. They planned to visit all the country's IVF clinics and research centres as part of this process. Pierre and his colleagues received this news with mixed feelings but welcomed it on the whole, because they believed it might allay some of the concerns of government ministers and therefore be helpful in countering Powell's significantly more conservative bill. At least they trusted the MRC and RCOG to act with scientific integrity.

Once again, and with intensifying reason, Alain and Fayette made clear to Pierre—and therefore Fran, indirectly—their expectations regarding the clinic's role in concealing the birth and transfer of their babies. Lena and Jake were of the same mind, already making plans to join her mother in Cornwall immediately afterwards. Lena declared she'd have the babies at home in private if the clinic refused to keep their birth a secret, warning Pierre, unnecessarily, he'd be risking the lives of her and the babies if she was forced to have a home birth. Pierre became increasingly concerned, caught between clients and his duty to the clinic to act with integrity. The blatant omission of his own making—the fact he hadn't discussed the Dubois' intentions regarding the birth registration of their babies with his CEO—began to eat away at him, fuelled by Fran's increasing insistence on a candid discussion with Giles Blenkinsop. He decided to ask Giles for a one-to-one meeting. But the next day he was summoned by the CEO for a discussion involving the clinical director.

Pierre and Gareth Townsend were sitting facing one another across the board room table, talking despondently about the political situation, when Blenkinsop entered, a sheaf of papers under one arm. Hastily he pulled out his chair and sat between them, spreading the documents before him. He nodded to each of them in turn. 'Gentlemen.' Pierre recognised his brisk, practical tone. He was plainly focussed on critical decision-making and in no mood for further complications. Pierre became aware of breathing more deeply than was entirely comfortable.

'As you know, we will need to submit information to the newly established VLA,' Giles began. 'The clinic faces yet another dilemma; the VLA requires a written application from us describing the particulars of treatment or research, not only that we wish to undertake but also that we are already providing. The question is how we should describe that we've successfully implanted a donor embryo into the uterus of a healthy surrogate as part of the assisted conception process for a patient? I would value your opinions.'

Pierre glanced at Gareth, giving him the opportunity of answering first. The man drew breath but hesitated. So Pierre spoke.

'I'm assuming we don't want to draw attention to the clinic's involvement with a surrogate at this point, even though it is currently perfectly legal,' he ventured. ''Owever, once a live birth is achieved, we plan to publish our results. We need the kudos and the favourable conditions for obtaining more funding, so we can't really omit this procedure from our report to the VLA'. He was acutely aware he hadn't offered a solution.

'I'm sure Giles isn't suggesting we omit to report this,' Gareth stated, eyeing the CEO. Pierre detected a hint of superiority in his tone. 'I'm sure I speak for all of us,' he continued, 'when I say being economical with the truth where it concerns our clinical reputation doesn't sit well.'

'No indeed,' Giles replied, nettled. 'I was not, for a moment, suggesting we exclude any procedure from the VLA report. I'm asking for your input on how we go about this whilst minimising the risk to the clinic. I'm sure you both appreciate the delicacy of the political situation.'

Gareth shrugged, turning his palms upwards. His tone had not altered. 'We simply describe the medical procedure in scientific terms. We're breaking the boundaries of what is technically possible here, for goodness sake. That far outweighs any concern regarding the involvement of a surrogate, in my opinion.'

Pierre sensed a growing impatience from his CEO and cut in. 'We 'ave to protect the participants in this procedure as well as the clinic. I assume we don't 'ave to disclose patients names?'

'We can rely on physician-patient privilege to ensure discretion,' Giles assured. 'Though obviously the couples will eventually be dealing with the authorities through the formal notification of adoption of the babies by the Dubois. But the clinic isn't involved in that. Nor, as you're both aware, are we mentioned by name in the surrogacy agreement.'

Pierre thought for a moment. 'Do you think the VLA will be acting independently? I mean, do they 'ave to share their data with anyone?'

Regarding the documents before him, Giles shook his head. 'That's not clear at this stage. I doubt they would specifically impart information on a surrogacy procedure but judging by the climate I'd say the VLA will want to be as transparent as possible.'

'As they should be,' Gareth voiced robustly. 'We are scientists, not politicians. We have a duty to act in an ethical manner and within the law, which we are doing. We're involved in this surrogacy purely on medical grounds and for the advancement of scientific research. We have nothing to hide. We should be concentrating our efforts on supporting the campaign against Powell's bill.'

Pierre nodded. 'I agree with you, Gareth. But you know 'ow information in the public domain can get twisted. We just 'ave to 'ope the activities of the VLA and the local Council will be entirely separate.'

'We're legally protected by the technical/ethical agreement, Pierre.'

'That's true,' Pierre replied hotly. 'But if information is misconstrued and we come under investigation then the arrangement is exposed, it could be difficult to separate the Dubois' IVF payment to the clinic from the surrogacy.'

The CEO gathered his papers. 'Thank you both for your opinions. Our report to the VLA on this procedure will be succinct and benefit focussed. I will also remind them the clinic is not a surrogacy agency and our excellent clinical reputation and the critical services we provide to patients should be born in mind when data-sharing, given the public's proclivity for sensationalism. I will share the draft with you for comment and any guidance that might come from the VLA in due course.' Giles viewed his clinical director. 'And, yes, we are stepping up our campaign activities. We can only hope ministers and the public, like the majority of the medical and scientific community, come to appreciate the immense health benefits of embryo research and IVF. Presently, it seems the clinic's entire *raison d'être* is teetering on the edge of Enoch Powell's axe.'

Chapter Twenty-four

Plymouth, England, May 1985

Mari had announced to Gerren she wanted a trial separation. Things had been difficult between them since Christmas and she'd been contemplating her feelings. When she'd walked out the morning after Boxing Day she'd driven for an hour or so considering what to do. She knew it wouldn't be long before Gerren went to the pub to meet his friends, so having made sure he'd departed the house she'd popped back, packed a small rucksack and taken herself off for a few days. It had been hard to find anywhere to stay, it being the season of jollity and relaxation, but she'd driven into the depths of Cornwall, eventually locating an isolated farmhouse bed and breakfast with one cosy room available in a small, converted barn. The location was perfect; she was the only guest and the family were friendly but kept a discreet distance. She could have contacted Xavier but chose to remain alone to try to think things through. She had spent her time walking the rugged coastline, curling up in front of the log burner with a book, enjoying the local cheeses with some good claret and listening to music on her Walkman. On New Year's Eve, guessing she might need cossetting, the farmer's wife, Morwen, had brought her a delicious hot meal of roast beef cooked perfectly, just pink in the middle, with roast potatoes, cauliflower cheese and home-grown parsnips, followed by a tasty apple pie. Morwen had invited her to visit the local pub with the family to see in the New Year, but Mari had gracefully declined; she didn't feel like celebrating and was enjoying her solitude.

Naturally Gerren had tried to persuade her to return, when she finally rang him to let him know she'd be away a few nights. Mari hadn't told him exactly where she was. If he'd known, he would have jumped into his car, driven down and insisted she accompany him home, the inference being it was all a tempest in a wine glass.

She had needed time to think. After some days she'd concluded she and Gerren should try to make things work, for the sake of all they meant to one another. She'd returned home and he'd made a big fuss of her, telling her how much he loved her and if she loved him too it was all that mattered.

A part of Mari still naively hoped she would be able to bring Gerren around to trying for a baby again. But as the weeks went by it became clear he didn't understand the depth of her feelings and wasn't willing to. He'd made more than one reference to the political situation: in a few months' time, he'd commented, the potential for using a donor egg might be withdrawn anyway. To her, this situation conferred intensifying urgency; to Gerren it was another deterrent in his defensive armoury.

Increasingly her feelings towards Gerren were shifting to resentment. She'd met with Xavier a couple of times during that period—with him it was always so loving and easy. Her love for him deepened while that for her husband waned. Without saying as much, Xavier had made it clear he would be willing to try for a child with her using a donor egg as long as the process remained lawful in the UK.

Eventually, and with difficulty, she told Gerren she was going to move out for a while. She needed some temporary space. Gerren was distressed and angry. He couldn't understand why he wasn't enough for her; why she had this obsession with having a child; why she couldn't accept they could make a perfectly happy life without children like other childless couples. She'd been unable to fully explain the intensity of her feelings, the craving, the desperation. But the fact he didn't understand her attested to a deficiency in their relationship. She knew she either had to get it out of her system or do something about it and in the meantime, it was pointless continuing to allow their marriage to deteriorate. That, at least, Gerren understood. So Mari moved out, temporarily renting a smart one-bed furnished flat in a large Victorian house in the Mannamead area.

In addition to Xavier feeling uncharitably over the moon at her departure from the marital home, however temporary, Alain was also pleased at this development. Xavier had spoken of Mari with him and Fayette, although he hadn't told their mother. To begin with, Alain hadn't been enthusiastic about their relationship, saying he didn't trust a woman with a foot in both camps. Part of his attitude was born of protectiveness towards his brother. He hated the thought of Xavier being taken advantage of. Fayette, on the other hand, had been more laissez-faire. Thousands of people have affairs, she had pointed out. Still, she'd warned Xavier against getting hurt. But, as Mari began her separation, Alain and Fayette were both hopeful this would be the beginning of a proper commitment to Xavier, as it was clear he adored her.

Mari began to have discussions with Pierre about the possibility of receiving a donor egg and what other treatment she might need if she were to try to conceive and carry a child. She confided that Xavier had expressed his willingness to assist, and she was contemplating it, but asked that Pierre keep this strictly confidential for the time being. Pierre told her he would do everything possible to help her but warned the IVF treatment of an ostensibly single woman was unlikely to be viewed favourably by the clinic, particularly in the current climate. He advised that IVF, already controversial, might not be approved outside marriage. While the newly established VLA was a non-statutory organisation, he explained, the clinic was now almost certainly bound to abide by the voluntary regulatory framework and gaining consent for a process could depend in part on the authority's idea of a suitable family. Pierre emphasised while he didn't agree with this sentiment, particularly in her and Xavier's case, the decision would be out of his hands. He said he'd already put the clinic in a delicate situation, as it had turned out, with the surrogacy case and he was unlikely to be allowed the same latitude in the near future. He recommended she decide about her future before trying to embark on IVF treatment. They both knew if she chose to divorce Gerren and marry Xavier this would take time and the final reading of Powell's bill was looming.

It seemed to Mari she would be thwarted whichever path she chose. She also felt guilty for trying to take such an analytical approach. The two men in her life were not numbered choices, to be dispassionately weighed and analysed, evaluated and scrutinised; they were human beings with sensitivities that could so easily be hurt. She listened honestly to her heart and finally understood it was telling her she no longer loved Gerren. Her feelings towards him stretched only to companionship but even that was strung with resentment, like fibres in celery, making her marriage unpalatable. Regardless of her yearning for a child, she realised her future lay with Xavier if she was to be happy.

Chapter Twenty-five

Plymouth, England, June 1985

On the 7th of June Commons MPs presented thirteen petitions containing four thousand and sixty-five signatures against the Unborn Children (Protection) Bill.

Having listened to the radio bulletin that evening, Mari telephoned Fran. She didn't trust herself to believe it. Fran explained, in addition to the intense lobbying, a certain amount of filibustering caused Powell's bill to run out of time, resulting in its defeat.

A frisson of excitement raised the hairs on Mari's arms. 'Bloody hell, Fran, this is incredible news. I'm so relieved, like a vast number of people I should imagine.'

'I know, it feels like a staggering reprieve.'

'How's Pierre? Have you talked with him? He must be delighted.'

Mari heard her friend's smile in her tone. 'I've just come from the clinic. You should see the elated expression on Pierre's face. They're all going about their business demonstrably flooded with relief and appreciation of the near miss.'

Mari was thrilled. Suddenly, her clouds of indecision were rent by a single potent desire as clear as sunlight. She had to tell Xavier face to face. They had a rendezvous arranged in London and Mari began to count the hours.

London, England, June 1985

They were to meet in their usual room in their customary hotel. They had long given up the pretence of booking separate rooms. Although the forward planning was sometimes tricky, it was comforting being able to envisage the surroundings of their liaisons and the space had come to feel like theirs, a private haven in a rough sea.

Mari arrived first. The turquoise and gold embroidered brocade curtains were half drawn against the late afternoon sun. She threw them back allowing sunlight to bathe the room with warmth. Setting her shoulder bag on one of the oak cabinets positioned next to the four-poster bed, she took out a bottle of Bordeaux, which she placed with two wine glasses on a table, cradled by two comfy chairs, in the window alcove. She sat with the sun on her back, staring into the room but not seeing, rehearsing what she would say to her lover.

It wasn't long before Xavier arrived, bearing a fragrant posy of colourful dainty freesias, her favourite flower. He threw his bag on the floor and came to her, beaming, arms open. '*Ma précieuse,*' he whispered into her ear, as she dissolved into his embrace.

Some moments later, as they disentwined, Mari took the flowers. She filled a tumbler with water and set them on the table next to the glasses. Xavier was chatting about his journey and asking about hers as he poured the wine, but she couldn't concentrate on what he was saying. Waves of adrenalin coursed through her body, causing her forehead to prickle and leaving her heart pounding. *Don't be silly*, she chided herself, *this is Xavier. You can say anything to him. He loves you.*

'Are you okay, Mari?' he was saying, prompting her to rejoin the moment. She refocussed her eyes and rearranged her fixed smile into an apologetic one. 'I'm sorry.' She shook her head. 'I was away in my head. I have something to say and I was thinking about it.'

Xavier's obvious concern at her words etched lines between his brows and his mouth fell open slightly. Hastily, Mari laid a hand on his arm. 'Nothing to worry about; it's all good,' she reassured. 'Let's taste this wine, shall we?' They sat beside the table facing one another, knees touching. She raised her glass and took a sip. 'To us.'

Xavier did the same, though still looking a little apprehensive. '*À nous.*'

When he had replaced his glass on the table Mari leaned forward, took his hands in hers and inhaled deeply. 'I love you, Xavier…' He made to speak but she cut him off. 'Please. Let me say this.' She took another deep breath. 'I love you and I want to live all my days with you; to grow old with you. I want to have a child with you; to grow your baby inside me. You have become my life, Xavier, and I never want to be parted from you.'

Xavier stared down at her hands for a moment and Mari realised he was squeezing them so tightly it almost hurt. Then he looked up and it was as if he could see into her soul.

'I will love you forever, *ma petite Souci!*' he declared, tenderness exquisite in his glistening eyes. 'I will always care for you. I'll give you anything you want within my power to give. I will give you a child if it is possible. You mean more to me than anything else in this world.'

They made love like wildfire. In the afterglow a peace pervaded her, suffusing body and mind. Mari's path lay with Xavier's and from this moment they would journey through life as one. As for the practicalities and difficulties, well, they would solve those together in the coming months.

Chapter Twenty-six

Plymouth, England, June 1985

Lena was beginning to experience heartburn and her back ached if she stayed on her feet for long periods. She'd had morning sickness with this pregnancy, which was hardly surprising with twins, but it had only lasted to the end of the first trimester. Heartburn, Pierre told her, was unfortunately common, the burning sensation in her upper chest triggered by increasing hormone levels and her expanding uterus. He advised her to keep to a healthy diet and drink plenty of fluids. Unfortunately, fluid was something she had a surfeit of, though mainly in her ankles. She'd now have to avoid curries, a fancy of hers, and had also been advised to cut out caffeine; how she would get by without her usual three cups of strong coffee in the morning she didn't know. Having halted her caffeine intake she was having headaches. Pierre advised plenty of rest, healthy snacks between meals and not skipping meals—to prevent her blood sugar dropping—but also that she continue to watch her weight gain. Eat little and often, he said, and keep hydrated. He warned her to let him know immediately if the swelling in her lower legs became excessive or increased suddenly.

She and Jake had unquestionably begun to feel the

stress of the surrogacy, particularly since her pregnancy had started to show, and Lena was sure this anxiety was contributing to her headaches. In her mind she fended off congratulatory comments and good wishes from friends and neighbours, while maintaining a cheerful exterior composure. She hated lying to friends but had no choice. Jake had tried to keep his wife's pregnancy a secret at work but somehow word had got around that Lena was expecting, resulting in slaps on the back and quips about his virility, as if he were the only expectant father in Plymouth. He increased the intensity of his search for an appropriate business opportunity in Cornwall. They wanted to be ready to move when the time came, to leave the inquisition behind and throw themselves into a brand-new life. If circumstances allowed, they hoped to relocate before the babies were born, staying at Lena's mother's house in the interim, enabling them to arrive in their new location as a one-child family. It would be tough leaving their friends but, since they couldn't tell the truth, they felt it would be easier to lie about the disappearance of their baby—no one else knew she was carrying twins—after distance and time had disjointed their friendships. They still had to decide what to say to George.

Lena and Jake had decided George should attend a nearby playgroup twice a week in the afternoon to allow Lena time to rest. After all, they could afford it now. As Lena's energy waned, her son's vigour increased. He was always bright and enthusiastic, with a keen interest in everything. Unusually for a two-year-old he rarely had temper tantrums except, for some inexplicable reason, when made to try on shoes. Lena would become more exasperated and embarrassed by the second as he lay on the floor of the shoe shop screaming and drumming his fists. However, once the purchase was completed and he was home he would forget all about the episode and, when Jake arrived back from work, George would run to him, holding out the new footwear, shouting 'Daddy, look, shoes. Shoes!'

It was one such day and Lena was dreading taking George for a much-needed new pair—he seemed to be growing so quickly. So she'd asked Fayette if she would go with them. Fayette had been visiting them; fortnightly at first then more frequently. Recently, she'd been helping around the house, despite Lena's protestations, but since Lena usually had her hands full looking after George and she didn't seem to have the energy to say no, she'd relented. In truth, she was thankful, not only for the practical assistance but because she was sharing the weight of responsibility for the little humans inside her. She and Fayette's singular bond was a natural precursor to a genuine friendship and their alliance was growing into just that, despite Lena's reticence. Several times Fayette had offered to look after George while Lena put her feet up, but Lena was wary of him becoming attached to the nice blonde lady who helped his mummy with the washing. Today, though, she hoped Fayette's presence might encourage George to behave himself in the shoe shop.

Fayette arrived bearing a large, lidded dish. ''Ello, Lena. I made cassoulet. Just re'eat it in the oven for an 'our or so at a medium temperature.' She smiled. 'Nothing to add, except maybe water.' She found a small space on the crowded kitchen worktop and set it down, then turned to kiss Lena on both cheeks.

Lena lifted the lid and inhaled. 'Mmm, smells delicious. Is that chicken?'

Fayette shook her head. 'Duck. I managed to find some. Cassoulet is a dish of south-west France. It is—'ow you say—a meal for farmers. This is the recipe of Alain's *maman*.'

'Wow. Thank ee so much. Yer so kind, Fayette.'

Fayette shrugged. 'I can do so little.'

Lena touched her arm. 'You've done so much. Look at my house fer a start; it hasn't been s' clean since before George was born,' she laughed.

'And where is the little man? Is 'e excited to 'ave new shoes?'

Lena raised her eyebrows. 'Er… I wouldn't say that exactly. T' be honest, I haven't told him where we're goin'. Y' know, not to make too much o' it. He's in his playpen in the livin' room, 'cause he's all ready to go an' I didn't want him gettin' dirty.'

Fayette hurried out of the kitchen and Lena followed, gathering their raincoats.

'*Coucou mon petit bonhomme*,' Fayette cooed, lifting George and swinging him in her arms, to his delight. 'Look, I brought you something.' Popping him on the floor, she reached into her shoulder bag and pulled out a small, grey and white, cuddly rabbit with big ears. '*Lapin*.'

'Lapa,' repeated George, grinning as he grabbed the toy with both hands, 'Lapa.'

'What do ee say, George?' prompted Lena, trying to keep the uneasy dichotomy of pleasure and disapproval from showing on her face.

'Ta,' said George, looking up briefly before putting the rabbit to his face.

'Fayette, ee shouldn't have, but thank ee all the same. Yer very generous.'

Fayette returned Lena's gentle smile. '"Is first French word.'

Lena looked at her watch. 'We'd better get goin'. The bus will be here in six minutes.' She bent awkwardly to thread George's arms into his waterproof jacket. 'No, put him down for a minute. You can have Lapan when you've got yer coat on.'

'I'll drive,' stated Fayette. 'No need for a bus. Let me take that.' She collected the pushchair that had been folded into the corner of the room.

'Oh, thanks, Fayette. That would be helpful. We got one o' those new booster seats but it's in Jake's car at work, 'cause I usually take the bus. No matter, I can sit in the back with him.'

As they drove into the city centre, they chatted about the next ultrasound appointment; Fayette accompanied Lena to every scan. The foetuses were developing normally and were of equal size; there'd been no sign of twin-to-twin transfusion syndrome. The two women had been thrilled to see their perfect tiny fingers and toes for the first time and their husbands had been equally uplifted by the images. By the end of April the clinic had been able to determine the twins were female. Recently the babies had gained weight and, to everyone's delight, the last scan had shown recognisable faces. Fayette asked Lena how she was feeling and she told Fayette about her backache and fat feet, though omitted to mention the constipation and the light pink streaks beginning to appear on her belly. 'Generally, I'm fine,' she said. 'As long as I can put my feet up every now an' then.'

'I can 'elp you with that. I'm 'appy to take care of George as often as you want,' Fayette stressed. She glanced at Lena in the mirror. 'Alain is at 'ome in Cahors at the moment. 'E is making a *chambre d'enfant* for the girls,' she said excitedly. 'You know what? 'E asked me what colour to paint it. I said it 'as to be pink; a pretty pink, not dark. With flowers,' she laughed. 'Alain said 'e can't paint flowers, but I will put them.'

'Hu hu hummm, pretty in pink…' Lena chanted. And Fayette chuckled and joined in.

In the shop, Fayette kept George occupied with his new rabbit while an assistant measured his feet and Lena searched for appropriate shoes. She returned with three pairs. He allowed her to slip on the first but began wriggling as she squeezed their ends. She decided there wasn't enough room for growth, so removed them and reached for the next pair, placing them sole to sole against those she'd taken off. They were the same shape. George began to screw up his face, heralding a wail. Fayette intervened, grabbing the last pair.

'Ooo, George, look what I 'ave for you. What a lovely bright colour red. You'll be so 'andsome wearing these. Will we put them on?'

Fayette blew out her cheeks and laughed at George's chortles as Lena slipped on the shoes and fastened the buckles. They fitted perfectly. The women exchanged knowing glances. As they stood, Lena gave Fayette a grateful hug.

Once home, Lena made a pot of tea while George ran happily from kitchen to living room in continual loops, modelling his new footwear. She and Fayette sat at the kitchen table while she peeled and chopped a banana into a bowl for George, pinching pieces for herself. The next time he ran a circle around the table she caught hold of him, lifting him onto her knees—she didn't have much of a lap these days. 'You'll wear them shoes out with all that runnin',' she chuckled. 'Yer wearin' me out just watchin' you. Let's have a cuddle and a banana shall we?' As George reached for the bowl, she pinched another piece, feigning a surprised face.

George giggled, popping a chunk into his mouth. 'Dat's for meee!'

Fayette was smiling affectionately at them. 'Alain and I 'ave decided to name the girls Suzette Adele and Sophia Fae,' she announced.

Lena's stomach lurched and she dropped the teaspoon she'd picked up to stir her tea with. It clattered onto the floor. One hand went to her belly as she felt multiple kicks. 'Oo.'

'What's wrong?' Fayette's tone was concerned.

Lena shifted George sideways momentarily. 'Quick, feel this.' She grabbed Fayette's hand and placed it to her. 'I startled them I expect. They're not moving as much now, less room I suppose. But they certainly did then. Did you feel them?'

Fayette glowed with happiness. She nodded, unable to speak.

When George had finished his snack, they moved to the living room so Lena could rest on the sofa for a bit. After a while, Fayette looked up from her position on the floor, with George, among the colourful wooden building blocks. 'George will 'ave sisters, in a way, won't 'e?' she beamed, reaching for Lena's hand and squeezing it. She refocussed on the toddler. 'That will be *très bien, mon petit.*'

She spoke again to Lena. 'As soon as Pierre says the babies can travel, we'll take them 'ome. I'll miss you. You will 'ave to visit us. George would love it. We don't 'ave the sea but there are some little lakes, with beaches, where children can swim safely. And of course we 'ave lots of sunshine.'

Lena felt a rise of panic and swallowed hard. 'Oh, I'm not really... I mean...' She searched for the words, but they wouldn't come. 'I'll miss you too,' she returned, realising she really meant it.

Later, while George was having an afternoon nap, Lena reflected on Fayette's words. She hadn't wanted to become too friendly with Fayette, suspecting she'd find it impossible to remain friends after giving up the babies. She'd come to understand she would need to cut off from the little ones completely for the sake of her sanity and found that a dreadful thought. But somehow her heart had absorbed Fayette's warmth and kindness and their alliance had become established before she became conscious of it.

Each time the babies had moved, particularly when Lena lay down, she had talked to them, caressing her belly, reassuring them. She spoke to them of their mother and father and told them she was looking after them until they were born. She often became tearful afterwards. She was desperately trying not to form a bond with the fast-evolving human beings inside her, but it was hopeless. Fayette always referred to them as 'the girls' but, on the occasions Lena had seen Alain, he'd asked "Ow are my babies?' His babies—the expression had begun to grate, although he had a perfect right. Once, out shopping, she had nearly bought a soft toy dog with floppy ears and found herself wondering which other baby comforter to purchase, before checking herself and walking out, her eyes brimming.

She would need to talk with Jake again and harden herself against what was to come. They needed to throw themselves into hunting for accommodation and preparations for leaving: the sooner the better.

Chapter Twenty-seven

Jake located an empty business premises for rent in Mevagissey, only thirty miles from Lena's mum in Polperro, or twenty if they used the four-car ferry from Fowey to Bodinnick. They figured initially renting premises and a cottage would be easier than trying to buy. They also spent as much time as possible interacting with George, who had commented more than once on 'Mummy's big tummy.' They'd decided to laugh it off and tell him nothing. 'Mummy's eaten too many pasties,' Jake would say; Lena now only wore large, Indian-print floaty dresses of the type that could hide a multitude of sins. They hoped George hadn't registered Fayette's words about sisters and Lena would warn her not to mention this again.

George was clearly enjoying playgroup. He already knew other toddlers in the local area, having been to play at their homes and they at his, but he was obviously having fun playing in a different environment and with new toys. Not yet having a brother or sister, having to share was something he could only further develop in the company of other children; it was taking time, but he was progressing.

George loved the sea and delighted in exploring the contents of rock pools with his parents. He'd imitate Lena and Jake as they peered into these wondrous miniature worlds and they'd show him limpets, mussels and whelks. He'd screamed with excitement the first time he'd seen a hermit crab unexpectedly popping out from its borrowed shell. If they spotted a small green shore crab or a tiny goby rapidly darting from the protection of one clump of seaweed or rock to another that was all the better. He loved catching brown shrimps with his fishing net, tipping them into his red castellated bucket and watching them swim until Jake or Lena decided they needed to be returned to their natural habitat. Once home from such excursions he would interpret what he'd witnessed as multi-coloured scribbles; lines, dots and circles, not quite a picture yet—Lena and Jake had that pleasure to come.

Jake played with George in the garden most days after work. George was learning how to kick a football, the resulting trajectory always indiscriminate, to the annoyance of Sammy who, more than once, had been curled fast asleep under the silver birch in the front corner only to be rudely awakened by a large blow-up plastic orb bouncing around his head. Whereupon he leapt up, disconcerted, and moved onto the roof of his owner's shed to lick himself and pretend indifference. When the ball wasn't in play Sammy sometimes allowed George to stroke him as long as there was no tail pulling. Lena and Jake were teaching their son to be gentle with animals, hoping one day to have a cat of their own—after they'd moved. Everything began to be 'after we've moved'. The phrase really meant 'after the twins have been born and given away,' but they couldn't say that aloud.

Friday the 28th of June dawned bright and warm and

innocent, discrete marshmallow clouds floating happily in a milky, wispy froth, slowly dispersing with the potency of the burgeoning sun.

Jake was saying goodbye to George, who was sitting in his highchair at the breakfast table eating eggy-bread soldiers.

'Bye-bye, my little man, be good for Mummy today.' He looked across the kitchen at Lena; 'I'll try and get away early this afternoon so we can go to the beach. It's goin' to be warm well into the early evenin'.'

'I hoped you might say that,' she replied, giving him a big smile. 'I plan to make toad in the hole fer a picnic tea.'

Jake grinned back at her. 'Excellent idea,' he said. He loved her way of making the sausages in batter with lots of tomato; it was delicious cold in slices.

'Beach!' exclaimed George through a mouthful of eggy bread.

'Yeah, beach!' answered Jake. 'I've gotta go to work now but we'll go to the beach later, okay?'

'Work now,' responded George, concentrating on playing with a bread soldier in his bowl.

Jake manoeuvred around the kitchen table to give his wife a kiss. 'Okay, gotta go, see you later. George, big kiss for Daddy?' The toddler looked up at him and threw open his arms. In each chubby hand he was clutching an eggy soldier. Jake gave his son a big kiss on his forehead, the cleanest bit of bare skin he could see. 'Love you both!' he shouted across the kitchen before closing the back door.

It was late morning. The toad in the hole was cooking and Lena had placed a kettle on the gas hob when the phone rang. It was Mari.

'Hi, Lena, how are you? I was wondering if you need anything? I've got shopping to do at lunchtime and could get things for you if you like. I could pop round with it later or sometime over the weekend.'

Before Lena could reply, the doorbell sounded. 'Hold on a minute, Mari,' she shouted towards the receiver, 'there's someone at the door. I think it might be my new catalogue. Don't go away.'

She left the phone off the hook while she walked along the hallway to the front door. It was her catalogue. As she signed for it, she could hear the kettle boiling; she'd forgotten to put the whistle on, so it was beginning to create a sauna in the kitchen. Simultaneously she caught the comforting aroma of sausages and realised the bake was due out of the oven. George had come to sit on the front step with his mid-morning snack of banana and apple pieces in his plastic bowl. As the delivery man retreated down the path to the front gate, Lena rushed back to the phone, calling to George, 'Stay there darlin', won't you.'

'Still there, Mari? Don't ee go away, I'll be back in a tick. Just have to take summat out of the oven.'

Lena glanced down the hallway—George was happily munching his fruit in the sunshine—before hastening back to the stove to remove the kettle and close the gas. Then she turned the oven off, grabbed a pair of oven gloves and bent to open the door, stepping back slightly to avoid the emerging whoosh of steam. 'Just comin', Mari,' she hollered towards the phone, as she took hold of the baking tray.

'Sammeee!' George's voice seemed to float through the air like the call of a distant gull. A shudder of apprehension moved through Lena's body and she turned to call her son.

Then she heard the appalling squeal of tyres. The sickening thud as vulnerable flesh and bone met rigid metal machine was something Lena would never forget as long as she lived. Time slowed and the world around her melted into a fearful haze; she was running to the front door and out into the garden with leaden legs, terror clawing at her throat, horror distorting her vision.

Front gate swinging carelessly; delivery man gone; no Sammy; no George.

She screamed for her beloved son.

Chapter Twenty-eight

The moment Mari heard Lena scream George's name she slammed down the receiver. Seizing her bag and grabbing her keys from her office drawer, she ran down three flights of stairs and out into the street to her car.

The journey through lunchtime traffic was nightmarish. She zipped behind other vehicles, slammed the brake, swerved aound corners, waited at excruciatingly slow traffic lights, sped up, slowed, and all the while her heart thumped and her throat filled with panic. Her mind conjured horrendous images and it was all she could do to keep her focus on the road as she swung the steering wheel this way and that through damp hands.

Finally she pulled up outside Lena's house and jumped out of the car. The gate was open and the front door ajar. Mari glanced around her but there was no sign of Lena or George, only a woman with grey hair who hurried across the road as soon as she saw Mari's car pull up.

'You a friend of Lena's?' the woman said frenetically. She was shaking and had to lean on the gate post.

Mari was desperate to get to the house. 'Sorry, I have to…' she replied distractedly.

'Are you Lena's friend?' the woman shouted. 'There's been an accident. I… I saw the whole dreadful thing. I called an ambulance.' She put her hand to her face, shaking her head. 'That little lad,' she spoke through her fingers, quietly now. 'He was so... limp. I pray he...' She couldn't finish but stood, staring through Mari, wringing her hands.

Mari's anxiety overcame her, leaving her trembling. She couldn't get her words out quickly enough. She gripped the woman's arm. 'What happened? Tell me! What did you see?'

Startled and overwrought, the woman took a step backwards and Mari had to let go of her. Then she took a deep, steadying breath. 'I answered the door to the postman then spied some roses that needed deadheading. I fetched my scissors and went back outside. The postman was coming out of Lena's gate. But he can't have shut it properly; the next thing I saw was George running towards Mrs Button's tabby sitting in the road.' There was a growing tremor in the woman's voice and her top lip quivered. 'He had his arms outstretched and he was shouting the cat's name. Maybe he was trying to chase it off the road or perhaps he's oblivious to traffic, I don't know.' She faltered.

Drowning in dread, Mari touched the woman lightly on the arm. 'Go on, please.'

The woman shook her head as her tears came. 'It happened so fast. I didn't even notice the car until it was there. She braked hard but it was too late. It was that car.' She pointed to a blue Ford located a short way off, half on the pavement at an awkward angle. 'We all rushed to George. He was just... lying there, with his eyes closed.' The woman looked into the road, recalling the terrible image. 'Lena was screaming. I ran back inside to call an ambulance. They came very quickly. Then the police arrived. They talked to the driver and to me. They took her away with them. I've got to go to the station later to make a statement.' She inclined her head towards Lena's front door. 'I pulled the door to but didn't want to shut it in case Lena didn't have her keys. I've been keeping an eye out.'

'Jesus!' Mari was fighting to stay upright. She half knelt, half fell onto the kerb where she stayed for some moments, face in her hands. *Oh God*. She took several deep breaths and clenched her fists. *Hold it together. Christ, Jake needs to know.*

The woman was offering her a cup of tea. Mari shook her head. 'No, thank you. I must… inside… phone Jake.'

'You've had a shock dear; we both have. A hot cup of something sweet will help. I'll make tea while you do what you need to.'

Dazed, Mari nodded gratefully and hauled herself to her feet. Turning towards the house she met with a tragic moment frozen in time—ants were feeding on pieces of apple spilled from a little upturned plastic bowl by the front door; in the hallway the telephone receiver was hanging lifeless on its spiral; a traybake was strewn across the kitchen floor.

She replaced the receiver and dialled Jake's number at work. There was no answer, so she left an urgent message with the switchboard operator for him to go to the hospital. She hoped he was already there or on his way. Hurriedly, she scooped up the batter and sausages, wiped the floor roughly with a tea-towel, ensured the oven was off and headed out, closing the door firmly. Jake would have keys even if Lena didn't. The grey lady was waiting for her at the gate with a steaming mug. She didn't want to stop but was thankful for a few sips of the hot sweet liquid and the woman's kindness. Then she jumped into the car and rushed to the hospital.

Plymouth, England, July 1985

Mari was devastated to learn George had been pronounced dead on arrival at the hospital. Lena was sedated and transferred to a private room at the clinic, where she was kept for three days under intense observation. Jake stayed by her bedside the whole time, taking turns with Lena's mum to rest in an armchair. Mari did what she could, coming and going discreetly, talking with Jake when he felt up to it, fetching essentials from their house, bringing them hot drinks and sandwiches, though no-one felt like eating.

The clinic staff were caring for Lena and Mari looked after Jake and Judy in the best way she knew—by being practical. Jake was in pieces. Lena was refusing to see anyone except her mother, Jake and Mari. She repeatedly uttered that she wished she was dead, she couldn't face the world now her little boy was gone.

'You'll find the strength to go on,' Mari heard one kindly nurse tell Lena and Jake, 'with the support of those who love you; you'll find the strength for the sake of your unborn children.'

Jake felt as though his insides had been ripped out and an unbearable anguish filled the vacuum. It pervaded every waking moment. When he managed to sleep, it suffused his nightmares. Trying desperately to cope with his grief, Jake's only other thoughts were for his wife's mental and physical health. So, on their return home, and during the following days, Pierre was allowed into the house.

Jake had several conversations with Pierre out of Lena's earshot. 'Could this bring on a miscarriage?'

'I can tell you, with constant care, there is no reason why Lena's pregnancy should suffer any serious effects. Although her immune system is vulnerable,' Pierre stressed.

'She's unable to sleep except in short bursts,' he told Pierre.

'And you?'

Jake shrugged. 'The same. But Lena's exhausted and her back aches all the time. And I'm really worried about her depression.'

Pierre laid a hand on Jake's arm. 'You're both grieving. It will take a long time.'

'I know, but she dunt want to go on.' His voice faltered and cracked so the last words were reduced to almost nothing. Every day the leaden shroud of despair threatened to pull him into oblivion. But he had to fight it; he must be strong for Lena and the unborn babies. He wiped the back of one hand roughly over his eyes and shook his head.

'Come on, let's go talk with 'er,' Pierre replied softly.

'Unsurprisingly,' Pierre told Lena gently, 'you're suffering an imbalance in serotonin production, which affects sleep, digestion and emotions, among other things, and you 'ave high levels of cortisol, which is a stress 'ormone. Consequently your blood pressure 'as increased. We can 'elp to some extent; I can arrange a prescription for you. I know you're not sleeping but try, at least, to rest as much as possible.'

Lena was looking at Pierre while he talked with her,

but Jake could tell she couldn't concentrate on what he was saying. She nodded occasionally but her eyes were vacant. He sat by her side, stroking her hand, repeating Pierre's advice; as much for himself as for her.

'Try to eat nutritious food regularly and maintain good 'ygiene,' Pierre was emphasising.

Jake nodded. 'Judy's a good cook, ain't she, Lena?' He raised his voice slightly and spoke slowly, as if to someone hard-of-hearing. 'Yer mum makes nice meals, dunt she? Not that anyone's got much appetite,' he mumbled to himself.

''Ow long will Judy stay with you?' Pierre enquired.

Jake shrugged. 'As long as it takes. She's a bloody saint. Dunt know what we'd do without her.'

'I'm glad, because I think you also need to be looked after, Jake,' Pierre replied kindly. 'You should both try to talk about your grief with family or close friends. You could also have some counselling. I'm going to give you the details of someone I know.'

Jake threw Pierre an astonished look. 'But... the agreement.'

Pierre held up a hand. 'In strictest confidence.'

Fayette and Alain were deeply concerned, not only for the wellbeing of the couple with whom their lives had become so intricately linked, but about Lena's health and their unborn children. Pierre had called Fayette every day since the accident with updates, explaining, although it was possible for a foetus to be affected by stress-triggered changes in the production of chemicals within the mother's body, for example with developmental delays or neuro-developmental issues, this was considered uncommon. There was no reason to worry, he insisted; Lena was being taken good care of.

Alain, who'd rushed back from France to join his wife, expressed his disquiet about Lena not wanting to see them, but Pierre assured them both her behaviour was not unusual for a woman experiencing intense grief.

Fayette gently reminded her husband how she herself had felt after each miscarriage. George's death upset her greatly. She longed to visit Lena to offer what comfort she could, but she understood. She prayed it wouldn't be too long before Lena could bear to see her.

George's funeral was intolerable; the exquisite service almost unbearable. The modest local church was brimming, funeral attendees standing in the side aisles and against the back wall. Fayette and Alain, Fran and Pierre sat at the rear, secreted amongst the multitude. Mari understood Lena didn't want to see them. The couple walked into the church behind the little coffin, Lena supported by Jake on one side and Judy on the other. Lena wore a flowing navy-blue dress which fell profusely from under her bosom. As they passed, Mari witnessed her friend's pain and her attempt to hide her pregnancy and was desperately sad.

Jake had asked Mari if she would give a reading and they'd discussed what she might say. But here in the church, as they sang 'Lord of all hopefulness,' she had to fight to remain composed, for their sake. She felt Gerren's arm around her and glanced up at him wretchedly as he squeezed her shoulder.

Before long Mari was in front of the congregation beginning her reading. '"There is no foot so small it cannot leave an imprint on this world." George's sweet little life touched the lives of many. He…' Mari's throat constricted and she struggled to read as her words blurred. Suddenly Gerren was there taking up the next sentence and they continued together, speaking alternately. And in that moment, she was glad he was by her side.

After they'd returned to their seats Mari wondered whether Gerren finally understood her longing to be a mother with the love of a child.

At the wake Lena and Jake were inconsolable, unable to celebrate their son's brief life. It was a purposely small gathering, just a few friends and family, at their house. Jake had briefly spoken with most of the funeral attendees, including many of his colleagues, outside the church. Lena had barely managed that, nodding to a few people as Judy led her to the car.

Mari busied herself, making drinks and handing round sandwiches. Lena's physical and mental exhaustion was plain. She looked around for Jake, who was engaged with people in the kitchen. Judy was talking with a couple she assumed to be Jake's parents. So she assisted Lena up the stairs and helped her into bed.

In the days leading to the funeral she had spent a lot of time with Lena and Jake, and also Judy, encouraging them to talk with her, to unburden. They mourned his wretched premature departure just as they mourned the non-existence of the child, teenager and man that he would have become, his achievements, joys and sorrows, his lovers and children.

Later that afternoon, the neighbour who'd witnessed the accident called to express her deep sorrow. In her hand she held a little red shoe.

Chapter Twenty-nine

Plymouth, England, August 1985

In the first weeks after the funeral it was as much as Lena and Jake could do to put one foot in front of the other. Then Judy returned home for a short while as she had some matters to take care of. They lived the semblance of a life, a grinding, laboured routine. Desolation had set in and the imminent birth of two babies they would have to give away was excruciating. Lena couldn't bury that and pretend it wasn't happening—every day she was reminded of another impending loss. The twins, in the final eight weeks of their development, moved often now. As they prepared to enter the world, Lena wished the world would engulf her, extinguish her, purely to stop the pain. She was an aching void, a soulless empty shell. George's death was her fault; if she hadn't left him on the front step… if she'd made sure the front gate was shut… if she hadn't been talking on the phone…

One afternoon, Lena could bear no more. In a haze of torment, she took a kitchen knife upstairs and ran a bath.

Having been to the local shop then hung the washing to dry in the sunshine, Jake came in from the garden and put the kettle on. On autopilot, he prepared the teapot and washed dishes, an anxious frown between his brows. With Judy gone, Lena was slowly shutting down. She wouldn't talk to anyone apart from him and her mother, not even Mari and certainly not a counsellor. He was terrified of losing his beautiful, once-vivacious, loving wife. She just couldn't cope. She was slipping away from him; soon she'd be beyond reach. Something had to be done.

Jake took Lena's tea into the living room. Seeing she wasn't there he called upstairs to her. When she didn't answer he checked the bedrooms—she'd taken to spending time in George's room. Finally he opened the bathroom door.

A cry rose in his throat, panic surging through his body. His wife was sitting, fully clothed, in the bath, one hand gripping a paring knife.

Lena looked up at him and her face crumpled. Then she released an agonised wail.

In two strides Jake was beside her, kneeling on the wet lino, checking her wrists, taking her face in his hands. 'Oh, my luvver.' He kissed her damp hair and tear-stained cheeks. He threw his arms around her shoulders and held her close, murmuring soothingly into her neck.

She drew a long shuddering breath. 'I couldn't do it; not t' them.' She opened her fist and let Jake take the blade. 'They kicked,' she whispered, placing a hand on her belly. 'They sensed…' the words caught.

Making encouraging noises, Jake helped Lena out of the bath, removed her wet clothes, dried her and got her into bed. She was diminished, a limp doll, eyes expressionless. He gave her hot, sweet tea and made sure she drank it. Then he climbed in beside her, settling Lena with her head on his lap.

Stroking her hair, he spoke softly. 'I love ee, Lena. So much. What happened… it's no one's fault, you must believe that. An' you're not facing this alone, my luvver. You have yer mum an' me. I'll always be by yer side, takin' care of ee; you can rely on that.' His eyes brimmed but he kept it from his tone. 'We're a team, you an' me; we always have been an' we always will be. We can get through this but we've gotta do it together.'

He wiped his eyes with a sleeve. 'You can't leave us, Lena. Think what that would do to yer mum. She's already mourning her grandson; to lose her daughter as well…' His voice broke. He spoke the last words almost under his breath. 'It would kill her… an' it would kill me.'

Slowly, she moved an arm across his lap. He found her hand and held it tightly.

When he was sure Lena had fallen asleep, Jake eased out of bed, carefully inserting a pillow under her head. Wiping remnant tears, he made his way unsteadily to the bathroom. With trembling hands he withdrew all the medicines from the wall cabinet into a wash bag, together with the nail scissors. Downstairs he removed the sharp knives from the kitchen drawer, placing them, with the medications, in an empty cake tin which he hid on the top shelf of a cupboard, well out of Lena's reach. He poured a large whiskey and sat, head cradled in hands, trying to rid himself of the bone-chilling fear that spread like a stain each time the image of Lena in the bath came before his eyes. His hunched shoulders began to shake as devastation surfaced in racking sobs.

The next morning, Jake did the only thing he could do—he gave Lena hope by way of ambiguity.

'Lena, my luvver, d'you want a cuppa? I'm makin' one.'

A barely imperceptible shake of the head.

'D'you want a coffee? I'm sure one coffee's not goin' to hurt.'

A flicker of interest. It was enough.

'Okay, I'm making us both one. Then we're gonna have a talk.'

She heaved a sigh and continued to stare out of the window as she lay on the sofa. The lady across the road was in her front garden pruning a yellow rose.

A minute later Jake returned to the living room with two mugs of steaming liquid and a small bowl of dried banana slices. Lena had an inexplicable craving for them; they were the only thing he could guarantee she would eat at the moment. During her previous pregnancy, he recalled miserably, she'd had a hankering for peanut butter. He thought the banana an improvement.

'Here you go.' He forced a smile, passing her the bowl so she'd have to move to take it. 'C'mon, budge up.'

Placing the coffee mugs on the low wooden table in front of them, he sat beside her on the sofa. 'I've been thinkin',' he told her earnestly. 'D'you remember my birthday? I don't mean the steak and the pub, I mean afterwards… when we got home.'

'Hmm,' came her uninterested response.

'I know we shouldn't have done what we did… well, what I did really… The thing is, Lena, I went to the doc's the day after, y'know, to ask what the chances were of… messin' things up, like. He told me condoms are about ninety-eight per cent effective if they're used perfectly, but he said obviously people aren't perfect an' sometimes the condom doesn't work properly, so he reckoned on average they're about eighty-five per cent effective. Eighty-five per cent, Lena. You know what that means? It means there's a fifteen per cent chance it was me who got ee pregnant.'

A glimmer of life appeared in Lena's eyes for the first time in weeks. Jake could see she was considering the significance of her husband's words. After some moments she gave a perplexed shrug. 'But I had two embryos put inside me, surely an embryo that's already formed outweighs the chances of sperm?'

Jake had considered this and was ready for it. 'That's as maybe, but it dunt alter the fact that there's a chance, however small, the twins could be ours. An', don't ferget, yer grandfather was an identical twin.' It was true, however improbable. The only lie he'd told her was he'd rung the doctor, to enquire about condom effectiveness, only that morning.

Lena's hands went instinctively to her belly. 'They've been lively today, but I think they're running out o' room.'

'Have they, my luvver? Can I feel?' Jake placed a hand on hers and held it there, resting on her bump. 'The way I see it,' he continued cautiously, 'is we've got a chance at a new life, a fresh start, with our new family. Somewhere a long way from here, some place completely different. We can't go on here, with all these memories. We could still have the lifestyle we dreamed of,' his other hand went to her belly, 'with our twins.'

'Our twins,' Lena repeated pensively. Then she shook her head as if she'd come to her senses. 'But what about Fayette and Alain?'

'We'd have to leave quickly. We wouldn't be able to tell anyone where we are—not our friends nor our families,' Jake replied plainly. 'If we want t' keep our babies we can't talk to Pierre or Fayette and Alain about it; they'd only pursue us, make us hand 'em over—we couldn't have that, could we?'

In her wretched state Lena was aware she couldn't reason clearly but desperately tried to comprehend the implications of her husband's words. She passed a hand over her forehead. 'I have t' think.'

During the next few days, Lena considered everything repeatedly. The fact of her grandfather being an identical twin seemed to fit somewhere, adding weight to Jake's opinion about the chance of the twins being theirs.

She began to remind herself the little kicking things inside her were a part of her; her blood flowed through their veins, she shared her hormones with them, the nutrients in her body were nourishing them, their lives depended on her. They were one with her; existed because she did. The more she thought about the possibility of her being their natural mother, the more determined she became to take care of them herself. She couldn't let them go; wouldn't. It was unthinkable.

The next evening she and Jake sat in the living room trying to force down tomato soup, although neither felt like eating.

'They can't have my babies,' she pronounced.

Jake choked on a sip of the warm liquid, sending him into a fit of coughing. When he'd recovered, his expression was solemn. 'You sure?'

She nodded. 'But I can't leave my mum, Jake!' There was panic in her voice.

Jake put an arm around her shoulders and kissed her head. 'You wouldn't have to. I talked with yer mum yesterday; she'd be willing to move with us. Obviously, she knows everything. I dunt know what we'd have done without her. We need her, but she needs us too, she told me so.'

'Really?' Lena was taken aback. 'She'd really uproot, leave her friends behind, sell the post office?'

'She'd do anythin' fer you, Lena, you know she would, anythin' to make you happy again. So would I.'

An appreciative, sorrowful smile, but a smile nonetheless, appeared on Lena's face, the first since George's death. 'What would we tell your parents?' she asked quietly.

Jake heaved a long breath and stared at the carpet, recalling George's funeral. He'd thought it impossible to feel more wretched, but he was wrong. His parents had been kind, his mother laying a hand on his arm occasionally, his father patting him on the back once or twice—as near as they came to hugging—although they had questioned as to why he hadn't invited his brother. He'd walked with them to their car to say goodbye and their uncommon gentleness encouraged him to share his business ambition. His mother's reaction was dismissive. 'You've had a terrible shock, Jake. It's not wise to make big decisions in your traumatised state. Rationality will return in time, believe me.' His father reacted according to his customary disposition. 'What the hell do you want to do that for? Work in a shop? You're a trained engineer for Christ's sake. What a waste of bloody education. Look at Jude. He's carving out a successful career for himself in the import/export business. He's shrewd, determined. Where's your perseverance, Jake?' Something inside Jake had broken. 'You just can't bring yerselves to do it, can you? To be supportive… just once. Even on the day of my son's funeral.' He'd turned his back and walked toward the house, knowing their relationship was finished.

'Jake?' Lena was repeating her question.

He looked at her tenderly. 'Oh, dunt worry about my folks. It's not as if we're close, is it? Far from it. I'll tell them you lost the baby and we need a complete change so we're startin' a new life.' He knew what he would write to them. He'd never be good enough for them. He didn't need them in his life anymore, just as he'd come to realise they didn't need him in theirs.

Lena's face adopted an understanding expression and she squeezed his hand. Jake felt a rush of gratitude and relief. The gentleness in her eyes was soon, however, replaced by anxiety. 'But what about the money? We've already had so much and we've spent some.'

Jake took a deep breath. They now had more than enough to start their new life. 'We need it to buy a house of our own and finance the business.' His tone was deadly serious, his voice quiet.

Having let his words sink in for a moment, she was shocked. 'Jake, we can't take their money and keep the babies!'

'Our babies.'

'Yes, our babies. But we can't take the money,' she repeated.

'We can't pay it back before we go, or they'll know we're leaving and try to stop or follow us. Either way, when the twins are born, they'll take 'em away from us.'

'Couldn't we send 'em the money once we're settled?'

Jake shook his head. 'They'd find out where we are. Look, the Surrogacy Arrangements Act came into force a couple of weeks ago. It bans makin' surrogacy arrangements for money, like we've done. I heard it on the news. It means Alain and Fayette are also implicated and even Fran.' He deliberately didn't remind her the law wouldn't be backdated. But he also remembered, from the news back in January, Norman Fowler stating the Adoption Act included criminal sanctions against payment for a child with a view to adoption. If their arrangement was discovered both couples were implicated.

She nodded, comprehending. 'But the money, Jake, we've been paid a lot of money—there must be some way. I don't think I could live with myself if I took their money. It's not right.'

Jake grabbed her hands, leaning towards her. His tone was gentle yet determined, his face bore a look of fortitude he hadn't showed her for a long time. 'Listen, Lena, you haven't been able to live with yerself these past weeks. You almost slipped away from me. I've been so worried... If you lose the twins as well...' He shook his head, tears welling in his eyes. He fought for composure.

Lena began to weep. 'I can't lose these babies, I just can't!'

'I know my luvver, I know.' Jake squeezed her hands. 'Look, you remember Fran saying birth mothers have legal rights under UK law. She basically said surrogacy agreements were unenforceable, didn't she? So we'd be legally entitled to keep the twins, particularly as there's a chance they're ours.'

Lena nodded.

'But there'd be a dispute,' Jake continued. 'Then it'd come out about the money and we know from what happened with Kim Cotton, the children would be made wards of court until a decision was made and it wouldn't necessarily go in the favour of the surrogate. That's why we can't risk bein' traced. We're all implicated, so no-one's goin' to say anythin'. Alain and Fayette will obviously try to find us, but they can't get the police involved because they can't put at risk bein' able to take the children back to France. They won't miss the money—they're rollin' in it. If they want £30,000 they just have to sell one of their many properties. But it gives us the lifeline we need. It's us or them, Lena; us… or… them.'

Lena was quiet a while. Then she said softly, 'Where would we go?'

Chapter Thirty

Mari was ringing Jake and Lena daily without response. After a few days she drove to their house in her lunch break. There was no sign of the car and the curtains were closed. She guessed they'd gone to stay with Lena's mother. Judy had stayed with them for nearly a month after the accident. A practical, kindly woman with a big heart, she and Mari had developed an unspoken empathy. Mari had done what she could to help Judy too; after all, she was mourning her grandson.

Back at her office she rang Gerren at work. Speaking with him felt awkward; she found her own tone stilted. 'Hello, Gerren. It's Mari. Sorry to disturb you. I just wondered whether Jake has returned to work?'

'Hi there, how are you, angel?' Gerren answered warmly. 'It's nice to hear your voice. How are you getting on in the flat—is there anything you need?'

Mari wanted to keep their conversation brief. 'Fine…thanks, and no. Have you seen Jake?'

'He's been signed off on sick leave for another week. He lets us know on a weekly basis at the moment. I was thinking of ringing him, but I thought, you know, if he wants to talk, he'd get in touch. Have you seen them?'

'I called by today but they're not at home. I expect they've gone to Polperro for a few days. Okay, thanks.' She was about to ring off, but Gerren spoke again quickly.

'Mari, please come home, so we can talk. I miss you. I'm sure we can find a way to mend our bridges.'

'Oh… Gerren, I'm not… ready yet. I need more time to think.' It was the only pretext she could think of that instant. In truth she was preparing herself to tell him she wanted a divorce.

The following week, when Jake hadn't turned up for work and there was no doctor's note, Mari felt concerned. Maybe he'd become lost in the unfamiliar pattern of present daily life, forgotten what day it was, what week even, she suggested to Gerren. She popped to their house; the curtains were still closed and the car missing.

The next day was the same: no Jake, no phone call, no one at home. Mari finished work early and drove to Polperro. She didn't have Judy's address but, as she ran the post office, she wouldn't be hard to find. It had rained heavily all day, purple-grey clouds settling stubbornly over the countryside until they'd discharged their load. However, once Mari arrived in the Cornish village an equally tenacious sun had breached the veil, sending shafts of warmth to highlight the painted cottages and shimmer amongst ripples in the harbour.

She parked the car and set off down the narrow combe towards the village centre. She walked the maze of narrow streets until she found the post office, a bright, white-painted frontage with two upper storeys of stone. The place was closed. Mari looked at her watch; a quarter to five. She moved closer to discover a small hand-written sign stuck to the inside of one of the two front windows. *Regret to inform – Closed until further notice – Due to family bereavement.*

Mari looked around her. There didn't seem to be an obvious door to the accommodation above. Perhaps it was around the back, but how to get there? There was an old-fashioned sweet shop next door. Rows of tall glass jars packed with brightly coloured confectionery sat in the window displaying their wares. She entered the shop to ask after Judy. The young girl behind the counter, an obvious summertime assistant, told Mari the post office had been closed for a month. When pressed for more information she shrugged, saying all she knew was that the neighbour's grandson had been killed. Mari deduced the girl lived above the shop and enquired after her mother.

'Mum!' the girl shouted, still looking at Mari. There was no response. 'Mum, come here a minute,' the girl tried again.

This time a tall full-figured woman with brown curly hair entered the shop through a door at the back. 'Go on, Sally. I can close 'ere.' The woman smiled at Mari. 'What can I 'elp you with? The fudge is on special offer—two fer one t'day.'

Mari looked at the neat pyramids of cubed fudge within the glass counter. *It won't hurt to oil the wheels*, she thought. She chose a mixture of vanilla and toffee flavours then asked whether the woman had seen Judy recently, explaining she'd met her while she was staying with her daughter. She and the shopkeeper agreed it was a terrible business.

'I think she must be in Plymouth with her daughter, 'cause I ain't seen her fer a while. I did see poor old Jake late one evening out of me bedroom window, but not to talk to. He was loading somethin' into a trailer out the back. I dunno what's goin' to happen about the post office. It needs to be open fer the folk round here.'

'Perhaps they'll put a temporary replacement in, you know, until Judy can manage it again,' Mari suggested.

'Perhaps,' the woman shrugged, 'but Judy owns the business so nothin' can happen without her say-so. I just hope it gets sorted soon; it's a fair way to Looe for folk to get their pensions. Don't get me wrong, though, I do hope Judy's alright. If you see her give her my best, won't you? Terrible business,' she repeated, shaking her head.

Mari could do nothing but return to Plymouth. For the next few days she kept an eye on Jake and Lena's house but there was no sign of life. Then she remembered her friends didn't own their house but rented it. She trawled the estate agents and rental agencies until she discovered the one that dealt with the relevant address. The slightly dishevelled proprietor informed her the current tenants had given notice and the house would be available in two weeks' time if she was interested in renting it.

'Did they leave a forwarding address?' Mari enquired.

'They did,' answered the man, 'but that's private information.' Seeing the disappointment on her face, he added 'But it won't help you if you want to find them: it's just a PO box.' Mari politely thanked him and left. The news alarmed her. She could understand them wanting to move house; perhaps it was too difficult to continue to stay where they were with their memories of living there with George. But, after how close they'd become, she was surprised they hadn't been in touch with their new address. She phoned Pierre and asked him whether they'd been in touch with him. They hadn't. Pierre told Mari that Lena was due for another scan in two days and he would talk to her then. Mari suggested perhaps Fayette and Alain might know where they were, but Pierre thought that unlikely; Lena hadn't wanted to see them since the accident.

Two days came and went. That evening Mari's phone rang. It was Fran.

'Lena didn't turn up for her scan today! Has she been in touch with you? Pierre phoned them several times but there was no reply. He hasn't told Fayette and Alain yet. Do you know what's going on?'

Mari told her friend she'd been trying to find them and had also tried to locate Judy, to no avail. 'I'm worried, Fran, it's not like Lena to disappear. I hope to God she's alright. I think I'll call on the neighbours and see whether they know anything.'

Fran agreed to phone around the hospitals and Mari visited Jake and Lena's neighbours. Afterwards she drove to Fran and Pierre's flat. Dusk had settled and the gloom echoed the shadows in Mari's heart. A crawling dread tightened her chest.

Pierre opened the front door with a grim look. He motioned her in. Fran placed a glass of whisky in her hand and they all sat in the living room to exchange information.

'Neither of them has been admitted to the hospitals in Devon or Cornwall,' Fran declared, trying to keep her frustration at bay, at least for the time being; she was waiting to hear what Mari had to say.

Mari shook her head, exasperated. 'They seem to have disappeared into thin fucking air! Someone saw a trailer parked behind the car for a few days; the woman across the road saw Jake put suitcases into the car late one evening and understood from him they were going away for a bit of a break; Lena's mum's post office has been shut for weeks and Jake was seen loading a trailer there too. What the fuck's going on?' She took a swig of the amber liquid. 'I mean, have they… done a runner?' Her hand shook as she held the tumbler.

'I don't know, but I'm beginning to think it looks that way,' Pierre grunted. 'Christ, what am I going to tell Alain and Fayette?'

'It looks like they don't want to be found; they've set up a PO box as their forwarding address for the rental agency,' Mari stated, resentment rising.

'Can we at least get hold of that?' Fran demanded.

'I tried: they refused. You can give it a go if you want. Obviously, we can't get the police involved,' Mari answered despondently.

'I'll put a bit of pressure on the rental guy, say I need it for legal reasons and threaten to look at his books if he's uncooperative.'

Pierre couldn't fathom Fran's reasoning. 'Why should 'e be afraid of that?'

'People often have something to hide. It's a common bluff.'

'It still doesn't get us any nearer to finding them,' Mari stated testily.

Fran strove for calm. 'No, but we could at least contact them, try to persuade them to talk to us.'

Mari nodded. 'What they must be going through,' she sighed, empathy returning.

'I 'ave to tell the clinic. *Mon Dieu*, what am I going to

say?' There was panic in Pierre's voice.

'Just tell them what you know,' Fran answered plainly. 'You can't do more than that. Tell them you're trying to locate Lena and Jake. Maybe give it a few days before you tell Fayette and Alain. We'll do what we can in that time to get in touch with them.' She regarded Mari, who burst into tears.

'I feel so guilty!'

Fran moved to sit by her friend on the sofa, placing one arm comfortingly around her shoulders. 'You've nothing to be guilty about. It's not your fault. None of this is anyone's fault.'

'It is,' Mari sobbed. 'I was the one who suggested that donor eggs and surrogacy might be a possible option for Fayette. I was the one who suggested Lena as the surrogate mother.' She wiped her wet cheeks with the backs of her hands but couldn't stem the flow. 'I was the one who was on the phone to her that day,' she uttered miserably. 'If I hadn't rung, Lena wouldn't have been so distracted and George might still be alive,' she finished quietly, covering her desolate, guilty expression with both hands.

Fran's grey eyes glistened at her friend's anguish. She gave Pierre a silent look that sent him into the kitchen for more whisky and drew Mari closer.

'Everyone entered into this with their eyes open,' she stated evenly. 'You were trying to help; Pierre and his colleagues were agreed on the way forward; Lena and Jake knew what they were getting themselves into, they know what their obligations are; Fayette and Alain were aware of the risks and what-ifs. That's why we set up the surrogacy contract.' Fran's tone was calm, but she felt her pulse racing in time with her heartbeat. She felt it her responsibility to try to enforce the agreement, though she knew it was a useless document since they couldn't take it to court. She would need to be present when Pierre met with Fayette and Alain. *Christ, what a fucking mess!*

Chapter Thirty-one

Fran succeeded in obtaining the PO box address from the rental agent. The city was London, but they were all aware the service could have been set up to redirect post anywhere from there. She tried to persuade the PO Box company to give her the forwarding address but was bluntly refused. So she wrote a short straightforward letter enquiring after Lena and Jake's well-being, informing Lena she'd missed a scan and reminding them to get in touch as soon as possible to arrange another.

Four days passed. No reply.

Pierre then wrote, saying he was concerned, asking after Lena's health and urging her to give him a ring to talk about any concerns either of them might have.

Still no response.

Eventually Pierre decided the dreaded time had come when he must inform his colleagues in the know at the clinic. He called a brief meeting. His news was met with varying reactions from disquiet to alarm and anger.

The financial director, Pascoe Newton, didn't respond as Pierre had imagined, with blame and disparagement. 'My position, and I speak purely from a financial and QA standpoint, is that we have already received a fee for the procedure, which has been carried out in accordance with the agreed protocol. So as far as I am concerned the clinic is neither owed nor owes anyone anything and we have fulfilled our contract.'

The clinical director, Mr Townsend, banged his fist on the table. 'Well, we can't publish now.'

'Per'aps we could still put out a short paper describing the procedure and stating that a pregnancy was achieved?' Pierre suggested.

Townsend jumped down his throat. 'Of course we can't bloody publish. Half the results are missing. If we don't have a healthy live birth the procedure—the success—isn't complete. What are we supposed to do, having made it publicly known we've used a surrogate? Tell everyone she's run away and we don't know whether she gave birth to healthy children and we don't know the state of her health? People will ask, for God's sake. We can't just give them half the story! No, it's dead in the water and some other group will beat us to it.'

Giles Blenkinsop had remained quiet throughout, a solemn look on his face. Finally he spoke, his tone uncompromising. 'With regard to the clinical aspects of this case my position hasn't changed. We attempted a worthwhile medical procedure, which has thus far been successful. This is something we can learn from. However, as we have previously discussed, the clinic is in a difficult position as far as the ethics are concerned,' he glanced soberly at Pierre, 'not helped by the unfortunate timing of national events. We will not publish this work, but we can draw from the experience. In time, my hope is that science will win out and the treatment of infertile couples through surrogacy will become more widely acceptable. If that happens, we will be in a strong position to be at the forefront of developments. However, I believe the risk that the surrogate mother will choose to keep the resultant child or children will remain, unless the law is changed, and the expectations of the intended parents must be managed judiciously. That said,' he addressed Pierre, 'I expect you to deal with Mr and Mrs Dubois in an appropriate manner so as not to bring the clinic into disrepute. Would you like me to be present at that meeting?'

'Thank you, but Fran and I will manage Fayette and Alain Dubois,' Pierre assured. He didn't want his director learning of their intention to register the children as their own and the subject was bound to come up in discussing the means by which they could search for the missing couple. In Blenkinsop's words lay a warning; nothing was to be made public or allowed to leak into the public domain, for that could damage the clinic's reputation. That meant no police but they couldn't involve the law anyway. 'We are also still trying to find the Lesters.'

Pierre wondered whether Mari would have spoken to Xavier but Fran said Mari would be taking her cue from him and wouldn't speak about it until she understood it was appropriate. That evening Pierre phoned Xavier.

At first, Xavier didn't believe it. 'I have to say it's not your funniest joke, my friend.'

'I'm deadly serious, Xavier. I'm sorry. I must tell Fayette and Alain. Can you be with them?'

'Jesus Christ, Pierre. This is for real? I felt so sad for them, losing their son. But... how can they do this to someone else, to Fayette and Alain who are desperate for their children? How can Lena and Jake not understand what it will do to them? Oh, God. They'll be devastated—

I don't know how Fayette will cope.'

'I'm so sorry,' Pierre repeated. 'We're trying to find them and we won't give up. But, in the meantime, Fayette and Alain need to know. Are you able to come over?'

'You know I'd drop everything if I could, Pierre, but I'm due in Lyon tomorrow and it's not something I can get out of, or hand to someone else. But I'll phone Alain after you've been to see them.'

Pierre contacted Alain and arranged to meet him at the Dubois' house the following day. He thought it best to deliver the appalling news in a private setting.

He and Fran arrived in the middle of a late summer thunderstorm. The temperature had been building over the past week and with it the air had become humid, the looming ominous clouds heavy with separating charge and lightening poised to strike. As Pierre and Fran emerged from their flat to make the short journey distant thunder heralded the onset of the squall. *What could be more appropriate?* Pierre thought to himself unhappily.

Fayette opened the door to them, looking pretty in a flouncy summer dress. Her smile fell briefly as she noted their sober expressions then reappeared, as a ray of sunlight temporarily veiled by cloud. She ushered them in. They kissed on both cheeks before she led them into the lounge. 'I'm making coffee; would you like some?' she said, trying to sound bright, though the anxiety in her eyes belied her voice.

'That would be lovely, thank you,' Fran replied affably.

"Ow is Lena? She 'ad another scan I presume?' Fayette made for the kitchen, speaking over her shoulder. 'You know I really think I should be there for all the scans.' Sounds of a kettle boiling and clanking china emerged.

'I think she senses something's wrong,' Fran whispered to Pierre. 'She's delaying the moment.'

He turned down his mouth and nodded. Rain began to buffet the windows and the rolling thunder caught up with the lightening, directly overhead now.

'Is Alain 'ere?' Pierre called to her. They were still standing awkwardly in the middle of the room.

"E's upstairs, on a call. I'll fetch 'im in a moment.' She reappeared, carrying a tray loaded with espresso cups and a coffee pot, together with a plate of biscuits and paper napkins. ''Ow are my babies?'

Pierre swallowed and nodded. 'All was well when I saw Lena last. They were still kicking occasionally, though running out of room to move much now—which is to be expected,' he added hastily. He felt a flush of warmth as his heart pounded, leaving his skin prickling. He hoped it wasn't noticeable.

Fayette placed the tray on a low glass coffee table and indicated to the sofa. '*S'il vous plaît.*' As they sat, Alain entered. He greeted them in a convivial tone. '*Bonjour. Ça va?*' They both rose again to greet him.

The pulse in Pierre's temples throbbed. 'I'm afraid we 'ave some… difficult news,' he began. 'There's no easy way to say this.' He raked a hand through his hair. 'Lena and Jake 'ave gone.'

'Gone? What do you mean? Gone where?' Alain retorted, annoyance shaping his countenance.

'*Disparu,*' Pierre clarified. 'Lena didn't come for 'er last scan. We're trying to contact them but we don't know where they are at the moment. 'Opefully…'

Fran laid a hand on Pierre's arm and he understood there was no point trying to minimise the blow by injecting optimism. Better to lay it down straight so they could all deal with the honest fact—Fayette and Alain's unborn babies had been abducted.

Fran recounted what Mari had told her and how they'd tried to reach the Lesters thus far.

Fayette emitted a heart-wrenching wail and, covering her face with her hands, sank to the floor, limp and sobbing. It was as if she were soaking into the carpet like a pool of multicoloured liquid.

'No, no, no!' Alain, mirroring the thunder clouds outside, looked as though he might hit Pierre but instead grabbed the nearest thing to hand, a white porcelain vase, and threw it at the back window, where it cracked the glass and shattered into a hundred fragments.

His action and the shock of sound caused Fran to flinch. She knelt to Fayette's crumpled body and stayed with her, one arm protectively across her back, the other stroking her hair.

'*Putain!* We 'ave to find them and quickly,' Alain yelled, his features puce.

'We 'ave about a month until the due date,' Pierre noted quietly. 'We will do all we can to locate them, we can assure you.' He thought of suggesting some reason behind the Lesters' actions; their son's death had most likely been the trigger. But there was no point. The two couples had entered into an agreement and the Lesters had broken it. Immeasurably worse than that was their missing unborn children. He didn't have to imagine their pain; he could see it in Fayette's shaking, crumpled body and Alain's agonized eyes.

Fran helped Fayette into an armchair, where her grief continued to emerge in cries and moans, as blood from a wound, until she was drained. Alain paced, fists clenched, considering their options. Fran stayed with Fayette while Pierre went into the kitchen to replenish the coffee. On his return he persuaded Alain to sit.

'They may be staying with relatives. We'll start with the telephone directories,' Fran stated. 'There's a collection of BT telephone numbers for the whole country in the London Library. Lester isn't a particularly common name. We'll need to make a list and ring each number.'

'There are tens of thousands of cities, towns and villages in Britain and we don't even know if they're in the UK,' spat Alain, gesticulating fervently with both hands.

Fran attempted to maintain a composed exterior, trying for appeasement, worried about coming across as supercilious. The muscles at the top of her neck were taut and a tension headache spread from the base of her skull. 'It'll be time-consuming but the directories are arranged by region, which helps a little.'

'If they're staying with relatives don't you think they will have warned their family not to give out any information?' Alain was far from being placated.

'You're probably right, but we 'ave to begin somewhere if we want to try and find them before the babies are born,' answered Pierre in a conciliatory tone.

'We could say Lena and Jake are the beneficiaries of a will, which is why we need to locate them. Relatives are often willing to talk if there's an inheritance in the offing. I know a… private detective,' Fran announced, her timbre, at first hesitant, grew more determined. She began to focus her anger at having been taken advantage of into an inclination to do whatever was necessary. 'In my line of work I meet all sorts of people. If we were prepared to involve a professional investigator, it would help with the legwork of the searches.'

Alain rose and paced some more. He turned, his eyes scrutinising hers. 'And what of the risk?'

'We'd have to consider that,' Fran agreed. 'Yes, it's possible they could uncover our arrangement, which would put ourselves at risk of being outed or blackmailed. But what is a private detective without a reputation for privacy and accomplishing the job?'

"Ow well do you know this person?' Alain returned.

'I've met him a few times. I believe he's genuine and effective. I'll do some digging around.'

Alain nodded curtly.

'After the babies are born,' Fayette spoke, wiping her face with the sleeve of her dress, 'they will 'ave to be registered. What 'appens then? Can we get the document? Will it tell us where they are?'

'That's a good point, Fayette,' Fran replied gently. 'Copies of every birth record in England and Wales are held at the General Register Office at Saint Catherine's House in London. There's an alphabetical surname index. We know when the twins are expected and the registration period in England is forty-two days,' she glanced at Pierre, who nodded, 'so we can search for births by the month of registration and surname; the registration district will be in the index as well, so that will give us a clue to roughly where they are. Once we've found the relevant birth records we can order copies of the birth certificates, which will give the date and place of birth and also the specific address of the person who registered it. We can do the same for Scotland and Northern Ireland.'

Fayette nodded. 'So if Lena and Jake cannot be found

before the twins are born, we can find them soon after,' she said, momentarily bolstered.

Fran hated delivering further difficult news but had to manage their expectations. 'The search is likely to take time, I'm afraid. Registrars from around the country send a copy of the births, marriages and deaths they've registered to the Registrar General in London every three months, so the records for September won't reach London until after the end of that month. Then the indexes must be produced. I checked with the General Register Office; the records used to be available in quarterly volumes, but from last year they're produced only on an annual basis which may mean we can't view the records for September 1985 until next January, unless we can somehow get a look at the third quarter's records in advance. We can try, of course.'

Fran's fleeting reassurance was deflated. 'January! *Mon Dieu*. We 'ave to find them before then.'

'I think the only other option before the end of this year is to ring all the maternity departments pretending to be a relative oo is unsure of which 'ospital Lena 'as gone to; but there are 'undreds of them and we can't be sure staff will release patient details,' Pierre contributed.

'Around three hundred,' Fran corrected, swallowing the last of her coffee and privately wishing for something a lot stronger. She shot her partner a look that said *try to be more positive*. 'But it's doable.'

'Yes, we must do that,' responded Fayette, repositioning to sit more upright in her armchair. 'With the 'elp of a detective.'

Alain was less reassured. What if she 'as the twins at 'ome?' He snorted. 'We don't even know if they're still using their own names, for Christ's sake!'

'An 'ome birth is unlikely with twins,' Pierre responded, his tone more upbeat. 'So we should 'ave a good chance of narrowing down the search. Fran will ask Mari if she 'as any photos of Lena and Jake.'

Fran spoke gently, 'I think it's unlikely they would use a false name to register the children's births. Whatever we might think of them they're not hardened criminals.' She meant the last to be helpful but it only made things worse.

'Well they're doing a good job so far,' Alain roared, spittle reaching the carpet. '*Putain*. They've stolen thousands of pounds and our only chance to 'ave children. If that is not criminal, I don't know what is!'

Fayette began to weep again. Fran chanced her hand on Alain's arm. He shook it off angrily.

'I'm sorry. I didn't mean…' Words deserted her for a moment. She looked at Pierre for support.

He spoke softly and earnestly. 'We will do everything possible in our power to find them,' he assured them. 'And we'll begin today.'

Chapter Thirty-two

London, England, March 1987

Mari exited St. Catherine's House and walked up Kingsway as far as Holborn tube station. She and Xavier had planned to meet at their hotel near St James's Park and grab a bite. She'd had a long day of client meetings from seven-thirty in the morning until three o'clock that afternoon and had then been checking birth records again in case the twins had recently been registered or she'd missed something in previous searches. Up to now she'd drawn a blank. There were no relevant entries for England and Wales; Xavier had been to Edinburgh three times over the past fifteen months to check the records held by the Registrar General for Scotland and she had twice visited the General Register Office of Northern Ireland in Belfast. She'd also been checking the consular records of overseas births in case Lena and Jake had travelled abroad. Their searches were focussed on Lena and Jake as they didn't know the twins' given names. In addition, they'd searched for Sophia and Suzette Lester, although they assumed Lena and Jake wouldn't have used the names chosen by Alain and Fayette.

Having not located Lena before or after the due date, despite their best efforts, including those of the private investigator, Fayette and Alain had decided to register the babies while the searching continued beyond the expected birth period. Mari had thought this unacceptable, but Xavier explained his brother and Fayette would need the certificates to record them as the parents, for when eventually the girls were found. As they didn't have to produce the children to register them but only had a finite window, they assumed they'd been born on the due date. Once back home with the children, entry of birth onto the French Civil Register would be made retrospectively, via a court judgement, using the false certificates, the reason being that the children had been residing in England. As the children would have French nationality and be living in France, Alain had reasoned that having a false birth record in England wasn't likely to have any consequence. Mari understood from Xavier that Alain and Fayette had stopped short of falsely registering the births with the French consulate in England because in the event— unthinkable though it was—that they never find their children there wouldn't be false records in the French system for them to deal with. Mari had prayed it wouldn't come to that. She was still entreating some higher force, though it didn't reconcile with being a non-believer.

As she headed for the tube station it spat with rain and bitter gusts whistled through the wide thoroughfare, crowded with traffic; red double-decker buses conveying commuters home from work, black London cabs taking people to stations, theatres, hotels and restaurants, pedestrians and bold London cyclists hurrying home, eager to be out of the chill and dampness. The naked trees lining each side of the street shivered in the icy spring shower. Mari pulled up the collar of her long, woollen navy-blue winter coat and tightened her mohair scarf, crossing and tucking the ends inside her lapels. It was too windy for an umbrella.

Her thoughts were so flooded with exasperation she couldn't think. They had tried every avenue of investigation their collective minds could conjure and been stymied at every turn.

During September 1985 Pierre, Xavier and the PI had split the task of contacting maternity departments countrywide but to no avail. The PI had located Jake's family, in Dorset, who had no clue where he was and seemed resentful, but not surprised, he hadn't been in touch.

During the last nineteen months, Alain and Fayette had scoured the Yellow Pages commercial phone directories archived in the London Library for engineering firms Jake might have joined, constructing an extensive list from which Fran and Mari had rung everyone. Mari recalled the missing couple had mentioned an aspiration to start a business selling outdoor gear, so Pierre and Xavier had drawn up a list of such businesses. She and Fran worked their way through it, telephoning each outlet, pretending to be interested in purchasing specific items of fishing tackle, asking the respondent's name under the pretence of wishing to ask for that member of staff personally when they subsequently visited the shop. Each time they drew a blank they asked whether a Jake Lester was employed there, saying he was friend who they believed worked in the area. She and Fran had become quite familiar with different rod types, power ratings, rod taper, guides, reels and reel seats. Again, this was laborious and could only be managed within working hours, which was often awkward for the two women, both engaged in demanding full-time employment. They had split the responsibility for different sections of the inventory by region. Mari had felt hopeful this line of enquiry might turn up relevant information, although this assumed the Lesters were still answering to their own names and their business, whatever it might be called, was advertised in the Yellow Pages. They hadn't turned up anything and suspected Jake and Lena were using assumed names.

The PI had checked all the post offices he could locate in London, brandishing a photo of Lena and Jake in case they were collecting their post personally. He was also some way through making enquires at all the banks in the major towns, beginning with the south-west and southern counties and working his way northwards. This onerous, tricky and seemingly never-ending task had not produced results to date. Alain was on the cusp of firing the PI—his funds were not limitless, as he often reminded them.

In the spring of 1986 Fayette had descended into a severe depression and Alain had taken her back to France. She needed to be in a familiar setting with his mother nearby and friends around her. She could no longer cope with living in a foreign country, struggling with the language and the consequent semi-isolation as well as with her grief. The others had assured Alain and Fayette they would continue to do everything they could to discover the whereabouts of their twins. Xavier was dividing his time between the UK and Alain, Fayette and his mother in France, spending most weekends in Britain.

Relations between Xavier and Alain had become strained. Alain distrusted Mari and did not endeavour to hide his feelings. He'd not wanted her involved in the search for his children, believing she'd done enough damage by suggesting her friend as a surrogate. His distrust had intensified into disapproval of her as an appropriate partner for his brother. Xavier couldn't persuade Alain otherwise and, given the situation, did not persevere.

Mari felt she had to assist in the quest for the twins but continued to keep her distance from Xavier's family; she hadn't yet met them and she and Xavier agreed it wasn't the right time for introductions. It felt wrong for them to be playing happy families in the circumstances. Consequently they hadn't made plans for their future, focusing only on the enormous task of tracking the children. Once the situation had been resolved they would consider their own lives. She and Gerren had continued to live apart and she'd told him she wanted a divorce but hadn't yet taken steps to instigate the process. Since he most definitely didn't want one, he hadn't taken any action either.

As she stood in a crowded tube train heading southwest on the Piccadilly line, Mari's thoughts turned, as they often did, to George's death. She was certain if the unthinkable accident hadn't occurred and George was safe and well with his parents, she and they would still be friends and the twins would be with Alain and Fayette, where they belonged. She remembered how Lena and Jake had adored their son; they would have given anything to keep him safe. She knew wherever they were they'd be taking great care of the twins. What they had done was inexcusable, but she understood why. Neither Jake nor Lena were malicious. She knew only too well why they would do their utmost to remain hidden, but she also believed they'd try to remain within the law. This aspect of her reasoning had fallen short, however, considering they'd stolen the money and there was no trace of a birth record. It was the law that all births in England, Wales and Northern Ireland must be registered within forty-two days and within twenty-one days if resident in Scotland. Even if the family was abroad, births still had to be registered and those of British citizens were recorded at the relevant British Consulate.

As Mari trod in the wake of thousands of others, changing tubes for the Northern line at Leicester Square, the name of the tube station fixed in her mind. An idea struck her. Their searches had included possible different spellings of Lester, but suppose they shouldn't be looking for a name that sounded like Lester at all? Perhaps they should be searching for a completely different name. What if Jake and Lena had indeed acted lawfully? She would need to visit St Catherine's House again to look at the index of birth records and locate the reference for George Lester.

A thrill of excitement passed like an electric current through her stomach and lightened her step.

Chapter Thirty-three

The next morning she and Xavier visited the archives as soon as St Catherine's House was open. Fortunately Mari's scheduled client meeting did not begin until after lunch and Xavier had the luxury of a free day. Over dinner the previous evening they'd discussed her theory and both were eager to check it out. They wondered why no one had thought of it. Mari knew George's date of birth, so they were quickly able to locate the relevant dusty volume that encompassed surnames beginning with L from the fourth quarter of 1982. They found the entry relatively easily; *Lester, George David*; Mother's maiden name *Gregory*; Registration district *Plymouth*.

Next, they searched for births registered under Gregory. They each took an index volume containing surnames beginning with G from the last two quarters of 1985. After ten minutes they looked at one another dejectedly.

'I was so sure I was right this time,' Mari uttered, the corners of her mouth turning down unhappily.

Xavier's brow creased with concentration. 'Okay, Jake and Lena registered George with 'is father's surname so we assumed they're married. We've looked for the twins under Lester, but 'aven't found them. If they don't 'ave a marriage certificate, we can assume Lena's last name would be Gregory. In that case, they could either register the children using Jake's surname or Lena could use 'er maiden name.'

'Yes, that's right,' Mari replied. 'At the very least, they would have needed proof of identification of Lena, as the mother; so if they weren't married, Lena would have used her maiden name. But we haven't found them under Gregory. I suppose she could have changed her name to something totally different or be using false documents,' she said flatly. 'But if that's the case we've no chance of finding her. Perhaps we'd should at least check the marriage records.'

Neither of them was sure how old Jake or Lena were; Mari figured she and Lena were probably about the same age but had never thought to ask. However, to throw the net wide they searched from 1970 through to the last available index volume, dated December 1986. Since the entries were recorded quarterly there were sixty-eight volumes to examine. Even between them the search took nearly three hours. A couple of thousand marriages to men whose surnames were Lester were recorded, however they could find no record of a Lena Gregory marrying a Jake Lester.

Mari leaned back on her wooden chair, hands behind her head, stretching her aching back. The furniture was not designed for comfort.

'We all assumed they were married,' she declared, her face a picture of despondency, 'and they never once corrected us. Lena must have signed the surrogacy agreement as Lester or Fran would have noticed.' She looked at her wristwatch; it was half past midday. 'I've got to leave in half an hour to get to my two o'clock meeting.'

She exhaled wearily. 'Bloody hell, we've reached another dead end.'

Xavier nodded, wearing a similar expression. Then his face brightened, hope supplanting gloom. 'No we haven't. This doesn't mean you're wrong, Mari, only that the babies were not born in England or Wales.'

Mari eyed him with renewed optimism, eyebrows raised. Then she groaned. 'But we'll have to go all the way to Edinburgh or Belfast to check the other records and we can't do that tomorrow, the offices will be closed for the weekend.' Frustrated, she sighed. 'It's going to be at least another week until either of us can get to Scotland or Ireland.'

'Leave it with me, I 'ave an idea,' was all Xavier would say. 'Go to your appointment and meet me in Covent Garden at the Crusting Pipe around six.'

Xavier had ordered a bottle of claret and a charcuterie and cheese board and was helping himself to the olives by the time Mari arrived in Covent Garden. She'd looked over the wrought iron railings protecting the inside perimeter of the upper level of vaulted arcades and spotted him dressed in his blue and white striped seersucker jacket over a white T-shirt and his Levi 501s. As she stepped elegantly down the wide weaving staircase to the lower courtyard, she could see him watching her and felt a familiar pleasurable sensation. It was a dry bright evening; the cool weather of the previous day having mellowed. The popular wine bar, set within three arched red-brick vaults and occupying one end of the quadrangle within the glass-roofed central market hall, was buzzing with folk appreciating after-work and pre-theatre drinks, some enjoying an early supper. Mari was thankful he'd chosen a table outside, preferring the fresh air after being cooped up all afternoon.

Threading towards him through an array of wooden tables she could see he was looking pleased with himself, which sent shivers of anticipation down her spine and raised the hairs on her arms. As she reached him, he stood to greet her, kissing her on both cheeks. He poured her a glass of wine and slid a large white envelope across the table, his mouth pulled into a wide grin.

She hesitated, almost not daring to open it, a whooshing pulse in her ears echoing her racing heart. He nodded at her. 'Go on.'

She slid a finger under the loosely gummed flap and took out the contents: a single piece of A4 paper, folded on itself. On opening it she saw it was a facsimile of an index of birth records, the header indicating births registered in July, August and September 1985. Xavier had managed to locate what they had long sought; there, among the handful of records of births recorded under the surname Gregory in that quarter:

Gregory – Suzette Rose
Gregory – Sarah Judy

The mother's maiden name was also given as Gregory.

Mari looked up at Xavier in surprise. 'Where? I mean, which register?' she uttered excitedly.

'Scotland,' he replied.

'Bloody hell.' She looked down at the entry again, to be sure.

'My "assistant" in Edinburgh assured me there were no other twins registered under the name of Gregory.' He smiled easily.

'How did you manage…'

'I can be very persuasive, as you know.'

She raised her eyebrows at that.

'I took 'er out for dinner the last time I was in Edinburgh,' he admitted sheepishly. 'It never 'urts to be on the right side of someone useful!'

'Hmm,' Mari smiled, 'clever.' She couldn't help feeling a tiny bit jealous.

'There is more,' he stated, pulling another envelope out of his jacket pocket and passing it to her.

Her heart was pounding so hard against her ribcage she thought everyone around them would hear it. When she looked at the contents Mari was almost dumbfounded. In her hands were facsimile copies of two birth certificates, one for a Suzette Rose and the other for a Sarah Judy. They had found the twins.

'You clever woman, you solved it!' He allowed her a few moments to regard the documents then, as she looked at him excitedly, moved nearer and threw his arms around her, holding her tight. '*Ma petite Souci*,' he breathed into her hair, 'what would I do without you?'

Mari's body trembled with the resonance of thrill and relief. She disengaged from Xavier, her eyes glistening, and examined the certificates once more. In the place and date of birth columns was written *September 20th, 1985; 8:10 a.m.* on Suzette's certificate and *8:25 a.m.* on Sarah's, and underneath, *Ullapool*. In the column headed 'Name and maiden surname of mother' was written *Lena Sally Gregory*. The column for the father's details were blank. Mari's eyes scanned the certificates to locate the vital information. The informant's details included an address in Ullapool.

Xavier had not wanted to telephone his brother straight away. Alain was hot-headed, he said, and was bound to go charging up to Scotland without a thought. Mari suggested he could at least tell Fayette and Alain they'd located the birth records and imply they were waiting for copies of the birth certificates before they could discover the location of the registrant.

That night they lay in bed within their comfortable hotel room discussing next moves. They hadn't wanted to speak too much about this at the restaurant for fear of being overheard.

'The first thing to do,' Xavier stated decisively, 'is to go to Ullapool and make sure they're still living at the address we 'ave for them. They could 'ave moved since then, of course. I will do this, because I'm the only one they don't know. They've never seen me and I won't arouse suspicion. If they are there, I can watch them for a while and discover where they work, oo they meet, oo they know and what their routine is. If they 'ave left Ullapool I can make enquiries about where they may 'ave gone.'

'I hope they're still there,' Mari declared. 'God forbid they've moved, otherwise we're back at the beginning.'

'Absolutely,' nodded Xavier, his eyebrows raised. 'Another reason not to build Alain and Fayette's 'opes too early.'

'Yes, you're right,' murmured Mari. 'Assuming they're still there, I take it you won't approach Lena and Jake?'

'Definitely not. As soon as I left them, they would likely disappear again.'

Possible scenarios were tumbling around in Mari's thoughts. 'Then I guess all of us—you, me, Fran and Pierre, Alain and Fayette—will need to go up there and face them, persuade them to hand over the children.'

'Hmm.' Xavier doubted this would work. 'What if they refuse?' he shrugged. 'We cannot physically grab the children from their arms. 'Ow do you say... 'ell would emerge?'

Despite the situation Mari smiled at his version of the common saying. 'Yes, I agree, we can't possibly do that. In any case, they could threaten to call the police and claim we're trying to steal their children,' she responded, frowning. 'But I suppose Fran has a copy of the surrogacy agreement.'

'Yes, but it isn't likely to 'ave any legal weight and if that becomes known then everyone is affected,' Xavier reminded her. 'And judging by what you told me of recent political events there is no guarantee the law will demand the release of the children. Remember what Fran said, Alain and Fayette could be fined or worse under the Adoption Act, even if not under the Surrogacy Act, if it's known they paid money for Lena to 'and over the babies.'

'Yes but because Lena and Jake took the money they'd also be implicated. So they'd probably prefer not to involve the police either,' Mari countered, turning to Xavier, propping up her head with one arm. 'But maybe Alain and Fayette would rather fight for the children in court legally and sacrifice having them on the French civil register?' She had another thought and sighed despondently. 'But then I suppose the fraudulent birth registration would be discovered and that would reveal their original intentions.'

'I think both couples would 'ave much to lose if it went to court. I'm concerned Alain will do something rash. 'E and I do not 'ave similar temperaments—'e has a severe temper and, given the situation, oo knows what could 'appen.'

Mari sighed and rolled onto her back, staring at the ceiling in the dim light afforded by the streetlights entering around the edges of the heavy curtains. 'Is it possible we could go without Alain and Fayette—I mean you and I, Pierre and Fran?'

Xavier snorted. 'I think you know the answer to that already. If you put yourself in Alain's skin, would you stay away? They 'ave his children and 'is money.'

'Hmm, I suppose not… although perhaps we could approach them first without telling your brother.'

Irritation became apparent in Xavier's voice. 'Alain and Fayette 'ave a right to know and anyway, if we don't obtain the children, Lena and Jake will disappear again with them.'

'Well, what else can we do?'

'I think we do not 'ave much of a choice,' Xavier answered sombrely. 'The only other option is to take the twins without Lena and Jake's knowledge.'

Mari was horrified. 'Are you talking about kidnapping them? You can't! No. That's a serious crime and, anyway, it's far too risky.'

Xavier shrugged. 'I cannot see another option. And as we've just discussed, I don't think Lena and Jake would launch a police investigation.' He counted on his fingers. 'They took the surrogacy money; they took the babies; they'd be worried a court might give custody to the biological parents—like Baby Cotton was given to 'er biological father—so they could lose the children anyway; and the notoriety would be terrible—think about the 'arassment Kim Cotton and others since 'ave endured.

Maybe each one of these things alone might not stop them getting police involved, particularly as Alain and Fayette would also be implicated, 'owever the combination of factors might be enough to stop them taking action.'

Concern drew lines between Mari's eyebrows and she shook her head. 'You're talking about what they have to lose, Xavier, but think about what they have to gain—two children; when they lost George they had none. Yes, there's a possibility they could lose the twins but, having run away, I bet they'd fight to keep them. They could say they signed a surrogacy agreement but then naturally conceived the twins and the law would be on Lena's side, as the birth mother, so they'd be more likely to get legal custody.'

'But if they try to argue the surrogacy agreement isn't valid, 'ow do they explain the money they were paid? That doesn't add up,' Xavier countered. 'And, anyway, blood tests would be done to prove the twins are Alain and Fayette's.'

'Hmm. Maybe Jake and Lena would threaten to get the police involved, as they know if the surrogacy became public it would ruin Alain and Fayette's chances of passing the babies off as their own, born naturally to them, in France. Maybe they'd hope Alain and Fayette would back down?' Mari suggested.

Xavier considered this then shook his head. 'Why would they believe the twins are worth any less to Alain and Fayette? They knew 'ow desperate they were for children. They still 'ave that desperation. No, everyone loses if it goes to court. My brother 'as a right to 'is children. The only way is to take them back.'

It was Mari's turn to shake her head. 'Kidnap's not a

valid option in my book,' she stated reproachfully.

'Well then, tell me 'ow you would approach the situation.'

'I think all six of us need to go and see them and we'll just have to contain Alain's anger somehow. They're reasonable people—well they were, at any rate. They were my friends. Perhaps I'd be able to appeal to them? Or maybe if Fayette talked with Lena…'

'They already made the decision to betray you. So what then—when they don't 'and over the babies?' Exasperation resounded in Xavier's response; anger was close by.

Mari had to admit she didn't know. 'Perhaps they'd give back the money, at least.'

Xavier's frustration boiled over. 'You think Alain wants the money?'

'Of course not, but… well… perhaps it would… enable them to try again,' she ended weakly.

'Huh, you think they would go through all this again. I don't think so,' he replied contemptuously.

'No, I'm sorry, you're right. And now the law has changed it wouldn't be easy to arrange,' she muttered.

'We're going in circles,' Xavier retorted dismissively. 'I think we should take this step by step. I will go to Ullapool in the morning.' He turned from her, indicating their discussion was over.

Mari lay in the dark, unable to sleep. Anxiety had her heart in its grip and her veins pulsed. The more she considered it, the more she concluded Xavier was probably right. *Taking the children has to be the most effective measure. But at what cost?* Her thoughts returned to the time of George's death. *I remember your grief, Lena; it was destroying you.* She imagined her one-time friends rising one morning to find the twins gone; hearing their anguished cries in her head, the breath caught in her throat and her abdomen contracted. *Christ! If you have to go through all that again... How could we do that to you?*

As Mari continued to wrestle with the situation, judgements of culpability surfaced. *But how did you and Jake think Fayette and Alain were feeling? How could you do that to them when they were so obviously desperate for a baby? And what about Xavier and me? We've put our lives on hold. We can't find any peace or be properly together until this disaster is resolved and we both want that so badly, Lena.*

She longed to be rid of this enduring, ruinous situation and the quicker the better. Nonetheless, at the thought of child abduction her flesh shivered, sending waves of panic through her stomach. The crime carried a maximum sentence of life imprisonment. *Is it worth the risk, Xavier? You seem to think so, although you're still several steps away from being faced with that final decision. But how can I let you risk everything—your life, our future together? I can't; I won't. I have to persuade you this is one situation Alain must handle on his own. Our future happiness depends on it.*

Chapter Thirty-four

Ullapool, Scotland, March 1987

Early the next morning Xavier took a train to Inverness. The journey was long and he didn't arrive until four that afternoon. He made a brief visit to the men's toilet on the station platform to don glasses and a false beard before jumping into a taxi and asking to be taken to any used car dealership in town. The taxi driver asked him what he was looking for. The man's accent was strong and Xavier had to concentrate hard to understand what he was saying, particularly since the driver had his window open and the streets outside were busy with traffic and Saturday afternoon shoppers. Xavier explained he wanted something cheap and the driver nodded and said something that sounded like, 'Och, aye, ah ken a place'.

The driver took him to a shabby used car business on a small industrial estate on the fringe of the city, where he picked out an old brown Ford Cortina with around 100,000 miles on the clock. The proprietor, a stubby man with broad shoulders and a belly to match, assured him the engine was sound. Xavier looked at the tyres and under the bonnet; the treads were in good condition and the engine was clean. He started the car, listening to the engine for a few seconds while checking the heater worked. It only had to do two hundred and fifty miles for what he had in mind.

'I'll take it,' he nodded.

He purchased the car with cash, giving a false name and address for the registration and licensing documents. The manager gave him the logbook and he swung his holdall onto the back seat and set off for Ullapool.

The day had been drab and gloomy and, by the time Xavier set off, it was almost dark. He drove slowly through persistent low-lying fog, arriving at his destination in a miasma of sea mist. Proceeding carefully into the town he looked for signs to the harbour, the indistinct glow of numerous headlights materialising through the brume.

Xavier located the imposing Edwardian hotel close to the quayside; he'd chosen there, rather than a B&B, hoping he could remain anonymous among its many rooms. The area had an eerie quality. He could hear water slapping against the side of the pier and boats creaking as they shifted on their moorings. He peered into the dank swirling fog but couldn't see more than a few yards in front of his hands. He turned towards the hotel; time enough to explore in the morning.

He woke early. The room was simply furnished but warm and the bed was comfortable. It being Sunday, breakfast would be served later so he showered, dressed warmly, donned his beard and glasses and stepped out into the fresh morning air for a look around. The dawn light was just beginning to supplant the darkness and all traces of the previous night's fog had disappeared. He walked the short distance to the quay. A stiff breeze blew across the grey waters of Loch Broom, on which bobbed hundreds of small boats. In the distance Xavier could see numerous large grey shapes rising ominously out of the sea loch and made out the twinkling of a multitude of tiny lights as the crews of a flotilla of herring-processing factory ships went about their business.

The pier in front of him was crowded with all manner of fishing boats and launches as well as lifeboats from the large ships being used as tenders, some tied directly to the wide stone promontory and others secured to one another, forming rafts of vessels radiating out like the fingers of an enormous outstretched hand. As it was early Sunday morning the quay was relatively quiet although a few people were up and about, some already engaged in maintenance activities on their crafts. Xavier, eager to locate Jake and Lena's house, moved on.

The road followed the gentle arc of the shoreline behind which lay the town, constructed on an easily navigable grid. The edges of the settlement stretched along the shore in both directions from the quay. He decided to follow the coastal road to his right. He figured it shouldn't be too difficult to find the place, which was on West Shore Street and therefore likely to overlook the water. He pulled up the collar of his leather jacket, tightened his scarf against the chill and walked around the bay with the water to his left. He found the road he sought almost immediately: *Sràid- A' -Chladaich-An-Iar*, West Shore Street. It curved away from him to a point of land that jutted into the loch. He passed the ferry port and a few austere commercial premises before coming to a long row of terraced houses, some rendered and brightly painted, others displaying their original two-hundred-year-old stone walls. Each relatively small cottage boasted two gable dormers denoting essential usable accommodation in the roof spaces.

Xavier searched for house numbers, but the dwellings bore names in place of mundane numerals. This was a problem because the address he sought had a number rather than a name. The cottages fronted directly onto the road, which came to an end at the point of the headland. However, he was able to walk further around the peninsular along the stony shoreline until he rounded the line of houses. Behind the buildings ran a succession of sizeable gardens backed by a low wall separating them from the extensive area of open grassland beyond, which looked as though it might be used as a campsite in the summer season. He noted some of the gardens were accessible via low wooden gates. A gravel path ran parallel with the backs of the houses then swept around to follow the shoreline adjacent to the grassland.

Unsurprisingly there was no sign of activity in the gardens; it was not yet seven-thirty. He decided to go back to the hotel for breakfast while considering his next move. He followed the grit track until it joined a tarmacked residential street leading to a wider thoroughfare with various two- and three-storey houses and several small shops. After ten minutes or so he arrived back at the hotel.

He was glad to be out of the cold for a while. Despite it being nearly April the weather was decidedly wintry, most unlike his native south-west France; even Lille and London were a great deal warmer at this time of year. He was looking forward to hot coffee and a hearty breakfast. The hotel's tartan-carpeted restaurant was brightly lit and he sat at a small table next to one of the many windows. He declined porridge, having experienced the surprisingly salty dish some years ago, in favour of a full Scottish breakfast. Xavier pondered what to do next as he leisurely enjoyed a substantial meal of fried eggs, black and white puddings, square wedges of sausage meat, bacon and griddled oatcakes. He would need to speak to the locals to determine whether Jake and Lena still lived in West Shore Street and locate their house. He could also investigate what Jake did for a living; he had noted the presence of a camping shop so perhaps they had set up their business after all, or perhaps he worked in the fishing industry. If they were in Ullapool he would need to learn their daily routine.

Having eaten, he rose and fetched his coat and a pair of binoculars from his room. Field glasses were not uncommon in this part of the world; he could pretend he was an ornithologist. He felt self-conscious sporting the false beard but considered it essential for security purposes. Once outside, he headed back towards the camping shop. There were no clues to its ownership in the name, which was Loch Broom Outdoor Leisure. Being Sunday, it was closed. Xavier checked the opening hours attached to the glass panelled door; he would visit again in the morning. He returned to the grit road leading along the backs of the houses on West Shore Street to see whether anyone was around. A man was placing rubbish in a dustbin near his back door but re-entered his house before Xavier could call to him. He looked at his watch; it was past nine o'clock. He strode around the peninsular to the front of the terrace and considered whether he should call at a cottage offering bed and breakfast then decided against it. If Lena or Jake opened the door, they would hear his French accent and might become suspicious.

Just then a generously proportioned woman with reddish-brown curly hair came out of a nearby front door. She smiled at him, her brown eyes twinkling, animating her kindly young face.

'Shame aboot the dreich weather,' she called across the street. 'Tis no' a day fur a stravaig!'

Xavier gathered she was commenting on the cold conditions but beyond that he had no clue. He nodded, smiled back and stepped towards her. 'Actually I'm looking for someone, a friend of a friend. I was told 'e lives around 'ere.'

'Ah canna stop; ah'm taking Alastair his breakfast.' She nodded at small tinfoil parcel in her hand. 'That's ma husband,' she clarified amiably. 'He forgot his bacon sandwich. Ye can walk wi' me if ye want. Ah hae to be quick, ah've left ma wee bairns in the playpen.'

Xavier caught her drift and stepped alongside her, taking the chance to talk. 'Do you know a Jake Lester?' he asked, treading quickly to keep up with her speedy pace. 'We 'ave a mutual friend. I'm just in Ullapool for a short while and I'd like to say 'ello.'

'Och aye, ah ken Jake and Lena pretty weel. They live next door. Though their name's no Lester ah'm afraid.'

Xavier shook his head and rolled his eyes. 'Tch sorry, I meant Gregory. That's great. Do they own the guest 'ouse then?'

'No, other side. Ah'm sorry but ye willnae catch them this morning, they're oot fur the day.' She turned towards the quay. 'That's me,' she indicated with her head. 'Ma Alastair's the harbourmaster,' she added proudly.

'Do you have their telephone number?' Xavier queried rapidly. 'I'd like to at least speak on the phone.'

'Och aye.' She related a four-digit number. 'Ullapool,' she added.

'Thank you. He won't know me but anyway I'd like it to be a surprise.'

'Aye, ah understand. Weel then.' She nodded goodbye and hurried towards the harbour office.

Xavier repeated the number to himself while digging a pen and a scrap of paper out of one of his jacket pockets. He scribbled it down, walked back up the road almost to the point, took out his little Instamatic camera and snapped a couple of photos of Jake and Lena's house from the front then did the same from the back. He noticed their low back garden gate was bolted and tied securely to its post with bailer twine—to prevent little ones escaping, he thought soberly, a grim image of a small boy running into traffic flashing through his mind.

He spent the next forty minutes wandering the town, getting his bearings, observing the main routes in and out from the northerly and southerly directions. He noted the location of a key-cutting shop and later timed the journey by car from there to the back of Jake's cottage. He returned to the hotel to collect his Ordnance Survey maps of the area. The area around Ullapool was inconveniently detailed on three separate sheets. He studied the Loch Assynt map, which covered the area north of Ullapool. He would have to locate an alternative port for what he had in mind, as Loch Broom was far too busy. Some years previously, he and a friend had spent a wonderful relaxing holiday camping in the Summer Isles, canoeing, fishing and exploring the freshwater lochs, upland moors and woods of the Assynt cnoc-and-lochan terrain. They'd visited Lochinver, which Xavier recalled as a lively fishing village, pretty as a picture but quieter than Ullapool. He decided to reacquaint himself.

He followed the winding road out of Ullapool along the shore of Loch Broom to its mouth then inland in a northerly direction through some old crofting settlements until it curved westwards towards the coast again, passing close by the jagged remnants of Ardvreck castle, a ruined tower house situated on the neck of a small promontory jutting out into Loch Assynt, which he remembered well for its raw vulnerability amongst the rugged resilience of the craggy mountains.

On the outskirts of Lochinver, he headed for the quay, positioned on the opposite side of the charmingly modest northern bay, and located the harbourmaster's office. The day had brightened, although the breeze was still keen, and a number of folk were about. He made enquiries of the harbourmaster, a tall, lanky man with an angular face, who told him where it was possible to hire a small cabin cruiser and purchase the nautical charts he would need, and confirmed he'd need an International Certificate of Competency.

Xavier tried not to let his dismay show. He wouldn't be able to hire the boat without an ICC. *Merde!* It could take him weeks, if not months, to join and complete a suitable training course and obtain a certificate. And even then, he wouldn't want to use his real identity. Near the quay stood a striking Georgian hotel constructed of dark stone with a round tower and distinctive stepped gable-ends. Xavier wasn't hungry but he could do with a hot drink and a chance to sit quietly and think. He ordered a whisky and a pot of coffee and sipped his drinks slowly, staring out at the grey water, a plan forming in his mind. He knew Mari had some kind of recognised boating licence. He didn't want to put her at risk, but it was clear he wouldn't be able to execute his scheme without her help. And if she was involved, he couldn't risk Alain being there too—he was too unpredictable. Having finished his coffee, he used the public telephone in a corner of the lobby to call her.

He didn't say much to begin with, speaking in general terms. 'They're there... I 'ave a number... I've seen the 'ouse... no, I 'aven't seen them yet.' Then he took the plunge. 'I know 'ow it can be done,' he said quietly, 'but there is a problem. I'm sorry, Mari, I need your 'elp.'

A while later, he breathed a relieved sigh as he replaced the receiver. It had been a difficult conversation. He hadn't wanted to discuss all the details of his plan at that moment, for fear of being overheard, but assured her it was watertight. He'd only wanted help with telephone calls and to borrow her ICC, but somehow they'd agreed she'd do more. Perhaps his determination to go through with it regardless had something to do with it. She'd wanted to lessen the risk to himself and the children.

He returned to his table to collect his coat. Tomorrow would bring fresh challenges, but he hoped it would be as fruitful as today.

Plymouth, England, March 1987

Mari replaced the receiver. For a few moments her heart continued to thump alarmingly and waves of adrenalin pulsed through her body, causing her forehead and palms to dampen with sweat and her stomach to churn. She rushed to the bathroom and vomited. Her hands were shaking as she made her way back into the living room to pour herself a large glass of brandy. As she sat on the sofa sipping the fiery, comforting, amber liquid, she contemplated what she'd agreed to do.

In her opinion there was no way Xavier could take the children without help. It would need two people to enter the property and get the toddlers rapidly and safely into the car with minimum noise. Xavier had conceded; he would enter, collect the first child and hand her to Mari while he returned for the second. Additionally, it would be impossible for Xavier to look after two babies and pilot a boat. She'd questioned why he wanted to escape by sea. He judged it the best chance of going unnoticed if the police were called, as he thought it less likely they'd monitor the waterways. She understood why he didn't want his brother involved—Alain was volatile and likely to want to confront Jake and Lena; also he wasn't subtle and was liable to take risks Xavier would not contemplate—and he couldn't ask Fayette to help without Alain's knowledge. Xavier didn't want Pierre or Fran involved either and Mari certainly agreed. She believed someone competent at boat handling and navigation should assist him, as the waters held hidden dangers, and had told him so. At first he'd been adamant that, beyond providing her ICC for him to imitate, he didn't want her embroiled in what was effectively kidnapping; however she couldn't endure the risk of him being caught as a consequence of struggling to accomplish the venture alone. She couldn't bear the possibility of losing him. She still felt a weight of responsibility for the dreadful situation and the children involved; she had to ensure they would be safe and well-cared for during the journey.

The more she considered the more there seemed to be

no choice but to aid her lover, for her own as well as his and the toddlers sakes. But the thought of ripping two young children from the people they knew as Mummy and Daddy, away from everything that was safe and familiar and comforting, and the effect this would have on her one-time friends, made her sick with self-abhorrence and fear.

Chapter Thirty-five

On Monday morning Mari hurried into work early. She'd promised Xavier she'd provide a couple of distraction phone calls and that meant talking to an insurance company and recording the patter on her Dictaphone so she could make notes. She was good at imitating accents but would keep the conversation with Lena to a minimum. Xavier only needed a minute or so. She felt a flicker of panic and the hair on the back of her neck prickled. She dreaded hearing Lena's voice.

Ullapool, Scotland, March 1987

Xavier awoke to the hustle and bustle of Ullapool's fishermen unloading the night's catch of herring and mackerel, lorries and vans coming and going, inflatable craft being loaded with provisions and the constant low hum of engines from the many vessels making their way to and from the klondyking ships in the deep waters of the loch. He had slept later than he'd intended, having been kept awake into the small hours—the hotel bar had been rowdy, full of men drinking keenly, intent on spending some of their hard-earned cash.

He telephoned his employers to tell them he had a family emergency and was likely to be away from work for at least a couple of weeks; as he had expected, they were extremely supportive. After finishing his filling kedgeree breakfast he made his way to the tip of West Shore Street and stood, using his binoculars to gaze out over the loch and back at the quayside. A weak sun had streaked the low, grey, bulbous clouds with a watery yellow tinge and the stiff wind of yesterday had been replaced by a gentle breeze wafting over the water.

It was a quarter to nine when the Lesters' front door opened. Xavier's stomach lurched. He swung his binoculars briefly in that direction, pivoting to face the loch again as soon as he'd established it was Jake—he'd studied the photographs intently—recognising his red-brown wavy hair and athletic stature. Jake was wearing a small green rucksack and strode purposefully down the road, turning left then right to weave into the village centre. Xavier followed at a distance, endeavouring to look as if he knew where he was bound. His theory about Jake's occupation was spot on; he watched as the man unlocked the glass door of the outdoor gear shop and entered its shadowy interior. After a minute or two the lights came on in the building and Jake reappeared at the door to turn the sign to *Open*.

Xavier paced the main street a while, keeping an eye on the front of Jake's store. A few people came and went. It appeared Jake was the only person working there. The previous day he had noted the opening hours did not include a lunchtime closure so judged Jake was likely to be tied to the shop for most of the day.

The clouds had begun to dissipate, the strengthening sun finding its way through broadening breaches in the steely vapour. The air in the sunlit spots was growing warmer. Xavier surreptitiously untied the twine securing Jake and Lena's back gate and sat on the grass within the comfort of a warm shaft of light not too far from their back garden, pretending to watch birds. He was hoping Lena might open the back door, but there was no sign of life for quite a while. Finally, after a couple of hours, he was rewarded with a sighting of her and the two children. She emerged with a basket of washing and proceeded to hang it from a length of clothesline stretching along the garden; as she did so two blonde-haired toddlers dressed warmly in trousers and blue-and-white-striped jumpers tottered about on the grass playing with what looked like a set of colourfully painted wooden blocks.

Xavier gasped involuntarily. These little beings were his flesh and blood. He felt incredibly protective and a tide of anger rolled through him, swelling like a wave heading for the shore. These children were his brother's—they belonged with his family in south-west France, not hidden here in the wilds of Scotland. His mouth set in determination, he walked quickly to the phone box he'd noted a street away. He spoke to Mari for a few moments then returned to his former lookout position. After a minute or two he heard a distant telephone ringing and watched as Lena gathered the children and ushered them into the house. If Mari managed her task effectively, he should have a couple of minutes.

He unlatched the gate into the back garden and swung it open, making sure to close it firmly behind him. He ran down the path to the back door and tried the handle. It was unlocked and he opened it just enough to see into the kitchen beyond. He could hear Lena on the phone in the hallway. The key hung from a nail on the wall the other side of the door, out of reach of the children. He pocketed it and stepped back though the garden, slipping a loop of twine around the gatepost on his way out. Then, walking as quickly along the grit track as he dared without drawing attention, he headed to the store offering a key-cutting service.

With the original and a copy of their back-door key in his pocket, Xavier made his way back to the rear of Jake and Lena's cottage, stopping once more at the phone box to call Mari. This time it was more difficult because the back door was shut; he couldn't hear the phone ring, so had to rely on his watch and hope to God the distraction would work. At the appointed time he gingerly approached the house again. He knew Lena would not be able to lock the back door but had no way of knowing whether she or the children would be in the kitchen. Mari's second call would be on the pretext of imparting a further piece of information that hadn't been discussed. Even if Lena refused to talk further, he'd still have ten or so seconds.

Xavier stood outside to the right of the door, listening intently. He thought he could hear a voice in the distance. He eased the handle down, opening the door just enough to confirm Lena was on the phone again. Pushing the door a little wider, he poked his head around it. A plastic swing bin stood in the gap between a worktop and the space the door opened into. Gently, he threw the door key into the gap, making it look as though it had fallen off the nail. He hoped Lena hadn't been looking for it but if she had she would think she'd simply missed it lying on the floor by the bin.

As Xavier retied the twine thoroughly around the

gatepost and walked away a surge of relief swept through him. He had accomplished the first stage of the plan. Ahead lay a huge challenge but, having set eyes on them, his determination to appropriate the children without Jake and Lena's knowledge had been validated. He would now monitor the family's movements and determine in which room the toddlers slept. He would keep an eye on the weather forecast, organise accommodation further down the coast and the hire of a boat from Lochinver—with the assistance of an ICC forged from Mari's certificate—choose an appropriate night for the endeavour and claim the twins—and the sooner the better.

Chapter Thirty-six

Ullapool, Scotland, April 1987

Ten days later, Xavier collected Mari from the last evening train into Inverness and they set off for Ullapool. They drove north-west, past Lochs Garve and Glascarnoch, between the mountains of Sgurr Mor and Beinn Dearg and onward in silence, not daring to look at one another, as if acknowledging the other person brought into unwelcome focus the reason for their presence; the terrible act which they were about to commit. Eventually, they came alongside Loch Broom, both still staring ahead as the headlights of the old Ford illuminated an occasional bend in the road, contrasting the harsh tarmac scar with the soft shapes of gorse and stunted trees edging the moorland that loomed above them on one side and the expanse of undulating, deep, dark water on the other. A light rain had begun to fall, diffusing the pale glimmer of a waning moon.

After passing through the hamlet of Leckmelm, Xavier pulled into a wooded track on the right, stopping when they were hidden from the main road. Finally he spoke. 'We can't arrive too early. I found this place during my last visit.'

The act of him speaking released some of the tension.

By meagre torchlight Mari poured cups of strong coffee from the thermos Xavier had prepared—they would not sleep tonight—and they discussed the plan. The following night they would stay in Balmacara, then Mari would catch a train back to Inverness and return to Devon the next day. Alain and Fayette would meet Xavier in Balmacara. Xavier would hand over the twins then walk into Kyle the next morning and take the boat back to Lochinver. He was adamant he would handle the boat on his own on the way back. He wanted her out of the area as quickly as possible. He planned to scrap the car when he arrived back in Inverness.

Reviewing the strategy felt unreal to Mari, as if they were merely talking about the plot of a film. They fell into silence again and Mari listened to the voice in her head which spoke of George's death and Lena's breakdown. She tried to counter its persistent accusations. *I know I'm righting a wrong; the children are Alain and Fayette's, not Lena's,* she told herself. *But Lena lost a child,* the voice said. *How will she cope with the loss all over again? It broke her before, she may not survive this.*

Then she realised there was a compromise.

Mari was compelled to share her thoughts. Her voice cut through the shadows. 'Xavier, I'm sorry but I have to say something. I'm so worried. Some part of me feels—no, truly believes—losing both twins is going to kill Lena.' Xavier turned to her, perplexed. He made to speak but she held a hand up. 'Please, just let me finish. I know we've discussed the what-ifs repeatedly and there are so many things to consider and so many possible consequences, but we haven't considered…' she paused, steeling herself to suggest something that filled her equally with horror and hope, '…a situation where both couples have a child.'

'What?' he replied, shock visible. 'Are you suggesting we take one twin and leave the other? Bloody 'ell, Mari!'

She put her hands to her face. She couldn't hold back the tears any longer. 'I know this sounds awful. I mean these are human beings and we're talking about them as if they're belongings. It's unbearable,' she cried. 'But if Lena was left with a child, I think that would save her, give her a reason to go on.' She dissolved into her sobs, her shoulders heaving. 'I'm sorry, I'm so sorry.'

Xavier pulled her gently towards him and enfolded her in his arms the best he could in the confined space, stroking her hair. 'I can't… I…' He heaved a sigh. He had no words.

Reaching behind, he grabbed a blanket to wrap around Mari, winding down the back of her seat until she could settle more comfortably. As Mari's sobs subsided in the semi-darkness he tried to focus on the awful task, stay alert to problems and minimise risk. His conscience goaded him. *We're here to return Alain and Fayette's children to their real parents* he instructed it doggedly. *I have to right the wrong Lena and Jake have done to my family.* Concern about Mari's safety surfaced. *You should never have involved her,* he reflected, guilt twisting his gut. *What if we get caught? What if Lena and Jake go to the police as soon as they discover the twins missing, despite the jeopardy?* He considered Mari's words. There'd seemed not to be any other way but maybe there was something in what she'd said. Perhaps there was a potential benefit of taking only one child. He doubted Jake and Lena would go to the police and risk losing the child they had left, especially if he warned them off. But he pushed the notion away. *You can't leave one of Alain and Fayette's children behind.*

Another couple of hours passed. Although Mari appeared to be sleeping, Xavier doubted she was. Even so, he didn't disturb her. He sat, in silence, unable to erase her words; it was all he could think about.

He shivered and held up his watch to the torchlight. Finally it was time. He started the car and was glad when a weak current of warm air reached his feet. Mari sat up, repositioning her seat. She glanced at him and he nodded noiselessly. They drove the short distance to Ullapool in silence, both dreading what must come next.

As they reached the outskirts of Ullapool, Mari pulled her silk scarf over her head and turned to Xavier. Her tense features were cast in shadow. He squeezed her gloved hand.

'*Ça va aller*. Don't worry,' he whispered.

They turned left and drove slowly along Shore Street, past countless pursers and mid-water trawlers awaiting their crews in the crowded harbour, behind which loomed the huge grey shapes of klondyking vessels anchored in the loch.

They continued along the shore almost to the end of the small headland then Xavier swung the car into a side street and around the back of a long row of small whitewashed terraced houses. It was two-thirty in the morning and the lane was quiet and dark.

Mari's stomach heaved and turned as a rush of anxiety swept through her body. Her hands were shaking as she pushed a stray tendril of hair back under her scarf.

Xavier cut the engine, donning his gloves before they exited the car quietly. His tall dark form was almost concealed within the inky dankness. Mari clenched her teeth, took a deep breath and stepped away from the vehicle. They trod carefully over a strip of grass between the road and a series of low walls running along the backs of the properties, separating the gardens from the grassland beyond.

She was terrified. Her stomach was constantly trying to visit her throat. She couldn't stop herself shaking. Stabs of guilt perforated her lungs making it difficult to breathe. Mari told herself to be angry. The twins belonged with their rightful parents. It's Lena and Jake who have wronged everyone. They all understood the reason, the trigger for their flight, but still the betrayal was done and the wrong must be put right. In the grip of fear, Mari became infuriated; with herself as well as Lena for putting her in this position. Anger was the only way to regain control, to calm her quaking limbs and steel herself for what was to come. The voice in her head persisted—*what if someone sees you? But we're dressed in black and I can hardly see six feet in front of me*, she countered. *But what if the babies wake up? What if Lena and Jake hear you?*

Xavier had located a wooden gate in one of the walls and was standing by it when she caught up with him. He lifted the latch slowly and moved cautiously up the concrete garden path dissecting the lawn. Mari hesitated then followed him gingerly towards the house, testing the ground with each small step, wary of tripping.

On reaching the back door he took a key from his jacket pocket and placed it in the lock. She watched him shrink into himself slightly, wary of making a noise, as he gently turned the key. The door opened without a sound and he took an audible breath.

Mari nodded to him silently, reached into her coat

pocket and handed him some white cloth overshoes which he placed over his own. She watched his tall frame disappear through the kitchen into a dark hallway as she waited just outside the back door. Blood pulsed in her ears, marking an eternity second by second. The waiting was unbearable and she wanted to scream. She put her shaking hands over her mouth, pressing them against her face.

Xavier located the twins' bedroom without difficulty, his previous surveillance paying off. The door was slightly ajar. With a quick glance across the narrow landing toward the other bedroom door, he entered the room, the dim nightlight casting a ghostly shadow on the wall. The toddlers were sleeping soundly on their backs, each wrapped shoulder high in a white blanket, each in an identical painted wooden cot. Their serene little features displayed contentment.

He let go of the breath he was holding and quietly swore to himself.

'*Fils de pute!*'

He ran his hands through his hair. He was facing the most important decision of his life and time had run out. He was deep under water, the weight of responsibility constricting his lungs. A torrent of judgements and emotions flooded through him, unwelcome, causing his body to shake. Anger struggled with guilt and fear, compassion with duty.

Instinct prevailed. '*Putain!*' he cursed again.

He stepped towards the nearest cot and carefully lifted the child along with her blanket. As he did so, he noticed her twin had opened her eyes and was watching him though the gloom. Her eyes widened as he stared back. He didn't wait another second but, cradling the child in his arms, rushed out of the room, down the stairs, out though the kitchen door and down the garden path.

Mari held out her arms for the child, looking at him in astonishment as he sped passed her. Then panic set in and she dashed after him.

They drove off at speed as a toddler's wretched wail hung in the dank night behind them.

Chapter Thirty-seven

West Highlands, Scotland, April 1987

They arrived in Lochinver in pouring rain. There were no lit streetlights among the ribbon of buildings on the east side of the bay or along the road which curved south-westwards towards the breakwater. However, a couple of bobbing lights shimmered weakly through the gloom from the harbour. On renting the Hardy cabin cruiser, Xavier had been told to expect fishing trawler activity day and night. Although commercial fishing was in decline, this was still the main business in the tiny West Highland settlement.

Xavier drove slowly around the bay in front of a long strip of small, whitewashed cottages until he reached an area where he could pull off the road by the water's edge. He turned in his seat to look at Mari on the back seat with the child in her arms. She put one finger to her lips. 'Shhh, she's asleep,' she breathed.

'We 'ave two choices,' he whispered. 'Either wait somewhere out of sight in the car, or transfer to the boat now. It's about three hours till dawn so if you still think we can't risk setting off until daybreak because of the rocks and unlit islands out there, we need to decide now whether we wait here or onboard.'

Mari shrugged. 'Do what you think is best.'

'Okay, let's go to the boat—the fewer people around to see us with a child the better. It looks like there may be a couple of fishing boats on their way in or out but they'll be occupied with their own business. Can you get 'er into that cot thing without 'er waking up?'

'I'll try,' Mari responded softly, 'but she seems happier being held. If she stirs, I'm just going to hold her and you can bring her carrycot.'

Xavier started up the Ford again and they continued in silence, following the road as it snaked around the bay past more houses, the tall stone-built hotel and a chandlery, until they reached the port. He swung the car onto the quayside and parked amongst a row of vehicles opposite the harbourmaster's office. The child stirred and murmured as Mari tried to replace her in the cot, but didn't wake.

'She must be tired,' Mari whispered, smiling pensively at the little round face which was just visible amid layers of blanket.

'I'm not surprised, she was crying most of the journey,' returned Xavier. 'I 'ope she stays quiet until we can get out of the 'arbour.'

Mari frowned. 'I thought we were supposed to be a family going on a holiday along the coast.'

'We are,' he confirmed, 'but the less attention we draw to ourselves the better. Come on, let's get 'er onto the boat.'

Xavier noticed Mari shiver; the night had grown cold as the damp set in. He assured her they could get warm in the cabin cruiser, where there was a gas stove and he had stored plenty of blankets. He located the boat, moored alongside a long metal-clad concrete quay which jutted out into deep water, and they carefully transferred themselves and the sleeping toddler onto it before he returned to the car.

He searched the inside of the car to make sure they'd left nothing incriminating; he had no intention of being caught. He checked the boot and found the second travel cot. A chill rushed through his body and his stomach turned. Christ, what would Alain say when he only delivered one child? He shook his head as if to fling the thought away. He'd deal with that later. Snatching the cot, he closed the boot quietly and locked the car. As the Ford wasn't registered in his name, he figured it would be safe to leave it among the other cars in this tiny fishing port for a couple of days.

The rain had diminished to drizzle, but the sky was still inky. Xavier climbed back on board and into the cockpit in darkness, having left the torch with Mari. He resecured the canopy and felt his way into the main cabin via a small set of steps. Once there he locked the cabin door, located the Calor-gas light he'd left in the galley and lit it with his cigarette lighter, adjusting the brightness to a subtle glow that reflected off the interior's polished wood surfaces, generating a rosy radiance. Mari was sitting in a small, white-cushioned seating area with the cot resting on a pull-out table in front of her. She'd found a quilt and blankets in the front berth and was cocooned within one. She looked up at Xavier anxiously as he busied lighting the stove and filling the kettle from a plastic water bottle. He smiled lovingly as he stepped towards her and kissed the top of her head. She turned her face upward, her mouth towards his. Longing languished in her eyes and drew her features into a pained expression.

Xavier recognised that look; it tore at his heart; desire for his touch, for reassurance, protection, but most of all for a child of her own. He perched beside her on the edge of the small cushion, softly kissed her lips and enveloped her in his arms, stroking her hair and whispering, '*Tout ira bien, ma petite Souci.*' She clung to him and he wished time would stop so she could remain in his embrace and be protected from the world indefinitely.

As the kettle boiled he left her side and returned to the stove. 'What we both need is an 'ot drink and some food inside us,' he said practically, spooning coffee into two plastic mugs. 'Then we should rest for an hour or so.'

'I don't feel hungry, but I'd like to shut my eyes for a bit,' she responded, yawning. 'Hopefully the little one will sleep for a while longer.'

He handed her a steaming mug and she cupped her hands around it, breathing in the comforting odour. She shut her eyes as Xavier melted butter into a pan and proceeded to fry bacon and eggs. The smoked bacon sizzled and spat in the fat, sending a delicious aroma around the cabin. Despite herself and the fact it was not long after three o'clock in the morning, her stomach rumbled. The warmth from the stove had begun to warm the little v-shaped space.

'There's a small electric 'eater, but I don't want to drain the battery. I don't know 'ow much charge it 'as. Once the engine is started we'll have diesel-powered 'eating,' Xavier remarked. 'It won't be long before it's warm in 'ere,' he nodded towards the front berth, 'then I suggest you put the cot on one bed and lie on the other.'

'Where will you sleep? You need some rest as well.'

Mari was concerned.

'I'll be alright. This table folds to make a bed between the seats.' He buttered bread and served up. ''Ere, eat this, you'll feel better for it,' he said, handing her a plate of hot breakfast. He carefully lifted the travel cot with its sleeping occupant and removed it to the berth then sat with his meal at the table, opposite Mari. 'Given the forecast and tides, remind me how long it'll take to reach the Kyle of Lochalsh,' he said, wiping bread around his plate.

'Well, it's about sixty-five nautical miles,' she answered between mouthfuls of yolk-laden bacon. 'Given the engine size this boat's top speed is about fifteen knots, but it won't be possible to go at top speed for most of the way. These are tricky waters and there are a few rocks on the charts which we'll have to make our way around. So I reckon it will take at least eight or nine hours. Dawn is around six o'clock; if we leave then we should be arriving at the Kyle of Lochalsh not far off high tide, which means the tide will be with us in Kyle Akin. Have you got the chart?'

He reached into his rucksack and unfolded a marine chart and she reminded him of the rocks and little islands they would need to circumvent, particularly in Kyle Akin, a stretch of water between Lochalsh and the Isle of Skye where there was a strong tidal flow back and forth.

Suddenly the sound of whimpering came from the berth, causing them to freeze and look at one another, hardly daring to breathe. But the toddler was just muttering in her sleep and the noises ceased after a minute or so. Aware they only had a couple of hours to rest, Xavier set the timer on his watch and they cleared the table, turned off the stove and went to their beds. Despite the anxiety pumping a heightened level of adrenalin through Mari's body, exhaustion dragged her consciousness into dormancy within minutes. Xavier lay awake awhile, his mind tossing thoughts like a tumble dryer, but eventually he too succumbed to sleep.

They were woken around five-forty by a wail and cries of 'Mummeee, Mummeeee!'

Mari jumped up and lifted Suzette out of the cot, holding her to her chest and rocking her. 'It's okay, darling. We're looking after you for a while.'

Suzette continued to cry, kicking her legs and moving her head from side to side. It was freezing in the cabin. Mari carried the toddler to her own bunk and tried to settle her down on her lap wrapped in a blanket but the moment she saw Mari's face she screamed again and called for her mummy.

Xavier offered her mashed banana in a small plastic bowl. 'I'm warming milk. See if you can get 'er interested in eating. That might take 'er mind off 'er mum. 'Ere, I also got these.' He put a large rust-coloured teddy bear and a brown stuffed dog on the bed. They were almost as big as Suzette. 'I should 'ave brought something from 'er cot…' he said ruefully.

Mari turned Suzette around on her lap to face the toys and made them bob around on the bed. The child continued to cry but reached one plump hand out to touch the dog. Its fur was long and soft and she curled her little fingers into it. Mari continued to talk to her in calming tones and eventually Suzette leaned forward, grabbed the dog with both hands and put her face to its flank. Over the next five minutes or so her sobs subsided as she played. Mari then managed to persuade her to have some warm milk and banana. She seemed hungry. Xavier had bought a packet of disposable nappies and a couple of sets of clothes; he located his purchases.

'Try these. I never knew buying nappies would be so complicated,' he grunted. 'They're sold according to weight, not age! I 'ope they fit—there's no alternative. At least you can buy clothes by age. Right, we've got five minutes before starting 'er up,' he warned, 'then I'll take over with Suzette.'

The contentment brought on by food and the toy dog abruptly disappeared as soon as Mari tried to change Suzette's nappy; she wailed again. Mari called to Xavier to help, so he held the dog above the child to grab her attention. It worked. They managed to change her nappy and pull a few clothes onto her squirming body; socks, trousers, a long-sleeved t-shirt and a jumper. They worked quickly while the sky turned a pale yellow as the sun rose slowly behind the mountains to the east of the harbour.

Mari entered the cockpit and started the engine, allowed it to warm until she was sure it was running smoothly then cast off the bow and stern lines and gradually moved away from the dock. The quay was busy with fishermen unloading their night catches. Everyone was occupied. She steered alongside the breakwater then out into the sea loch aiming west-south-west, avoiding the protuberance of Glas Leac in the middle of the water and heading south of the much larger Soyea Island. Passing A' Chleit island, she made for the first big headland of Rubha Còigeach. Rounding this, she turned south-west for the double headland protecting Loch Ewe.

She was glad to focus on a task that needed her full attention; to put thoughts of the toddler out of her mind for a while, albeit with difficulty, to ensure her safety.

Thin streaks of cloud tinted pink by the sun's rays had painted themselves across a blueing sky. A light south-westerly breeze wafted towards them and the boat rose and fell in the slight swell. The air temperature had risen to five degrees according to one of the gauges. It was warmer in the canopied cockpit, protected from the wind; however, she still felt cold despite her four layers including a thick woollen jumper and waxed jacket.

She opened the door to the cabin, poking her head through to request a mug of coffee and tell Xavier she judged it safe for him to take over at the helm for a while. She'd set a course and he should just keep the boat following it. The escaping warm air comforted her chilled face for a few moments—the diesel-powered heating obviously working well. Xavier and the child sat on his makeshift bed playing with paper and crayons he'd taken from his stash of purchases. He was drawing animals and naming them and Suzette was repeating the names. In some cases she knew the animal before being told. She kept repeating 'dog' and pointing at the toy.

'She seems taken with the dog,' observed Mari. 'They didn't have a dog, though.'

Xavier nodded. 'Hmm. Per'aps someone they knew 'ad one. I'll make you a sandwich with that coffee then we'll swap.' He climbed off the bed and stepped toward the galley, keeping one eye on Suzette. 'She's a wriggler. If I don't watch 'er every second she'll be off the bed, crawling around the floor and into all the cupboards,' he said in an amused tone. 'Also, she keeps repeating something that sounds like *ayah*. I don't know if she's asking for something. Any clues?'

Mari turned down the corners of her mouth. 'No idea, sorry.'

'Oh, well,' he shrugged, then changed the subject. 'Where are we?'

'Just passing the Summer Isles.'

'I'll come and look, they're beautiful. I'll bring 'er with me.'

'Wrap her in a blanket, it's cold out here,' Mari warned.

To their left an archipelago of dark shapes rose out of the silver-blue sea, silhouetted by the eastern sun. Like a family of giant sleeping seals, some considerable in size and other smaller isles barely visible above the water, they basked under the flushed sky. In the distance the crags of Ben Mor Coigach rose magnificently.

'I wish we 'ad time to explore the islands,' Xavier spoke regretfully. Suzette was wide-eyed and fidgeting in her wrappings. He repositioned her in his arms. 'I stayed on Tanera Mor, the largest one, a few years ago. It was so peaceful. I canoed around some of the isles. You can see otters and seals and even… hmm… what do you call those creatures like… umm… *dauphin*?'

'You mean dolphins?'

'Yes, but not them.'

'Porpoises?'

'Exactly. You can see them in the summer 'ere. And there are lots of birds and wildflowers. I'd love to show you,' he continued, enthusiasm burgeoning in his voice. 'Per'aps we could come back one day for an 'oliday.'

Mari's eyes flashed. Her rare temper had been ignited by his spark of normality. But things weren't normal. The situation they were in was as far from normal as she could bear to contemplate. She knew it was unfair to take her feelings out on him. His justification for what they were doing was rectification and retribution. She'd agreed to help because of her part in the original plan and because she loved him. He had repeatedly told her she was not to blame; she felt guilty all the same and with just cause, she believed. But what they were doing now—stealing a child for God's sake—was wrong too! How could he even contemplate coming back to visit, for pleasure, this place where they'd committed such an act? It would be forever tarnished to her.

She bit her lip and held out her arms. 'Give her to me. You take over steering,' she told him curtly. She took Suzette below, banging the cabin door shut.

Her emotions were all over the place. One minute she was fully supportive of Xavier, feeling nothing but tenderness towards him; the next, her heart ached with yearning for a baby—for a few reckless moments when they'd boarded the boat, thoughts of taking the child for herself flitted through her mind; leaving her home and estranged husband and running away with Xavier somewhere far where they would never be found, though in reality they could never deprive Alain and Fayette of Suzette. But the next moment she was racked with guilt and fear, her stomach somersaulting and her throat tight. She had to get a grip on herself. She took a deep breath and told herself firmly they were set on this course—they had discussed it at length and agreed. She should try to remove her emotions from the situation. She would get on with what they had to do then return home to her life, an existence that had nothing to do with any of this.

Mari spent the next few hours keeping Suzette occupied and fed, making hot drinks and food for herself and Xavier and trying to rest. At regular intervals she checked they were still following the correct course. Occasionally she took the helm whilst he used the head. They opened the cabin door to allow a little of the warmth to reach him in the cockpit. Xavier concentrated on steering and avoiding other vessels, particularly the large klondyking ships from Eastern Europe emerging from Loch Broom loaded with mackerel. Once they were west of the headland at Rubha Reidh Mari set a new course southward towards the inner sound between the Isle of Skye and the mainland. West of the mouth of Loch Torridon she took over the helm again. Suzette had fallen asleep to the gentle rocking of the boat and the steady judder of its engine. Xavier began clearing away so they could disembark quickly once they reached Kyle of Lochalsh.

The strengthening sun had dissipated the cirrus clouds as Mari steered the boat past the islands of Rona and Raasay and east of Eilean Mòr. The grey and white rocks of the isles, topped with yellow lichen and hosting clumps of furry sea ivory, rose out of the sea, water lapping at their bases. Further from the water she recognised cushions of grey-green sea pinks awaiting their flowers, which gave way to patches of heather. Guillemots, gannets and fulmars circled and dived in the sound, paying no heed to the boat's dishonest cargo.

Mari was concerned about the rocks north of Eilean Bàn at the entrance to Loch Alsh, so chose a course south-west of the little island before heading for the harbour. The tidal stream in Kyle Akin was with them but the port ahead was busy and there were several cruising yachts, small fishing boats and supply vessels in the water, as well as two large ferries crossing between the mainland and Skye. Mari managed to navigate their approach and, with Xavier's help, moored alongside a pier opposite a large hotel on the waterfront. The water was choppy with the wash from vessels coming and going from the large railway pier nearby, making disembarking tricky. Luckily Suzette was still asleep, so Mari could lay her in the travel cot. She placed a little blue knitted hat on the child's head, obscuring her wispy blonde hair then pulled the hood of her own coat over her head and wrapped a scarf around her neck and mouth whilst Xavier donned his false beard and glasses, making him seem yet more like a stranger. Between them they carried the cot and their bags the short distance to the taxi rank outside the station.

Xavier had arranged the rental of a cottage to the north of the nearby village of Balmacara. Less than fifteen minutes later they were alone again outside a small, whitewashed building with little brown dormer windows set in its grey tiled roof. Located up a rough narrow track off the tarmac lane, the cottage nestled into a hillside and was surrounded by pasture liberally peppered with rowan trees. It was perfectly secluded. Mari gave a heavy sigh of relief as Xavier closed the front door, cocooning them in a safe haven.

But Xavier couldn't yet relax. He still had to face his brother, who was expecting to receive two children.

Chapter Thirty-eight

Xavier walked into the quiet village of Balmacara, where there was a pay phone and a shop for him to buy supplies. It was the first time he'd been alone since meeting Mari in Inverness nineteen hours ago; the first time he'd truly been with his thoughts. As he walked between the charming, whitewashed houses with their pretty gardens his situation felt unreal. Here was he, calmly strolling around this idyllic backwater in the late afternoon sunshine, a kidnapper with a stolen child and a married lover stashed a mile up the road. For a few moments he felt as if he was playing a character in a story written by someone else, observing himself, detached and impassive. Everything around him was so normal, yet he was trapped in a waking nightmare, partly of his own making. When his task was completed—when he had given the child to his brother—he would go home to France but what he had done would follow him for the rest of his life. He would never be able to escape his conscience. He would always be culpable and fearful of being apprehended. He wished to God he'd never become involved. But it was no use wishing; he had to hold his nerve.

Three days previously he had summoned Alain and Fayette to Scotland, warning them to make the long journey by car rather than use the train. He hadn't told them his exact plans as he hadn't wanted to chance Alain turning up during their implementation, predisposed to impulsiveness and liable to go off on his own tack. Xavier had planned everything meticulously with as few risks as possible for the sake of them all. Alain and Fayette had stayed the preceding night in Fort William and were awaiting his instructions. Their call was brief. Xavier gave his brother their location and refused to be drawn by Fayette in the background excitedly shouting questions about the children.

As he re-entered the cottage, Xavier shouted to Mari, 'We 'ave under two hours!'

She appeared from the living room, distraught. 'She's been wailing ever since she woke up. But I've managed to feed her our last piece of bread and a bit of cheese. She keeps saying *ayah* and calling for her mum. It's breaking my heart, Xavier!'

Xavier stepped towards her and encircled her in his arms, holding her tightly. 'You know where she belongs now,' he said softly, kissing her hair. 'Fayette and Alain will take good care of 'er. She'll be so precious to them. She will be greatly loved, you know that. It's nearly over for us now. By the time they get 'ere, you'll be on your way 'ome.'

Mari turned her tear-stained face towards him and nodded her assent, taking comfort from his embrace. They kissed; a long, impassioned touching of lips and hearts and souls. They knew it would be the last time for a while.

Just then Suzette crawled out of the living room into the hallway and looked up at them. Her little cheeks were red from crying, but her face now wore a blithe expression. She sat on her bottom, turned and pointed back into the room. 'Dog,' she said, then turned to look at them again and gave a big smile.

Xavier grinned back, relieved to see her mood had improved. Mari's face lit in a radiant smile as she bent to pick Suzette up, returning to play with her and the toy dog. Xavier recognised she wanted to interact with the child for as long as possible before she had to leave.

He rustled them up a cheese omelette and they ate sitting on the sofa with Suzette, Mari feeding her pieces of apple and pretending to give some to the dog as well.

After a short while he looked at his watch. 'It's nearly four-fifteen. You'd better get going. You can call a taxi from the village.'

'I think I'll walk,' Mari announced. 'The route along the main road is just three miles but it's only about two miles further if I continue up this lane and circle around the back of the hill behind us.' She reached for their road map. 'It looks like a narrow road most of the way until Badicaul, then I'll not be far from Kyle.'

'Hmmm.' Xavier didn't like to think of her wandering the countryside on her own, but determination was written on her face. It was unlikely anyone would be looking for her and it would be a quiet route with less chance of being noticed. Alain shouldn't be coming from the direction of Kyle but it was best not to take any risks.

'It won't be dark for about three hours,' Mari continued. 'I'll have plenty of time and the trains to Inverness are frequent. In any case,' she shook her head briefly as if to dismiss his concern, 'I need to clear my head and make peace with myself before sitting on a crowded train.'

So it was decided. Mari would walk to the station in Kyle to catch a train to Inverness. Xavier would see his brother and Fayette on their way then deliver the Lesters a threatening phone call. He'd walk into Kyle the next morning before taking the boat back to Lochinver.

Mari donned her thick jumper again, packed her remaining belongings into a rucksack and was about to pull on her walking boots when the crunch of tyres sounded on the gravel drive.

'Jesus, it's not Alain already, is it?' she exclaimed, peeking around the net curtain at the kitchen window. 'Christ, it is. They're early.'

Xavier looked around from the sink, his face set with panic. '*Merde*!' He knew Mari would not want to meet Fayette and Alain for the first time here, now. Plus her involvement in the kidnapping must be kept from his brother; it was a security policy and he wouldn't let Mari relinquish that protection.

They glanced around the room, their eyes resting on a door under the staircase which led to a broom cupboard. Mari threw in her rucksack and walking boots and followed rapidly. There was just enough space for her to crouch between a bucket and a vacuum cleaner.

'Give me enough time to get out!' she whispered. 'Take them into the other room.'

Xavier nodded and closed the door. A knocking sounded from the hallway.

'Wait!' Mari hissed, 'my coat!'

Xavier ran to retrieve her raincoat from a hook by the front door, dashed back and threw it into the cupboard. 'Love you!'

Her reply was lost as he shut the door again and walked quickly to the front entrance, trying to compose himself.

Alain and Fayette were standing on the stone step wearing jovial expressions. Their southern French tans weirdly out of place in northern Scotland. On seeing Xavier Alain threw open his arms and kissed Xavier on both cheeks, patting his brother on the back as he gave him a hug. '*Ahhh, bonjour mon frère! Ça va?*'

'*Pas vraiment,*' Xavier replied grimly, turning his attention to his sister-in-law. '*Bonjour Fayette. Entres. Il fait froid n'est-ce pas?*'

'*Oui,*' she laughed, shivering, '*il fait très froid en Ecosse!*'

Xavier took a deep breath as he ushered them into the living room where Suzette was playing with the teddy bear. '*Voila Suzette,*' he declared as assuredly as possible.

Tears spilled from Fayette's pained blue eyes and her expression radiated love as she moved slowly towards the toddler. Sinking to her knees in front of the sofa, she beamed at Suzette, gently taking hold of one tiny hand. Suzette's little fingers curled around her forefinger as Fayette stroked the back of the child's hand with her thumb. She glanced at Xavier for the briefest of moments, glowing with elation.

Alain stood motionless, watching his wife, compassion and rapture rooting him to the ground. At length Fayette took Suzette in her arms and, holding the child to her breast, rocked her slowly from side to side. '*Mon bébé, mon bébé,*' she repeated, over and over. Wiping tears from his eyes, Alain joined them on the floor, encircling them both in his arms. They stayed there for some moments, a new family.

Xavier turned, tiptoed out of the room and poked his head into the kitchen. There was no sign of Mari. He was returning to close the door to the living room so he could check the kitchen cupboard in relative safety when Alain pulled the door open again, grinning. '*Merci*' he said gratefully; '*merci!*'

Then came the question Xavier was dreading: 'Where is her sister?'

Alain followed his brother into the kitchen. Xavier hoped Mari had been able to make her escape.

Mari had been trying to put on her boots and lace them up in the dark confines of the cubby-hole without making a noise. She'd found this impossible and had had to open the door slightly, allowing in a chink of light and affording more space to manoeuvre. With her boots secure, she'd made it across the room to the back door and attempted to pull back the bolt, but found it was rusty. She thought she could work it free, avoiding the squeal of metal on metal, if she rubbed soap into the joints. She'd got as far as dripping washing up liquid around the pin when she'd heard footsteps in the hallway and had dashed back into the cupboard, pulling the door closed using a hook on the inside from which hung a couple of dusty aprons. Shortly afterwards she heard Xavier and Alain enter the kitchen.

'Xavier, is she sleeping? Is she upstairs?' A hint of uneasiness had crept into Alain's tone.

Xavier turned around to face his brother and took a deep breath. 'She's not here,' he replied purposefully.

Alain shook his head in disbelief, his quiff of dark curls bobbing back and forth. 'What do you mean she's not here?' he asked, incredulous. 'Where is she?'

'I didn't take her,' Xavier answered quietly.

Alain became angry. Clearly, he couldn't believe what he was hearing. 'What were you thinking? Why the hell didn't you take both children?' he responded heatedly, gesturing in astonishment.

'I… I couldn't. I just couldn't,' Xavier faltered then regained his conviction. 'Lena and Jake would have likely gone to the police. I believe leaving one child guarantees they won't.'

'You can't barter with my children,' his brother thundered.

Mari's words echoed in Xavier's head: *losing both the twins will kill her.* 'I…' Xavier began but changed his mind. Alain would never understand.

Alain was enraged. 'What! You fucking bastard! You know what we've been through because of them, not to mention that huge amount of money!' he screamed. 'You are absolutely unbelievable! Jesus!' He hit his fist against the kitchen wall.

'I'm sorry.' Xavier didn't know what else to say.

'You know what I think?' Alain bellowed. 'I think this was Mari's doing. I bet she suggested leaving one child for her poor bereaved friend,' he retorted nastily. 'Where is she?'

'She's not here. I didn't want her involved,' Xavier snapped.

'Too late for that, brother,' Alain sneered. 'She was involved from the start. It was her idea, remember? You know, I bet she had a hand in this whole situation. She and that Lester woman probably shared the cash. Christ, it's enough to buy four houses up here. Mari wanted Lena to be left with a child, so she has a chance to play mother, to make up for her own childlessness. Can't you see you've been played! For God's sake open your eyes!'

'That's bullshit! She would never have done that! All

she wanted was to help. She's spent the last twenty months feeling guilty. Jesus, Alain, she's been helping me track them down! It's taken all this time to find them and I never stopped looking, not for a moment. You know that!' Xavier returned adamantly.

'No, no, no!' Alain shouted with increasing forcefulness, 'Mari and the Lesters, they've conned us. Where are they? You tell me where they are and, by Jesus, I'll make them pay!'

'Alain, calm down! This is madness. If you go charging in there, you'll put us all in jeopardy. As things are they're not going to talk—I've made sure of that. I've been careful and I was well prepared, plus they don't know me. If you show up now, you'll be noticed, I guarantee,' Xavier warned. 'Take Suzette and go back to France. Live your life!'

'When you told me you'd found them after all this time, we agreed a plan. You've only delivered half of it. I want the other half and I'm going to get it. She's mine; I have a right to have her,' Alain threatened.

'Jesus, Alain, listen to yourself! These are lives we're talking about, ours and theirs: children, not commodities!'

'Don't you think I know that?' Alain roared. 'Christ, have you any idea what we've endured, what Fayette has suffered?'

'I'm sorry. I know it's been horrendous,' Xavier answered regretfully.

Alain lowered his voice, but it was full of menace. 'So where are they, Xavier?'

'For the last time Alain, don't risk everything!' Xavier entreated. 'If not for you then for Fayette, for Suzette!

Alain took hold of Xavier's jacket at the neck and

shoved him hard against the kitchen wall. 'Fucking tell me where they are!'

Xavier had borne enough. He'd lived this nightmare for nearly two years and he'd risked everything for his brother. He wanted to be out of there, out of his brother's life. If Alain was going to fuck up, he wanted to be nowhere near. He snapped.

'Ullapool,' he replied flatly. 'But if you get caught, it's on you—both children. Do you understand! Do you? Because I've done my best for you and now I'm washing my hands of it. You're a fool if you go anywhere near the Lesters again,' he finished reproachfully.

The kitchen door opened fully and Fayette appeared with Suzette in her arms. Suzette's little round face wore an anxious look and her bottom lip trembled. 'You've frightened her,' Fayette accused tearfully.

'You can blame your brother-in-law for that,' Alain declared contemptuously. 'He hasn't got the balls to do what's necessary and now I have to finish the job.'

'Alain, please! He's been trying to help us.' Fayette was careful to keep her voice calm for the sake of the child, although she was shaking.

Xavier turned to Fayette. 'I'm so sorry,' he said sadly. 'I had a split second to make the decision and I couldn't do it. I just couldn't take both of them.' Not waiting for a reaction, he walked past her into the hall and started up the stairs. 'I'll get her things,' he uttered miserably.

Fayette wrapped Suzette in a little all-in-one outdoor suit she'd brought and placed the knitted bonnet over her fine hair and delicate ears whilst Alain loaded the car with all the items Xavier had bought for her. All the while Fayette murmured reassuringly to the child, who seemed to have taken to her. When Xavier appeared in the doorway Fayette looked up at him, bestowing a gentle, non-judgemental smile. 'How do you know her name?' she whispered. 'How do you know this is Suzette?'

'Their names were on the cots,' he replied simply.

'Thank you,' she said quietly. It was heartfelt.

Xavier watched as Fayette placed Suzette into the cot on the back seat and climbed in beside her. Alain returned from the car for a moment to stand beside him.

'I'm going to take Fayette and Suzette down south then I'm going to Ullapool,' Alain stated doggedly. 'And you should know—I am doing it for Fayette.'

'Leave! Now! Take your family and go!' Xavier turned his back on his brother; Alain did the same.

It had been nearly impossible for Mari to maintain her composure, trapped as she was in the understairs cupboard, listening to the toxic fraternal exchange. Distress had quickly turned to fury at Alain's hateful words. How dare he accuse her of betrayal! It sickened her to think someone believed she could behave so wickedly. After all she'd done for Xavier's brother! She didn't even know him. She'd only become involved as an act of kindness because she loved Xavier and so deeply understood the pain of not being able to have children. Was she so obsessed with having a child it could skew others' perception of her to that extent? Because of Alain, she'd turned into a kidnapper: a criminal. She'd wanted to rage at Alain, to drum her fists on his chest and scream, to remind him of the huge risk she and Xavier had just taken—for him. Not to mention the heartache she'd experienced at ripping a child from its parents, listening to her cry for hours, unable to provide sufficient comfort, becoming emotionally attached then having to give her to someone else.

She could bear no more. She had to get out of the house and away from the venomous situation that had poisoned her life for two years and would continue to do so if she didn't cut it out of her existence. She would never be free of it if she stayed with Xavier and she would never be accepted into his family because of her role in shaping it.

While the others were preoccupied in the living room and outside the front door, Mari slipped out of the cupboard, quietly closed the kitchen door and turned her attention to the bolt on the back door. The washing up liquid had done its job and, with jiggling, she moved the fastening back. She turned the key in the mortise lock and flung the door open, rushing out into the cold early evening air. On reaching a low wire fence at the garden boundary she leapt over with ease and didn't stop running until she'd made it to the protection of a group of rowan trees on the hillside a few hundred yards from the cottage. Stopping briefly to catch her breath, tears streaming down her cheeks, she took one last look behind her before making her way through some dense heather scrub and another area of woodland onto the lane north of the village just before it cut behind the hill. Thus she began her miserable journey to Kyle, to Inverness and ultimately back to meagre normality.

Chapter Thirty-nine

Xavier trudged back into Balmacara, the appalling row with his brother still raging in his head. After Alain had sped away, his tyres spitting up gravel to pepper the windows, Xavier noticed the open door in the kitchen and realised, his heart plummeting, Mari would have overheard the argument, including Alain's accusations. He ached to hold and reassure her but knew it'd be a while before he could do that again. He felt utterly miserable and tried to concentrate on the few remaining tasks.

With each stride, he became more determined to deliver such a frightening warning to the Lesters it would guarantee their silence and make them leave Ullapool without delay. He had to prevent Alain from blundering into their lives to abduct the other twin and no doubt getting caught, which would put them all at risk. He must protect them all but especially Mari. He was sure Suzette's sister would be safe and happy with Lena and Jake. It was the best solution for everyone.

By the time he reached the phone box Xavier was convinced he'd done the right thing. He glanced around. It was quiet. The pulse in his temples throbbed as he stepped inside and dialled the number hurriedly scrawled on a piece of paper, crumpled from being thrust into his jeans pocket.

After only three rings there was a crackle then a low, choked male voice. 'Yes.'

It wasn't a question. In that single word Xavier heard fear and resignation. He steeled himself and chose as few words as possible.

'Stay silent, no police, or I'm coming for the other one,' he growled, inwardly disconcerted at how like a stereotypical villain he sounded. He heard a sudden anguished cry in the background. 'Leave Ullapool… disappear… or you'll lose 'er as well.'

Silence.

'You understand?' he snarled.

'Yes,' came the voice, strangled with emotion. 'How is she… Suzette?'

Xavier spoke angrily. 'She's where she should be, with 'er parents.' He hesitated. 'She's fine,' he added, a modicum of empathy creeping in, uninvited.

He heard stifled sobbing and felt a momentary rush of guilt and sorrow. But his rage quickly resurfaced as he invoked Fayette's anguish at the disappearance of her unborn babies and the intolerable situation in which Lena and Jake had placed him.

'Never speak of this. You're lucky to 'ave her twin. Get out now! You 'ave twenty-four 'ours.' He slammed the receiver, his hands shaking.

Before returning to the cottage, Xavier called at the village shop and bought a bottle of Talisker. Once back at the cottage he indulged in the peaty, smoky, amber liquid until he lost consciousness.

Cahors, France, April 1987

Xavier arrived home a few days later to find a letter from Mari . From the postmark, she'd sent it soon after leaving Scotland. Her words became seared on his mind:

My darling Xavier,

In the days since Scotland I have been in turmoil. In trying to do what we thought was right we have caused yet more pain. Now when I think of you, I can only see that time; the darkness, the anxiety, the fear.

For a few beautiful moments during the brief hours with Suzette it was as if we were a family. In those moments all I wanted was to run away with you and the baby and live a life free of the past. Of course, that was not possible. The loss I felt having to give up Suzette has turned me inside out, leaving me raw and vulnerable, even though she wasn't mine and I'd barely known her. I try not to imagine how Lena must be feeling.

There's no question of my understanding we took action with good reason and picturing the joy on Fayette's face softens the guilt I feel, a little. However, I can no longer think of you without pain in my heart. It is for this reason I can no longer continue our relationship. My desperation for a child and the guilt and agony at what we did are almost too much to bear. I have to try and shut all that away, for good, and can only do so without you. I am so sorry, my darling, but for me there is no going back.
Mari

It was as if a chasm had opened beneath Xavier's feet and his whole life had fallen into it.

He telephoned Mari at work. The first couple of times the phone rang without being answered. He persisted. The third time she picked up.

'Mari,' he uttered anxiously.

'Xavier, please, there's no point…'

'Please, Mari,' he interjected. 'We need to talk about this,' he pleaded. 'We can't just… stop.'

She sighed. 'Xavier, I can't. I've explained why. It's… too painful.' Her voice was carefully controlled.

'You told me you felt more alive than ever before when you were with me,' he countered gently, trying to breach her armour, to reach her core. 'More yourself.'

'More alive,' she replied sadly, 'and more desperate, vulnerable. I can't live like that.'

'You won't 'ave to,' he entreated. 'The pain you feel now, it will lessen in time. We won't 'ear from Lena or Jake ever again. Alain's anger will cool. We will all be able to continue with our lives.'

He sensed she was shaking her head. 'It won't ever be the same,' she whispered. 'Too much has happened, been said. It can't be taken back or undone.'

'Please make a life with me, like we planned,' he implored her. 'I love you, Mari.'

'Love is overrated,' she replied coldly.

'You don't believe that, I know you don't.'

'I'm not the person I was, Xavier. I've been torn apart and I can't put myself back together with you in my life. This is the end of it.' All traces of emotion had left her voice. 'If you truly love me you won't contact me again. I wish you well and hope one day you'll be happy.'

The phone went dead and Xavier was left alone, desolated, with the wreckage of his life.

Chapter Forty

Cahors, France, 4 June 2018

Xavier lay awake, shifting, unable to sleep although he felt exhausted. Strangely, a part of him was relieved to have finally shared the truth with Suzette's twin. The burden he'd carried for thirty years seemed lighter. However, reliving the nightmare had drained him. He wondered whether he sought validation from Sarah for his decision to leave her with Lena and Jake—perhaps, though it hadn't manifested. He was infuriated Sarah had chosen not to believe him, though he wasn't surprised. Placing himself in her skin he could understand why the words of a stranger wouldn't weigh as heavily as her trust in her parents. However, it was imperative she believe him. He no longer thought she'd alert the police to the kidnapping. But, in her current frame of mind, God knows what she might say to Suzette when they met.

It was obvious Sarah and Ben needed time to reflect; anyone in their position would. In any case, as he'd pointed out, she could easily get a DNA test to prove her genetic identity. Meanwhile, he retained the upper hand as Sarah longed to meet Suzette so, as they had no idea where she was, they were unlikely to disappear.

A shaft of moonlight, shining through a chink in the

heavy brocade curtains, illuminated a patch of limestone wall, causing it to glow like honey in a jar before a fire. By rights he should talk with Alain and Fayette before anything was said to Suzette, but he hesitated. Sarah had approached him; he controlled the situation and he wanted to remain in control to limit the damage. He'd developed a good relationship with Suzette since she'd reached her mid-teens and he wanted their bond to remain.

His mind wandered to Suzette's sixteenth birthday. He'd been invited to a family gathering in honour of her approaching adulthood, her *soirée débutante*. He and Alain had hardly spoken for the best part of fourteen years and he hadn't visited or been invited to his brother's house for a long time. Fayette had asked if he could be there for Suzette's sake and hers and his mother had summoned him in no uncertain terms. He'd been unsure of how Alain would receive him, so had arrived in a state of trepidation. Alain had managed to maintain a civil enough composure throughout the meal. However, when his brother had retreated outside to smoke and Xavier had accompanied him, Alain had begun to quarrel, stress lining his features and strain in his voice.

'For Christ's sake,' Xavier had retorted, 'can't you let it be, for once? It's Suzette's sixteenth birthday.'

'But it's not, is it?' Alain had shouted. 'Not her actual birthday but the one I falsely registered before we knew when her real birthday was. Thanks to you we can't even celebrate on the date of our own daughter's birth,' he roared.

'I am not to blame. At least you have a daughter, thanks to me,' Xavier had countered, his voice raised to match his brother's.

Their mother had appeared at the heavy wooden kitchen door. She'd looked at one son then the other and spoke in a furious whisper, her grey curls shaking as she shook her head. 'Keep your voices down. You want Suzette to hear? This feud has gone on long enough. Xavier did what he did and had his reasons. The past is the past and you both must live with it. You have a birth certificate from 1985, Alain; you registered a date, obtained the court judgement and got it properly recorded in Cahors, as you wanted—that became her birthday and she doesn't know any different. It hasn't impacted her life and it shouldn't affect yours. For God's sake,' she crossed herself, 'it's been sixteen years; it's time you both buried the sorrow and looked forward or you'll never enjoy the present.' With that she'd turned her back on them and shut the door behind her.

From then, Xavier recalled, Alain had been at least civil, if not warm, towards him. He visited more often and forged a friendship with his niece. They saw one another increasingly frequently, Suzette even visiting London with him on a few occasions, which always thrilled her.

Xavier turned onto his back and stared at the wooden beams. He'd chosen this room—in the *pigeonnier* of his old stone farmhouse—for his bedroom, as it was the highest floor of the house, affording the best view with windows on three sides of the tower flooding it with light from sunrise to dusk, which was wonderful in the depths of winter. Tonight the bright moonlight played around the timbers, casting shadows.

An image of Suzette in London floated into his mind. It was four weeks ago, a few months after he and Mari had found one another again. Suzy had visited London with her husband, Gabriel, and he'd arranged to meet them for dinner. Mari had also decided to join them, having steeled herself to meet Alain and Fayette's grown-up daughter. 'If I'm going to be a part of your family,' she'd told him, 'I might as well start now.' They'd enjoyed a delightful evening in a West End restaurant serving fusion food. Xavier was overjoyed to observe Mari and Suzy connecting straight away. Two significant women in his life; it was important to him they could bond. However, at one point in the evening the conversation had turned to childhood memories and Suzy had recounted she'd had an imaginary friend 'Ayah'. On hearing this Mari had turned pale and soon excused herself from the table. When, after some minutes, she hadn't returned he'd gone looking and had found her outside, smoking. Surprised, he'd enquired whether there was anything wrong; he thought she'd given up cigarettes. 'Don't you remember?' she'd asked him, her eyes glistening. 'On the boat and in the cottage, Suzette kept saying "ayah"? I didn't understand then, but now I think she was calling for her sister.'

His mind back in the present, Xavier sighed heavily and looked at his watch; it was nearly half past three. He'd be desperately weary in the morning. He'd have to contact Ben to find out what condition Sarah was in. Then he could decide how to proceed. God almighty—how was he going to break the news to Suzy?

Chapter Forty-one

Xavier had arranged to meet his niece on Monday evening after she finished her shift at the laboratory, where she worked as a cytologist. He was thankful Suzy's employer prohibited staff from sharing their professional profiles on the internet for security reasons. From Xavier's perspective a beneficial outcome was that Suzy was hard to trace on the internet. That, together with the fact she didn't post personal information on social media—he wasn't sure whether this was owing to caution or because it just wasn't her bag— meant Sarah hadn't been able to locate her online; a fact for which he would ever be grateful.

He'd thought it best to go to Suzette's apartment in the centre of Cahors, where they could talk in privacy. She split her time between there and Saint-Cirq-Lapopie where Gabriel stayed in the accommodation above his rented woodturning workshop and gallery during the summer season, as he often worked in the evenings. Gabriel would be merely forty minutes if Suzette needed him following Xavier's revelation.

Xavier gazed around Suzette's living room while she poured them both a beer. He liked what she'd done with the place since she'd taken it over from her parents. She'd successfully married the old building with a modern interior. *She has her mother's eye*, he thought.

She beamed at him as she brought their drinks through from the kitchen and set them, with olives, on a low table in front of the sofa. As they exchanged news for a few minutes, she asking him about Mari and he about Gabriel, Xavier's insides were doing somersaults. Finally he could wait no longer. He inhaled deeply. 'I have something important to tell you.'

She pulled a mocking face which said *that sounds ominous* but her expression quickly transformed to trepidation, reflecting his own.

He cleared his throat. 'I deliberated whether this should come from your parents but decided I should give you the news, as certain… events… have recently occurred which your parents are, as yet, unaware of.'

Suzette listened quietly as Xavier began from the point when he'd first met Mari. He didn't hide Mari's involvement; he wanted his niece to understand her selfless part. He also wanted her to appreciate the circumstances in which she'd been separated from her twin sister. However he didn't tell her he'd threatened the Lesters, compelling them to disappear so Alain couldn't take Sarah from them, jeopardising everything Xavier held most dear—he could never admit his part in their escape. He hadn't told Sarah and he hoped Lena and Jake wouldn't divulge that they'd been forewarned—once they knew it was he who abducted Sarah, they'd know he'd made the call. But he'd done them a favour and warned them never to speak of it; he didn't see why they should do so now. Neither did he mention his brother's accusations against Mari—there was no need to burden Suzy with anything else.

As Suzette tried to absorb her uncle's words, her emotions constantly shifted; shock, bewilderment, sorrow, compassion. She had no idea her mother had suffered miscarriages and it pained her to think of what her parents went through. That Lena had carried and given birth to her, she found extraordinarily generous. When her uncle revealed two baby girls had been born, her hands flew to her mouth. 'A sister? A twin!' Alarm quickly replaced her astonishment. 'Oh, but what happened to her?' she whispered, gripping Xavier's hand, her eyes glistening. He placed his other hand over hers reassuringly while he continued.

When she learned Lena and Jake had absconded with her and her sister Suzette was devastated. She cradled her head in her hands. 'Jesus! My poor parents. How could Lena and Jake do that to them? I'm sorry for them, losing their little boy, but to take someone else's children…'

'I believe Lena wouldn't have been able to go on living if she'd had to give you both up,' Xavier said quietly. He resumed his narrative, pausing at the point where Suzette had been handed to Alain and Fayette.

As she heard Xavier admit he'd made the decision to leave her sister, Sarah, behind, Suzette filled with anger. Though her uncle explained his reasons she couldn't believe he would abandon her sister to the people who had stolen them from their real parents. 'How could you?' she cried. 'You betrayed Maman and Papa. They must have been desperate to have us. You talk about Lena's needs and that leaving Sarah behind was like some kind of… insurance—what about my parents? What about me?' Her bitterness sliced the air between them. She rose abruptly and crossed the room, distancing herself from him.

He shot her an anguished look.

'I need a few moments alone,' she said, entering her bedroom and closing the door quietly. She was struggling to place the blame solely at one person's door: the Lesters, her uncle, her father—what action had he taken to retrieve Sarah? Why hadn't her parents told her about her twin?

She focused on her breathing to slow it down, before re-entering the living room. 'All the time I could have spent with my sister,' she said to Xavier, shaking her head despondently. 'I feel so…' she strove for the right words and reached for the remains of her beer. Her hand trembled as she held the glass.

'Cheated,' she stated finally, the word emerging through a tight throat.

'I'm sorry,' Xavier lowered his head.

'Did Papa try to find Sarah?' she uttered through a curtain of tears, her voice reduced to a croak.

Xavier nodded. 'Yes. I believe he went to Ullapool but the Lesters had vanished without a trace. I think he kept looking for a long time. It wasn't as easy to track people in those days. I'm truly sorry, Suzy. This is why I wanted you to understand the reasons why we all acted as we did; it was complicated and the threat of criminal prosecution hung over all of us, as it has done for thirty years. That is until yesterday… when Sarah caught up with me.'

Suzette gasped, her skin rippling into gooseflesh. 'You've seen her? You've spoken with her?' She laid a hand on her uncle's arm. 'Is she here, in Cahors?'

Xavier told her how Sarah had discovered him and Mari and tracked him to France. 'She wants to see you,

Suzy.'

Suzette released a deep breath. 'Oh my God. That's…' The revelations and myriad emotions became too much and she put her hands to her face and sobbed like a child.

It was a few minutes before she regained a semblance of composure. Her uncle had not tried to comfort her, no doubt sensing her need to vent, but when she raised her head, his face was racked with concern.

He reached out his arms to her, blinking back tears. 'The last thing I wanted to do was to hurt you.'

She nodded. 'I'm… overwhelmed.' She returned his hug briefly then heaved a sigh. 'It won't do me any good trying to blame anyone. What happened is heart-breaking but, at the same, it's amazing I have a twin sister. So where is she? What's she like—is she like me?'

Xavier rose to retrieve another couple of small beers from the fridge. Settling himself beside her again he reached for his phone, locating a photo of Sarah that Ben had sent him.

Suzette inhaled sharply. 'It's like looking in a mirror! We've even got similar hairstyles.' She zoomed in, peering at the screen as she moved the photo. 'She's got dark streaks in her hair and she doesn't have a mole on her collarbone'.

The corners of Xavier's mouth turned up. 'That's the only difference I've seen.'

'When was this taken?'

'This morning.'

Suzette gazed at the image, with fondness. 'She looks wistful, contemplative; she's not quite facing into the lens.'

'You have the same look sometimes,' Xavier remarked softly.

She turned to him, smiling. 'Yes, I know. Gabriel has caught me unawares. He printed and framed a black and white photo of me wearing that same expression. It's on his bedside table.' She took a gulp of refreshing beer. 'I have to meet her. I need to know her. We're part of one another; two halves of a whole.'

Xavier shot her a relieved smile as he too reached for his second beer, 'I'll bring Sarah to you'

'I agreed to mind Gabriel's gallery tomorrow morning while he finishes a commissioned piece. Is it possible for you to bring Sarah to Saint-Cirq-Lapopie? We could meet after lunch in the courtyard at the back of the gallery. It's very private, we won't be disturbed there.'

Xavier nodded his agreement. 'It's the perfect place,' he said gently.

Suzette jumped up and headed for the bedroom. 'I have to be with Gabriel,' she called over her shoulder. 'I have to tell him face to face.'

Xavier waited by the door between the bedroom and living room as his niece threw a few things into her overnight bag.

'It's strange,' she reflected, 'Sarah and I shared a life for a year and a half, but I don't remember playing with another version of myself. Oh!' She dropped the bag she'd just packed, her hands flying to her mouth.

'What is it?' Xavier stepped towards her anxiously.

'I've suddenly remembered my imaginary friend's name.'

Chapter Forty-two

Saint-Cirq-Lapopie, France, 5 June 2018

Suzette sat at a round table in the shade of an old rambling wisteria which twisted and turned over a metal frame, covering half of the small, flagged courtyard. Her heart thudded as she glanced frequently toward the gated passageway rounding the side of the cottage, leading to the front lane. She looked at her watch for the hundredth time; it was nearly two pm. She'd closed Gabriel's gallery an hour ago and made a goat's cheese and walnut salad for their lunch, though she'd hardly eaten any. Gabriel had retreated to his workshop and she could hear the comforting rhythmic sound of a carving chisel against wood. The medieval village spilling down the cliff-side hummed with visitors but the thick walls of the stone buildings surrounding her buffered their busy sounds. She continued to wait anxiously in the oasis of calm.

The squeak of a wrought iron gate reached Suzette's ears and she sat forward, upright, pixies somersaulting in her stomach. Suddenly she was face-to-face with herself; a replica, wearing an identical look of astonishment. For a few seconds Suzette's surroundings dissolved and the two of them remained alone in a void. She noticed Sarah trembling, as was she, however the rapture on her twin's features matched the joy in her own heart.

Suzette's tears spilled over as Sarah stepped forward and uttered a timorous '*Bonjour.*' Then she was holding her sister's hands and kissing her. 'Oh, *mon Dieu*. Hello, Sarah, *ma précieuse soeur!*' She felt Sarah's arms around her, clasping tightly, and returned her embrace. '*Merci,*' she wept, '*merci.*'

Then the strangest thing happened. Their thirty years apart vanished as Sarah whispered 'Ouzi' and she responded tenderly, 'Ayah.'

That first afternoon Suzette and Sarah spent hours sitting in the sunshine talking, each beginning to gain a picture of the other's life and of the people closest to them. Ben was exploring the village and Xavier drove to his brother's house on the other side of Cahors to deliver the news.

The women discovered how similar they were, not only physically but also in character and mannerisms, likes and dislikes, beliefs and approach to life. They swapped stories of their childhood and teenage years, boyfriends, lovers and how they came to be with Gabriel and Ben. Together they laughed and cried and quickly discovered an unassailable bond.

Suzette showed her sister photos of her parents and spoke extensively of them, acutely aware of Sarah's difficult position . She tried to alleviate Sarah's distress and help her prepare for an encounter with Fayette and Alain.

Sarah stressed she wasn't ready to meet Suzette's parents that evening—she couldn't yet think of them as her own family. Suzette was heartbroken for her sister.

As shadows lengthened and the sun hid beyond the

darkened crags and the roman-tiled roofs of dwellings high above, Ben and Gabriel joined them. They continued getting to know each other over a bottle of Chateau Lagrezette and delicious platters of cheese and charcuterie with olives and warm bread. In addition to their love of Suzy and Sarah, Gabriel and Ben began to discover numerous commonalities, including a passion for fitness and sport, appreciation of gastronomy, a strong element of determination and a positive outlook.

'I love 'er *forte volonté*—'ow you say, will-power?—but also 'er *douceur*,' Gabriel remarked at one of the candid points in the conversation, inclining his head toward Suzy.

'It's the same for me with Sarah.' Ben smiled tenderly. 'And I love her stubbornness but also her compassion.'

'We like to 'ear all these compliments,' Suzette grinned, reaching for her sister's hand.

'Yes, you should both have more wine,' Sarah laughed.

The four of them chatted and chuckled as night descended and the moon cast its radiance into the courtyard, highlighting each of them with an incandescence matched only by the glow Suzette felt in her heart. And every time her eyes met Sarah's, she knew her sister was feeling the same.

In the small hours, Suzette drove Sarah and Ben back to their hotel. Xavier had phoned earlier to arrange to collect them, but Suzette insisted she would take them then return to her flat. As Gabriel had bent to kiss her goodnight, she'd beamed at him.

'It's been a good day,' he whispered.

'It's been wonderful,' she replied.

Cahors, France, 6 June 2018

Suzette had offered Sarah and Ben the spare bedroom in her apartment so the next morning they left the château and joined her in Cahors. Sarah cautiously agreed to accompany her sister to meet Alain and Fayette at the family home that afternoon. As the hour came nearer Sarah's apprehension intensified until, fifteen minutes before they were due to leave, she was overcome with panic.

She ceased pacing their bedroom and sat on the bed. 'I can't do it,' she exclaimed to Ben, 'I can't go. I'm not ready.'

Ben sat beside her, took hold of her trembling clasped hands and placed his other arm around her shoulders. 'You don't have to do anything, sweetheart,' he said softly. 'Tell me what you're afraid of.'

'These people, they're strangers. I don't know how to be with them. I can't… be their daughter, I'm Mum and Dad's daughter: Sarah Lester.' She began to sob quietly. 'I love Mum and Dad.'

Ben pulled her gently towards him, so her head came to rest on his shoulder. 'You're not being disloyal to Lena and Jake and you don't have to be anyone other than who you are,' he said, stroking her hair. 'You were born to Lena, nothing changes that. She and Jake raised you in a loving, supportive family and gave you everything they could. They will always be your parents. Try to think of Alain and Fayette differently.'

'But… what my parents did…how can I face Alain and Fayette?' she uttered.

'You're not accountable for what happened,' Ben reminded her tenderly. 'You're your own person with your own feelings. You have your life and they have theirs; the two spheres are about to overlap but you're in control of who you allow into your circle and how you interact with them. Just be yourself.'

Sarah sat upright, wiping her eyes with the backs of her hands, considering his words. 'I suppose this is like an adoptee meeting their biological parents for the first time,' she reflected.

'Exactly,' replied Ben. 'I know Alain and Fayette didn't give you away—obviously they wanted you very much—so you don't have any hurtful feelings of rejection to deal with, but you've lived an independent life for thirty-three years. You're meeting them on your own terms.'

She turned to Ben and nodded. 'Will you come with me. I want you there.'

'Of course, sweetheart.'

While Sarah prepared herself, Suzette strode restlessly around the living room, plumping cushions and repositioning ornaments. She felt her sister's uneasiness as she placed herself in her twin's situation. She slowed and deepened her breathing. She longed for Sarah to feel comfortably part of the Dubois family, to be easy in the company of her parents and happy in their love, though she recognised this might take a long time and the path would be stony. At some point, Suzette supposed, she would meet with Lena and Jake. She hurriedly dismissed the thought with a shake of her head. She wanted to focus on Sarah, her remarkable, loving, determined sister, whose dogged pursuit of the truth, despite the risk to herself, led to this extraordinary mutual discovery, wonderful for them both but, for Sarah, also devastating. She would support her twin in every way possible, today and all the days of their lives.

As Sarah stepped out of the bedroom, ready to leave, Suzette hugged her reassuringly, whispering 'They 'ave no expectations.' Sarah was reminded she wasn't alone. With Ben and Suzy at her side, she concluded, she could face anything.

Sarah anticipated Fayette becoming emotional, but in the event, Alain's behaviour surprised her. On entering the extensive old manor house Suzette ushered her into a large modern kitchen-diner. Ben hung back by the door. Fayette turned instantly from the cooker, beaming, her expertly cut bobbed blonde hair wafting in the wake of her movement. Approaching Sarah, she took one hand in both of hers. 'Welcome to our 'ome,' she smiled. 'We 'ave longed to meet you. But let me say, we are just as nervous as you must be. Come.'

She led Sarah to stand next to a long polished-granite dining table. Touching the top of her arm affectionately, Fayette added softly 'Please don't worry—we will not try to claim you; we just want to know you and for you to come to know us.'

Somewhat relieved, Sarah smiled and nodded. 'I would very much like to know you.' She turned her attention to Alain, who was standing awkwardly on the other side of the table, staring at her.

'*Bonjour*,' she acknowledged politely.

He nodded, unable to speak for a moment. Then he spoke hesitantly, his voice croaky. 'Sophia Fae, *ma fille chérie*.' Whereupon he collapsed onto a chair and wept.

Taken aback, Sarah looked at Suzette, who, also surprised, glanced at her mother. Her eyes glistening, Fayette threw Sarah an encouraging nod as she went to her husband. 'You 'ave a French identity, *chérie*,' she clarified. 'I told Lena we planned to name you Suzette Adele and Sophia Fae. While we searched for you, Alain registered your births in England, as French *nationales*.' She helped Alain to his feet and encouraged everyone to the table, beckoning to Ben. '*S'il vous plaît*, come join us, Ben.'

While Fayette greeted Ben, Alain busied himself with fetching glasses and chilled wine, aided by Suzette, who, Sarah noted, took the opportunity to give her father a hug. Having regained his composure, Alain returned to the table and proceeded to pour. 'We 'ad to give the date as the day you were supposed to be born and say the clinic in Plymouth was your birthplace,' he explained, his timbre still slightly husky. 'Of course, we only registered Suzy in France.'

Sarah's features resisted her internal frown. 'So I have birth certificates in two different names, one true and the other false?'

'Well, you could say they both contain false information,' Alain grunted. Fayette shot him a look of warning. 'But, yes, your Scottish one is legal.'

'*Mais...* this means I 'ave another certificate also?' Suzette asked, her eyes wide with surprise.

Her father smiled sadly. '*Je suis désolé, ma belle.*'

Fayette reached for her daughter's hand. 'It was the only way to register you in France,' she explained.

Suzette breathed slowly, as realisation struck and her eyes filled with tears. 'So...when is my actual birthday?'

'Twentieth of September,' Sarah interjected, '*vingt septembre*,' she added to be clear. She felt a jolt in the depths of her stomach as her sister's shock resonated with her. She grabbed Suzy's other hand and held it tightly. 'You were originally named Suzette Rose but you're French so Suzette Adele is much more suitable.' She glanced at Fayette and Alain before turning back to her twin. 'Your French certificate is the one which matters, registered by your true parents.'

Suzette stared into the middle distance and the room fell silent. Then she disengaged her hands and stood, knocking her chair backwards. She eyed her parents. 'Unbelievable! All these years and you didn't tell me.'

A torrent of French that Sarah didn't understand spilled out as her sister walked from the room. Anxious, she sought Ben's hand. Fayette rose and went after her daughter, placing a comforting hand on Sarah's shoulder as she passed.

Alain's eyes glistened as he took a gulp of wine. 'It is difficult for everyone,' he muttered thickly. 'The joy we felt when we 'eard you 'ad found us was… beyond words. You 'ave brought us so much 'appiness, I cannot tell you. We also 'ave to deal with the pain of the past which 'as landed at our feet once more. And we must 'elp Suzy come to terms with what she knows now.' He took another steadying mouthful of wine. 'And you Soph… Sarah. 'Ow are you?'

Sarah gave Alain a kind smile. 'I'm okay, I think. I seem to have felt every possible emotion but finding Suzy is the best thing that's ever happened.' She paused. 'And I want you all in my life… now and always.' She wiped away a tear as Ben squeeze her hand.

Outside on the limestone terrace, in the dappled shade of a rambling grape vine, Suzette stood with her mother under the pergola, a light breeze cooling her tears. 'I could have helped,' she uttered sadly.

'Helped? But how, sweetheart?'

'I would've helped you search for her... when I was old enough.'

Fayette shook her head. 'It would have consumed you,' she replied gently.

Suzette let go of her mother's hands to wipe the wetness from her cheeks. 'I'm so sorry about your miscarriages, maman.'

As Fayette cupped her face, Suzette registered the shadows beneath her mother's beautiful eyes but also the fine lines at their corners which deepened as she smiled. 'It's all in the past. We have you. That's what matters. We have one another. And now... your sister... it's a little miracle.'

As they hugged, Suzette heard her mother whisper, ' "The longer we dwell on our misfortunes, the greater is their power to harm us".'

They walked back to the house, arm in arm. 'Voltaire?' she guessed.

'I believe it's been misquoted over the years, but he said something about giving substance to evil by dwelling on it,' Fayette replied.

Suzette squeezed her mother's hand. 'It's a good philosophy. Did it help?'

'Eventually.'

The door opened and Fayette and Suzy returned to the table. Suzy's eyes were moist, but her expression calm.

Sarah turned to her sister. 'Actually I think we're lucky,' she smiled supportively, 'we can celebrate twice.' She shot Suzette a quizzical look. 'What is the date of your... French birthday?'

'*Le vingt-deux*, twenty-two,' Suzette returned, managing a smile.

Ben, who had been silent, leaned forward in his chair and raised his wine glass. 'I think we should celebrate Sarah and Suzy's birthday for three days every year. While the situation may not always be easy, it's wonderful you have all found one another. So I say cheers to that!'

'Yes, cheers,' Sarah echoed.

The others raised their glasses and toasted in unison, '*Santé.*'

France, 8 June 2018

Sarah and Ben were sitting on the plane, sipping rather insipid coffee. Ben was watching a sports programme on his iPad. Sarah stared out of the window. They had left the vineyards around Bergerac and were now heading over the forests of the Haute-Vienne. Although her eyes were directed towards the greenery below her focus was elsewhere; so much had happened over the last few days.

A stewardess interrupted Sarah's thoughts, gesturing towards her empty cup. She glanced at her watch; they would be back in England before long. She gazed into the swirls of light-grey cloud some way beneath the plane. It hadn't occurred to her Suzette could have a birth certificate different to the one she had unearthed or that she herself could have a somewhat fraudulent birth record, giving her an identity as a French national. She snorted incredulously. Sophia Fae. She silently repeated the name to herself. It sounded faintly exotic; a name redolent of a film star or fashion designer. Just as a fae was a mythical being, she reflected, Sophia Fae didn't exist either. One question nagged at her. She tapped Ben on the arm, signalling him to pause his video.

'Something's been bugging me. When a baby is registered in the UK, that must have consequences,' she said, when he'd taken out his ear buds. 'I mean, when they come of school age, if they didn't turn up at school surely questions would be asked?'

'You're thinking of Alain's false registrations?' Ben replied.

She nodded.

Ben thought for a moment. 'Well, you were both registered as French citizens, born to French citizens. So I think it would be natural for an authority to assume you'd moved to France. I wouldn't expect any cross-checking of English and French registers.'

'Hmm. I suppose so. But what about Suzy's Scottish birth registration?' Sarah returned. 'Wouldn't UK social services get involved if a registered child wasn't sent to school? Or, at least, start asking questions?'

'I wondered about that too,' Ben nodded. 'The thing is, for a Local Authority to pick up on the fact two children were born in Scotland and only one child turns up at school somewhere different would imply all Local Authorities are joined up and check birth registers. I did look briefly on the internet but didn't find anything linking birth register and local authority school registration. And remember, this was in the eighties.'

'Yeah,' she concurred. 'And I suppose people often

relocate, perhaps moving abroad with family.'

He patted her hand before replacing his earphones. 'No need to worry about your mum and dad getting into trouble. It all happened a long time ago.'

As the pilot began their descent, Sarah's thoughts turned to her parents. They were due home in three days. She'd been in touch with them infrequently during the past week, blaming the poor signal and a busy schedule, as they had done earlier in their trip. She couldn't stand making small talk with them while bearing the weight of undisclosed truth and knew the next few days would pass frustratingly slowly. She kept playing out conversations with them in her head, but that only served to make her more anxious and she knew discussions never progress in reality as rehearsed when you're cast as both accuser and defence. Sadness had begun to replace anger, pain to supplant resentment. Soon she would have to face them and their relationship would change forever.

Chapter Forty-three

Malvern, England, 11 June 2018

Ben had offered to accompany Sarah to her parent's house to provide moral support. They would be expecting to see him too, however Sarah preferred to face them alone. Their cruise ship had docked that morning and they'd driven up from Southampton. She'd decided to leave work early to arrive in Upton around four in the afternoon. Her mum and dad would have had time to unpack and settle themselves by then. As she neared their house the now all too familiar stomach-churning commenced and she arrived in a state of apprehension. She took several deep breaths before climbing out of her Prius, repeating the mantra, *You're in control* to herself.

Lena and Jake were all smiles and hugs as she entered the hallway. Despite the situation she found herself glad to see them. As she followed them into the living room, she nervously checked the pocket of her leather jacket, her fingers touching the edge of the photo she was carrying, printed by Suzy for her.

Sarah waited while Lena made a pot of tea and fetched a bowl of dried nuts. 'Polynesian chestnuts,' her mother said, 'try 'em, they're delicious.'

'We brought you a few things from our travels, love.'

Jake inclined his head towards a collection of small, wrapped objects on the coffee table. 'Hope you like 'em.'

Sarah nodded, impatient to impart what she had to say. Her mother began talking enthusiastically about Tahitian food when she interrupted.

'Mum, Dad, leave that for now. I have something to tell you.'

'Oh,' Lena responded, her commentary halted by the urgency in Sarah's voice. She appeared surprised for second or two before a large grin appeared. 'Do I have to buy a hat?' she raised her eyebrows excitedly.

Jake wore a concerned expression. He could see from his daughter's solemn countenance she had something serious on her mind. He placed a hand on Lena's arm in warning.

'Suzette is alive and well and living in France,' Sarah blurted out, 'and I've met her.' She retrieved the photo from her pocket and pushed it across the coffee table. 'I know everything,' she said quietly.

Lena's hands went to her mouth. 'Oh my God! Sarah, darlin'!' Her eyes closed momentarily in anguish.

Her father was staring at her, his features set in shock. It was a few moments before he recovered sufficiently to utter, 'How did you...'

'Xavier Dubois, Alain's brother,' Sarah interposed. 'I told you I'd overheard him in a café and he was with the woman who mistook me for Suzette. You insisted it was a coincidence. You said Suzette was dead. You continued lying to me.' Sarah couldn't keep her mounting resentment from her tone. 'I have a twin sister and you kept that from me... all this time!'

Lena's eyes brimmed. 'Was it this Xavier who took her

away?' she whispered.

Sarah hesitated but the time for secrecy had long gone. Her parents weren't a threat to Xavier, just as there was no longer danger to them from Alain. Honesty was essential now. 'Yes,' she replied, 'and the woman I bumped into in Malvern turned out to be Mari.'

Her mother emitted an agonised cry which ripped through Sarah's heart, though she stayed resolutely where she was. 'Were you ever going to tell me the truth?' she asked bleakly.

Jake picked up the photo of the two girls. They were standing with their arms around one another, heads bent together, their identical features glowing with joy. Passing the picture to his wife, he regarded Sarah through watery eyes. 'I'm so, so sorry we had to deceive you.' Pain was instantly obvious in his expression, pulling at the muscles around his eyes. 'Yer more precious to us than life. We couldn't bear t' part with you. After George... yer mum... well... she couldn't...' He shook his head sadly.

Lena's thumb was gently stroking the faces of the twins in the image, tears streaking her cheeks. Now she carefully placed it on the table and moved to where Sarah sat. Crouching in front of her she took both of Sarah's hands in her own. She spoke slowly and her tone was earnest, intense. 'Whatever you think of us, we love you more than anythin' in the world. I grew you both inside me and I gave birth to you. You may not have my DNA but yer still a part o' me. I gave you life and... you saved mine.' She squeezed Sarah's hands and then hugged her tightly.

Sarah cried softly. 'I know you both love me,' she managed to whisper, 'but I'm angry and resentful and those feelings aren't simply going to vanish. I was so shocked at what you did. Although I'm beginning to understand your reasons, it all still feels like a huge betrayal.'

Jake wiped away an escaped tear. 'You said you knew everythin' but there's somethin' you dunt know.' He looked towards his wife for acquiescence. She nodded.

'There is a chance you might have our DNA,' he pronounced. 'It's small, but a tiny possibility.'

His words hit Sarah like a punchbag. 'I don't understand,' she sniffed quietly, wiping her eyes with the backs of her hands. 'How? Tell me; tell me everything!'

That evening Ben and Sarah curled up on the sofa with a bottle of Pinot Noir. Sarah related her parents' account of events. She and Ben agreed the possibility of her being Lena and Jake's daughter was extremely remote, even given the fact of her great-grandfather and his brother being identical twins. Then they discussed whether Sarah should tell Suzy. On one hand they believed she had a right to know; on the other, did they have the right to implant uncertainty, however minute? Suzy was clearly happy—why paint clouds on her horizon?

Sarah decided she must be candid with her sister. Their relationship had to be based on openness and honesty. For too long their lives had been—unbeknown to them—shrouded in secrecy. Together they would decide what to do.

Chapter Forty-four

Malvern, England, 28 December 2018

Sarah drove to Upton in the afternoon half-light to visit her parents. She had significant news for them.

She and Ben had spent Christmas in France. Together with Suzy and Gabriel, Xavier and Mari—now his fiancée—and Xavier's mother, they had stayed with Alain and Fayette. For many reasons it was a momentous occasion, not least because the two brothers tried hard to reconcile their differences. Mari was also being introduced to the family and Sarah had been able to spend quiet time getting to know her. They'd taken to each other straight away, their first antagonistic encounters firmly in the past. They'd all enjoyed a happy few days, eating, drinking and laughing.

Sarah was slowly forming a relationship with Alain and Fayette, having spent a couple of long weekends with them and her sister during the summer and autumn. They were kind and loving. She couldn't think of them as her parents though; it was more comfortable regarding them more like godparents of whom she could grow fond without feeling disloyal to Lena and Jake. Although her relationship with her mum and dad was subtly different now, the change was not appreciable—at least to outsiders. She'd managed to follow in Ben's footsteps, her core confident self-reliance once more governing her actions.

As she pulled onto their driveway, Sarah felt a frisson of excitement. Suzy had struggled with unwanted resentment towards Jake and Lena for months but now wanted to meet them and move forward. She'd confirmed that morning she and Gabriel would be arriving in Malvern tomorrow.

Sarah's mum and dad greeted her with kisses and they settled in the lounge by the cosy wood burner. The coffee table was stacked with plates of fruit and cheese, mince pies and Christmas cake. Sarah added a bottle of Portuguese Porto she'd bought in Cahors.

'How was yer Christmas, love?' Jake enquired.

Sarah smiled. 'It was really enjoyable, thanks Dad. I know it was difficult for you two, knowing I was with them but I hope you enjoyed yourselves too.'

Lena glanced hesitantly at her husband. 'Yes, we had a lovely quiet time, didn't we, Jake? How's Suzette? We want to hear all about it.'

Sarah described her Christmas. While she was keen to normalise the situation, she was also sensitive to her parents' feelings. They listened and nodded, making polite sounds of acknowledgement.

'Sounds like a good time was had by all,' Jake stated when Sarah finished. She sensed adopted joviality in his tone and was eager to tell them the wonderful news about Suzy. However, first Sarah wanted them to explain something Suzy had raised.

'Can I ask you something?'

'Of course, love,' Lena replied, taking a gulp of port.

'After Suzy was taken, how did you disappear again? How was it that Alain couldn't find us?'

Her mum looked taken aback, though Sarah thought it an obvious question.

Jake answered. 'We moved around quite a bit at first. Yer granny joined us when we found a place where we felt safe. We had to get false identity documents. We couldn't use yer mum's name any more.'

'How on earth?'

'My brother,' Jake interjected.

'I didn't know you had a brother,' Sarah exclaimed.

'We never speak of him.' Lena rose abruptly and left the room. Sarah heard the kettle boiling.

'Jude's not a nice character,' her dad explained. 'He operates in a shady world. That's how I knew he could help us, for a price of course.'

'You had money,' Sarah muttered, trying to keep her tone even.

An uncomfortable expression crossed her father's face. 'Yes, we did. Love, you have to understand how desperate we were.' He sat back in his armchair and sighed. 'But we should never have asked Jude for help. We only told him we'd stolen some money, not about… you know.' He inhaled deeply again. 'Some time later he tried to blackmail us.'

Sarah shook her head. 'Unbelievable!'

'What he hadn't bargained for was yer dad bein' able t' give as good as he gets,' said Lena, returning with a pot of coffee.

'I threatened him with goin' t' the police with what he'd been up to fer years—things he'd forgotten he'd boasted t' me about in the past,' Jake explained. 'He backed off after that, we moved again an' we haven't heard from him since.'

'After a few years we settled in Upton,' Lena said. 'By the time you were school age, we felt it was safe enough t' use yer dad's surname again.' She gave Sarah a faltering look.

Sarah laid a comforting hand on her mum's arm. Her tone was positive. 'It's in the past now. We all want to move forward. And speaking of that, we'd like to be with you on New Year's Eve.'

'Oh, that's lovely. What time were you and Ben thinking of coming? I'll make dinner,' Lena smiled.

Sarah beamed. 'You'll need to plan for six…because…Suzy and Gabriel will be coming too.'

'Oh my God!' Lena's hands flew to her face, her eyes brimming. She turned to Jake, who'd frozen. 'Oh my luvver,' she cried.

Jake swallowed audibly and moved to sit beside his wife. As her parents absorbed their erstwhile daughter's reconciliation with past events, Sarah saw a tsunami of relief and released guilt in her mother's expression. Then Jake's arms were around Lena and she was shaking as she sobbed in his embrace.

Malvern, England, 31 December 2018

As Sarah pulled on her cashmere dress and dried her hair she could hear laughter from the spare bedroom, where Suzette and Gabriel were also dressing for the New Year's Eve celebration. It was the first time they'd visited Malvern and they loved the place. The previous day they'd walked on the snow-capped Malvern Hills and Sarah had delighted in pointing out her favourite spots. Later they'd warmed up with boozy hot chocolate before visiting one of their favoured old inns for mulled cider and a hearty supper. She looked forward to sharing more treasured places with her sister. Most of all they loved simply spending time together.

Sarah rose from her dressing table to close the curtains and noticed a car parked a few yards away, the occupant dimly lit by a glow she assumed to be coming from a mobile phone, a rising trickle of smoke emerging from the driver's window. She couldn't make out the registration but had the feeling she'd seen the same car several times over the past few days, always after dark. Her brow wrinkled momentarily. It couldn't be anything to do with Alain, could it? She pushed the thought away. After all these years, she didn't think so, though her parents still owed him a lot of money. But if he wanted to locate Lena and Jake, he could just ask her or Suzy. She shrugged. Maybe the person in the car was waiting to collect a neighbour. Even so, she would mention it to Ben. She returned to her preparations.

As she donned her makeup she glanced at her watch. They would soon be leaving for Upton. Suzy had told Sarah she wished to thank Lena for bringing her into the world. They had a special bond, she said, that could never be broken. Sarah appreciated it would be an emotional reunion for her mum and dad and was thrilled Suzy was finally able to find a connection with them within herself. She understood how significant Suzy's words would be for her mum and felt proud of her sister for recognising that too.

As she put on her necklace—a silver chain, adorned with dogs, that Ben had given her—she wondered what the new year would bring. She and Ben loved dogs and had talked about adopting a rescued animal once they were sure they could fit their respective working patterns around it. It would be wonderful to walk on the Malverns with a dog. She smiled to her reflection in the mirror. It really was incredible how similar she and Suzy had turned out to be after thirty years apart, even down to their taste in men. Gabriel was charming and so like Ben.

Suzy would be with her any minute—they had an important decision to make and had been putting it off ever since she'd shared Lena and Jake's confession with her twin. They'd had several difficult conversations about how they felt. Understandably, Suzy believed it improbable her parents were not Alain and Fayette. Sarah was honest that she cherished a hope, afforded by ambiguity, that she was the daughter of Lena and Jake. Thus far the status quo had been infinitely preferable to undergoing a DNA test. However, each faced the challenge of coping with the uncertainty in a different way and both women knew they had to be prepared to live with their joint decision.

There was a knock at her bedroom door. 'Come in,' Sarah called.

Suzy popped her head around the door. 'Now?'

Sarah nodded. Her sister entered, closing the door behind her. She wore tailored black trousers with a turquoise silk blouse. 'You look gorgeous,' Sarah grinned.

'*Toi aussi*,' Suzy beamed.

It had become their standing joke.

Sarah rose and they hugged tightly. Eventually when parting they remained holding hands. Understanding suffused the space between them and they both acknowledged it with a nod.

'No test,' Suzy affirmed.

'No test,' Sarah concurred.

'But if one of us wants to know in the future, we talk again,' Suzy confirmed.

'Absolutely,' Sarah agreed.

'I 'ave something else to tell you.' Joy lit Suzy's smile.

Sarah's heart leapt.

As Sarah descended the stairs she reflected on her sister's words. Suzy had asked her to be godmother and she couldn't wait. She wondered whether it would ever be possible for Lena and Jake to be in the same room as Alain and Fayette; she doubted it. But, between them, she and Suzy had begun to heal the wounds seared into the lives of those they loved three decades ago.

The four of them convened in the living room for an aperitif, laughing as the champagne cork hit the ceiling and holding out their glasses as Ben tried to fill them before the bubbles spilled onto the carpet.

Ben held up his glass. 'To family,' he toasted, 'and the future.'

Sarah raised her glass in salutation then added, 'To sharing the rest of our lives.'

'*Partager nos vies*,' Suzy echoed.

Outside in the dark a man stared through binoculars at the silhouetted figures. He shivered and pulled the upturned collar of his winter overcoat closer around his neck against the cold. Dropping the field glasses through the open window of his car, he walked a few yards up the road, keeping low against the grassy bank of the hillside between the road and the houses. On reaching Sarah's car, he bent and placed something underneath it before moving slowly away.

www.ingramcontent.com/pod-product-compliance
Ingram Content Group UK Ltd.
Pitfield, Milton Keynes, MK11 3LW, UK
UKHW040944110326
468872UK00003B/800